MIDNIGHT CLEAR

ALSO BY KATHY HOGAN TROCHECK

FEATURING CALLAHAN GARRITY:
Strange Brew
Heart Trouble
Happy Never After
Homemade Sin
To Live and Die in Dixie
Every Crooked Nanny

FEATURING TRUMAN KICKLIGHTER:
Crash Course
Lickety-Split

MIDNIGHT CLEAR

A CALLAHAN GARRITY MYSTERY

KATHY HOGAN TROCHECK

HarperCollins*Publishers*

This is a work of fiction. Although some Atlanta locales are real, others are fictitious. Names, characters, and incidents are the product of the writer's imagination and any resemblance to real events or actual persons, living or dead, is entirely coincidental.

HarperCollins books may be purchased for educational, business, or sales promotional use. For information please write: Special Markets Department, HarperCollins Publishers, Inc., 10 East 53rd Street, New York, NY 10022.

FIRST EDITION

Library of Congress Cataloging-in-Publication Data

Trocheck, Kathy Hogan, 1954–
    Midnight clear / Kathy Trocheck. — 1st ed.
       p.   cm.
    ISBN 0-06-017543-5
    I. Title.
    PS3570.R587M54   1998
    813'.54—dc21   98-20321

98 99 00 01 02 ❖/RRD 10 9 8 7 6 5 4 3 2 1

For Sallie Gouverneur, agent, friend, despot, co-conspirator.
Vaya con dios!

ACKNOWLEDGMENTS

The author wishes to thank the following people for their generous help, advice and expertise: Donna Crosby Sloan and Robert Waller for legal advice, Major Mickey Lloyd of the Atlanta Police Department, Jim Auchmutey of the *Atlanta Constitution* for memories of Funtown, and Barrie and Bobby Aycock of Glen-Ella Springs, who gave me a quiet place to hide. The Columbus family of St. Petersburg, Florida, supplied the original Tom and Jerry recipe, the Davis family shared tears and beers. Martha Winzeler minded the store. Katie and Andy Trocheck were the inspiration for Tot n' Joes. As always, Tom Trocheck did everything, including the Blue Christmas.

1

We had a real dime store when I was a kid. Not a Kmart or a Target, but a Woolworth's, where you could buy wonderful things like a live goldfish and bowl for your brother, or a bottle of eau de toilette in a satin-lined box for your mother, or a ceramic ashtray in the shape of a clown's head for your dad. One year, instead of the usual box of chocolate-covered cherries, I bought my mother a plastic snow globe for Christmas. Only I was so excited about spending a whole dollar on her that I made her unwrap her gift two days early.

I shook the globe hard and little white flakes of something that looked like snow swirled around in the perfect little world encased in plastic. Inside that snow world there was a tiny church with a white steeple, and a green fir tree, and a minuscule ice-skater. "See," I told Mama. "It's a snowstorm."

When the snowflakes settled, I grabbed the globe out of her hand and went to shake it up again. Even then, I guess, I preferred a world in constant motion. But the globe flew out of my hand and bounced off the mahogany chest of drawers. The plastic covering cracked, fluid seeping out all over the bedroom carpet. I don't remember crying, but I can remember being certain I had spoiled Christmas.

"Never mind," Mama told me. "I like it better this way. Who ever heard of snow in Atlanta at Christmas?"

For years, the snow globe came out with the Christmas decorations and it held a place of honor on the coffee table, along with a lumpy red candle my sister made as a Brownie project, and the genuine Italian ceramic manger scene my brother Kevin bought one year when he was flush with money from his newspaper route. The crack was never mentioned, although it grew wider every year until one year, in my early teens, it broke in two in my mother's hand as she was unpacking it. Edna took the pieces, taped them together, wrapped them in tissue, and tucked them back in the cardboard Rich's department store box where she kept all her Christmas decorations. It never got unpacked after that year, but she never threw it away, either. I think she thought it would eventually heal itself.

"You're using up a whole, perfectly good pound cake for that mess?"

Edna put down her mixer and peered over my shoulder. I was cutting finger-sized slices of pound cake and layering them in the bottom of my grandmother Alexander's big cut-glass bowl. I was preparing English trifle. You would have thought I was cooking haggis or water buffalo or something. My mother sniffed her disapproval and turned up the volume on the CD player. She knows I can't stand Perry Como—so there was Perry, blaring in my ears about how there was no place like home for the holidays. Perry didn't have a clue. His mother probably never came unhinged if somebody cooked something new in their kitchen.

Edna went back to her corner of the kitchen counter, where she proceeded with her Tom and Jerry batter. Edna is famous for her Tom and Jerrys. She got the recipe decades ago from an Italian family in our old neighborhood, and every year since, at Christmastime, we make quarts and quarts of the stuff to give away as gifts and to serve at Christmas Eve dinner, along with the fruitcake and the pound cake and the Coca-Cola baked ham and the ambrosia made with real, honest-to-God grated fresh coconut.

Most people these days don't even know what a Tom and Jerry is. It's probably better that they don't. All those uncooked eggs, along with heavy whipping cream, confectioner's sugar, brandy, rum, and cognac—a nutritional nightmare. And that's just the batter. To make the actual drink, you heat up a tot of the batter with a cup of milk—

whole milk, of course—and toss in a stout dose of bourbon. Not for the weak of heart, literally.

So the beaters were whirring and Edna was cracking those eggs like a fiend, tossing the eggshells right at me, not caring that she was splattering me with egg yolk and beaten cream. I could complain, but that would be picking a fight, sure as anything.

That's what you get for getting above yourself, I could hear her thinking as she pelted me with shells. Miss Smarty-pants. Miss Too-good-for-Jell-O-salad. Miss Dried-apricots-in-the-fruitcake.

"This office Christmas party was your idea, you know," I said loudly.

Her shoulders stiffened, but she didn't turn around.

Edna and I run a cleaning business called the House Mouse, right out of this same kitchen where we were currently holding our annual Pillsbury bitch-off. The house is a cozy little Craftsman bungalow in an in-town Atlanta neighborhood called Candler Park. Well, inside it's cozy. Outside, the neighborhood is sometimes a little edgier than we would have wished. Last year, we ended up chaining our wreath to the front door after it was stolen twice in the same weekend. But I'm optimistic that things are changing for the better. I'd decided on an Elvis Presley "Blue Christmas" decorating motif this year, with yards of silver garlands and festive strings of blue chasing lights and a spotlit portrait of a pre-Vegas Elvis smiling down from its perch atop the porch roof, and I think even the homeless guys who sleep in the vacant house on the corner were leaving us alone, out of respect for The King.

The girls who work for us love Christmas. Edna had been baking nonstop since the day after Thanksgiving, we'd worn holes in our Perry Como/Andy Williams/Nat King Cole/Bing Crosby CD collection, and the tree in the living room was already swamped with wrapped gifts. Even Cheezer, our only male House Mouse and resident oddball, loves the season. Everybody was in the Christmas spirit. Even, for once, me, Julia Callahan Garrity, owner and president of the House Mouse, not to mention Callahan Garrity Investigations.

Usually I think of Christmas as just one long headache. Our clients always want to switch their cleaning schedules around, traffic is a huge hassle, I hate malls and shopping because I never know what to buy anybody, and nobody ever buys me what I really want. I always end up spending too much, eating too much, and pouting too much. Christmas never meets my expectations. It hasn't, not since the watershed year I was twelve and I got a ten-speed bike and a ski jacket with a fake-fur collar and my first stereo. After that year, Christmas was just something to endure.

This year though, things were different. I found myself humming along with the radio. The girls were healthy and working hard and the House Mouse, for once, seemed fiscally sound. Edna was in good shape, too. We'd started taking regular morning walks around the neighborhood in the fall, and had kept it up until it got too cold for both of us.

I'd finished my shopping, too, and Christmas was still a week away. I had mail-order catalogs and a single marathon power-shopping day at Rich's to thank for my current sense of well-being.

And my love life was just fine, thank you very much. Andrew MacAuliffe and I had been together more than five years. We'd weathered his fling with his ex-wife and my brush with breast cancer, and more close calls with disaster than I like to recall. We've had tough times together, Mac and I, but we've finally come to the realization that we're better together than we are apart. Besides, we had to stay together for the dogs. His black labs Rufus and Maybelline produced a litter of five fat, wiggling puppies a year ago, and one—the runt of the litter, naturally—had stolen into my heart while I wasn't watching. Of all five puppies, Tammy Faye whimpered the longest, barked the loudest, and peed the most often on the floor. She was irresistible. Since he lives in a log cabin in the woods with plenty of space for the dogs to run, Mac has physical custody, but Tammy Faye knew, and I knew, that she was mine.

This year, for once, I really wasn't being the Grinch. Edna was the one who was getting all twitchy about this clambake. I was just trying to be practical.

"It would have been a lot easier to just give everybody a fifty-dollar Christmas bonus," I pointed out to Edna. "Maybe pick up a cheese ball and some chicken wings and call it a night."

Edna's lips tightened.

"We promised them a Christmas party. They're all excited. Ruby went out and bought herself a new hat. Cheezer says he might bring a date. And you know how worked up Baby and Sister are. Neva Jean's taking them for their hair appointments first thing in the morning. Are you gonna call them up and tell them they got all cut and curled just to sit home and watch *Christmas with Kathi Lee*?"

"We'll have the damned party," I assured her. "But would it kill you if I made something new?"

Nobody in our family ever made anything you could call fancy. Our cooking was substantial, solid, Southern. Nobody ever made anything new. Every holiday dinner, every Sunday supper, had a set menu in our family. Thanksgiving meant turkey, Christmas meant ham, Easter was leg of lamb, Monday night was vegetable soup and corn bread, Fridays meant macaroni and cheese or Mrs. Paul's frozen fish sticks. I can still remember the heady feeling that pervaded our kitchen that first time in the early nineties when Edna served chicken burritos. You would have thought she'd discovered penicillin.

But I'd had trifle at a dinner party somewhere, and I'd been besotted with it ever since. I'd waited a whole year to try out that trifle recipe. I'd made custard—from scratch. Set aside one of our famous lemon pound cakes to cut up and sprinkle with the twenty-dollar bottle of sherry I'd been hoarding. I bought imported English raspberry preserves, apricots, kiwifruit, strawberries, and fresh raspberries so expensive I had to look the other way when the cashier at the grocery store rang them up.

"The girls don't like fancy stuff like this," Edna said, waving her hand at the cut-glass bowl. "It's pretentious. You'll make them feel funny. Besides, we've got my pound cake and fruitcake, and Ruby's fudge, and all those boxes of candy customers have been dropping off. All these desserts will put them in sugar shock."

"I made a veggie platter," I said stubbornly. "Anybody who doesn't want my trifle can eat celery and carrots."

"Fine," Edna said. "Makes no difference to me. It's your house. Your business. You do as you please."

She took a dishcloth, ran it under the faucet and started mopping up the counters. Then she reached under the sink and got a bottle of Fantastik.

We Garritys are generally nonviolent people. When we fight, it's usually either with words or, worse, with silence. Not Edna. Her favorite weapon is a bottle of spray cleanser. She spritzed the entire countertop. I had to take my trifle and move it over to the kitchen

5

table to get it out of her line of fire. She took the dishrag and began swabbing the countertop. Her jaw was set, her eyes narrowed. This was war.

I decided to ignore her. With deliberate ceremony I dribbled the sherry over the pound cake and poured over it a thin layer of custard. I was concentrating on cutting up the kiwifruit when I heard the knock at the back door. I looked up. Edna kept spritzing and muttering to herself.

"Knock, knock," a deep voice called.

Edna dropped the bottle of Fantastik, right on to the floor. Her eyes were riveted to the back door.

It had been years, but I knew that voice.

"Knock, knock," he called again.

"Who is it?" I answered.

Edna was trying to untie her apron, but she was only knotting it worse.

"Sam and Janet," the voice boomed out.

Edna's hand jerked badly and she knocked the cognac bottle to the floor, along with the bag of confectioner's sugar. When she picked it up her face was covered with a fine white sheen of sugar.

"Sam and Janet who?" She coughed as she said it.

The beautiful bass voice boomed the answer. "Sam and Janet evening. . . You will meet a stranger. . ."

2

"Well, stranger!" Edna threw the back door open and enveloped my brother Brian in a hug that left them both breathless.

Brian was a good foot taller than our mother, and he grinned over her shoulder at me. I stood rooted in the doorway, wondering what I should do. How many years had it been since we'd heard from my baby brother? Daddy had been dead a little over ten years. Brian had shown up out of nowhere the day of the funeral, too. Riding a motorcycle, full of tears and apologies for not knowing about Daddy's long, lingering illness. He wouldn't stay at Mama's house that night, said he'd be more comfortable in a motel, but would call in the morning. He'd missed ten years' worth of mornings by my count.

But by Edna's reckoning, her baby boy was back, and it was Christmas a week early.

"Look at you," Edna cried. "You're skin and bones." She wouldn't let go of him, hugged his neck again, rubbed the sleeve of his navy blue nylon windbreaker. He leaned down and picked up a huge plastic sack full of lumpy objects.

"Christmas presents! I may be a Wandering Jew, but Brian Garrity never skips out on Christmas presents!"

"Oh, now," Edna started.

He took a step toward me and gave me a quick, awkward hug. "Jules," he murmured. "You smell like likker.

7

I punched his shoulder playfully. "We've been cooking. Anyway, you smell like beer. Same old Brian."

He smelled of stale beer and stale cigarettes and something else. Something odd, sort of flowery or powdery. He was taller than I remembered, and thinner by at least fifty pounds. His hair, worn in dark brown, shoulder-length curls when I'd seen him ten years ago, was cut in a close-cropped crew cut that showed a surprising amount of gray for a man who was only thirty-six. His face was tanned and weathered, the skin of someone who'd spent a lot of time outdoors.

I had to hug myself to keep warm. The cold and damp from the back stoop was already seeping through the thin soles of my bedroom slippers.

"Come on out to the truck," Brian said, pointing to the driveway. "I got a surprise."

"You're a surprise," Edna said. "That's enough for me for one night. Why didn't you call and let us know you were coming?"

"Just you wait and see," Brian said. A rusty black Toyota pickup was parked in the driveway behind my new van. Brian walked over to the passenger side and flung it open wide.

"Looky here," he said proudly. "Look what I brung y'all."

I peeked in the truck. At first I thought it was a pile of dirty laundry. Given Brian's past history, I was expecting laundry. Or maybe Amway samples, or a case of beer that had "fallen off" a truck somewhere.

But then the lumpy pile of clothes began to stir. A little girl sat up, blinked, looked at Brian, then Edna, then me. She had pale blonde hair, nearer silver than gold, and it stood up in ringlets on top of her head. Her eyes were big and dark and solemn. She was dressed in an oversized men's white undershirt and a diaper. My brother reached out his arms to her and she squirmed away.

"Mama," she whimpered.

"Sweet Jesus," Edna said sharply, edging closer to the truck to get a better look. She steadied herself with one hand on the hood of the truck.

"Brian, is this your idea of a joke?"

Brian scooped the child up in his arms.

"Joke's on you, Grandma," he said, winking at Edna. "Y'all. This is my daughter, Maura. Maura Jean Garrity. I been telling her about how Santa Claus loves to come visit little girls at their grandma's house. Ain't that right, Aunt Julia? Don't Santa Claus come right down the chimney at Grandma's house at Christmas?"

"All the time," I said dryly. "Grandma is Santa Claus's girlfriend."

"Noooo," Maura wailed. "No Santa Claus!" She was squirming in Brian's grip.

Edna reached over and took the child in her own arms, smoothing her hair with one hand, rubbing her cheek against the little girl's. "It's all right, darlin'," she crooned. "Grandma's here. And Santa won't come in tonight."

"She's soaking wet, Brian," Edna said. "And cold. She's like a little Eskimo baby."

Edna hustled the child into the kitchen. By the time Brian and I caught up with her, Edna had Maura propped on the kitchen table and was wrapping her in a big bath towel she'd just pulled out of the clothes dryer in the adjacent laundry room.

"How old?" Edna demanded, rubbing Maura's tiny pink feet between the palms of her hands. "Two?"

"She was three in September, right around your birthday, Mama," Brian said.

"You don't have any idea when my birthday is," Edna said briskly. "I was born in October. You say this child is three? Mighty tiny for three. And still in diapers? We've got to get her in some decent clothes before she freezes to death."

"She's fine," Brian said. "Maura's a big girl, aren't you sweetheart? We'll get her all the clothes she needs in the morning. Right now, she's doing just great in her daddy's T-shirt. A T-shirt was good enough for all of us kids for a nightgown, wasn't it, Jules?"

"Callahan," Edna said quickly. "Everybody but me calls her Callahan now, Brian."

"They have since college," I pointed out. Of course, Brian hadn't actually been around me since I was in college, but he had to know anyway.

"Whatever," he said, shrugging.

"Finish warming her up, then give her a little cup of milk, Jules," Edna ordered. She threw a quick look at Brian. "She does drink out of a cup, doesn't she?"

"Sure," Brian said. "I told you, Maura's a big girl now."

9

I poured a couple of inches of milk into one of those plastic go-cups they give you when you buy a Coke at the convenience store, and Edna stepped into the laundry room and started rooting around in the cupboards.

Maura sipped her milk, holding the cup with one hand and tugging at one of the silver curls with the other.

Edna came out of the laundry room with a faded, blue fleece sleeper, which I recognized as once belonging to one of my brother Kevin's boys, who are now eight and ten. She had a pair of thick, white cotton training underpants in the other hand.

"Come here, sweetheart," she cooed to Maura, taking her onto her lap. She started to unfasten the tape on the diaper.

"Uh, Mama, that might not be so good an idea," Brian said.

"Are you telling me this child isn't potty-trained?"

I rolled my eyes. I remembered well this stage with my two nephews and with various other unsuspecting mothers and their toddlers over the years. Edna Mae Garrity is a potty Nazi. All four of her children, she liked to brag, had been completely toilet-trained by no later than eighteen months. Edna was the kind of person who stopped women in the diaper aisle at the Kroger to deliver sermons on the subject. Pull-Ups—the kind of disposable diapers designed to allow children to pull their diapers up and down like underwear—were, in Edna's well-voiced opinion, even worse an abomination of the industrial age than instant iced tea or canned biscuits.

Brian picked up the bottle of sherry I'd been using for the trifle and knocked back a long swallow.

"Hey," I said, snatching it away from him. "That's for my trifle."

He wiped his mouth with the back of his hand and grimaced. "Tastes like crap anyway. Where's the real stuff?"

I handed him the bourbon bottle. "Is this more what you had in mind?"

He poured himself three inches and plopped down on one of the oak kitchen chairs.

"Daddy," Maura said. Edna had zipped her into the sleeper and was rocking gently to and fro, humming some wordless song that sounded a lot like "Mona Lisa."

Brian blew her a kiss. "Daddy's good girl. Let Grandma take you night-night."

"No night-night," Maura said, her lower lip starting to tremble.

"We'll stay right here by Daddy," Edna said. "Just rest your eyes now, sugar."

Edna hummed and Brian sipped and I watched. Before two minutes had passed, Maura's milk-pale eyelashes started to droop, then flutter. Her heavy, steady breaths filled the warm, light-filled kitchen.

My brother got up to refill his glass. He held up the bottle to offer me a drink, too, but I shook my head no. It was amazing. Here we all were in my kitchen, a week before Christmas. My brother had turned up from nowhere after a hiccup of ten years. You'd think he'd just gone down to the corner store for a pack of cigarettes.

Brian reached over and rubbed a fleece-covered toe. "Best little girl in the whole damn world."

"Where'd you get that baby?" I said, unable to hide my curiosity.

He laughed. "The usual way. Don't tell me you hadn't tried it yourself, Jules. You're no old maid."

"Whose is she?" I asked. "Where's the mother? Where have you been all this time, Brian Garrity?" My voice got louder and more insistent with each question. He was drinking my bourbon. I deserved some answers.

"Shh!" Edna said fiercely. "You'll wake her up." She pushed her glasses down to the end of her nose and gave Brian that look. "Is she really your child? No fooling around now, son."

"She's mine," Brian said firmly. "You get a look at her toes? Look exactly like mine, especially that long little toe."

Edna wouldn't let him off the hook. "Who's the mother? Does she know you've taken the baby? What's this all about, Brian?"

Brian took a pack of cigarettes from his shirt pocket. It was a blue work shirt, faded and in need of washing. He shook a cigarette out and lit up.

"I'm the daddy. That's the most important thing for Maura. And no, her mama don't know where she's at. Her mama don't know nothing but partying and whoring around." He looked around for an ashtray, but I didn't offer one, so he cupped his left hand and flicked ashes into it.

"Shay doesn't deserve to know where my baby's at. Shay don't care nothing about this little girl. All she cares about is that big shot real estate broker she works for and screws on the side. Partying. Smoking dope probably. Sleeping with men in the same room with my baby daughter. You see those clothes Maura had on? Her other clothes were wet when I picked her up. That's all the extra clothes they had in her diaper bag at the day care. Not even a pair of shoes and socks. Not even a goddamn jacket."

"Shay," Edna looked down at Maura's upturned face. The sound of her soft breaths filled the kitchen. "Not Shay Gatlin. Are you telling me this is Shay Gatlin's child?"

"'Fraid so," Brian said.

I tried to keep my face expressionless. Talk about a blast from the past.

Shay Gatlin had lived down the street from us, growing up out in the suburbs in Sandy Springs in the sixties and seventies. Her mother, Annette, had been the neighborhood tramp, a bottle-blonde divorcée with an endless supply of no-account boyfriends moving in and out, and Annette's only child a detail the mother didn't seem terribly interested in.

Shay was a tough little stray, the kind of kid who'd show up on your doorstep right after school and stay through dinner and on into the evening until Edna insisted it was time for her to go home. Edna probably fed Shay most of the hot meals she ate in her childhood, with Colonel Sanders and Ronald McDonald providing the rest. Shay had been just a kid when I left home for college, what, seven or eight? She'd be in her late twenties now, at least seven years younger than Brian.

"She told me she was on the Pill," Brian said, dipping a finger into the bowl of Tom and Jerry batter. "You remember how skinny she always was? She didn't even show until she was seven months gone. That's when she told me. Said she quit taking the Pill cause it made her gain weight. By then, it was too late to do anything about it. We got married as soon as I knew. Well, pretty soon after. Right after Maura was born. My name's on the birth certificate. I made sure of that, Mama."

Edna sucked in her breath, glancing down at the baby. Her face softened as she traced the outline of the child's ear with her fingertip. "My first granddaughter," she said. "And I didn't even know."

3

We sat up past midnight. Brian drank bourbon, I asked questions, Brian ignored most of them. Edna watched, enraptured, as Maura slept, wrapped tight in her arms. Her curiosity was killing her, I was sure, but she'd evidently decided to leave it up to me to be the one to ask all the questions. Eventually, I heard a short, exaggerated snort. Edna's head shot up and she blushed, embarrassed at being caught snoring.

"Some things never change. The old lady still snores like Popeye," Brian drawled.

"And you're still a smart-aleck horse's ass," Edna retorted. With effort, she heaved herself out of the rocker. She shifted the sleeping child in her arms, and kissed the top of Brian's head. He had the grace to blush.

"I reckon you won't leave without her, will you?" she asked. "Callahan will get you some sheets and blankets. I'll put Maura down in my bed. Poor thing. She's worn out." She shuffled off down the hallway, toward her bedroom.

"You see that?" Brian stood up and stretched. "I knew Mama'd do that way. I feel better already, seeing Mama with my baby. Now I know I've done the right thing. OK by you if I sack out on the sofa?"

"Fine," I said. "Is this, uh, a temporary arrangement?"

He hooted. "You mean, am I trying to move in with y'all, dump the baby on you? No, Jules. It's just for tonight. See, me taking Maura was kind of a sudden decision. The place I'm staying, I'm not exactly set up for kids yet. I need a day or two, get a crib, see about a baby-sitter, all that kind of thing. And I thought it was high time Mama met her granddaughter."

"You're crazy," I said flatly. "You can't just take a baby from its mother. I don't care what kind of mother she is; you don't do that, Brian. It's called kidnapping. The cops will throw your butt in jail."

Brian ran his hand over his chin, where the stubble was decidedly gray.

"Shay's got no right to have Maura. She's a unfit mother."

I looked him over. He was underweight, unwashed, more than half drunk. From the look of the junk in his pickup, I had an idea the place he'd been staying was right there in that truck.

"Like you're a fit father," I said.

He didn't flinch.

"Where were you?" I asked. "What the hell has happened with you, Brian?"

"I've been around," he said simply, shrugging. "I'm gonna go get some clothes out of the truck, take a shower, hit the sack."

He headed for the back door. Just like he had ten years ago, after Daddy's funeral.

"No," I said simply. "I'll get you some towels. I'll wash your clothes for you. I'll even fix you something to eat. But you're not going to sleep until I get some answers."

"Shit," he muttered under his breath. "I shoulda gone to Maureen's." He put his hand on the doorknob. "I'm just going to get my stuff. OK? Let me get a shower and then you can give me the third degree. Swear to God."

"Deal," I said.

But I stood in the doorway and watched him get his stuff.

"Still a cop, huh?" he said, when he was back inside. "What was that you were saying about food?"

"Scrambled eggs, bacon, toast."

"Biscuits would be better," he countered.

"I'm not your mama," I reminded him. "And this is no diner. Take it or leave it."

• • •

I scrambled half a dozen eggs, fried eight pieces of bacon. The bread was getting a little moldy, but I scraped off the green parts and made him four slices of toast. I left the milk jug on the table in front of him.

He sat at the kitchen table, took his knife and cut the toast in neat triangles. Just like Edna had always done for us. His hair was wet, his eyes red-rimmed from the soap and shampoo. He'd put on a clean brown flannel shirt and left the shirttails sticking out, and he reminded me for the first time of the kid brother who used to hog the Frosted Flakes box every morning.

"Everybody's still pissed at me, huh?" he asked, picking up a slice of bacon and nibbling at it.

"Kevin told Edna you were probably dead. That she should quit waiting for you to come home."

"My big brother," Brian said sourly. "What a guy."

"What'd you expect?"

"I never meant it to be so long," Brian said. "Daddy dying, I couldn't handle that. Guy I knew said he could get me a job working on one of those oil rigs, out in the Gulf. Good money. Fifteen, twenty bucks an hour, he said. But my bike broke down before I got to New Orleans. Time I got there, they'd given the job to somebody else. Let me tell you something, Jules. People in Atlanta think it's hot here, they've never been to New Orleans in July. Christ! It's like being melted alive."

"You were in New Orleans all this time?" I asked. "How'd you hook up with Shay?"

"Nah. Hell, I only stayed in New Orleans a couple weeks. Let's see. From there I went to Houston. You ever see pictures of that big SunBanc building, looks like a pyramid made out of aluminum foil? I helped build that. Company I was working for got some contracts out in San Francisco, so I spent a couple years there. Then my boss quit that company, got a job in Seattle, so I went up there for about six months. Never did see a full day of sunshine. Atlanta was looking good when I got back here. I tell you, I got down and kissed that ugly red clay, I was so glad to be back home. And wouldn't you know it, the first friendly face I see when I get back to Atlanta, it's little, skinny ole Shay Gatlin. I go into the bar at the Marriott down at the airport, there she is, sitting on a bar stool, sipping a glass of white wine. She knew me right away, but I had no idea who she was. I mean, you wouldn't know her, either, Jules. She was a fox."

I'd fixed myself a cup of tea, and I sipped it slowly. "You said Maura's three. So you moved back here—what, four years ago? And you've been here that whole time? And you couldn't bother to pick up the phone and let anybody know you were alive?"

He poured himself a tall glass of milk. "What would it have changed?" he asked. "Shay moved in with me. We were living down in Jonesboro. Some of the time, I didn't have a job. Some of the places we lived weren't so great. Was I gonna call you up and say 'Hey, y'all come on down here to the trailer park, and by the way, could I borrow fifty bucks?'"

"We're family," I said. "We've all been broke before. Out of work. Nobody cares where you're living, Brian. For God's sakes, what do you take us for?"

Brian drained the glass of milk, wiped his face with a wadded-up paper napkin. He leaned forward.

"Look. I'm not like y'all. I'm not into all this family mess. I don't ask for nothing from nobody and I don't expect nothing. Besides, after I got together with Shay, well, I could just hear what you and Maureen and Mama would say about her. That she was trash. Maybe she is—yeah, well, she definitely is—but I didn't need to hear it from my family."

"Where's Shay now?" I asked. "What happened that made you take Maura and leave?"

He got up from the table and scraped his scraps into the trash. "I left six months ago," he said. He took his plate to the sink and started washing it. It was a side to my brother that I'd never seen. Growing up, he'd been the consummate slob, leaving a trail of clothes and toys and trash in his wake.

"She was screwin' around on me. I knew it for a long time, but I wouldn't admit it to myself. I caught her once, sneaking into the apartment when she thought I was asleep. Had her panties in her purse. After that, I left. Shay couldn't afford the apartment without me. Her and Maura moved in with Annette and her boyfriend, Chuck, a couple months ago. They're living down there in Jonesboro, one of those big condo complexes right near the airport. Chuck's a lawyer. Slicker than cat shit."

"Annette's still around?" I didn't hide the surprise in my voice.

"Still claiming she's thirty," Brian said. "She tells people Maura's her sister's kid. Hey, you'll get a kick out of this. Annette's a cop."

"No way."

"Well. A security guard. At the airport. She's got a gun and everything."

I could imagine Annette Gatlin with a Colt Malt Liquor in her hand, but the idea of her patrolling the airport with the real thing was a scary thought. "Remind me to hop a Greyhound next time I leave town," I said.

He laughed.

"Is the divorce final?"

"Not that I know of," Brian said. "Chuck's her lawyer. Her and Annette think they run the world. She's working as a secretary for some real estate tycoon down there in Clayton County. Guy owns half the county. He's big in politics, pals around with all the lawyers. That's how Shay got temporary custody. All those judges down there buddy around. A working man like me doesn't have a chance."

"Shay's got custody of Maura?" I asked sharply. "Full custody?"

"I'm supposed to get her every other weekend," Brian said, looking around for something to dry his dishes. "It is so fucked up you wouldn't believe it. Chuck got the judge to say I can only have Maura for the day. Not even overnight."

I sighed. "You big moron. Shay's lawyer probably has a warrant out for your arrest for violating that custody order."

He shook his head vehemently. "You don't know Shay. She probably hasn't even figured it out yet. That day care, it's a twenty-four-hour-a-day operation, 'cause of all the people who work over at the airport. Shay drops Maura off, and Annette's supposed to pick her up. But hell, you know those two. They go out and party half the night. Imagine that? A mother-daughter team of sluts?"

"So get a lawyer," I said. "The way to get a custody order changed is not to kidnap your three-year-old."

"Lawyers cost money. I already owe my guy sixteen hundred bucks—and that's what he charges for screwing up my life and giving my little girl away. So I said, 'fuck it.' Shay's so dumb it's pathetic. I followed her this morning, watched her drop Maura off at day care. This afternoon, I followed her when she left the office. You know where she went? The Day's Inn on Riverdale Road. Why's a mother need a motel room when she's got a condo two miles away? So I went over to the day care, and I told the chick working there, Shay had a late appointment and needed me to pick up Maura. No problem. You shoulda seen Maura's face when she saw it was Daddy picking her up. Like a little beam of sunshine."

"Like felony abduction," I said. "You've got to call Shay and tell her where Maura is."

"I didn't come here to get lectured to," Brian snapped. "This is just for one night. Tomorrow, I gotta go to work, pick up my paycheck. Then I can pay the deposit on this new place, and get us situated."

"And what then?" I demanded. "Just go into hiding, like some damn outlaw on the lam? Get real, Brian. Get a lawyer. Let us help you. We're your family, dammit. We want you and Maura in our lives."

"Then mind your own business," Brian growled. He got up and headed toward the den. "I'm going to bed."

4

In the morning there was an oil puddle in the driveway where Brian's truck had been parked. The truck was gone. But Maura was sitting at the kitchen table, propped up on a stack of telephone books, happily spooning cream of wheat into a face already smeared with what looked like grape-jelly covered toast crumbs. Edna sat across the table from her, drinking coffee and admiring her new grandchild.

"She's the smartest young'un I've ever seen," my mother announced.

"What about me?" I asked. "I always thought I was the smartest young'un you'd ever seen. You told me I could read by the time I was four."

"That was before Maura," she said, giving me a dismissive wave. "Show Aunt Callahan how smart you are, sweetheart," Edna coached.

Maura put her spoon down on the tabletop and her dark eyes took me in, faded flannel pj's, sleep-matted hair, red and black Georgia Bulldog bedroom slippers. I was a mess. Aside from the food on her face, however, Maura was a picture of good grooming. She wore a red-and-white striped long-sleeved shirt and a pair of red corduroy overalls. The clothes were clean but faded. Her hair had been combed and clipped with a red plastic barrette in a curly topknot on top of her head.

"No Callahan," she said calmly.

I yawned and poured myself a cup of coffee. "You're right, Ma," I said. "She's brilliant. Must be Shay's gene pool."

"This young'un knows all her numbers," Edna said. "Even her phone number, including the area code. And right before you came in, she was singing 'Rudolph the Red-Nosed Reindeer.'"

"Where's her daddy?" I asked.

"Gone when I got up. And I got up at six," she said. "He left a note, though. Had to go to work. But he said he'd call before noon."

"Daddy?" Maura said, cocking her head to one side. "Daddy's bad."

Edna raised an eyebrow at me. "Wonder where she heard that?"

"It's a big mess," I warned my mother, gesturing with a nod of my head toward Maura, who was listening intently. Maybe she really was a little rocket scientist. Hell, the Garrity side must have contributed something to the kid's DNA. "I tried to talk to B-R-I-A-N last night. He won't listen. You-know-who has custody. Legal custody. He's not even allowed overnight visits, Ma."

Her face paled. "Good Lord. What kind of lies has Shay been telling about him?"

"He's broke," I said. "No money for a lawyer. And he has no intention of taking our friend home or telling her M-O-M where she is."

"We'll give him the money," she said, as though that would solve everything. Get his life back on track. I've known that S-H-A-Y since she was this one's age. She's not fit to raise a cockroach, let alone a child. And as for that Annette—"

"Shh," I cautioned. But it was too late.

"Granny Annie!" Maura said, twisting a strand of hair that had escaped from the topknot. "Where's my Annie?"

"At work," Edna said, patting her hand. "But Grandma's here. And Aunt Callahan. And we've got lots to do this morning. Can you help Grandma?"

You had to hand it to Edna, she was smooth.

"Can we watch *Barney*?" Maura asked, looking from Edna to me, not sure who was the boss of this outfit.

"Sure," Edna said. "Whatever that is."

"It's a kiddy show. The star is a big purple dinosaur who sings and dances," I said. "Kids love it. Personally, it makes me want to puke."

"Maybe we'll watch *Barney* after we go to the store," Edna told Maura. "We're having a party tonight! A Christmas party. And you get to help make the cookies. How about that?"

"Store?" Maura's face brightened immediately. "Buy me a toy?"

"Groceries," Edna said. "But maybe we can get you a treat."

I coughed tactfully. "Uh, Ma. You can't take Maura to the store. You don't have a car seat in your car."

Edna frowned. "I've got seat belts in my car. I'll strap her in good and tight. She doesn't need a special seat. And it's just up to the Kroger. Not even a mile away."

"State law," I said. "Children under six have to be in child safety restraints."

"Pooh," Edna said. "I raised four kids and they hadn't even invented seat belts."

"Yeah, but Maureen's still got a scar on her forehead from where she hit the dashboard Jesus, that time you had to slam on the brakes to keep from hitting the Shoemakers' dog," I reminded her. "Anyway, we've got to talk Brian into taking Maura back to her mom as soon as possible. If this child has a single tiny scratch on her, you know they'll blame him. And us."

"All right," Edna said. She kissed the top of Maura's head. "You stay here and watch *Barney* with Aunt Callahan. Grandma will be right back."

"Hey," I said, "I didn't volunteer to baby-sit. I've got a lot of errands to do this morning."

"Never mind," Edna said. "You can bond with your niece while I'm gone. Be nice, now. And don't forget to put her on the potty right after you clean her up from breakfast. All this cereal she's had, she should be ready for a really big job."

"Potty?" I put down the banana I'd been peeling. "I didn't sign on for potty duty. Definitely not. You can just put her back in a diaper, Ma, until you get home. I spent my whole childhood cleaning up Brian's butt. I'm not starting over on his kid's."

"We're out of diapers," Edna said. "I was going to pick some up at the store. Just until we get her schedule working smoothly."

My mother took a damp washcloth and gently dabbed Maura's face with it. The child wriggled and shook her head and giggled, but Edna had dealt with much tougher customers than this kid. "Come on, now," she coaxed. "Let's get this pretty face cleaned up." Edna clamped down on Maura's left hand, but she unwisely left her right hand free.

Plop. Edna looked up, surprised. A tablespoonful of Cream of Wheat was sprayed across the crown of her head.

"Shit," Edna said, putting her hand up to feel it.

"Shit!" Maura agreed.

It took five minutes of scrubbing to get the hot cereal out of my mother's highly teased pink bouffant. "Now I got flat hair," she complained, looking at herself in the bathroom mirror. "Can't have an office Christmas party with flat hair. I'll run by the beauty parlor after the store and have Frank wet it down and comb it out nice."

"Uuuuh," Maura sang out.

Edna gave her a fond glance. Maura was seated on the toilet, the red corduroy overalls hanging down over her feet. "Good girl," Edna said. "Make a big potty for Aunt Callahan. She'll be so proud."

"She'll be so disgusted," I muttered. "This is why I never had kids, you know."

We stayed in the bathroom for another ten minutes after Edna left. Maura making noises like an elephant in childbirth, me making encouraging noises. But there were no really encouraging signs that Maura was about to achieve big potty status.

"Almost done?" I asked, leaning wearily against the bathtub.

She shook her head. "Read me a story."

A story. The kid liked to read in the bathroom. She was definitely a Garrity.

"Stay right there," I said, dashing out into the living room to look for reading material. "Story," I muttered. "Need a story for Maura."

We were woefully short on children's literature. No *Cat in the Hat*, no *Madeline*. Kevin's kids didn't come over very often, and when they did, they brought their own handheld video games to combat the boredom of being at Grandma's house. The coffee table held a stack of old magazines, *TV Guide, Reader's Digest, Atlanta Magazine,* like that. I seized one and ran back to the bathroom.

"Here," I said, holding out a year-end double issue of *People* magazine. "It's got Princess Diana and Michael Jackson. Hours of reading entertainment."

She spread the magazine across her lap and flipped through the pages. "Barbie!" she said excitedly, pointing to a photograph of Heather Locklear hanging on the arm of a menacing-looking rock star.

"Kid's good," I said.

I turned on the water in the shower. If we were going to spend the morning in that bathroom, I might as well get clean while we were doing it.

"You stay right there while I take a shower, OK?" I said, stepping into the tub. "Let me know when you make big potty."

"OK," Maura agreed.

I was still nervous that she might decide to get up and leave and do God knows what. I remembered the last time I'd baby-sat for one of Kevin's kids. I'd gone into the house to answer the telephone and in the minute I was gone, the little vandal had managed to get the garden hose turned on full power so he could "wash" my van. With all the windows open.

"Let's sing," I said. If I could hear her voice, I rationalized, she couldn't be getting into too much mischief.

"Row, row, row your boat," I warbled.

"Gently down the stream," she answered.

"Merrily, merrily, merrily, merrily, life is but a dream."

We sang, and I sudsed up. I poured a capful of shampoo in my hair and worked it into my scalp. Maura's high-pitched little voice went on and on about rowing down the stream. I lost track of the verses, thinking about my prodigal brother and his idea of a Christmas surprise. I washed my hair twice, rinsed it with conditioner, and then stood for a long time under the stream of hot water, trying to sort out my emotions. I stepped away from the water, lathered myself up, then let the water sluice the soap away.

"Merrily, merrily, merrily, merrily," Maura said, a little out of breath.

My right hand slid across the flesh of my left breast, felt the slight pucker of tissue from the lumpectomy I'd had six years ago.

The water was scalding hot but I felt myself go cold all over. I left the water running, stepped out of the tub, and stood, dripping wet and naked in front of the bathroom mirror. I wiped at the fog-steamed mirror. Maybe the mirror would tell me something my fingertips couldn't. But there was nothing new. A slice of red puckered tissue hiding a mass of free-floating cancer anxiety.

I do the breast self-exams every month. Sometimes the anxiety and fear bubble up from nowhere and I panic. Calling my surgeon helps. Talking to Mac helps. I keep the mammograms under the bed, and when the panic strikes, I pull them out and examine them, to reassure myself I'm clean.

But sometimes, usually in the shower, the panic hits. I pressed the breast again with my fingertips and tried to remember how everything should look.

Maura was still sitting on the commode with the *People* magazine opened to a pictorial history of Liz Taylor's hairstyles and necklines. She didn't seem all that surprised to see her aunt emerge dripping wet and naked from the steam clouds of the shower to poke warily at her own bosom.

I did a breast self-exam exactly the way my gynecologist showed me, only ten times more intensively than usual. It took longer, too, because I had to stop two or three times to deal with the dry heaves that kept overcoming me every time I tried to form the word "cancer" in my brain. I had to puke in the bathtub, because Maura was still taking her own sweet time about that potty business.

She read and sang, and I puked.

"Row, row, row your boat," she repeated. And then, finally, as I was struggling to get dressed, she said the words. "Oh, looky. Big girl. Good girl."

I wiped my mouth on a bath towel and swallowed hard. She hopped off the commode so I could get a look at what she'd accomplished. It was everything Edna had hoped for.

Maura got to flush the toilet. She did that, and I clapped, and we sang "gently down the stream," which seemed mightily appropriate.

Then I knelt down unsteadily on the tile floor and helped her pull up my nephew's too-big underpants, and snap the shoulders of the red overalls, which I realized had been his, too, six or seven years ago.

She was so proud of herself. Her hair was as damp as mine from the steam, and her cheeks as pink as mine from the heat. She patted my cheek, and then, with a chubby forefinger, repeated what she'd just watched me do, poking my left breast, directly on the lumpectomy.

"Boo-boo," she said. She kissed her fingertip, then pressed it to my scarred breast. "Better?"

"Better," I said. I took a deep breath.

"Sing some more," Maura begged. "More."

I stood up and we sang the last verse.

"Life is but a dream."

5

Maura and I decided to play house. Clean the house, that is. We put my grandmother's special crocheted lace tablecloth on the dining room table and took Edna's fancy cut-glass wine goblets out of the china cabinet. We cut out the sugar cookie dough on the kitchen table: stars, hearts, a reindeer, a candy cane, and a Christmas tree. Maura really did know all the words to "Rudolph the Red-Nosed Reindeer."

"Shh," I said, holding a finger to my lips. "Don't tell Grandma you sang it to me."

I cut up the vegetables for the relish tray for that night; Maura got to mix the Lipton's onion soup mix into the sour cream for the dip. She flung onion dip all over the kitchen, screaming with glee each time a glob landed on me. We split a bag of potato chips; they were the baked kind, so I felt they were fine for a toddler.

We were having a high old time grating the cheddar for the cheese ball when Edna staggered in the back door under the weight of an armload of groceries.

Maura took a long calculating look at all the grocery sacks. "Treat?"

"Just like her Daddy," Edna said, giving her granddaughter an indulgent peck on the cheek. "Did you make potty for Aunt Callahan?"

"Big potty!" Maura boasted.

"It was impressive," I admitted. "I was going to save it, but . . . "

"Never mind," Edna said quickly. She held her pocketbook out to Maura. "Look in Grandma's purse," she said, putting down the last armload of supplies.

Maura reached for it and I gave a start. "Your gun," I said, feeling faint. "It's not . . . "

"It's hidden up in the A-T-T-I-C," she said. "First thing I did this morning. Baby in the house, you think I would have something like that around? All she's gonna find in that purse is a bag of M&M's."

"Candy!" Maura said, bringing up the brown and white bag. She ripped the top of the bag, sat down, and spilled the bag's contents into her lap. She started sorting them by color, red in this pile, orange there, yellow, green, and blue.

"When'd they start making blue ones?" Edna asked, peering down at Maura.

"Right after the last bag of candy you bought for your other grand-children," I said, starting to unload the bags. "Some grandmother you are."

I was trying to stuff everything into the refrigerator when the phone rang. Edna picked it up, listened, and tried to talk.

"Now, wait a minute," she said. Her voice had a strangled, unnatural tone.

"Say that again? I don't understand. Don't talk so fast."

Edna's eyes met mine. Her lips formed the soundless word: Shay.

The voice on the other line was agitated, speaking so loudly I could hear the stream of profanity from where I stood. Maura was oblivious, sorting her candy into color categories, popping them one by one into her mouth, appreciating the stains left on her hands.

"Now, Shay," Edna said. "That's just crazy talk. Calm down, please. Nobody's kidnapped your baby. She's sitting right here on the floor, happy as a clam. No, I will not put her on the phone." Edna's lips were pursed into a grim line. "You're too upset. You'll get her all upset."

"Give me that phone," I told my mother. Edna shook her head, but I held out my hand, and finally she handed it to me.

"Shay?"

"Who the hell is this?"

"It's Callahan."

"I heard you were calling yourself that now. Who the hell asked you to butt into my business?" she snarled. "I'm gonna have all your asses under arrest for conspiring to kidnap my baby. You better do what I told your mama. Put that sorry-ass brother on the phone right this minute."

Her voice was low and throaty, deep as a man's. I'd forgotten that about Shay. As a kid, she'd always dressed in jeans and a T-shirt, and with that surprising deep voice, lots of people had mistaken her for a little boy.

"He's gone to work," I said. "But Maura's fine. Edna and I are watching her. She's good as gold. No trouble at all. He said he'd be back here around noon. I'll have him call you as soon as he gets in."

"Your brother's the one who's in trouble," Shay said, interrupting. "He thinks he can kidnap my kid and get away with that shit, he's nuts. I got a court order right here that I'm looking at. Signed by the judge. And I can have a sheriff's deputy go out to where Brian works and have him served; locked up if he doesn't hand over Maura. And my lawyer's gonna get a restraining order put on him, too, saying Brian can't have the baby at all, since he pulled this kidnap shit."

"He just wanted to see the baby, that's all. He didn't think you'd get this upset."

"Upset?" she shrieked. "He kidnaps Maura from the day care, lies about me, and disappears for twenty-four hours? I didn't sleep all night, worrying about where my daughter could be, whether she was warm enough, whether she'd eaten or had her vitamins. I was frantic."

"Brian misunderstood," I said, pissed at her goody-goody act. "He happened to see your car parked at a motel near the airport, right after you got off work. He thought he was doing you a favor, picking Maura up, so she wouldn't have to spend so many hours at the day-care center."

"He followed me?" she shrieked. "My God. He's stalking me now. I knew it. That son of a bitch is stalking me. And he's got a gun, too. You know he's violent, don't you?"

"I don't believe that," I said coolly.

"There's a lot you don't know about your brother," Shay said. "You and all that Garrity crowd, think you're better than everybody else. Let me tell you something, Brian Garrity is no saint. He's a drunk, and a criminal. He hit me, I dealt with it. But when he tried to hurt my baby that's when I drew the line. That's when the judge drew the line, too. I got a news flash for you, Julia Callahan Garrity. That brother of yours is a child-abusing pervert. What do you think about that?"

"I think you're a pathological liar," I said calmly. "I'll tell Brian to have his lawyer call you."

"What lawyer? Where'd he get money for a lawyer?"

"This lawyer is an old family friend," I lied. "I thought you'd have been notified by now. Brian is filing to have the custody order amended. If you'll give me your lawyer's name and number, I'll have Brian's lawyer call him right away."

"I don't know what you're trying to pull, but it won't work," Shay said. "You just tell that brother of yours that I want my baby back here at my apartment by five o'clock today. And he better bring my check, too."

"What check?" I asked.

"Child support," Shay snapped. "He's three months behind. They got a deadbeat father statute in this state, you know. If I don't get that check along with my baby, and I mean today, Brian goes to jail. It sure as hell won't be the first time."

She slammed the phone down. I heard another click on my end of the line before I hung up.

Edna came in from the other room. She'd been listening in. "Lying little troublemaker," she said. We both looked at Maura, who was still playing with her M&M's. There was a dark stain on the front of the corduroy overalls, but Maura hadn't seemed to notice.

"Your turn," I told my mother, scooping Maura up in my arms and handing her over to Edna.

"In a minute," she said. "You told her Brian has a lawyer. An old family friend. You're not thinking of who I'm thinking of, are you?"

"None of the lawyers I deal with do domestic law," I said. "They all hate divorce work. Ferd just sort of popped into my mind."

"I guess so. Him being divorced and remarried four times himself," Edna said tartly. "You think he'd do it, help Brian?"

"If he's still in practice," I said, shrugging.

"If he's still alive," Edna said. "That's what I'm wondering about."

6

Ferd Bryce was still alive as far as directory assistance was concerned. They gave me a number for a residence in Cumming, a former country junction that's experienced a population explosion in the past ten years as the city expanded northward.

The phone rang and rang, but nobody picked up. "Trust Ferd not to have an answering machine," I told Edna.

"At least he's got a phone now," she said. "Remember after he got back with that second wife, for the second time, he made her get rid of the TV and the microwave, wouldn't even let her have an electric blanket?"

"That was his third wife," I corrected her. "Susan the second. He got into that back-to-nature stuff in a big way while he was separated from Cindy, number two. I'll bet that's why he's moved to Cumming. To live up in the woods to get away from all the Democrats and left-wing nutjobs."

Edna chuckled. "Joke's on him. All the nutjobs have done moved up into the woods. They got a higher crime rate in Forsyth County than we got right here in Candler Park. Keep calling, though, Jules."

She glanced over at Maura, who had been cleaned up and was now sitting on the kitchen floor, happily stacking all our plastic containers into a Tupperware tower.

"I can't believe how normal this child is. We've got to get her away from Shay and Annette. Right now. Before they turn her into what they are."

Even though I'm a private detective, I rarely do domestic work. Divorce is too messy. Too emotional. I know a little something about the business, though, and I know how child custody usually works.

"Don't get your hopes up," I warned her. "Judges in Georgia want mamas to raise their own babies. If one judge has already restricted Brian's visitation privileges, Shay must have some bad stuff on him. Even somebody as good as Ferd, even a former judge like Ferd, might not be able to change that."

But that wasn't what my mother wanted to hear. She got a package of hamburger out of the refrigerator, dumped it in her big blue mixing bowl, then got busy chopping the onion and green pepper for her famous sweet-and-sour meatballs.

"No matter what she says Brian has done, I promise you, Shay and that mother of hers have done worse," Edna said, pinching off bits of meat and rolling them between the flattened palms of her hands. "You're a private detective. You'll just have to get busy and catch them at it. Hang out at that motel. See who she's shacking up with. Borrow that video camera from that lawyer buddy of yours again."

I sighed. "It's not that easy. Brian still has to take Maura home. Even if we get him a lawyer and even if I run round-the-clock surveillance and find out Shay's running a white-slave ring out of that apartment, in the meantime, she's got custody."

Edna snorted. "It's ridiculous."

I hadn't dared tell Edna what was really worrying me. Shay's accusations about the kind of life Brian had been leading all these years. What did I really know about my brother? Was he capable of violence? The old Brian was sly but good-natured. If you caught him in a lie, he'd bluff his way out of it if he could. He and Kevin used to trade pummeling on a regular basis, but that was different. They were brothers.

At 12:30 the phone rang. We both jumped to answer it. Edna had hamburger meat all over her hands, so I won the toss-up.

It was Brian. He was calling from a pay phone, and the background roar of traffic almost drowned him out.

"Callahan? How's my baby doing? She keeping Mama running?"

"Where are you?" I asked.

30

"I got hung up on the job," Brian said. "I still got to go by the new place, leave a check for first and last month's rent. Could be another hour or two. Is there a problem with Maura?"

"She's fine," I said, lowering my voice. "Shay called, Brian. She figured out you'd be here. And she knows where you're working, too. She's threatening to have the cops pick you up unless you have Maura back at her place by five today."

"Bullshit," Brian exploded. "I'm not taking her back over there. No matter what. They can just lock me up, if that's what it takes, but no baby of mine is going to live like that."

"Let me talk to him," Edna said. She grabbed the phone away from me.

"Brian? Honey, I don't know what kind of trouble you're in with that girl, but I do know we need to get a lawyer looking into this," Edna said quickly. "Me and Callahan put in a call to Ferd Bryce. You remember him? Daddy's friend that was a divorce lawyer for so long, and then a judge?"

I could hear a long stream of angry invective. Edna sighed, handed the phone back to me. "He never would listen to reason, once he got that temper up," she said.

"Brian."

"Never mind about Shay," Brian said angrily. "She's just blowing smoke about cops and lawyers and stuff. Thinks she's Perry Mason cause her mother sleeps with some crappy little lawyer down in Jonesboro. She's at work, I know 'cause I rode by there on the way to my job. Her Cutlass is parked right there. So she ain't going out looking for Maura right away. Anyway, she's terrified of driving into Atlanta. 'Fraid a colored guy will carjack her. Annette's working night shift, two till eleven. So y'all just sit tight. I'll come pick up Maura as soon as I can cut loose of this job. Tell Maura Daddy's coming for her real soon."

"What about Shay?" I persisted.

"I'll deal with her," Brian said. Then he hung up.

I'd heard about the terrible twos, but nobody ever warned me about a three-year-old. Or maybe they did, but since I wasn't in the market for one, I just didn't listen.

It probably wasn't the best day for me to be baby-sitting, anyway.

My nerves were rubbed raw by all the preparations for the damned office Christmas party, and now my brother had come back into our lives and dumped a truckload of troubles on us.

Maura was meek as a lamb until Edna tried to feed her lunch. Peanut butter and jelly had been standard lunchtime fare at our house my whole life. But Maura cringed from the little sandwiches—with trimmed crusts—as though she was facing a live boa constrictor.

"No, no, no," she hollered, pounding the table with her spoon. She threw a sandwich across the room, then followed it up by tossing her cup of milk overboard, too.

I looked at Edna. "What was that about normal?"

"This is normal," Edna said grimly.

We tried applesauce. No go. Carrot sticks. Maura nibbled, chewed, spat it out. Vanilla wafers. Scrambled eggs. Graham crackers. Canned fruit cocktail. Out of desperation, Edna even offered her a meatball. Maura stabbed it repeatedly with her spoon, then swept the remains onto the floor with the rest of her discards.

"Let's give her a dose of NyQuil and call it a day," I suggested.

"I give up," Edna said. She fixed Maura with her look, the ones us kids used to dread. "Do you want me to feed you myself, young lady?"

"Nooooo," Maura howled. She arched her back and launched herself backwards, tipping over the chair and landing, screaming, on the kitchen floor.

We both lunged for her at the same time. Maura sat up, saw the effect her act was having on us, and started to wail like a banshee.

Edna tried to cradle the child in her lap, but Maura wriggled away. She stood in the middle of the kitchen floor and proceeded to pitch a rare old fit.

"She's on a roll," I told my mother. "What do we do now?"

Edna's eyes narrowed. "If she was mine, I'd turn her over my knee and pop her one. But they call that child abuse these days. So, instead, we'll just ignore her."

"Ignore her? It sounds like we're torturing cats in here," I said.

Edna grabbed my hand and pulled. "Come on in the dining room. We'll put out the plates and napkins and silverware. Just act like she's not even here."

Maura had stamina, I'll say that for her. She continued to howl for nearly an hour. Her lungs must have been ready to burst. Then she wandered into the dining room, where she stood in the doorway, sniffled, and sucked her thumb while twining a lock of hair around her finger. "No, no," she cried, every time one of us glanced her way. "Bad Grandma. Bad girl."

Once I nearly gave in and picked her up, but Edna wouldn't let me.

"She's almost done," Edna said. "Let her cry it out."

At three o'clock, Maura wandered out of the room, and it was suddenly quiet. "She's down," Edna said, giving me a triumphant thumbs-up.

As usual, my mother was right. We found Maura curled up, one finger twisted around her hair, the thumb of her other hand inserted in her mouth, fast asleep on the den in the sofa.

"Thumb-sucking," Edna said, clucking in disapproval. She unfolded the blanket Brian had left neatly folded on the arm of the sofa, and tucked it around her sleeping granddaughter. "We'll have to get to work on that. None of mine ever sucked their thumbs."

7

The two of us watched the phone and the back door the rest of that afternoon; we cooked, cleaned, polished silver, and cooked some more. I got the big crystal punchbowl out of the attic and Edna mixed the punch. I made a quick run to the Korean grocery store for ice and more beer. If Brian was around tonight, I thought, we'd need it.

It was after five when I got back.

Maura was still asleep, and Edna was making the sauce for her meatballs—chili sauce and grape jelly. "He hasn't called," she said, answering the question I hadn't asked. "What are we going to do?"

The party was supposed to start at six.

"I'm gonna try to reach Ferd one more time. You go take a shower," I said. "Put on that Christmas sweater you've been saving for something special. And if Shay calls, we'll just lie like crazy."

Maura was just starting to wake up when we heard a car in the driveway. "Good," Edna said. "That ought to be Neva Jean. She promised to get here early to help set out all the food."

Maura's face was pink and flushed from where she'd pressed it against the sofa while sleeping. Her hair was softly mussed. She looked around and yawned. Which made me yawn. Edna scooped her

34

up in her arms. "Now she's feeling sweet, aren't you darlin'?" Edna cooed, her voice so syrupy it made me want to gag.

"She's wet," I pointed out. "Aren't you ready to give in on this potty-training deal yet? At least during naps?"

We heard a car door close. "You go out and help Neva Jean," Edna ordered. "She's supposed to bring some folding chairs and some new appetizer recipe she's trying out. I'll get little missy here cleaned up. I picked her up a party outfit while I was out. A little green velvet elf's suit. Wait till the girls see my baby. They'll eat her up with a spoon."

Neva Jean McComb was my first House Mouse. I'd acquired her along with the pink Chevy van and a half dozen regular clients when I cashed in my retirement fund from the Atlanta Police Department and went into the cleaning business eight years ago. She was bossy and unreliable and her love life with Swannelle McComb was even more bizarre than anything the supermarket tabloids she adored could ever invent. But she could whip a three-thousand-square-foot house into shape in just under two hours and do as many as five houses a day—as long as we kept her supplied with Mountain Dew and a radio tuned to the country music station.

Today she and Swannelle had packed enough food into the back of his pickup truck to feed Pharaoh's army.

"What is all this?" I asked, eyeing the cardboard boxes of foil-wrapped casseroles, Tupperware containers, and brown paper shopping bags. "You opening a restaurant?"

Swannelle gave me a wink and reached over and patted Neva Jean's size eighteen rump, which she had packed into what appeared to be size ten black velvet toreador pants. "She's sumpthin' ain't she?" he said, leering at her. "It just ain't right how some women got it all—looks and smarts—plus one hell of a cook."

"Now, quit," Neva Jean said, slapping his hand away. "We got to get this casserole into the oven before it starts coagulating. And I don't want my Jell-O salad freezing, neither. It makes the Cool Whip rise to the top."

Neva Jean gave the orders for assembling the food on the buffet, and Swannelle did as he was told, smiling and bowing and scraping in a most un-Swannelle-like manner.

"What's with him?" I asked, when we were alone in the kitchen.

"It's Christmas," she said. "He's got his eye on this six-thousand-dollar golf cart, and he knows I won't let him buy it unless he treats me right."

I wiped my hands on a dishtowel and opened the oven to take a peek at the mystery appetizer she'd been bragging about. It was still covered with foil, and a thick red sauce was bubbling over the sides.

"Golf? Since when does Swannelle play golf?"

"He doesn't," she said, taking off the faux leopard-fur jacket she'd worn into the house.

"Wow," I said, eyeing the rest of her ensemble. Neva Jean had dressed herself the way some people trim a Christmas tree. She'd piled her blonde hair on top of her head in a teased-out French twist, and pinned a sparkly gold star at the peak of the bouffant. Her tunic was green satin, reaching just above her knees, with row after row of gold fringe punctuated with silver dollar–sized red and gold spangles.

She did a little pirouette. "That's not all." She mashed one of the spangles. All along the rows of gold fringe, tiny white lights began blinking off and on.

"Instant party," I said.

Neva Jean beamed, literally. "I had to send away for it. Sixty-six dollars. And then—you believe this?—batteries weren't included. I had to swipe 'em out of three of Swannelle's remote controls. He thinks I forgot to pay the cable bill again."

"What was that about the golf cart?" I prompted.

"Oh yeah," she said. "You know Swannelle got himself another DUI last month. So they revoked his driver's license for six months. Which, excuse me, but I don't think wine coolers should count on blood alcohol. Me personally, three of those Kiwi–Key Lime ones just barely give me a buzz. But the Georgia State Patrol don't see it that way."

She sighed. "I been driving him to the bowling alley, and the American Legion, the shop, everyplace. Somebody at the American Legion the other night told him about golf carts. See you don't have to have a driver's license to drive 'em. And they got real fancy ones now. Swannelle likes the ones with the built-in beer cooler on the back. And you can get 'em customized with CD players and gun racks and everything."

"Is that legal to drive around on the streets?"

She waved her hand. "Who knows? It's just for six months. I'm thinking of letting him get it, just to keep from making one more trip to that damned bowling alley."

"Get what?" Edna asked, walking into the kitchen. She was in red. Maura, true to her promise, was all in green velvet, from a tiny cocked hat to a pair of miniature green velvet boots with gold bells on the toes. Maura stared at Neva Jean, clutching Edna tightly around the neck. I guess she'd never seen a talking Christmas tree before.

Neva Jean was speechless for about half a second.

"Well, gwacious," she said, trying unsuccessfully to pinch Maura's cheek. "Who is this widdle pwincess?"

Edna preened. "This is Maura Jean Garrity. My granddaughter."

"Long lost granddaughter," I added. "My brother Brian's little girl."

There was a commotion in the hallway. "That must be Cheezer," Edna said. "He was going to pick up Ruby and Baby and Sister."

"Let me hold the baby," Neva Jean begged.

I stared at her in surprise. Neva Jean has never been a baby person. She's never made any pretense about that. "I don't need kids, pets, or houseplants," she'd always say when anybody asked her about why she'd never had children. "The only thing taking up oxygen in my house is me and Swannelle. And some days, I'm not even certain I want to share my oxygen with him. You know what I mean?"

Edna handed the baby over and Neva Jean stared into Maura's eyes with nothing short of adoration. "She's precious," Neva Jean declared. "She looks just like you, Callahan."

"She doesn't look a thing like Callahan," Edna said. "Callahan's all Garrity. Got that black hair and the Garrity earlobes. This baby looks like my side of the family. She's Rivers through and through."

While my mother was listing all Maura's finest points, the kitchen started to fill up with the House Mouse staff.

"Looky here, girls," Neva Jean called. "Look what Santa Claus left for Edna and Callahan."

Everybody had come dressed to the nines. Ruby, who usually favored shapeless dark dresses and black crepe-soled work shoes, had obviously dipped into her best church finery. She wore a winter-white wool dress and a huge white turban with a veil that draped over her forehead and a red orchid the size of a dinner plate pinned to her bounteous bosom.

The Easterbrooks sisters, Baby and Sister, weren't about to be out-done by Ruby. Miss Baby wore a long, blue velvet gown with big puffy sleeves, a sweetheart neck, and a huge chiffon bow at the waist. The dress hung limply from her bony frame, the neck fastened with safety pins for modesty. Miss Sister had opted for a more casual look: a vivid red sweater, baggy red sweatpants, and sneakers, topped off with a red fur Santa hat.

Cheezer, our newest and only male House Mouse, had fashioned a look that could only be called neo-grunge formal. He wore his usual threadbare jeans and black Converse high-tops, a faded flannel shirt, and a rusty black dinner jacket with satin lapels.

"Merry Christmas," Edna called. "Everybody, I want you to meet—"

"What's that Neva Jean got there?" Sister interrupted, peering at Maura through her thick spectacles. "That some kind of pet mon-key?"

Miss Baby elbowed her sister in her bony ribs. "Hush up, fool. Look like Neva Jean done adopted herself a baby. Neva Jean, where'd you get that baby at?"

Edna flushed bright pink. "That's my granddaughter, girls. Her name is Maura Jean."

"Margarine?" Now it was Sister who was doing the poking, although Cheezer was on the receiving end. "I never heard of a white baby named Margarine." Her cataract-dimmed eyes gleamed mis-chievously. "But then I never knew nobody white or black named Cheezer, so I guess they's lots I don't know about in this world."

"It's a nickname," Cheezer said. "Cheezer. For Charles." He wisely decided to change the subject. "Hey, Edna, cool outfit. I didn't know you had a granddaughter."

Edna reached out for Maura and Neva Jean reluctantly handed her over. Maura buried her face in Edna's shoulder. All the attention was making her suddenly shy.

"I didn't, either," Edna admitted. "Not until last night. She's my youngest son's child. We're just baby-sitting while Brian gets settled in his new apartment."

"Where's her mama at?" Baby said loudly.

"Uh, she's, uh, at work right now," I said. "Does anybody need anything to drink? Beer, wine, eggnog? Ruby, we made a fruit punch especially for you."

But Maura was not to be distracted. Her lower lip started to tremble, and she began tugging at one of the pigtails Edna had so lovingly tied with green satin ribbons. "Mama? I want my mama."

"After a little bit," Edna promised, patting her back. "Let's go in the dining room now, and see what's good to eat. Let's have a taste of Grandma's pound cake. How about that? A big ole piece of cake for Grandma's best girl."

"And trifle," I chimed in. "Aunt Callahan made trifle especially for you, Maura."

Edna rolled her eyes. "As if this baby would know what trifle is."

The oven timer began buzzing then. "That's my appetizer," Neva Jean said. "I hope everybody's hungry!"

"Somebody say something about eggnog?" Miss Sister asked. "That the kind with whiskey in it?"

The doorbell rang then. "That'll be Mac," I told the staff. "He was going to pick up the honey-baked ham on his way over. I better go give him a hand."

Finally the girls started to move toward the dining room. But they all stopped short when the doorbell rang again, and then again. Now somebody was beating with their fists on the door.

At first I thought it was some guy who'd turned up at the wrong address for the wrong Christmas party. It had happened before.

"Open up," a deep voice called. "Open up. I know you're in there, you damn Garritys."

My scalp prickled. Edna froze. I'd heard that voice just once in twenty years. But it had been earlier today.

8

I ran to the dining room and peeped out the front window. The sky was deep blue, not yet dark, but past sunset. Parked at the curb, directly under the streetlight I saw a silver Cutlass.

"It's Shay!" I hissed.

"Who?" Sister asked, looking from me to Edna. "You want me to let Mac in? It's gettin' cold outside."

"No, Miss Sister," I said quickly. "It's not Mac."

"You sure?" Edna knew but didn't want to know. She tiptoed over to the window to get a look for herself, then backed away quickly, as though she'd come too close to a hot stove. But it was too late.

"Mama," Maura whimpered.

"Christ!" Edna said. "How the hell did she find us?"

"Doesn't matter," I said. "Brian's not back. There's nothing we can do. We've got to give her back, Edna."

"The hell you say," she snapped.

Our party had come to a dead stop. The girls, Swannelle, and Cheezer stood there and stared at us.

"Act like it's a party," Edna commanded. Then she was rushing down the hallway toward the kitchen. "And you haven't seen me or Maura," she called over her shoulder.

"What are you doing?" I called after her. "That's Shay out there. The jig's up, Edna."

"No it's not," Edna called. She was in the hallway between the kitchen and the bedroom. She set Maura gently down on the floor. "Stay right there," she instructed her. Then she reached up, pulled on a rope, then stood back and let the attic stairs unfold. She was scrambling up them with a speed I hadn't known she could muster. Maura stood at the bottom of the steps looking alarmed.

"Come on, sweetheart," Edna coaxed. "Let's see if we can find Daddy's old toys up here. Aunt Callahan's, too. There's a whole big box of dolls up here. Climb up here right quick so Grandma can show you."

The toys and dolls part helped her make up her mind. Maura climbed the folding stairs as easily as a monkey.

"Now close that hatch," Edna instructed me.

"And do what?" I asked, my hands on my hips. "Tell Shay I don't know where her three-year-old went? She's obviously not as stupid as Brian thinks she is. She found her way here to the house. She knows we've got Maura. Come on down, Mama. We're just going to have to give her up. Temporarily. OK?"

"Pull up those stairs," Edna ordered. "I don't care what you tell her. Just lie. You're good at that. All the Garritys are."

She reached way down, and tugged impatiently at the steps. The doorbell was ringing.

"Go," Edna said. "Don't let her in the house. Get rid of her."

The doorbell rang twice more as I was folding the stairs up, a third time while I was in Edna's bedroom, stashing Maura's diaper bag and clothes under the bed. I ran back into the dining room, gasping for breath.

"What should we do?" Neva Jean asked.

"Act like you're having fun," I said. "It's a damn Christmas party, right?"

Now Shay was pounding at the door again.

"I know y'all are in there," she called. "I've come to get my baby. Open up, you damn Garritys."

"We've got a signed court order," called a deeper, definitely male voice. "And we'll get a sheriff's deputy over here if we have to. Don't be stupid, Miss Garrity. Open the door."

Our guests stood rooted to the spot, all of them watching to see what I'd do.

I opened the door.

• • •

The last time I remember seeing Shay Gatlin was the first time I ever heard a kid use the F-word. Hell, I was eighteen at the time and I'd never used it. The girl who lived across the street from us, a little prisspot named Stephanie, had gotten a pink Strawberry Shortcake bike for her birthday, and she was the envy of the neighborhood that summer. All the little girls on the block were congregated in her driveway, while Stephanie rode around and around them in circles, showing off her strawberry-colored bike with the horn and the handlebar streamers and even a license plate bolted to the back that read Stephanie.

"Lemme ride, lemme ride," all the little girls were calling, jumping up and down. But Stephanie sailed around and past them in a pink blur. Until Shay Gatlin could stand it no more. The next time Stephanie brushed by Shay was the last. I saw Shay, six inches smaller, grab the kid by her ponytail and throw her to the pavement. While Stephanie howled about her scraped knee, Shay hopped on the pink bike, rode it down to the end of our street, and then back up. The little knot of girls stood watching her, half fascinated, half terrified at what she'd done. After one fast circuit, Shay came pedaling back to Stephanie's house. She jumped off at the curb and let the bike go smashing against the sidewalk.

"There's your fuckin' bike," she called out, sticking her tongue out and waggling it at the group of girls. She stalked back toward her house, a bedraggled brick rancher at the very end of the block.

Shay's eyes narrowed when she saw me. Although it was bitter cold outside, about twenty degrees, she wore no coat over her red cowl-necked sweater and black wool leggings, which were tucked into the high leather boots. If she'd had a sleepless night, it didn't show. Her face was flawlessly made up, green eyes expertly lined and mascaraed. Her shoulders were hunched together against the chill wind that blew across our front porch, her gloveless hands clenched tight against her side. She radiated fury.

The man standing beside her was tall, at least six-foot-six, with salt-and-pepper gray hair, a handlebar mustache, gold wire-rimmed glasses. He wore a serious blue suit with pointy-toed, black snakeskin cowboy boots.

"Where's Maura?" Shay demanded, looking past me into the house.

"With Brian," I said, trying to block her view. "He picked her up a little while ago."

The older man shook his head. "That boy's gonna be in a world of trouble."

"Shit," Shay said, stomping her foot. Even with two-inch heels on the boots, Shay was a foot shorter than me, still petite—though from the looks of her dark roots it had been a while since she'd been a natural blonde. She looked up at me, her face full of hate.

"I don't believe you," she said finally. "Chuck, she's lying."

Shay turned around, as if to go, then whirled quickly back and tried to shoulder her way past into the hallway.

I threw my arms out and took a half-step foreword, onto the porch.

"I said she's not here," I tried to keep my voice calm, but heard it echo, so loud I wondered if old Mr. Byerly across the street would hear us. "If you've got a problem, you better discuss it with Brian."

"You bet I've got a fuckin' problem!" Shay snarled. "My baby is in your house. And I'm gettin' her right now. I've got my lawyer here, so don't try anything funny. Come on, Chuck."

She tucked her head in to her chest, and rammed right into me, knocking me backwards, but not down. She was in the house in an instant, stomping around in those big black boots. "Maura!" she called loudly. "Maura?"

Her lawyer followed right behind her, a smirk plastered on his face. He gave me a patronizing nod. "Chuck Ingraham," he said. "As Shay mentioned, I'm her attorney. Down in Clayton County, folks are real serious about child abduction. Judge Bingham happens to be a personal friend of mine. If you're hiding that child from her mother, who has sole legal custody, I warn you, I'll have the judge cite the whole lot of you for contempt of court," he drawled. "I'd advise you not to interfere in this matter."

"And I'd advise you to tell your client this is private property," I retorted. But he kept walking.

Neva Jean and Swannelle were standing in the doorway of the dining room. She was feeding him a meatball on a toothpick. They both gave Shay and her lawyer half-baked smiles.

Baby raised a gloved hand and gave the intruders a regal wave. "Howdy-do," she called politely. "How 'bout some eggnog?"

"What did you do with my baby?" Shay said, ignoring the offer.

Her face was pale; the heavily made-up eyes glittered with malice, her rosebud mouth twisted into an odd, suspicious smile.

I grabbed for her arm, but she was too fast. She darted down the hallway toward my bedroom, kicked the door open. "Maura?"

When she found the room empty she moved on to Edna's, kicking the door open, standing in the middle of the room, kicking at the bed with the same venom she'd kicked at that pink bike years and years ago.

I held my breath, but the house was silent except for the staccato tap of Shay's boots on the wood floors. Nervous laughter and canned-sounding conversation drifted from the dining room.

I had a mental vision of Edna, huddled somewhere overhead, her hand over Maura's mouth. What had my mother gotten me involved with now?

"I told you she's not here," I said, breathing hard. "In case you haven't noticed, I'm having a party, and I don't remember inviting you. Get out, or I'll call the cops and have you both arrested for criminal trespass."

"Chuck, show her the papers. She thinks we're bluffing."

Ingraham reached into his inside jacket pocket and pulled out a single sheet of legal-sized paper. She snatched it out of his hand and waved it in my face. "See this? It's the custody order. Chuck said y'all might try to pull something like this. You think you're so damn clever, you and the old lady. As soon as Brian disappeared with Maura, we knew right where he'd run with her. Who else? Mama and big sister. But you're messing with the wrong person this time, Julia Garrity."

I snatched the papers away from her. Ferd would need to see them if he was going to help Brian. Then I clamped my hand down on Shay's elbow and started steering her toward the door. "I'm not messing with anybody," I said. "This is between you and my brother. Now I'll thank you to get out of my house."

Chuck Ingraham raised his eyebrows, but followed us toward the door.

She wrenched away from me. "It really pisses you off, doesn't it?" she asked, lifting her chin. "Me and Brian getting married. Him marrying into white trash. I bet it really got Edna's goat when she found out who Brian was married to."

"Get out," I said as unpleasantly as I could. "You're trespassing. I don't know how they do things down in Clayton County, Mr. Ingraham, but it's against the law up here in Atlanta. And I know a few judges myself."

Ingraham gave a martyred sigh. "Let's go, Shay," he said.

Shay shot him an evil look, but he shook his head, as if to tell her her tantrum was getting her nowhere.

"I'll go," she said finally. "But Brian better have Maura at my place by the time I get home. And tell your mama don't get attached to my little girl. 'Cause this will be the last time she'll get her hands on my baby."

Shay did her best flounce. Ingraham was right behind her. I slammed the door. It was all quite theatrical.

She backed the Cutlass down our driveway doing forty miles an hour, jerked the car into forward and laid rubber as she peeled away.

"Woo-wee," Sister said. "That l'il hussy was some kind of mad. Who'd you say she was?"

"My sister-in-law," I said. "Soon to be ex. I hope."

I went back to the hallway and stood under the attic door. "Coast is clear," I called wearily, heading for the pull-down steps. "Come out, come out, wherever you are."

9

Edna scampered down the attic steps as quick as her slightly arthritic limbs would take her. Maura sat crouched at the top of the pull-down stairs, like a frightened possum, a doll clutched under her arm. All of us stood at the foot of the stairs, looking up. Her dark, disturbed eyes stared down at us.

"Come on down, sweetheart," Neva Jean called softly. Maura shook her head vigorously.

"Come here, little lamb," Sister called. "Come give us some sugar." Maura shook her head again.

"You want me to haul the little ankle-biter out of there?" Swannelle asked, putting his beer bottle down on the hall table and starting toward the stairs.

"Leave her be," Neva Jean said, swatting at Swannelle. "She's probably scared to death. Probably thinks you're the boogeyman."

"I think she likes the dark," Edna said, brushing at a wisp of cobweb hanging from the neckline of her sweater, then peering up at the child. "All the while we were up there we could hear Shay down here ranting and raving. I told her we were playing hide and seek and she should stay real quiet so she could win a prize. I was sure she'd start hollerin' the minute she heard her mama's voice. I found a box of old toys. She picked out one of those army dolls. I think it was Kevin's. After that she never made a peep."

"That's G.I. Joe," I said, starting up the stairs toward my niece. "Come on down, Maura," I said, reaching up my arms toward her. But she only scooted farther back, away from the stair opening.

I climbed all the way up into the attic, stooping to keep from hitting my head on the exposed ceiling beams. I pulled the chain on the bare-bulb ceiling fixture. The attic was gloomy, cold, cluttered with the bits and pieces of unnecessary belongings too good to discard, festooned with cobwebs, the rough wood plank floor littered with the carcasses of dead insects. It was the sort of place that should terrify a child. God knows I didn't like it much myself.

Maura put a finger to her lips and smiled conspiratorially. "Me hide," she whispered, ducking down behind a cardboard box.

"You win," I said, clapping my hands. "Game's over. Let's go downstairs and see what kind of prize Grandma has for you."

She cradled the G.I. Joe doll tenderly, stroking it like a cat. He was naked and even in the dim light I could see the battering he'd taken from my brothers. A hand was chewed off, and somebody had used a black marker to draw on the genitalia the doll's manufacturer had omitted. Predictably, he'd been given a whopper. Lucky Joe.

"Maura?" I extended a hand toward her.

"Cake?"

"Lots of cake," I promised. "Cake and candy and trifle and all kinds of goodies. And you can bring G.I. Joe to the party, too."

"Cake." It was decided. I handed her down feetfirst to Swannelle.

"About damn time," he muttered. I couldn't disagree.

Playing Anne Frank apparently hadn't bothered Maura a bit. Cheezer and the girls loved on her and petted her and passed her from lap to lap. Edna and I were the ones who were totally unnerved.

"You think she'd really have Brian thrown in jail?" Edna asked worriedly, sipping from a glass punch cup full of Tom and Jerry. I took a paper napkin and dabbed at her milk mustache.

"Can you blame her?"

Edna bristled. "You taking her side against your own brother?"

"I'm not taking anybody's side about anything," I said. "Where's Brian? He promised to be back here by noon. It's the same old story. And he's put the both of us in a horrible position. Same old Brian."

She slammed her punch cup down on the dining room table, spattering droplets of white liquid all over the damask cloth. "Don't you start," she warned. "He's my son. He's home. That's all I care about. Everybody else can go straight to hell."

"You two fussin'?" Neva Jean elbowed between us, holding her casserole in a pair of giant oven mitts. "Come on, y'all. It's Christmas. We gotta party down."

Edna glared at her and then at me, and an uneasy quiet descended on the room.

"Hey!" Neva Jean said. "I want everybody to taste what I brought. Tell 'em, Swannelle."

Swannelle's spoon poised over the casserole. "Wait'll you taste it. Swear to God, it's the best thing you ever put in your mouth." He leered at Neva Jean. "Almost."

"Smut-mouth," she said, blushing. "No, really, Callahan, I want you to taste it."

I looked down at the oblong glass dish. The contents were vaguely lumpy, blanketed in crust-embedded, rubbery orange cheese. A maroon sauce bubbled up around the edges. I took a fork and poked at it.

"Yummy," I said, trying to sound enthusiastic. "Looks fantastic."

Ruby was at my side now. Though a Bible-thumping teetotaler, she too was sporting a milk mustache. And her turban was listing to one side. It didn't take a P.I. license to tell that she'd gotten into the Tom and Jerrys.

"Mmm-mmm," she said in her high childlike voice. "What you call that, Neva Jean?"

"Sloppy tots," Neva Jean said.

Ruby spooned some onto her plate and took a taste. She rolled her eyes and smacked her lips in ecstasy. "Mercy. What all is in there?"

The others crowded around too, ladling the sloppy tots onto their plates, tasting and proclaiming its grandness. Even Cheezer. "Bitchin'," he said. And then, "There meat in here?"

"Nothin' that won't cure what ails you," Swannelle assured him.

"Couldn't be easier to make," Neva Jean said. "You just take the big bag of frozen Tater Tots. Ore-Ida. Lay it out in your pan. Then you get you a pound and a half of hamburger meat. Fry that up real good, drain it on paper towels, put it back in the skillet. Mix the meat up with two cans of sloppy joe stuff, and pour that over the Tater Tots. Now you sprinkle two cups of grated cheese over the sauce. Top with two cups of crushed up Fritos. Bake it for thirty minutes and—"

"What about the sour cream?" Swannelle asked, his brow furrowed. "You didn't say nothin' about the sour cream."

Neva Jean paused between bites of the sloppy tots, chewed, and dabbed at her lips. "You could put dollops of sour cream on top," she offered. "After it comes out of the oven, you know, for an extra zip. But now, that's a lot of extra fat, and I'm kinda tryin' to watch my weight, so I left it off tonight."

We ate and drank and I suppose everybody else had a good time, but I could hear myself laughing too loud. All the food we'd lovingly prepared and presented tasted too . . . Something. Edna stayed in one corner of the dining room and pretended I didn't exist. She was the hostess with the mostest, toting Maura around on her hip, leading everybody in the singing of off-key Christmas carols.

She stood Maura up on the dining room table and had her sing "Rudolph the Red-nosed Reindeer," and the girls, as Edna predicted, ate her up with a spoon.

"Look just like that Shirley Temple gal, don't she?" Sister asked, feeding Maura a morsel of cake.

"Sure does," Baby agreed.

I made another trip into the kitchen to refill my glass with lots of ice and Jack Daniel's and just enough water to keep things interesting. I had a headache coming on, so I swallowed some aspirin and downed it with the bourbon, and then I fixed myself another drink and sat myself down on the kitchen floor with half a can of dry roasted mixed nuts. I ate the cashews first, the peanuts last. The nuts were salty so I fixed another drink and that was the end of the Jack Daniel's. The phone rang. Out in the dining room, Swannelle was murdering "We Three Kings." I let the answering machine pick up the call.

"Mama?" It was Brian.

"Screw you," I mumbled, craning my neck to see the kitchen clock. It was ten o'clock.

"You there? Jules?"

"Callahan," I said, still not picking up the phone.

A pause, like he didn't know what to say or do next. "Anybody there?"

I sighed and picked up the phone. "Where are you?"

"Look," he said. "Let me talk to Mama."

"She's busy," I said nastily. "Taking care of your kid."

"Screw you," Brian said. "Something's come up. Tell Mama I'll be by in the morning to get Maura. She's OK, right? Not crying or nothing?"

"Shay was here," I said. "You remember her? Your wife? Maura's mother? She's apparently got a lot more brains than you have. She figured out where the house was and came looking for her daughter. She had her lawyer, that Chuck guy, with her. I told her Maura was with you. Edna's idea, not mine. That's the last lie I tell for you, asshole. If you're not here first thing in the morning, I'll take Maura back to Shay myself."

"That bitch ain't gettin' her hands on my kid," Brian said. "Let me talk to Mama, Callahan. I'll get this straightened out."

"Too late. Mama can't fix your screwup this time, Brian. I won't let her. Did you know she had a heart attack two years ago? Damn near died?"

"Mama was sick? I didn't know."

"You didn't care. You're not into family, remember? Edna's sixty-seven. She's too old to be hiding out in the attic like a criminal. You've got till eight in the morning."

"You leave Maura right where she is," Brian said. "I'll be over first thing. Pick up my kid and get out of your hair, and you can go back to minding your own damn business and I'll mind mine."

"Fine with me," I said.

I hung up the phone and lay my head back on the kitchen cabinet. The wood was smooth and cool to the touch. I closed my eyes and listened to the girls saying their good-byes in the other room. I heard Cheezer fire up his mail truck out in the driveway, heard it stall, and then catch. Heard the sound of Edna humming and talking softly to Maura as she tried to coax her out of her elf suit and into a nightgown and the bed.

After a while, maybe half an hour, Edna came shuffling into the kitchen in her bedroom slippers. She dumped a load of dirty dishes in the sink with a deliberate clatter. I kept my eyes closed. The headache was closing in on me. It felt like my head was being squeezed by giant pliers.

"Brian called," I said. "Something came up. He'll be here to get Maura in the morning."

"What's wrong?" her voice was tense.

I opened my eyes, pulled myself rather unsteadily to my feet. "Ask him," I said.

10

The piece of paper with Ferd Bryce's phone number was lying on my bedside table. It was late and I was more than half-drunk, but I dialed the number anyway. He picked up after the second ring.

"Y'ello," his voice boomed. "Who's speaking?"

"Ferd?" Of course it was Ferd. I sat up straight and tried to concentrate. I hadn't really expected him to be home. "It's Callahan. Callahan Garrity."

"Well, gawddamn," he drawled. "Callahan Garrity. Now that's a name I hadn't thought about in a long time. How's your mama and them?"

"OK," I said. "Edna's pretty good. She lives with me, you know. We live in Candler Park. Maureen and her husband live up near you, in Roswell. Kevin's married and got a couple kids. He keeps busy—"

"Candler Park? You're living over there with all the hippies and radicals," Ferd said. "You need to get out of that city. Move out here like I did, out to God's country."

"We're pretty happy here, Ferd," I said.

"You still a cop?" Ferd asked. "Last time I saw you was right after you got your detective's badge, wasn't it?"

"Probably," I said. "I quit the force seven years ago. I've got a P.I. license, but mostly I run a cleaning business."

"Well now," he said, coughing politely. "That's interesting. How

51

come you're calling me out of the blue on a Friday night? Not that I mind. I don't go to bed until two or three anyway. I got a computer, and I'm usually on the Internet. I was just fixin' to sign on when you called."

"It's about Brian," I said.

"He in jail?" Ferd was good about getting down to business.

"Not yet," I said. "At least, not as far as I know."

I told him about Shay and Maura and the custody order and Shay's accusations. And about how we'd hidden Maura from Shay and her lawyer, and Brian's distrust of lawyers in general.

He listened carefully, asked a few questions. "You say a judge down in Clayton issued the order?"

"Yeah," I said. "Shay's mother, Annette, works for a lawyer down there, too. Chuck something. He claims he's buddy-buddy with all the judges down there."

Ferd coughed. "You can have Brian call me tomorrow. Don't know how much help I'll be. Maybe we can find him a lawyer who's tight with that courthouse crowd in Jonesboro. But in the meantime, tell him my advice is to take the kid back. Right away. If he's jailed for violating that custody order it'll work against his own best interests."

"Thanks, Ferd," I said. "About Brian. He, uh, well, we don't know much about where he's been or what he's been doing for the last ten years. Don't tell Edna I told you, but my sense is he's had some problems."

"I been knowing your mama for thirty years," Ferd said. "She's a good lady. Do anything for her kids."

"That's the problem," I agreed. "She won't hear a word against Brian. And she's already made up her mind about getting Maura away from her mother."

"Child custody's never easy," Ferd said. "Used to hate those cases when I was on the bench. I'll tell you the truth: Not many judges in this state are gonna take a child away from the mother. Not without some real serious cause. The best Brian might hope for is shared custody."

"I'll tell him that," I said. "When I see him. If he'll listen."

"Have him call," Ferd said. "You be sweet now, you hear?"

• • •

Visions of sugarplums did not dance in my head. The throbbing between my temples was more like tap-dancing elephants. I slept fitfully, finally got up at six in the morning. Since I was awake anyway, I reasoned, I might as well get busy cleaning up the party mess. Make amends with my mother.

I smelled coffee brewing before I got to the kitchen. Should have known Edna wouldn't rest long with a sink full of dirty dishes.

She was drying the cut-glass bowl with a linen tea towel. All the rest of the dishes were washed and put away, the counters and floors sparkling.

"I was gonna do that," I said lamely.

"I've been up since five," she said, pouring me a cup of coffee. "I'm not used to sleeping with a three-year-old threshing machine."

I took the coffee cup and sat down at the table. She sat down opposite me.

"What are we going to do about Maura?" she asked. "And what is the matter with your brother?"

I tried to choose my words carefully. "It's not our choice," I said. "You know that. This is something Brian is going to have to take responsibility for. And we both know . . ." I stopped and started over, trying not to sound as judgmental as I felt. "He makes a lot of promises. He means well, but—"

"Your brother would not hurt a fly," Edna said. "Down deep, he is a good boy."

"A man," I corrected her. "Brian is a grown man, Mama. A father."

"A good father. He loves that child."

"He dumped her here yesterday and disappeared," I said. "He hadn't laid eyes on us for nearly ten years, and he drops off his three-year-old as casually as if she were a load of dry cleaning."

"He needs our help," Edna said, sipping her coffee. "And I intend to do whatever I can."

I got up and roamed around the kitchen, looking for something to eat. "Any pound cake left?" I asked hopefully.

"I was saving a piece for Maura," Edna said. "She's got her daddy's sweet tooth. There's plenty of fruitcake, though. And some cookies in the cupboard."

I found the chocolate chip cookies and bit into one. It had an odd, herbal taste. Psychedelic. I spat it out in the sink. "Where'd these come from?"

She raised an eyebrow. "Cheezer brought them. He said they were an old family recipe."

"What, the Manson family?" I gathered all the cookies on the plate, wrapped them in the foil, and dumped them in the trash. I took a big gulp of coffee to try to wash away the taste. "Make sure Maura doesn't get into those," I warned her. "And remind me to give Cheezer a talk about the evil weed."

"What about Maura?" she repeated.

"I called Ferd last night," I said. "He's agreed to try to help Brian. But he was adamant. Maura has got to go back to Shay."

"No," Edna said, shaking her head. "I won't let that happen."

"Listen to me," I told her. "It's only until Ferd can petition to get the custody changed. As soon as Shay knows Brian has a real lawyer working for him, that there's a possibility she'll lose custody, she'll clean up her act in a hurry. She'll have to. I'm a P.I., remember? I'll be all over her butt like white on rice, asking questions at her apartment complex, watching her office. I don't care what Brian says. Shay's got plenty of street smarts. Clearly, she loves Maura and doesn't want to lose her."

"Shay Gatlin doesn't know what love is," Edna said. "Her and that mother of hers. Annette Gatlin. When I think of those men, parading through her house, all hours of the day and night . . ." Edna pushed her coffee cup away. "Annette's behind this," she predicted. "Wait and see. Those two just want to use Maura to hurt Brian. Hurt us," Edna said bitterly. "You heard her yesterday. "They hate us."

"Mama!" The wail coming from Edna's room was heartbreaking. "I want my mama."

Edna put her coffee cup down with a clatter, and started for the hallway. "She's only three," I said. "You can't just snatch a child that age and expect her to forget her mother. It's not natural. It's not right."

Maura was sitting in the middle of the bedroom floor, stark naked. She pounded the floor with the naked G.I. Joe doll. "Mama!"

"Maura," Edna cried, bending down to pick the child up. "We're right here, sugar. Right here."

I looked around the room. Maura's wet diaper was on the floor in front of Edna's dresser. The little pink flannel nightie was flung on the bed. There was something else on Grandma's bed, too. I pointed at it and tried not to laugh. "The potty-training seems to be going really well."

Edna gagged. "Maura!" she said sternly. "Did you make poo-poo on Grandma's bed?"

"No," Maura said. She held out her doll. "Joe made poo-poo."

It took us an hour to get the bed stripped, the sheets washed and Edna's mattress scrubbed and disinfected. I gave Maura a bath and somehow wrestled her into a set of my nephew's outgrown T-shirts and overalls. Maura fed herself two bowls of oatmeal, then we had to give her another bath and scrape the oatmeal off the kitchen floor.

"Whew," Edna said, emerging from the bathroom with her freshly scrubbed granddaughter in tow. "I'd forgotten how much energy they have at this age."

"Selective memory," I said.

Maura wasn't the only one who had freshened up. I took a good look at G.I. Joe. He'd changed too, acquiring what looked like a gauze diaper, wrapped expertly around his waist and legs. I gave Edna an inquiring look.

"Joe doesn't want to have any more accidents," she explained.

She opened the kitchen cupboard, and Maura sat down on the floor and pulled out all the pots and pans she'd played with the day before. Edna heaved herself down into a kitchen chair.

I pointed at the clock. "He's not coming."

She knew what I meant. "Give him another hour."

"Then what? Another hour? Then we all go back up to the attic when you-know-who shows up here with an arrest warrant? No. I'm taking her home."

She bit her lip. "I don't think I can stand it."

Clash. Maura had the lids to two saucepans, banging them together like cymbals. She got up, handed them to Edna. "You play, Grandma."

Edna banged the lids together half-heartedly. "I'm going with you," she vowed. "I want to see that place she lives in for myself. Let her know Edna Mae Garrity is watching every step she takes."

"We ought to have a car seat," Edna said, glancing over her shoulder at the backseat of her big Buick. She'd bundled Maura into a brand new bubblegum-pink snowsuit, strapped her into the seat belt in the middle of the seat, and then cushioned her on either side with our biggest sofa cushions. "We can stop at Target on the way there," Edna suggested. "They've got 'em on sale. I saw it in the paper. And maybe I could get some clothes for that nasty doll of hers."

"Target's not open yet," I reminded her. "No more stalling. We'll buy a car seat on the way back. After we drop her off."

"You sure you got the right address?" Edna asked, for the third time. "Maybe we oughta wait till Brian gets here. Or maybe we should call, make sure Shay's home. Maybe she and that mother of hers are still out carrying on. It's Saturday morning, you know."

"I got the address off the custody papers Shay gave us yesterday," I said. "It's an apartment complex on Tara Boulevard. Anyway, I don't want to tip her off that we're coming." I patted the purse on the seat beside me. "I've got my camera in there. We're gonna document everything we see."

It was after eight o'clock. Sunrise had been brilliant—streaks of gold and pink and blue, the winter sun dazzling off the bare treetops outside our kitchen windows. But the sun had disappeared, and Atlanta's winter-long drizzle had set in. The gray-flannel skies seemed only a shade or two lighter than the dun-colored landscape. The Buick's windshield wipers struggled against the slanting rain. Maura, oblivious to the bone-chilling depression settling over Edna and I, hummed something that sounded a little bit like "We Three Kings."

Jonesboro and Clayton County have a special spot in the Atlanta tourism world. For one thing, it's where Hartsfield International Airport, the second busiest in the world, is located. For another, it's the place where Margaret Mitchell planted Scarlett O'Hara, smack in the middle of her fictional version of the antebellum South.

Saturday morning traffic on Interstate 75 was light. I made it to Clayton in less than thirty minutes, the Tara Boulevard exit five minutes later.

Margaret Mitchell would have thought she'd landed on Mars. Once Clayton County had been considered part of rural Georgia—red clay fields and piney woods, with the railroad tracks running right through the middle. Now Tara Boulevard was six lanes, lined with the usual detritus of shopping centers, apartment complexes, and Coming Soon billboards, all of it directly in Hartsfield's flight pattern. I could see six huge jets streaking across the horizon in front of me; up in the puffy gray cloud cover there were bound to be dozens more, all of them circling around the approach to the airport.

"Look for Twelve Oaks Plaza," I told Edna. "From the street number, I'd say it's on the right."

Her face was drawn and tear-streaked. "Some place to raise a child," she said, blowing her nose into a tissue. "Breathing in jet fumes and engine exhaust."

I'd been thinking the same thing. "On the right," I repeated.

She pointed ahead to the next traffic light. "That's it."

Twelve Oaks Plaza was the name of the street and an apartment complex that seemed to stretch out for half a mile on both sides of the gray cedar Twelve Oaks sign on the corner.

"You know who lived at Twelve Oaks plantation in *Gone With the Wind*, don't you?" I asked Edna.

"I have no idea," she snapped. "I'm not thinking about books. I'm thinking about the welfare of my grandchild."

"Ashley Wilkes," I told her anyway.

Edna twisted around in her seat so she could watch Maura, who was herself bouncing up and down, bobbing her head to whatever song she was humming. She didn't seem to sense she was home, but then, she was so petite, she couldn't see out the window.

I made the right turn into the apartment entrance, and then glanced down at the address I was looking for. Building 4565.

We cruised slowly for what seemed like two or three blocks. All the buildings were alike: slanted-roof blue cedar boxes, either two or three stories tall. The top two floors of each building had small balconies; the bottoms had what looked like a walled patio. They looked affordable, respectable, mind-numbingly monotonous. Twelve Oaks Plaza was like a self-contained village. We passed a convenience store, a swim and tennis club, even a small fenced playground with a swingset and a rusty-looking slide. Edna tsk-tsked.

Building 4565 was at the end of a cul-de-sac. I parked in an empty space in front of the building, but left the motor running.

A jet roared overhead. I had to put my lips directly on Edna's ear so that she could hear over the racket.

"She's probably gonna be really pissed that it's us dropping Maura off instead of Brian," I told Edna. "She told me on the phone yesterday that he owes her back child support, too. I don't want Maura to hear her mama bitching me out. You stay out here with her, OK? As soon as Shay's cool, I'll come and get both of you."

"I'm not leaving until I see the inside of that apartment," Edna repeated.

"I'm not asking you to," I said. "Be back in a few minutes."

Shay's apartment was on the ground floor, at the back of the building. A piece of masking tape attached to the doorbell said Ingraham/Gatlin. I rang the doorbell and waited. I'd taken the camera out of my purse and put it in the pocket of my ski jacket. The back of the apartment building got no sunlight and the only light fixture in the hallway had a smashed bulb. It was cold and damp, and I shivered and pulled up the collar on my turtleneck sweater. I rang the doorbell again, and knocked.

"Shay?" I hollered. But the jet roar was so loud I could barely hear my own voice. I doubted anybody inside could hear me out here. "Shay?"

Even though I'd worn thick wool socks and boots, my feet were getting cold. I walked to the end of the hallway. It let out on the back side of the apartment building. The land sloped off sharply, into a deep, kudzu-engulfed ravine, separated from a small strip of lawn by terraced stacks of landscape timbers.

Staying close to the building, I could see the patio that logically led off of Shay and Annette's apartment. The cedar fence around the patio was about six feet high, but it had rotted in places, and boards were missing. I tugged at the patio door. It was rain-warped, but pulled open. The patio was concrete, stained with oil, and crowded with a pink tricycle, a rusted barbecue grill, a red beer cooler, and a couple of aluminum lawn chairs. A sliding glass door led into the apartment, but the filmy white drapes were drawn tight.

"Shay?" I sidestepped a plastic sand bucket and some flowerpots full of long-dead houseplants. A bag of potting soil spilled over onto the patio and around broken shards of clay pots. A rusted screen door had come off the track and was leaned up against the outside of the door. I moved it aside, then stood by the sliding glass door, cupping my hands to the glass to try to see inside.

I could see what looked like a living room. One small lamp on a coffee table beside a sofa provided the only light in the room. The place was a wreck, trash and clothes strewn everywhere. There were three empty beer bottles on the table with the lamp. I was glad my camera had a flash.

"Shay! It's Callahan!"

I pushed on the handle. The sliding glass door moved jerkily on the rusted metal track. I started to push the curtain aside, but something—a nagging feeling of unease—stopped me.

"Shay?" I stepped back from the sliding glass door.

"Excuse me?"

I whirled around. A small black woman in a green flannel robe stood in the doorway of the patio. She looked to be in her early sixties, with pink rollers in her hair wrapped with a black chiffon scarf. She wore red rubber thongs on her bare feet.

"You looking for Annette and them?"

"Yeah," I said, wondering if the neighbor thought I was breaking into the apartment. "I'm, uh, Shay's sister-in-law. Brian's sister, Callahan. We were supposed to meet this morning, but she's not answering her door."

She nodded a polite greeting to me. "I am Mrs. Jimmy James. You'll have to excuse my appearance. I heard somebody hollering over here, and I just come right over. In case of an emergency or something."

It was then I noticed she carried a garden rake in her hand. Probably to rake me to death in case I happened to be an armed intruder.

"Have you seen Shay this morning?"

"Probably they're all hungover," Mrs. James said, pursing her lips in disapproval. "If that's what they calling it these days. They were all partying pretty good over here last night. Them and their boyfriends. I called over here at 2 A.M. and told Annette I'd call the po-lice if they didn't cut out that music and fighting. She knows I'll do it, too. That quieted things down a little bit."

"Does Shay usually work on Saturdays?" I asked. "Or does Annette?"

"I don't know when they all at work," the woman said, shaking her head. "I like to mind my own bidness."

I knew I'd found that most valuable of all jewels. A nosy neighbor.

"Oh, really?" I said. "Annette and Shay, they're pretty popular, huh?"

"Popular," she said, sniffing. "Some folk call it popular. Some call it indecent. Got mens living here in front of that little child. I seen things you don't want to know about."

I pushed the sliding glass door open. She stood right there in the doorway, watching me, rake poised. My fingers clamped and unclamped on the camera in my pocket. If Annette and Shay were gone, maybe I could get some photos of what their apartment looked like. If it was anything like what Brian said, that was the kind of thing a judge might consider in a custody action.

I stepped inside. The air was overheated, stale. As a former cop, my eye had been trained to look for criminal details. And as a cleaning professional, I'd developed a hypersensitive nose. Shay's apartment smelled like cheap red wine, dirty diapers, and kitty litter. Mrs. Jimmy James stepped into the living room right behind me.

She made clucking sounds. There was a faint scurrying from the front of the apartment. We both bristled for a second, Mrs. James whirling around to see if we had company.

"Roaches," I said, finally, pointing toward a corner of the living room where a trash basket overflowed with pizza boxes, beer cans, and McDonald's wrappers.

"I knew they was coming from over here," she said, banging her rake on the floor. "I ain't had no bugs till this crowd here moved in."

I took my camera out of my pocket, tested the flash, and then started snapping photos. Shot number one was the trash basket. Shot number two was the sofa, where it looked like the family's dirty laundry had been accumulating for weeks. Maura's tiny socks and pants and shirts spilled onto the floor from black plastic trash bags.

"What's that for?" Mrs. Jimmy James asked. "I thought you said you were family."

"It's for my scrapbook," I said, and I kept shooting, moving to the front of the apartment, into the tiny galley kitchen, which was a horror unto itself, heaped as it was with dirty dishes, half-filled Chinese take-out containers, and a catbox so ripe it made my eyes water. I could only stand to take two shots in the kitchen, but if they came out, they would speak volumes about the surroundings in which my niece had been living.

Mrs. Jimmy James followed behind me, muttering about calling the apartment manager, stomping her foot every once in a while to scare off the roaches.

A short hallway led off the right side of the living room toward what should have been the bedroom wing. There were three doors. The bathroom door was ajar. I peeked in, snapped a still life with diaper pail, dirty laundry, and scum-crusted sink.

Faint music played from behind one bedroom door. Mrs. Jimmy James was right on my heels.

"Shay?" I called loudly. "Wake up, Shay. It's Callahan."

"It's Mrs. Jimmy James," Mrs. James called. "You need to wake up and clean this place up, young lady."

There was no answer. I opened the door. The room was cloaked in darkness. It smelled like hairspray, baby powder, and sour milk. I felt around on the wall for the light switch, then flicked it on, but nothing happened. Just enough light came in from the hallway that I could make out the unmade bed with a table and a lamp beside it.

I walked over to the bed, nearly tripping on piles of clothes and shoes unseen in the darkness. I switched on the lamp. Heard Mrs. Jimmy James's rake fall to the floor.

A weak pool of yellow light flooded the bed. Shay's bed. She lay on her stomach, her thick blond hair splayed over the pillow, covering her face, which was pointed toward the doorway. Her eyes were closed; the black satin sheets pulled up right below her shoulders.

"She ain't sleepin'," Mrs. James said. "Is she?"

I touched Shay's bare shoulder and found it as cold as I'd expected. Now I could see the blood pooling on the sheet, and on the quilted bedspread. "No," I said. "She's not asleep. Could I please use your telephone?"

11

Mrs. Jimmy James walked right up to the side of the bed, leaned over and pressed her fingertips to the wrist of Shay's outflung right hand.

"Don't!" I cried.

Mrs. James seemed surprised at my outburst. "She dead," she said calmly. With one finger she lifted the edge of the sheet. "Poor thing. Look like to me, she was cut with a knife. Somebody killed her good."

"We've got to call the police," I said, glancing nervously around the room. Was it merely a pigsty, or had Shay struggled with her killer? And how recently? The bedspread had been pulled up over her shoulders, as though to cover the body. Although clothes and toys were strewn around the room, the furniture looked to be in place. For the first time I noticed the white crib shoved into a corner. A faded yellow afghan hung over the crib's side. On the floor at the head of the crib was a stuffed animal. I leaned over and picked it up. It was a loppy-eared hound dog, its fur rubbed off in places, one eye gone. Its owner had loved it near to death. I tucked it under my arm. Maura was going to need something to love.

I made myself focus on the bed. On Shay. I was a cop once, a detective even, but never in homicide. I'd known cops who could stand over the corpse of a child and crack jokes, who could eat a slice of pizza while watching an autopsy. Violent death would never be familiar to me. I swallowed and stood beside Mrs. James, looking down at Shay. I felt a faint buzzing in my ears, could hear my breath slow and catch at the brutality in that room.

Even in death, Shay looked angry. Her pink lips were pulled down at the corners, the mascara slightly smudged. I held my breath, moved the sheet a bit. Mrs. James was right. I could see a deep slash below Shay's shoulder blade. There must have been others, too, but I'd already seen enough.

Shay's resemblance to Maura was startling, disturbing. The short, upturned nose, the pouty mouth. Even the coloring was the same. The three-year-old's mother was dead. Where was Brian? Christ. Had he done this?

"We've got to get out of here. Call the police," I repeated. But first, I had to get outside to the car, let Edna know what had happened. We had to get Maura out of here, before the police arrived.

"Think I don't know that?" Mrs. James headed for the door. "We got a killer loose around here. I'm gonna call 911. Lock up my door and call the apartment manager, get me a deadbolt put on my door. Peephole, too."

I stuck my hands in my pocket and remembered the camera. "You go ahead," I told Mrs. James. "Call 911 and give them directions. I'll be right along. I just want to see if anything was taken."

She gave me an odd, puzzled look.

"I used to be a police detective," I said reassuringly. She looked doubtful, but she left.

I took the camera out and began snapping pictures, starting at the door, working every angle of the room. My stomach was queasy. I had to force myself to focus on the bed, on Shay, on the blood spatters on the headboard and wall. There were ten exposures left on the roll of film. I clicked them off rapid-fire, then hurried out the open sliding glass door. Just for a minute, I stood there on the patio, letting the chilly gray drizzle wash over me, wishing it could wash away the scent of death, the grim memory of what I'd just left behind.

Edna had gotten Maura out of her makeshift car seat and moved her to the front seat, where the two of them were engaged in a hot game of peekaboo.

I tapped on the window. Edna looked up, startled, rolled the window down. "What's wrong?"

"Everything," I said, mouthing the words so that Maura wouldn't overhear. "Shay's been murdered."

"Oh God," she said.

Maura climbed up onto Edna's lap, giggling, sticking her tongue out at me. So we were friends. I made a half-hearted silly face. Silly is hard when you've just seen a corpse. I pulled the stuffed hound dog out of my jacket and held it out to her. "Is this yours?"

"Poochie," she cried, grabbing the dog and hugging it tight. "My Poochie."

"Grandma's going to take you home so you can give Poochie a nap," I told my niece. "Sit in the back now and let me buckle you up."

She obligingly climbed into the backseat. I fastened the seat belt and tucked the pillows around her again. I walked around to the driver's side of the car.

"Go home. Call Ferd," I said. I handed her the camera. "Put this somewhere safe, like the bottom drawer of my dresser. And if you hear from Brian, tell him—"

"What?" Edna was alarmed. "What's going on, Julia?"

"Not in front of Maura," I said, drawing my words out so she would understand the seriousness of the situation. "Call Maureen. Maybe she's seen Brian. If he calls, tell him we need to see him. Right away. Tell him he's got to get together with Ferd. Now go. The cops and the ambulance will be here any minute. I don't want you two getting caught up in this."

I pounded the driver's side door. "Go!" I repeated.

Mrs. Jimmy James had already stepped up security measures. She kept the chain on the lock and made me show her my P.I. license before she'd unlock her apartment door and let me in. It was a good thing she didn't notice the license had expired six months ago.

"The police are on the way," she said, locking the door behind me.

I looked around her living room. It was hard to believe it was the exact same layout as Shay's. The place was spotless, crowded with an overstuffed suite of furniture, ruffled draperies, and walls full of family photos. On top of the television was a framed snapshot of a tiny

towheaded girl in a ruffled yellow dress, holding an Easter basket—
Maura. I looked inquiringly at Mrs. James.

"My little angel baby," Mrs. James said sadly, shaking her head.
"Who's gonna tell her about her Mama going to heaven?"

Heaven? I wondered.

"Maura's with my mother right now," I said. "Were you good
friends with Shay, Mrs. James?"

"Maura's the only reason I stayed here after that crowd moved in
next door," Mrs. James said. "That Annette and her boyfriend? Did
you say you were kin to them?"

"No, no," I assured her. "Maura's daddy is my brother."

"That's all right then," she decided. "I don't like to talk bad about
people, but those folks were trashy. It like to worried me to death, little Maura being over there with those people."

"You baby-sat for her?" I asked.

"Two, three times a week," Mrs. James said. "That Shay stayed out
in the streets. Her mama, too. Sometimes, they called me up and had
me go over to the day care, pick the baby up and bring her back here
and keep her all night. Not that I minded."

"Look here," she said, motioning toward a love seat. A small plastic
laundry basket held a stack of coloring books, a margarine tub filled
with crayons, and a Raggedy Ann doll. "That's Maura's. She loves to
color. And go to the store. Never saw a baby loved to go to the store
like she does."

I heard a siren. My time was running out. "When did you last see
Shay?" I asked. "Last night?"

"Didn't see her," Mrs. James said. "I was watching my programs on
the television. I heard people coming and going over there, door
opening and closing, and all that racket. Like I said, I called Annette
about that noise. I talked to her. Didn't talk to Shay."

"Who all was over there?" I asked.

"Ooh," she said, fanning her hand. "The boyfriend. Chuck. He
lived there. I heard him. Heard Shay laughing and carrying on.
Another man. He been over there before, maybe. Can't say. You know,
I mind my own bidness."

"What about a tall, thin man? With short curly hair, starting to go
gray? Looks a little like me? Drives a black pickup truck? Was he
there last night?"

I didn't have a photograph of Brian, didn't even have a clear mental picture of how he looked these days, or what he might have been wearing.

"I don't know," Mrs. James said. "Like I said, I mind my own bidness. But I can't say I saw a truck last night. Can't say I didn't, neither."

Mrs. James and I stood at the sidewalk in front of the apartment building, huddled together under her umbrella. She'd put on real shoes and a pair of gold-rimmed eyeglasses and a sweater, and fussed a little with her hair. "TV folks always interview the neighbors," she explained. The first cruiser came screaming around the mouth of the cul-de-sac on two tires. It was a dark brown Clayton County police department cruiser. Right behind it came more Clayton County sheriff's squad cars and two teal green Crown Victoria sedans, and behind that was an ambulance.

Mrs. James waved with both arms. "Right here," she called out. "Dead body right here."

The Crown Victoria sedans each carried a pair of detectives. Mrs. James took one pair inside Shay's apartment to show them the body. I got to stand out in the cold, in the parking lot, to give a statement to the other pair.

Despite the rain, people began to drift out of their apartments, to stand around and speculate on what was going on. Both the detectives were white. One was dressed in Saturday morning sweats. He looked to be in his early thirties, with light brown hair and a handlebar mustache. He was short and compactly built, with a dark blue windbreaker thrown over the sweatshirt, like he'd come directly to Twelve Oaks Plaza from his workout at the gym. His partner was older, with grayish-yellow hair that stuck out over his ears. He wore a black wool blazer over baggy gray flannel trousers, shiny black loafers. He wore the widest, reddest, ugliest necktie I'd ever seen.

The gym rat handed me his business card. It had an embossed gold shield. The card said his name was Gerald P. Tuohy and that he was an investigator for the Clayton County police department. The older man gave me a curt nod. "I'm Lawrence," he said. I couldn't tell whether that was his first or last name because he didn't offer a card. I didn't offer mine, either.

"You the one who called?" Lawrence asked.

"That was Mrs. James," I said. "She lives next door."

"But you found the body," Lawrence said. "That right?"

"We found it together," I corrected him.

"Did you know the deceased?" Tuohy asked.

"She's my sister-in-law," I said. "Her name is Shay Gatlin."

Tuohy was writing it down. Lawrence was listening to me, but his eyes were everywhere, watching the people drifting by, the cops going in and out of the apartment, the cars cruising slowly past.

"Look," I said. "I used to be on the job. The victim is a white female, approximate age twenty-eight. I came over here this morning to talk to her, nobody answered the door. I went around back, which is where I met Mrs. James. We entered the apartment through an unlocked sliding glass door from the patio, walked around, found the body in a bedroom, at approximately 9:45 A.M. From what little I could see, she'd been stabbed in the upper back, right shoulder blade. No weapon in plain sight, but of course, I didn't want to disturb the scene, so I exited by the same door I entered. As far as I know, nobody has been in or out of the apartment since your people were called. Her mother's name is Annette Gatlin. I think she works as a security guard at the airport. Now, instead of all the questions, why don't we save everybody some time, and just let me go write out a statement. Could we do that? "

"You were a cop? Where was that?" Lawrence asked.

"Atlanta P.D.," I said. "I was in property crimes. You could call my old captain. C. W. Hunsecker."

Tuohy shook his head. "Don't know him."

"You wouldn't," Lawrence said. "Didn't I hear he took early retirement?"

"Disability," I said. "He got shot on the job a couple years ago." It didn't seem pertinent to mention that he was trying to save my ass at the time, or that it was my fault he'd nearly died trying.

Lawrence shrugged, looked at Tuohy. "You wanna take her back to the office, let her give you a statement? I want to go inside, take a look around."

Tuohy's face fell.

"Let her wait," he said. "You can do that, can't you?"

"Sure," I said. "I love waiting in the rain."

They let me wait in Mrs. James's apartment, while Mrs. James was outside giving interviews to the television camera crews that had picked up the call from their police scanners.

I called the house. Edna answered. "Did he call?" I asked.

"No," Edna said. "Nobody's heard from him. What happened there, Jules?"

"Shay's dead," I said. "Stabbed. The cops are here, I've been questioned once, and I'm going to go give a statement at the Clayton P.D. Did you call Ferd?'

"I knew it was something like this," Edna said. "When you were taking so long in that apartment, I knew it was something awful."

"Very awful," I said. "What about Ferd?"

"I told him what I knew," Edna said. "He gave me a beeper number."

"Call him back. Ask him to meet me at the Clayton police department office. The detectives' names are Lawrence and Tuohy." If I was going to go give a statement about finding a body, I wanted a lawyer in my corner.

"The police won't think . . . You won't have to talk about Brian, will you?" Her voice cracked. "He wouldn't. I know him."

Maybe she did. I didn't. "I'll do what I can," I said. "I gotta go."

12

The nameplate on his desk identified my interviewer as Detective L. D. Lawrence. He'd lost the jacket, rolled up his shirtsleeves. He had a cigarette tucked behind his ear. A nice touch.

"Your friend had multiple stab wounds," he said, looking down at the open notebook on his desk. "Somebody was very upset. You have any thoughts about that?"

"Not my friend," I said. "My sister-in-law. I hadn't seen her in years. I wouldn't know who might be upset with her."

His eyebrows were much darker than his hair. He raised one now. "Your sister-in-law? But you hadn't seen her in years?"

"We're not close," I said. I was watching the clock on the office wall behind Lawrence. It was close to noon. I figured it would take a full hour for Ferd to get here from Cumming, if he was going to show.

Lawrence caught me looking. I had a feeling there wasn't much he missed. "You expecting somebody?" he asked.

"My ride," I said.

I heard a commotion out in the hallway. Soft weeping, a woman's voice, a man making comforting sounds. Tuohy opened the door and stuck his head in. "I've got the mother and her boyfriend here. We'll be in the captain's office. All set here?"

"We're good," Lawrence said, his voice dismissive. I saw a blur of silver hair, a petite woman in a dark blue uniform. I recognized Chuck Ingraham from his visit the day before. But I wouldn't have known Annette. This was the neighborhood blonde bombshell? From where I sat, she looked like a meter maid.

Lawrence wheeled his chair out from behind the desk, kicked the office door shut.

"You know her?" he asked, gesturing toward the door.

"A long time ago," I said.

"Him?"

"We've met."

"But you showed up at their apartment this morning, took it upon yourself to break in when nobody answered the door."

"I didn't break in," I reminded him. "The back door was unlocked. I didn't go in until Mrs. James came over. Didn't she tell you that?"

"We have Mrs. James's statement," Lawrence said. "But she'd never seen you before this morning. Doesn't know who might have entered Miss Gatlin's apartment before she got there."

"I didn't kill Shay," I said. "I didn't enter that apartment until Mrs. James came around to see who was looking for Shay."

He looked at the notebook. "I've got that written right here. What I don't have is a reason why you went over there this morning."

Where was Ferd? I really didn't want to start airing the family linen to this detective. But I also didn't want to refuse to answer his questions or make him overly suspicious of me. After all, I hadn't done anything wrong.

"I needed to talk to Shay," I said. "About my niece."

"That's the three-year-old? Maria?"

"Maura," I corrected him.

"Never heard a name like that," Lawrence said.

"It's Irish. We, I mean, the Garritys, we're Irish. It's like Mary, but in Gaelic, I think."

"Talk to her about what?"

"Custody," I said. "She didn't want to share custody. I wanted to discuss that with her."

"You a lawyer?"

There was a knock and the door opened. A female deputy in brown uniform stood in the hall. Ferd Bryce was beside her. "Detective? This gentleman says he needs to speak to you."

Lawrence wheeled his chair out again, took a look at Ferd, and gave her a look. "I'm busy."

"I'm Ms. Garrity's attorney," Ferd said, stepping inside the office. He stuck out his hand. "Judge Ferdinand Bryce. Retired, of course. How ya doin'?"

Lawrence looked at me, scowled. "You feel the need for a lawyer?"

"I feel the need," Ferd said, looking around for a chair. "You got any coffee?"

Lawrence grudgingly went for coffee. I gave Ferd a quick, heartfelt hug.

He'd changed drastically, shed maybe sixty or seventy pounds, so that his jeans hung loosely from his hips and loose folds of flesh hung like wattles from his neck and chin. His thick shock of dark wavy hair had gone totally white and was thinning at the temples, making his wide forehead and high cheekbones even more pronounced. Once he'd been a big, bad grizzly of a judge. Now he looked like an aging, yet still noble, Cherokee chief.

Even in paint-spattered blue jeans, cowboy boots, and suede jacket.

"You dieting?" I asked.

He coughed. "The big C. They took part of my left lung two years ago, made me quit smoking. I'm fine, for an old fart. Catch me up quick, will you? Before the detective gets back."

I told him about finding Shay, about the apartment, and about the roll of film I'd shot of the apartment. "I thought it might be useful for the custody petition," I explained. "Then, after we found Shay, I just shot the rest of the roll."

"Gawddamn," Ferd said. "You think the neighbor will say anything about that?"

"Don't know," I said. "They took our statements separately. The neighbor lady is quite a pistol, Ferd. Didn't turn a hair when she saw the body. She's the one who lifted the sheet and saw the stab wounds."

"Maybe it wasn't the first time she saw the body," Ferd said.

"No, I don't think . . . "

"You let the cops decide that," Ferd instructed me. "When Lawrence gets back, you cooperate. Tell him what you saw, what you did. Leaving out the photography for now."

"What about Brian?"

"You don't know anything about Brian, and that's the truth," Ferd said. "Don't volunteer anything he doesn't ask about directly. I'm just gonna sit here and act interested. We'll give him another ten minutes, and unless he has something substantial, we'll tell him his time is up."

"They've got Annette and her boyfriend here," I said. "The other detective brought them in."

"Annette?" Ferd frowned.

"Shay's mother. They were all living together in the apartment. The neighbor said they had a noisy party last night. She heard their voices, but didn't actually see anybody."

"Including Brian?"

"I gave her a description. She said she didn't think she'd ever seen him."

Lawrence brought in a cardboard holder with three cups of coffee, handed them over, and sat back behind his desk.

"I just talked to Detective Tuohy," he said, stirring his cup with a pencil. "Mrs. Gatlin, the victim's mother, seems to think your brother killed her daughter. Her boyfriend—gentleman's name is Chuck Ingraham, he's one of our local attorneys—corroborates that. In fact, Mr. Ingraham claims your brother Brian kidnapped that child you've been so concerned about."

I glanced over at Ferd. He closed his eyes and gave the slightest shake of his head.

Lawrence hadn't missed Ferd's gesture.

"Do you know where Brian Garrity is?" he asked. "Where he was last night?"

"No, but—"

Another brief knock at the door. Tuohy came in, handed a computer printout to Lawrence, gave me a smirk, and left.

Lawrence ran his finger down the print on the page. "This is interesting," he said, looking from me to Ferd, then back to me.

"Your brother's got himself a record. Assault and battery, making terroristic threats, couple of drunk and disorderlies. You know he put his wife in the hospital last year? Mrs. Gatlin says he tried to choke Shay. She got away from him, but he did blacken her eye and give her a couple bruised ribs."

My heart sank. I felt nauseous. My mind wandered back to the apartment, to Shay, her blood spilt on the black satin sheets. I thought about Brian and the resolve in his voice. He'd told me. "I'll deal with her." Had he?

"May I?" Ferd had his hand out, asking for the computer printout. Lawrence gave it to him. Ferd took a pair of bifocals out of his jacket pocket, perched them on the rim of his nose. I scooted closer, looked over his shoulder at the printout.

It was from the GCIC, the Georgia Criminal Index Center, and it listed half a dozen arrests for Brian John Garrity. The first arrest was 1992, the most recent a year ago.

Ferd put his finger on the latest arrest for drunk and disorderly. "You said Brian allegedly put Shay in the hospital last year? Did she file charges?"

Lawrence snatched the printout from Ferd.

"Her mother says she was terrified of Brian Garrity. Wouldn't file charges because she was afraid he'd kill her or harm the baby. That's when Ms. Gatlin moved in with her mother."

"He'd never touch that child," I said hotly. "He adores her, and Maura adores him. I don't believe he hit Shay, either. He'd never hit a woman."

Ferd put his hand on my arm.

"All right, then," he said, standing up. "Unless you have anything else, Miss Garrity has some other business to attend to today." He handed Lawrence a business card. "You can phone me if you need to speak to her."

Lawrence tossed the business card onto his desk. "I'm not done. Where is your brother, Ms. Garrity? Where can we reach him?"

I shrugged, and before I could say anything, Ferd was nudging me toward the door.

We wound around a narrow linoleum-floored passageway looking for the front door and the parking lot. There were more office doors, all of them closed and locked, but everything seemed to dead-end into another hallway. Somebody should have been thrown in jail for what they'd done to the old Clayton County courthouse.

A bronze plaque on the wall told us that the original red brick courthouse had been built in 1898 to replace an earlier courthouse that had burned down. The only visible remnant of the old building was the truncated clock spire that peeked above the hideous junk the county had tacked onto the building over the years. There had been additions in 1962 and 1971, and maybe even more, all of them slapped in place without regard to form or function. We went up short flights of stairs, took a couple of elevators, finally found our-selves in an abbreviated lobby area.

"Gawddamn," Ferd said. He was breathing heavily, his mouth ajar.

"Look," I said.

Annette Gatlin and Chuck Ingraham were sitting on a wooden bench in the lobby. She leaned against the man, wiping her eyes with a crumpled tissue. She saw me at about the same time I saw her.

She jumped up and came charging over to me.

"He killed her!" she cried, giving me a weak shove. "Brian killed Shay."

Ferd put an arm around my shoulders and tried to gentle me past her.

"No, damn you," Annette cried. Her eyes were red-rimmed, her makeup streaked. "I saw her," she sobbed. "I saw what he did to my baby."

"I saw her, too," I said quietly. "Brian didn't do that, Annette. He couldn't."

Annette's friend eased over to her. Ingraham's thin hair was sprayed and combed over a bald spot he wanted to believe wasn't there. "You don't know Brian Garrity," he said.

"You don't, either," I told him.

"Where's Maura?" Annette demanded. "Where's my granddaughter?" She grabbed the boyfriend's arm. "Chuck. Tell them about the custody order. What the judge said."

Chuck Ingraham's Adam's apple bobbed above the caramel-colored turtleneck sweater he wore. "There's a custody order in place," he said, speaking to Ferd instead of me. Shay had legal custody. We want the child returned, today. Immediately."

Ferd hitched the shoulder strap of his briefcase, then hitched his pants. "You're an attorney?"

"I'm Annette's attorney. And a friend of the family."

"My condolences," Ferd said, tipping his head slightly. "As you're aware, Georgia code states that in the event of death of a custodial parent, the surviving parent is entitled to custody."

"No fuckin' way. He killed Maura's mother," Annette twitched with anger. "That's not right, is it, Chuck?"

Ingraham nodded. "Technically. But it's left up to the judge's discretion. I'll call him this afternoon. Get Detective Tuohy to speak to him. Brian is a suspect in a murder. I doubt a judge would give him custody."

"We'll see," Ferd said. He nodded, tucked my arm in his, and we walked outside, where the sun didn't shine and the birds didn't sing—and Ferd couldn't remember where he'd parked his car.

13

Ferd was huffing and puffing by the time we found his dusty maroon Mercedes, which he'd parked in a handicapped parking spot in the sheriff's lot all the way at the back of the courthouse complex.

He got behind the wheel, rummaged around in his pockets, brought out an orange plastic inhaler and took a couple of puffs. After a minute or so, his breathing seemed to get easier.

"Don't ever get old," he advised me.

"Brian's in deep shit," I said. "Can you do anything?"

He shrugged. "Depends on whether or not he killed his wife. If he's guilty, I can't help. I won't. Twenty years on the bench, I put enough scum back on the streets. Then, I had no choice. Rules of evidence, sentencing guidelines, all that bullshit. I'll talk to him. If I think he's telling the truth, we'll take it from there. If he's not completely truthful with me, you'll have to find somebody else. What about you?"

"Me?"

"I watched you in there with that detective. Very cagey. Are you hiding Brian? Hiding anything other than that roll of film you told me about?"

"No," I said. "I'm only doing this because of Edna. And the child."

"Not for you?" Ferd started the Mercedes. It was a seventies model, big and leathery, and the engine started without a hitch.

"If Brian's a killer, I want to know," I said.

• • •

We drove back to Twelve Oaks Plaza. Yellow crime-scene tape fluttered around the perimeter of Shay's building, and a uniformed sheriff's deputy stood by his cruiser in the parking lot.

"Crime scene guys must have finished up," I said. They hadn't taken long. "Wonder if they found the murder weapon?"

"You happen to get that neighbor's phone number?" Ferd asked.

I had. In fact, while I was in the apartment, I'd noticed her phone list, printed in large block letters on a sheet of paper taped to the wall near the phone. There hadn't been time to copy it. I reached into my jacket pocket and pulled out the folded piece of blue-lined notebook paper.

It had all her important numbers written down: doctor, pharmacy, eye doctor, apartment maintenance man, some people only listed by first names, probably friends or neighbors or relatives, and—the reason I'd borrowed it—Shay's, Annette's, and Chuck's numbers at work, and the number for Maura's day-care center.

"Too bad there's not a number for Brian on there," Ferd said. He handed me a little cellular flip-phone. "Want to call your mother? She's pretty upset."

I called. Upset was a mild way to describe the state Edna had worked herself into.

"Maura's asleep," she said. "What on earth has happened?"

"Shay was stabbed to death," I said. "In her bed. I just finished giving the detectives my statement. They, uh, wanted to know why I was there, so I told them it was a custody dispute. They asked a lot of questions about Brian, Ma."

"He called," she said. "Thank God, he's OK."

"He's OK? Where the hell is he? Did you tell him about Shay?"

"He already knew," Edna said. "He'd heard it on the radio. Honey, he was so upset, he was crying. It near to broke my heart."

"*Where is he?*" I repeated, loudly. "Where has he been?"

"He had some kind of problem at his job. His check wasn't ready, and he had to wait around for his boss to get there, and then, when he went to the place he'd just rented, the manager tried to hold him up for more security deposits and so forth. He said he didn't get his stuff moved until late last night. He thought it would be too late to call. So he slept on a mattress on the floor, and he was coming to get Maura when he heard about Shay on the news."

"Why didn't he call?" I shouted, pounding the dashboard in frustration.

"The phone wasn't hooked up yet," Edna said. She made it all sound so reasonable.

"The cops think he killed Shay." There. It was out. "Did you tell him to get over to our house right now? That Ferd needs to see him?"

"I told him," Edna said, sniffing. "He's afraid, Jules. He says Annette is out to get him. They tried to have him thrown in jail a couple times, making up lies about him."

"He's been to jail," I said bluntly.

"I already know all about that," Edna said. "It wasn't his fault."

Talk about denial. "Is he coming over? Did he give you a phone number?"

"He wants to talk to Ferd," Edna said. "Talk about what Ferd can do to make sure Annette can't take Maura away from him. He said he'd call back about four o'clock today. Can Ferd be here?"

I looked over at Ferd. "Can you be at our place at four?"

"I guess."

We decided it would be all right if I called Mrs. James from the car. Just a few friendly questions.

"Mrs. James? This is Callahan Garrity calling. I'm sorry to disturb you after such an awful morning, but my mother and I are watching Maura, and we had a couple questions we wanted to ask you. About Maura."

"My angel baby," Mrs. James said. "She doing all right? Annette was just over here asking all kind of questions. She's all worked up. And the police won't let 'em in that apartment. Not even to get some clothes or nothin'. She asking me about where you took that baby to. Tried to get me to say you went in there by yourself. I told her twice. Ain't nothin' wrong with my hearing. And if you'd gone in that place, I would have heard you."

"Thank you," I said. "I appreciate that. And Maura is fine," I said. "We haven't told her yet. Mrs. James, I need to call the day care to let them know Maura won't be there Monday. Could you tell me the name of it?"

"KidzKare," she said promptly. "Over there off Riverdale Road. Miss Sandy, that's the name of Maura's teacher."

"I'll call them and let them know," I said. "And maybe I should talk to Shay's boss, too. Do you happen to know his name?"

"Dyson Yount. He's a big man down here in these parts. What you call a real estate magnate. Owns half of Clayton County, that's what Shay told me. And she was his right hand. She told me that man was crazy 'bout her. I reckon that's right. He come over here a little while ago. All tore up about Shay. I gave him a Coca-Cola and let him use the phone."

"Ask her about the murder weapon," Ferd coached.

I bit my lip. If I got too inquisitive, Mrs. James was likely to tell Annette or the cops that I'd been snooping around.

"That was a terrible thing that happened to Shay," I said soberly. "Terrible. I can't imagine who would want to hurt her like that."

"That's what I told the police," Mrs. James said. "She got a lot of friends. Lot of men friends. Maybe one of them got mad about all her boyfriends. All I know is, I'm getting me a peephole, and putting a stick on that sliding glass door. My nephew, he's bringing me a shotgun, keep by my bed till they find the crazy man who done this to that girl."

"I'm sure the police are working very hard to find him," I said.

"Huh!" she said. "I don't know about that. They poked around out here, but they gone now. Had a whole slew of men out there stomping around in the kudzu back here. Looking for that knife, I reckon."

"Did they find it?" I asked eagerly.

"Don't guess they did. They messed around for a while, then they quit. Right now, there's just the one sheriff out in the parking lot. Keeping folks away. Listen here. I got to go now. The Channel 46 news is coming on, and I got to tape it. You give my angel baby a kiss for me, you hear?"

"I hear," I said. "Uh, Mrs. James, is there anything in particular Maura likes to eat?"

She laughed heartily. "That's a fussy-eating child. Reckon you found that out. I don't believe Annette and them ever cooked anything regular for her. She likes fast food, Happy Meals, pizza, hot dogs. I got her to eat little baby carrots, if I gave her something to dip 'em in. And celery sticks. She'll eat that pretty good. Sometimes she'll eat a little bit of fruit."

"All right, that's a start. Thanks," I said. "Would it be OK if I called you again?"

"You call anytime at all. Except during my programs. Try grits."

"What?" I asked, confused.

"Grits. Maura loves grits. Put some butter on 'em. Maybe just a sprinkle of sugar."

"We'll give it a try," I said.

Mac's Blazer was in the driveway when we got home. I'd completely forgotten we'd made a date to finish up his Christmas shopping.

He was sitting at the kitchen table eating a bowl of soup.

"I'm sorry," I started.

"Edna told me everything," he said. "I needed an excuse not to go to the mall."

I introduced Ferd to Mac. "Ferd and Daddy were best buddies," I said.

"Jack stayed with me through three divorces," Ferd said, pulling a chair up to the table. "I miss him more than I ever missed any of those gals."

Edna came into the kitchen trailed by Maura, who dragged her stuffed dog on the floor behind her. Edna gave Ferd a quick hug and a peck on the cheek, then insisted on fixing him a bowl of soup.

"It's my homemade vegetable soup," she said, ladling it out of the pot. "There's corn bread, too. I remember you love corn bread."

Ferd patted his stomach. "Why couldn't I have married somebody like you, Edna Mae? Somebody who could cook?"

"'Cause you weren't interested in home cooking," Edna retorted. "As I recall, you were interested in good looks and good times."

"That's true," Ferd admitted.

We ate soup and talked strategy. Edna managed to coax Maura into eating three or four mouthfuls of soup, and three slices of corn bread. When Maura had finished, she tottered off to the cupboard and pulled out her pots and pans.

"We've gotta get her some real toys," I said. "Mrs. James says she loves to color."

Edna's eyes flickered. "Can we keep her?" she asked Ferd.

"For now you've got physical custody. And possession really is nine-tenths where that's concerned," Ferd said. "With Shay dead, Brian is entitled to custody, pending a lot of other stuff."

"Like what?" Edna bent foreword.

Ferd coughed discreetly. "You sure you want to go into all this?"

"Mac's family," I told Ferd.

"I've never met Brian," Mac said. "Maybe Ferd's right. I could just go watch the ball game in the den."

"Never mind," Edna said. "Answer my question, please Ferd."

Ferd drummed his fingers on the tabletop. "Shay's family could petition the court to award custody of the child based on the child's best interest and welfare."

"Welfare?" Edna hooted. "Those people aren't fit to keep a cat."

"When I have those photos developed, they should show the kind of environment Maura was living in," I said. "The apartment was filthy. Garbage, overflowing catbox, dirty clothes. There wasn't even a sheet on Maura's little crib. And the neighbor told me they never cooked regular meals for Maura. She was usually left at day care, or with Mrs. James, who baby-sat for her two or three times a week."

"She's still wearing diapers," Edna said indignantly.

"We'll tell all that to the judge," Ferd said. "But it's probably not going to be enough. You all need to realize that this thing may get ugly."

Uh-oh, I thought. Here it comes. I was glad Ferd would be the message-bearer and not me.

"What's that supposed to mean?" Edna asked. "They're going to tell a lot of lies about Brian, he already warned me."

"He has a criminal record," Ferd said as gently as he could. "Assault and battery. Drunk and disorderly. Some other things, too. Not to mention the fact that the family has apparently already started pointing the finger at Brian for Shay's murder."

Edna folded her arms across her chest. "He didn't do it. We can prove he didn't do it. He's not violent. Not Brian."

"We'll get to that," Ferd said. "But there are financial concerns, too. I understand he was behind on his child support payments. And that his recent employment record may be pretty spotty."

Edna's eyes were blazing. "We are Brian's family. I am that child's grandmother. Whatever we have is hers. If this is about money, tell us."

"I don't know what it's about yet," Ferd said, reaching across the table to pat Edna's hand. "I just want you to know the possibilities."

"Maura's staying right here. Right where she's at," Edna said, looking over at the child. "Nobody's taking her anywhere. Not while I'm around to stop it."

14

Mac was sitting on the kitchen floor, helping Maura build another of her Tupperware towers. He's a civil engineer by training, so it was a very complicated tower, utilizing all our wooden spoons, an egg-beater, a round wooden cutting board, and some wooden clothespins Edna had dug out of the junk drawer.

"Look, Maura," he said brightly. "Here's the observation tower. And here's all the people looking down." He made a clothespin dance across a catwalk he'd made from wooden spoons. I was seeing a new side of Mac. It was fascinating.

I looked over at Edna. "Who's going to tell Maura?"

Her face crumpled a little, her hands reached automatically for her deck of cards. Since she quit smoking, Edna keeps an almost constant game of solitaire going. Now she laid out the cards, flipping them over so fast I could barely see the numbers and symbols.

"How do you tell a baby her mama's never coming back?" she asked. "Even if she's a lousy mama?"

We both looked to Ferd, who was brushing corn-bread crumbs off his denim work shirt. "I'm a lawyer, not a shrink," he said. "Shouldn't her father be the one to tell her?'

"Should be," I said.

Edna shook her head. "Brian's no good at that kind of thing. He gets all emotional. He couldn't even say Shay's name on the phone today. He asked me to do it. I tried half a dozen times. She's just a baby. How can I tell her that?"

"Has she been asking about Shay?" I wanted to know.

"Not much," Edna said. "When I put her down for her nap, she just said it once. 'Mama.' She hasn't cried or anything. Maybe we'll just wait. Keep her busy and happy. We'll take her to see Santa Claus, drive around and look at the lights. After Christmas. Then we'll tell her."

Ferd coughed and his face reddened.

I got up and poured him a cup of tea, brought it back to the table and set it in front of him.

"Ma," I said, as gently as I could. "We might not have Maura that long. Everything depends on Brian."

Edna wanted to talk money to Ferd, so Mac and I took Maura in the living room to look at the Christmas tree.

We always get a Fraser fir. Scotch pines, grown locally in the South, are much cheaper, but for us, the smell of Christmas is the smell of a Fraser fir. Besides, the needles stay on the tree longer—or at least that's what I tell myself to justify the twenty-dollar price difference.

This year we had the blinking colored minilights on the tree. Edna's choice. I like the big, old-fashioned outdoor lights we'd squirreled away from my childhood, but this year it was her turn to decorate the tree. So we had the red pipe-cleaner star tree-topper one of my brothers made in fourth grade instead of the imported Italian bisque angel I'd bought at a ritzy boutique, and great tacky handfuls of tinsel instead of the beaded gold roping I'd picked up at the same boutique.

I turned off the lights in the living room and Mac plugged in the tree. The lights splashed polka dots of blue, green, pink, and yellow on Maura's face as she stood, awed, by the sight of the tree. She reached out and touched a silvery ornament, catching it in the palm of her hand. It was a glass kitten, playing with a glittery pink ball of fur.

"Mine," Maura said firmly.

"Go ahead, Maura," Mac coached. "You can look at it." He unhooked the ornament and handed it to her.

I winced. The ball was one of our oldest ornaments, one of the few that had survived all the family Christmases with four rowdy kids and two dogs. Once there had been kittens, puppies, pale yellow chicks, and a baby lamb, all made out of the delicate hand-painted glass. The kitten was all that was left.

Maura turned it over and over. She held it up to the lights so they would blink against the glass. "Kitty cat," she told Mac.

He picked her up in his arms. "What's the kitty cat say?"

Her little pink mouth was perfect for the job. "Meow-meow."

Mac kissed her soundly on the cheek. "Smart girl. What does the doggie say?"

"Woof-woof."

He rewarded her with another kiss.

"And the cow?"

"Moooo," she said, drawing it out and laughing at her own cleverness.

He looked over and gave me a big wink. "I think this little girl needs to go Christmas shopping with us. What do you say, punkin? Want to go to the store with Aunt Callahan and Mac?"

She nodded vigorously. "Big Mac."

I had to laugh. "Mrs. James says she loves fast food. That must be why she's so taken with you, Big Mac."

"Little girls love me," Mac said. He set Maura down and put his arms around my neck. He brushed my hair off my forehead and kissed my ear. "How about the big girls? How do they feel?"

I returned his kiss, breathed in the sharp clean smell of him. Mac doesn't wear perfume or aftershave, but he uses some kind of soap that drives me wild. "This girl's in love," I said. "But I really am too tired to go Christmas shopping. How about tomorrow?"

"I was going to go cut down my tree," he said. "Maybe you guys could go with me. We could all pile in the Blazer. Me, you, Maura, Rufus, and Maybelline."

"Where do we put the tree?" I asked.

"Tie it on the roof," he said quickly. "What do you say?"

I looked down at Maura. She was busy picking ornaments off the lowest branches of the tree, trying to shove them in the pockets of her overalls. "Mine, mine, mine," she sang.

"It depends," I said. "It all depends on my damn brother."

"You never talked very much about him," Mac said. "What's he like?"

"I don't know very much," I said. "From what he told me, he's moved around a lot since my dad died. He and Shay got together when he moved back here. According to him, Shay didn't tell him she was pregnant until she was seven months gone. They got married after Maura was born. He's been working construction jobs, from what I can tell. He says he's moving into a new apartment. I got a feeling he's been living out of his truck until just recently. He's broke. He's no angel. What else do you want to know?"

"Who killed his wife?"

I walked over to the tree, picked a candy cane off one of the branches, and handed it to Maura, who'd been standing on her tiptoes, trying to reach the candy.

"The neighbor is a snoop. Which is a help. She says Shay had lots of boyfriends, and that she and Annette were pretty wild. Annette's boyfriend was living there with them. Another thing I forgot to mention to Ferd. The neighbor said Shay's boss came over to the apartment today. Mrs. James says he's a 'big man' down there, whatever that means."

"Sounds like a start," Mac said. "Do the cops know any of this?"

"They took Mrs. James's statement," I said. "I hope she talked about the men. Of course, the man they're most interested in is Brian Garrity."

"You haven't told Edna everything, I take it."

"I couldn't," I said. "You see how she is about him. Blind love. That's Edna Mae Garrity. Annette claims Brian was violent toward Shay. According to her, he beat Shay up so bad last year, she had broken ribs and a black eye. Had to be hospitalized."

"Christ!" Mac said with distaste. For a big guy who loves to hunt and fish, he's really a marshmallow. Hates violence, especially against women or kids.

"Funny thing, though," I said. "Lawrence, the detective, showed us Brian's rap sheet today. Just to make a point about what a hard case Brian is. Ferd noticed there was no arrest for the incident Annette told the cops about. He asked, and the cop got all testy about it. Annette told them that Shay didn't file charges because she was afraid Brian would kill her or even hurt the baby."

"But she filed charges against him the other times?"

"We don't know that much about the other arrests," I said. "Looks like some bar fights, public drunkenness, that kind of thing."

"Sounds like Brian's the Garrity family bad seed," Mac said quietly.

"Prodigal son," I agreed.

15

Edna wouldn't let anybody near the phone, even though we have call waiting and two lines coming into the house. At 4:30, the phone rang and she jumped on it like a tick on a dog.

"Brian?"

"Let me talk to him," I said.

Edna shook her head no.

"Maura's fine," she said. Her voice dropped. "We haven't told her anything yet. Thought you'd want to do that yourself."

Edna listened and her face grew thoughtful. "Son. We need you here," she pleaded. "Ferd can't help you unless you help him."

Her face arranged itself in folds of sadness and what I thought might be resignation.

"What about money? You got enough to live on?"

She handed the phone to Ferd.

"Brian?" His voice was too loud for our small, overheated kitchen. "What's this about, buddy? Sounds like you got some serious troubles."

He listened to Brian's explanation.

"We're working on that. Right now, you've got physical custody of your daughter. And as long as nobody challenges that, we're all right. It's a good idea to let the child stay here with your mama and sister. Stable environment, all like that."

Brian must have asked what the police knew about Shay's murder.

"She was stabbed to death. They had cops canvassing the area in back of the apartment this afternoon. We don't know if they found anything. And they've been questioning the neighbors."

Ferd took a small notebook out of his inside jacket pocket, uncapped a slim silver pen, and jotted notes as Brian talked. He looked up at me once, his eyes darted briefly toward Maura. I got his meaning.

"Ma," I said. "Mac wants to take Maura Christmas shopping. How about if you go along with them? He doesn't really know anything about dealing with a little girl."

"I'm staying put." Edna folded her arms across her chest. She was digging in for the siege.

Ferd covered the receiver with one hand. "Go on, Edna," he urged. "Be good to get out of the house. Callahan and I can take care of things here. We're gonna work on strategy. You guys go on and hit the stores." He lifted one hip, took a worn billfold out of his pocket, extracted two twenties. "Here. Buy something for the baby from me. Like the song says, you need a little Christmas, right this very minute."

Maura came over and put her arms around Edna's waist. "Store. We go to the store." She stood up on her tiptoes, grabbed Edna's pocketbook from the kitchen table. "Come on, Grandma. Store."

Edna allowed herself to be dragged out to the mall with Mac and Maura, only after Mac reminded her of all the things that could be bought for little girls. Doll, toys, books, and clothes. He had a twenty-year-old daughter who lived with his ex-wife in California, but he was always shopping for gifts for Stephanie. Guilty dad syndrome.

"An EZ Bake Oven," Edna decided. "Child loves to play house."

"That's so sexist," I complained. "They probably don't even make 'em anymore. I can't believe you want to turn your granddaughter into a little Martha Stewart at this age."

"An EZ Bake Oven and a tricycle," Edna continued. "A shiny pink one. With a bell."

"I never had me a pink tricycle," I said, sulking. "Daddy brought home that big, ugly red boy's bike. I hated it."

"We needed something everybody could use once you outgrew it," Edna said. "That bicycle had a lot of miles on it. Good and sturdy."

"I hate good and sturdy," I said.

• • •

Ferd continued his conversation in whispers until he heard Mac's Blazer pulling out of the driveway with the Christmas shoppers.

"We've got some hard stuff to talk about, my friend," he said, standing up and stretching. "Stuff we can't very well discuss on the phone. We need to meet."

"I'm coming, too," I said, loud enough for Brian to hear on his end of the line.

Ferd looked at the kitchen clock. "I gotta be home in an hour to take my pills," he told Brian. "Tell you what. You know the old Red Barn, right there on U.S. 19 in Roswell? Used to be a fried chicken joint? It's a yuppie fern bar now. Meet us there at five. Can you make it from where you are?"

Ferd coughed and his chest rattled, like something had come loose in there. His face reddened, he grabbed a napkin and held it to his mouth.

"No? Five fifteen then. You got any papers from this other lawyer, anything like that, bring it with you. Oh yeah. We'll need rent receipts, pay slips, and canceled checks. Anything to prove where you were on Friday and Saturday. Anything that proves you're a hard-working, regular-paycheck kind of doting daddy."

I took the phone from Ferd. "Brian? This is important. Don't screw around on us now."

"I already talked to Ferd," Brian growled. "Mind your own damn business, OK?"

"I found Shay's body. It's my business now," I said. "See you at the Red Barn."

Ferd headed north on I-75 to I-285, the perimeter highway that winds like a lazy lasso around Atlanta. I was following in my new Ford Econoliner van, but it was no match for the Mercedes' powerful engine.

At least my van was running. The year before, a case I hadn't wanted to take, and never actually felt like I had solved, had paid off in an unexpected way: found money, twenty-five thousand in all. I used some of it to retire the old pink Chevy van and I bought a "pre-owned" 1995 Econoliner. Edna insisted our trademark House Mouse colors of pink and gray should be retained. So I caved in and did it.

Neva Jean had begged me to let her have Swannelle weld a big pink mouse onto the front of the van, as a hood ornament. But I'd held my ground. I do have some sense of decorum.

I had a vague idea of where the Red Barn should be. It was one of the last vestiges of the old, small-town Roswell. Years ago, it had been a country breakfast joint, a place that opened at 6 A.M. and closed at 2 P.M., after the last of the locals sopped up the last of the country-fried steak with the Red Barn's famous cat-head biscuits. After Mrs. Winners and McDonald's decided to serve frozen reheated flapjacks and cardboard biscuits, the Red Barn's wheezy brand of service couldn't compete with food that was crappy but fast. Later it was a used car lot, then a barbecue restaurant. Its previous incarnation made it a country-cute weekend brunch spot.

I'd grown up in a suburb just south of Roswell. A bedroom community called Sandy Springs. Lots of red-brick ranch houses or red-brick two-story Georgians, tons of kids in the neighborhoods. My parent's idea of middle-class nirvana. Daddy was a sales representative for a company that made rug backing. The mill that produced the rubber backing was down in south Georgia, in a tiny town called Hazlehurst. The carpet mills were in Dalton, up in north Georgia, and as far away as Spartanburg, South Carolina, and Burlington, North Carolina. The first of every month, Daddy went down to Hazlehurst to file reports and meet with the bosses. The last of the month, he went to visit the buyers at the carpet mills. In between, he was home with us, coaching Little League baseball, cleaning gutters, making us attend church at St. Jude's on Sundays, attending his Rotary Club meetings on Wednesday morning.

Come to think of it, those meetings had been at the Red Barn. Rotary was where he'd met Ferd, an up-and-coming lawyer who liked the things Jack Garrity liked: baseball, Democratic politics, backyard cookouts with the neighbors. We went to the beach every year for a week, usually Myrtle Beach, sometimes Panama City. One year Ferd and his first wife, Joanie, went with us to the beach. Joanie stayed by the hotel pool and drank mai-tais, and Ferd ignored her. They got divorced shortly after that.

It would have been faster to take Georgia Highway 400 to get to Roswell, but out of force of habit, I got off 285 and turned north on Roswell Road. I wanted to go by the shopping center with the Winn-

Dixie, where I had my first summer job. The McDonald's where we used to hang out after Friday night football games. The county park where we'd parked our butts on those baseball bleachers for hours on end every spring and summer.

I passed Abernathy Road and tried to look down it, past a shopping center that had been a grove of pines when I was a kid. Somewhere, past all the urban congestion that had sprung up in twenty-five years, was the entrance to the subdivision where I'd grown up. I wondered if Brian had come this way, too. Or if he even remembered the name of the street.

Then I was crossing the Chattahoochee River. The sludgy red-brown water churned with the wind. It was high from all the rain, spilling out of its banks. That's how the Chattahoochee works, either flooding in the winter or slowed to a death trickle every summer when the rains disappear.

Right before I got to what people think of as the village of Roswell—a congregation of old stores and warehouses left over from the days when the town was a busy cotton trading crossroads—I spotted the Red Barn on the left. I pulled in. The lot was half full. No sign of a dusty black pickup truck. I parked beside Ferd's Mercedes. He got out of the car, locked it, and we headed for the front door. I deliberately slowed my pace to match Ferd's halting limp. He grasped my arm as we went up three short log steps. Just how sick was he?

Maybe two dozen people were clustered at tables in the bar. The main dining room had been closed off. The waitress explained they were serving only "our bistro menu" because the place closed at 6 P.M.

Ferd ordered us both a Jack Daniel's and water. It made me smile. Ferd had been the one to introduce me to Black Jack. When I was eighteen, at a family party, he fixed me a drink the way he always liked his: ice, water, Black Jack. He'd looked defiantly at my daddy, who was turning the steaks on the grill, sipping from his ever-present can of Budweiser.

"She's gonna drink, Jack," he said. "It's a fact of life. Better she drinks the good stuff, doesn't puke her guts out on those stinking wine coolers or that other crap the kids drink."

"Want something to eat?" he was asking now. He pushed the paper menu toward my side of the table. The offerings were nothing inspirational. Bar food. Chicken wings, deep-fried jalapeño peppers, baked potato skins, chicken nachos.

"Maybe some nachos," I said. "If you'll share them with me?"

He nodded. "Bring two forks," he told the waitress. "But I'll have gas all night after this."

When she was gone, we took turns watching the door, looking for Brian.

"If he stands us up this time, I'll go out and hunt his ass down and hand him over to the cops myself," I said.

Ferd sipped his drink. "He doesn't seem to grasp the seriousness of the situation he's gotten himself into. He kept telling me he can't believe anybody would think he'd kill his wife. Has he always been like this? You think he's been doing heavy drugs?"

"He did a lot of experimenting with drugs in high school," I admitted. "But so did everybody else. He wasn't doped up Friday night, as far as I could tell. A little drunk maybe."

"Did he make any threats against his wife to you?" Ferd asked. "Tell you he planned to do her harm? You think he's a vengeful kind of guy?"

"He said he'd fix her," I said. "He was just enraged that Shay could keep him from seeing Maura. And I think he was so frustrated with the way the legal system had screwed him, he'd decided to take matters into his own hands. Taking Maura must have been a last-minute decision. He didn't have her clothes or toys or anything. I think he saw an opportunity and seized it."

"Maybe he saw another opportunity Saturday night," Ferd mused. His big bucket-shaped head drooped a little. "Maybe he found Shay alone, they fought, he killed her."

The front door of the restaurant opened.

"Let's ask him," I suggested, waving to get my brother's attention.

He nodded at me, stepped to the bar, got a beer. He stood there for a few seconds, his eyes glued to the basketball game on the television set mounted over the bar. Georgia Tech was playing Florida State, and the Yellow Jackets were burning up the Thiller-Dome.

"Christ," I muttered. "Nothing's changed."

"Brian," Ferd bellowed. "The meter's running, buddy."

My brother shrugged, put a couple of crumpled ones on the bar and then ambled over, pulled a chair over from a nearby table. "I was listening to the game on the radio on the way over here. You still follow ACC basketball?" he asked Ferd.

Ferd knocked with his knuckles on the table. "Hello? Brian? This ain't happy hour we're having here, Budrow. We're trying to figure out how to keep your ass out of jail. You want to give us a little help?"

Brian scowled, reached into his jacket pocket and brought out a wad of limp, wrinkled papers, which he slapped down on the table, right in the middle of a water ring from our drinks.

I moved the papers, sopped the tabletop with a wad of paper napkins.

"My pay stubs, rent receipt, all that kind of shit."

"What about canceled checks?" Ferd asked, sifting through the papers.

"No checks, no banks," Brian said. "I'm on a strictly cash basis. Makes life easier. That way, Shay and her old lady couldn't stick their nose in my business."

"And you have no real financial records," I said, hearing the sourness in my own voice.

"I get along," Brian said.

I picked up one of the pay stubs. It was a perforated inch-wide strip of paper, not typed, but handwritten. Brian Garrity, pay period 12-18-97, $650. I couldn't make out the signature. I handed it over to Ferd, who was scanning similar strips of paper.

"What company is this?" Ferd asked, his pen poised above his notebook.

"J. T. Quality Homes," Brian said. "We're putting in a hundred and twenty-five units down in South Fulton. Subdivision called Autumn Chapel. All this shitty weather lately, we couldn't pour foundations and the framing crews were backed up bad. That's why I had to work Friday and Saturday, pouring concrete. Worked some this morning, too. I'm supposed to run down there this afternoon, but looks like I can't make it now."

Ferd put a pen on the scribble on the stub. "This the boss?"

"My boss," Brian said. "Randy Pryor. He's superintendent. Some other jerk-off owns the company."

"And he can vouch that you were at work the times you just said?" Ferd asked.

"Randy's OK," Brian said. "He knows what a hard time Shay was giving me. She was always calling the construction trailer, raising hell about money. He started giving me extra hours, when he could, so I could get the money together for my new place."

"This is the apartment you were moving into Saturday night?" Ferd asked. "Where is it?"

"It's actually a mobile home. Down near the site," Brian said coolly. "You guys order any food?"

"Nachos," I said. "You can have mine if the waitress ever brings our order. I'm not hungry anymore." I dug around in the scraps of paper looking for something like a rent receipt, came up with an envelope with writing on the back: December rent $400 Pd.

I turned the envelope over. It was one of those Publisher's Clearinghouse envelopes, addressed to A. L. Mobley. "Is this your landlord?" I asked.

"Who? Al? He's the park manager. Asshole."

Ferd took the envelope from me. "Not signed. Not dated," he noted, his voice dripping with sarcasm. "I suppose you paid in cash?"

Brian nodded. "I told you, that's how I operate. But hey, call Al. He'll tell you I was there."

"He lives on the premises?" Ferd asked.

"Sort of," Brian said. "He was there Saturday, evicting some old bag who kept setting her place on fire, smoking in bed."

"Anybody else see you there?" Ferd asked. "Neighbors? Anybody help you move your stuff?"

"All my stuff fit in one pickup load," Brian said. "You been through divorce, Ferd, right, man? I was lucky to get a sleeping bag and the clothes on my back. Shay threw away a bunch of my shit. I wasn't paying attention to neighbors. I got over there late, after six, place was dark. No power, no hot water, no phone."

"And you stayed there all night?" I asked.

"I guess," he said, his eyes watching the television now.

"Don't guess," Ferd said sharply. "Did you stay there all night?"

Brian put a finger up, held up his empty beer mug so the waitress could see his neediness. "Heinekin," he said.

"Brian!" I said sharply.

"I went out for a couple hours, OK? The place was cold, dark. No TV. This dump isn't wired for cable. I went out, got a pizza, watched a ball game. I didn't go over to Shay's, and I didn't stick a knife in her."

"And you didn't bother to call us and check on your daughter, either," I said angrily.

"Where did you go?" Ferd demanded. "Did anybody see you? It's important, Brian."

But Brian's attention had wandered again. Now he was looking not at us, and not at the television, either. He was looking at the door, and a tall, ruddy-faced man who was staring right back at Brian.

"Fuuuck," Brian said, drawing the word out. "Dyson fucking Yount."

16

"Yount?" Ferd's back was toward the door. He scraped the chair around for a better view.

"Shay's boss." Brian put his head down on the table, his arms crossed over it, as though his not looking at the man would mean the man could not see him. "Fuck," said his muffled voice.

Yount picked his way through the empty tables and chairs in the bar. He stood by our table, looked down his nose at Brian as though he were a piece of questionable halibut.

Brian raised his head. "What the fuck do you want?"

"Just doing a favor for Annette," Yount said. He had the thick careless drawl of a man educated someplace he is sure is the Harvard of the South—Duke, Vanderbilt, Emory, someplace like that. He took a thick, sealed white envelope and slapped it on the table. Brian pushed the papers away.

Yount was handsome, if you liked thick wavy hair and full, rather feminine lips and the kind of jaw you see on Calvin Klein underwear models. The tortoiseshell eyeglasses were modish, like prop glasses, to lend the air of authority.

He nodded at Ferd. "It's a petition for an emergency custody hearing. Judge Bingham has already agreed to hear it. Wednesday. Two o'clock."

"What's that mean?" Brian asked Ferd. "You said they couldn't do this. Shay's dead. I'm her father. Nobody else is getting my kid."

Ferd held up a hand, cautioning Brian to be quiet. "Are you a lawyer, sir?"

"Concerned friend," Yount said. "Mrs. Gatlin wasn't sure where to serve this." He gave Brian a withered look. "Mr. Garrity here doesn't seem to have any permanent address."

"I got an address," Brian said gruffly.

"I'd advise you people to pack the child's belongings," Yount said, his voice icy. "Judge Bingham doesn't take kindly to letting minor children be raised by their mother's murderer."

He ran a hand through the thick wavy hair, adjusted his glasses.

"I told Shay it would come to this," he said, his voice hoarse. "She knew you were stalking her. Driving by the office. Watching the apartment. I told her. He'll kill you. She thought the divorce would end it. She was talking about taking Maura and moving. Florida, maybe. To get away from you, once and for all."

Brian jumped up from the table, knocking his chair backward onto the floor. He grabbed Yount by the shoulder. "I didn't kill her," he said, his voice scarily quiet.

Ferd stood up quickly, pushed himself between Brian and Dyson Yount.

Brian backed up only a little.

"Me and Shay were through. I knew that. I knew a hell of a lot more than y'all thought I knew. Stalk her?" He gave a joyless laugh. "I didn't need to stalk Shay. She didn't even have the decency to sneak around, the slut. She liked to rub it in my face. That she was fuckin' you. Fuckin' anybody who wanted some. I watched the office and I watched the apartment. Not because I gave a damn about Shay. All I wanted was my daughter. I got her now. And I'll be goddamned if I let that whore Annette get her hands on her."

Yount looked past Brian, at me. "Your brother beats up women," he said, his lip curling in disgust. "Is this somebody you want raising a three-year-old?"

He turned and walked out of the bar.

The food came and Brian ordered another beer. Ferd shook his head, told the waitress, "Bring him some coffee."

"The fuck?"

When the waitress was gone, Ferd took his pad and silver pen and tucked them into his pocket. "If I'm going to help you, we've got to get some things straight. First off, one beer. That's your limit. None would be better, but I'm a realistic man."

"You're drinking," Brian whined. He pointed at my nearly empty Jack Daniel's. "Callahan's drinking."

"We're not suspects in a homicide," Ferd said. "You are. You also have prior arrests for DUI and public drunkenness. Do you think Dyson Yount is psychic? That he just showed up here tonight, hoping you'd be here? He's got an investigator following you, or following Callahan. One wrong step, one beer too many, you'll get picked up again for DUI. And you'll lose this child you claim to love. You understand?"

Brian started to say something, then changed his mind.

Ferd looked at his watch, then picked up his fork and began quickly picking apart the nachos. He wolfed down half a dozen forkfuls while we watched, washed it down with half a glass of water.

"I've got to go home and take my meds," he said, wiping his mouth with a linen napkin. He got some money, put it on the table.

Ferd gave Brian his stern, Judge Bryce stare.

"Get your phone hooked up and give the number to your mother and your sister. Give your sister your address, and the name of that pizza joint you claimed to be in on Saturday night. Tell your boss we'll need to talk to him. Open a bank account. Your mother and I discussed money earlier tonight. She wants to help with your finances."

"I'm not taking money from my mother," Brian said, setting his jaw in a way that made me think he'd been watching Edna's body language.

"You're going to have to," Ferd said. "We're not just worrying about keeping you from being charged with Shay's murder. We've got to prove that you're a responsible, tax-paying wage earner. That you're a fit parent. That it is in the best interest and welfare of Maura that you have custody of her. You understand all that, Budrow?"

"Yeah."

"Good." Ferd stood up, handed Brian his business card. "That's got my cell phone and my beeper number on it. And the unlisted number at home."

I looked up at him with astonishment. This was a man who hated technology, who wouldn't even own a television for five years.

Ferd saw my surprise. "I'm playing the stock market a lot. Have to keep in touch with my broker."

"Brian," he continued. "I expect you'll be hearing from those investigators down in Clayton County. Probably a man named Lawrence. If they call, or show up, call me. No matter where or what time. You call me. And you don't say a single damn word until I get there and give you the OK."

Brian sipped his cup of coffee, making a face. "All right."

Ferd slipped on his raincoat. "I'll talk to you tomorrow. Do me a favor till then, would you? Stay out of trouble."

We worked out an arrangement, my brother and I. Scraped half the nachos, half the guacamole, half the sour cream, and half the salsa onto a bread-and-butter plate. Split it right down the middle. I could tell he was dying for a beer. Instead I asked the waitress to bring us more water. The salsa was canned, but it was really hot.

We ate quietly, if not companionably. Brian watched the Tech game. I watched him.

When the food was gone and the game was finished, there was nothing else to do.

"Callahan?" Brian's work-reddened hands turned his napkin over and over. "Mama's really been sick?"

"She was," I said. "She'd been having problems for a long time before she admitted it to me. Forty years of cigarettes, greasy food, and raising four kids. She's a bonanza of risk factors."

"What do the doctors say?" he asked.

"It's a lot of mumbo jumbo," I warned. "The heart attack was caused by mitral valve prolapse. She's got coronary artery disease. They replaced one of the valves with a piece of a pig. The good news is, she can walk up the front steps without having to take a half-hour rest. The bad news is, she wants to root in the mud all day and won't come unless we call 'Sooey.'"

Brian smiled wanly. "Guess you all think I'm a real shithead."

It was too late in our relationship to start playing games. "We wanted to tell you about Mama. Maureen kept saying, 'You're a detective, track him down.'"

"But you didn't."

"Edna wanted us to. Right before the surgery, when we weren't sure if she'd make it. But there wasn't time. It came up so fast; they had to do emergency surgery. Even if I had known where to look, there wouldn't have been time."

"And you didn't want me to come home anyway." The way he said it—not a question, just a statement—hurt. I blushed, bit my lip.

"You walked out right after Daddy died," I reminded him. "Edna always had this fantasy. That you'd come home. Every Christmas, an extra package under the tree. She never said, but I knew it was a shirt or something. In case. In case of Brian. And on Mother's Day. If we took her out to dinner, she'd come right home, listen to the answering machine. In case you called. What if I had tracked you down, told you Mama was sick? Would you have come? Brought Shay home for Sunday supper?"

"Maybe," he said. He took a drink of water. "But she's my mother. I deserved to know, didn't I? What if she'd died?"

"You want the truth?" I asked. "You were the least of our worries. Keeping her alive, that's what Maureen and I were thinking about. Kevin, too. Her next EEG, her next stress test, what drugs she could tolerate, when she could start cardiac rehab. That's what we were thinking about. Not Brian Garrity."

"I was thinking about her," Brian said, rubbing his temples with those long, callused fingers. "The night Maura was born. I wanted to call Mama so bad. I was scared. Maura was so tiny. And she was yellow. Nearly orange. The hospital said it was jaundice, but they kept her three extra days. And I wanted Mama to come over there, hold her and rock her and make her all right."

"Why didn't you?"

He shrugged. "Me and Shay had a fight about something. And Annette was there. Shoving me out of the way, just taking everything over. Bossing the nurses, bossing Shay, bossing me. I couldn't bring Mama into all that."

I laughed. "Edna Mae Garrity could outboss and outshove Annette Gatlin any day of the week. I can't believe you didn't know that."

He shook his head no. "Christ. Mama always hated Annette when we lived in the old neighborhood. Always. And Annette hated her right back. When Shay and me started going together, Shay wouldn't even tell Annette at first. She knew there'd be a big fuss."

"Family feuds," I said. "The Hatfields and McCoys. The Capulets and the Montagues. The Garritys and the Gatlins. Guess you guys thought you were real star-crossed lovers."

"Star-crossed nothing," Brian said. "I just wanted to get in her pants."

17

The house was empty when I got home. There was a message from Edna on the answering machine. She and Mac were going to stop for dinner on their way home from the mall. And yes, they'd found a dandy tricycle for Maura.

The house was chilly. I put on my flannel nightgown and slippers, threw a quilt over my shoulders, made myself a cup of Irish Breakfast tea.

Edna had left all the Christmas lights burning. She thinks it scares off bad guys. I tell her it's a fire hazard when nobody's home, but secretly, I love to sit in the dark and look at the lights.

So that's what I did now. I put a stack of Christmas CDs on the player, the soft, instrumental ones, and I lit all the red candles Edna had lined up on the mantel, and I put a match to the gas logs in the fireplace.

If I pull my favorite big, squashy armchair up to just the right spot in front of the fireplace, I can also get a good view of our front porch. I could see the glow from our Blue Christmas light display, and Mr. Byerly's wooden Santa and reindeer all lit up on his front yard. It made me feel good, knowing Elvis was up on our porch, smiling out at Dasher and Dancer, et al.

I pulled the quilt around my shoulders and sat back in the armchair and did absolutely nothing. The first CD on the stack was a favorite, the Atlanta Symphony Orchestra conducted by Robert Shaw.

I hummed along, watched the reflection of the candles and the fire-light in the big gilt mirror over the mantel. The tea was hot and sweet, half cream, half sugar.

I should have been making a list of all the stuff I'd need to do on Monday. Ferd had made it clear that he expected me to do all the investigatory groundwork to prove my brother had nothing to do with Shay's murder. Brian had begrudgingly given me his phone number at work, with the warning that I was not to call unless it was an absolute emergency. "Like if something happens to Maura."

I thought about how Brian changed when he talked about his daughter. The old cockiness disappeared and his face was suffused with tenderness. "I can't tell her about her mom being dead," he con-fessed to me. "I just can't. She's my baby. It kills me when she cries. Could you do it? Please, Jules?"

"Sure," I said. His not being man enough to do the right thing didn't bother me, I guess because I'd never expected that much out of him. Because I still didn't think of him as being a man.

He was eager to hear what she'd been doing, what she'd eaten, how she'd slept, did I notice how smart she was?

"She's got Edna wrapped around her little finger," I told Brian. "Mac, too. They were taking her Christmas shopping this afternoon."

He'd reached into his jeans, taken out a roll of bills. All ones, I noticed, feeling guilty about my snoopiness. He counted off ten ones, handed them across, looking embarrassed.

"Tell Mama, buy her something. A toy, maybe. With the rent and utilities and gas for the truck, there's not much left right now," he said apologetically. "I want you to know, I'm gonna be doing the right thing by Maura. Soon as I get my feet back on the ground, I'll pay you and Mama back for what you been doing. Things will be dif-ferent."

I tried to push the money away. "You don't need to do this, Brian. Keep the money. Maura has all the toys she needs. She loves playing with the pots and pans. Mama was going to buy her some crayons at the store. Mrs. James, the baby-sitter, told me Maura loves to color."

He took my hand, put the bills in my palm and closed my fingers over it. "Get her some coloring books and all like that. Tell her Daddy bought 'em for her."

"I'll tell her," I'd promised. It was a start. But buying some crayons and a coloring book wouldn't begin to fill the hole left by a dead mother and an irresponsible father.

And then there was the problem of Annette. Like it or not, we were all going to have to deal with Annette, and Chuck Ingraham, her lawyer. Shay hadn't even been buried yet, and we were already getting ready to claw each other's eyes out over the only thing of value she'd left behind—her daughter.

The quilt slipped off my shoulder and I was suddenly chilled. My hand went to my left breast. It was nothing. Scar tissue, that's all. I was due for a mammogram again in February. It could wait until then.

Wait. I hate to wait. Waiting meant putting my fate in somebody else's hands, waiting meant letting those bad cells hang around and insinuate themselves into my healthy body.

The firelight and soft music tricked me into sleep. I woke when I heard the key turning in the back door. Groggily, I made my way back to the kitchen.

Edna had an armful of packages, Mac had an armful of Maura, slung over his shoulder. Her head was nuzzled in the nape of Mac's neck, a favorite spot of my own, her eyes closed tightly. He kissed me on the forehead and I smelled candy cane.

"Put her down on my bed," Edna whispered. She set her shopping bags down on the floor and the two of us followed Mac and Maura into Edna's bedroom.

I turned back the covers and Edna slipped the sleeping child into a diaper and a pair of sweatpants. "Wish we'd had these when I was raising young'uns," she said. She stroked Maura's hair, pulled the cover over her shoulder.

The child's eyes fluttered. She sat up and looked wildly around the room. "Mama?" Her thumb went to her mouth and huge tears welled in her eyes. "Where's my mama?"

"Oh God," Edna said. "I can't do this."

"Brian won't," I said flatly. "Guess that leaves me."

I sat on the edge of the bed and kissed Maura's forehead. Her face was candy-sticky, her cheeks salty with the fast-spilling tears. I gathered her into my arms and held her, rocking gently to and fro.

"Maura?" I said. "Do you know how to say your prayers?"

"Huh!" I heard Edna whisper. "You think those Godless hussies ever said a prayer?"

"Now I lay me?" Maura asked, twisting around to look up at me.

"That's right," I said. "Let's say our prayers together."

"Bath," Maura said. "First we have bath and then we say prayer."

"Well, I'll be," Edna said. She went into the bathroom and I could hear water running. When she came out, she had a wet washcloth. She sat down on the bed beside us. "It's pretty late for a bath, sweetheart," she said. "Let's just wash your feet tonight."

"Bath," Maura said stubbornly.

Edna shrugged. "None of mine ever begged for a bath," she said.

We took Maura in the bathroom and ran a tubful of warm suds. She undressed herself, stepping daintily out of the diaper, and allowed me to pick her up and set her in the tub. "I'll get some clean pajamas," Edna said, leaving the room.

Maura splashed around, submerged herself in the water, reemerged, blew suds at me. We were having a fine time playing find the washcloth.

"Where's my mama?" she asked.

This time there was nobody around to answer the question. I could hear my heart thud, my mouth go dry.

I put my mouth under the faucet and got a drink, then I sat back down on the tile floor beside the tub.

"Your mama had to go away," I said, my voice sounding high and scratchy.

"No go," Maura said, slapping her hand on the surface of the water.

I almost stopped. Who was I to give this child the most devastating news of her life? I wanted to run from the room, call somebody, a shrink, or a doctor, or a priest or somebody who had the right kind of heart and mind that could form such words. My own heart was feeling unnaturally small and stunted lately. My long-lost brother was back, and I wanted to be glad and love him and welcome him back, and help him find his way back home. All I could feel was annoyance, impatience, resentment. What was wrong with me? I felt maybe one of my ventricles was pinched, an artery that should have been pumping love and understanding was blocked off, leaving my emotions as tepid as day-old dishwater.

"Mama had to go," I said chokingly. "To be with the angels. In heaven. Do you know about heaven?"

"Maura's an angel," the child chirped. "Mama's angel."

I fished the washcloth out of the water and dabbed at her face with it.

"You are your mama's angel," I said. "But now, Mama will be watching you from someplace far away. You won't be able to see her anymore. But she'll see you."

"Daddy go bye-bye?" she sobbed. I caught one of her tears with my pinkie finger, let it roll down my wrist.

"Daddy will be back," I said. "Daddy will take care of you now. Daddy and Grandma and me, and Aunt Maureen and Uncle Steve."

"And Uncle Mac."

I turned around. Mac was standing in the door of the bathroom, Edna cowering behind him, dabbing at her eyes with the sleeve of Maura's pink pajama top. "We'll all take such good care of you," Mac said. He handed me a bath towel.

"Come on, honey," he said to her. "Let's say our prayers now."

18

It was only 7 A.M. when the doorbell rang. We were sipping our coffee, Edna and I, enjoying the quiet before our ward woke up and started to rock our world.

"What the hell?" Edna muttered. She tightened the belt on her bathrobe and went to the front door. I ran my fingers through my tangled curls and was right behind her. It was a good thing, too, because our early morning visitor turned out to be Annette Gatlin.

She was dressed to kill in a severe black suit with a white silk blouse and a short skirt. She had the kind of legs I hate to see on other women, which meant they were flawless, and she knew it, too. She was peering in through the window in our front door, jaw jutted out in defiance.

Edna assumed the same pose when she saw who it was. "What do you want?" she called loudly.

"I want my granddaughter," Annette said angrily. "You've got no right to keep her from me, Edna Garrity."

"The hell I don't," Edna shot back.

I took Edna's elbow in mine. "Let me deal with her," I whispered. "You go call Ferd. Ask him what we should do. I'll stall her."

"Don't let her in," Edna warned. "I don't want her grabbing Maura. No telling what she might do if you open that door." She scurried down the hall to the phone.

I stood so that Annette could see me. "Maura's still asleep," I said, trying to keep my voice down. "She had a long day yesterday. A long night. We told her about Shay last night. She cried herself to sleep."

"So did I," Annette said fiercely. "We're burying Shay this morning. Putting my little girl in the ground. Maura needs to be there. She needs to see her mother one more time."

"In a coffin?" I pulled at the neck of my robe. "Are you insane? She's only three, Annette."

"That's the sickest thing I've ever heard in my life." Edna was behind me, the phone pressed to her ear. Her eyes were blazing.

"Let me in, damn you," Annette said through clenched teeth. She reached into the black leather pocketbook that hung from a chain on her right shoulder, brought out an envelope. "I've got an order from the judge. You better hand my granddaughter over right this minute, or I'll have the cops here so fast your head will spin."

"Let me see that." Before I could stop her, Edna was opening the door, reaching for the packet of papers.

"Wait," I started to push the door shut, but Annette caught me off guard. She shoved past me into the hallway.

"Maura!" Annette called, half-running down the hallway, her heels tap-tapping a maniac Morse code against the old oak floors. "Maura, it's Annie. Wake up, precious. Annie's here to get you."

Edna dropped the phone onto the hall table and went after her, but Annette was younger and faster. And meaner.

"Hello? Who is it? Who the hell's there?"

I could hear the roar from the discarded cordless phone. I picked it up.

"Ferd, it's Callahan. We've got a situation here. Annette just showed up with a piece of paper she says is an order from the judge saying she can take Maura. To Shay's funeral, for God's sake. She can't do that, can she?"

"A judge?" Ferd's voice was thick with sleep. "What judge?"

"I don't know," I said. "She just barged in here and went after Maura, like a heat-seeking missile. Edna's trying to stop her. Maura's still asleep."

"Annie!" I heard Maura's voice from the back bedroom. So she was awake.

"Come on precious," Annette said loudly. "Annie's gonna take you for a ride."

"No, you're not," Edna screamed. "You get away from her. You're not taking her anywhere."

"Ferd? Can I call you right back? I've got to go back there and referee before those two kill each other."

I put the phone down and raced back toward the bedroom. Maura was cowering on the bed, thumb stuck firmly in her mouth, big dark eyes watching her two berserk grandmothers engaged in a tug-of-war over a tiny black velvet dress.

"I'm going to dress my grandchild and take her to that funeral and let her pay her proper respects to her mother," Annette said, trying to pull the dress away. "Don't you mess with me, Edna Garrity. I warn you. You've ruined my family, you and your murdering son. I won't let you take my grandbaby, too."

Edna clung to the sleeve of the dress like a drowning man to a life raft. "Family? What family?" she shrieked. She looked over at me. "Call the police, Jules. Tell them a crazy woman has broken into our home and is trying to abduct my granddaughter."

"Stop it," I said, snatching the dress away from Annette.

Maura shrunk deep into the pillows, pulling the quilt up over her eyes. "No, no, no," she cried, her voice muffled by the covers.

"Look at her," I said, pointing at the cowering child. "She's terrified. You should be ashamed. Both of you."

Edna, at least, was contrite. "Oh Lord," she said, covering her mouth with her hand. "What are we doing?"

Annette sat on the side of the bed and reached for Maura. "Come on, honey," she cooed. "Don't be scared. It's just Annie. Annie wouldn't hurt her baby."

"Outside," I said loudly. "Both of you. In the kitchen."

I marched the two women down the hallway to the kitchen.

Edna stood with her back to the refrigerator, ready to make her stand if she had to. Annette took up a position in the doorway, ready to make another run to grab up Maura and escape.

"Let me see that order, please," I said, reaching out my hand for the paper Annette had flashed at us.

I'm no lawyer, but the document looked genuine. In essence, it ordered us to allow Annette Gatlin to have special twenty-four-hour custody of the minor child Maura Jean Garrity, for the specific purpose of attending her mother's funeral service. The judge was Payne

Bingham, the Clayton County judge who would be hearing Annette's petition to get permanent custody of Maura.

"Looks real," I told Edna. I handed her the court document, then called Ferd back. He picked up in the middle of the first ring.

"I tried calling Judge Bingham," Ferd said. "Too early, of course. Read me what the order says. Word for word."

"Be right back," I told Edna. "You two behave."

I walked the phone into the living room, where the women couldn't hear me. I read the order just as Ferd asked.

"You'll have to let her take the child," Ferd said.

"To her mother's funeral?" I cried. "It's the cruelest thing I ever heard of. The poor kid is back in the bedroom hiding under the covers. She's already hysterical. Ferd, I don't think Edna will let her go. She'll go to jail before she hands Maura over to Annette."

"Nobody's going to jail," Ferd snapped. "That's why you've got a lawyer. To keep you out of jail. Now, let me think." There was a brief pause. "The order doesn't mention a time you have to hand Maura over, does it?"

"No," I said, rereading it. "It just says on this date."

"All right," Ferd said. "Obviously they're not having a funeral service this early in the morning. Annette's just trying to catch you off guard. Ingraham probably told her to give it a try. Tell her you've got to get Maura calmed down, then dressed and bathed, and feed her breakfast. That ought to take an hour or so, right?"

"It takes an hour just to scrape the oatmeal out of her hair," I said wryly. "Then what?"

"Tell Annette you'll meet her somewhere, to turn the child over to her. See if you can just take Maura to the church where the funeral is. Promise to have her there on time."

"Why?" I asked.

"That should give me time to try to call the judge, reason with him that it's not in Maura's best interest to attend her mother's funeral," Ferd said. "I've got a lady friend, she's a psychotherapist. I'll see if I can get her to draft a quick letter and fax it to the judge, outlining all the reasons that this is a poor idea."

"But the judge already signed the order," I said. "Will he listen to us at this late date?"

"I don't know," Ferd admitted. "But we'll give it a shot. At the very least, you get this situation between your mother and Annette defused, get them away from the child while you calm her down."

"Makes sense," I said. "All I have to do is figure out how to get Annette to agree to it. Right now, it looks like it'd take dynamite to get her out of here without what she came for—Maura."

"You're a conniver," Ferd said. "I know you'll think of something."

"Thanks a lot," I said. "I think."

"Call me as soon as Annette leaves, and we'll finish working out the strategy," Ferd said.

Instead of going back to the kitchen, I made a detour into the bedroom. I pulled back the covers, but Maura was gone. There was a warm, damp spot where she'd been.

"Maura?" I said quietly. "Maura?"

I checked under the bed, found nothing more than Edna's house slippers and her spare pair of reading glasses.

I spun around. Edna's old-fashioned walnut highboy and lowboy sat too low to the floor. Even Maura couldn't have fit under them. I checked the closet. Lots of flowered polyester, no three-year-old. The bathroom was empty, too. I checked the bathtub, even Edna's narrow linen closet.

I darted into the hallway, looked up and down. Raised voices coming from the kitchen. Edna was telling Annette exactly what she'd always thought of her. The words "bottle blonde" and "low-class roundheel" seemed to be getting a good workout.

I ducked into my bedroom, looked high and low, was about to go alert the grannies and put out an all points bulletin when I noticed something odd sticking out of the wicker laundry basket in the corner of my bedroom. It looked like the leg of a hairless stuffed hound dog. And there was a lot more laundry than I remembered being there earlier in the morning.

"Poochie?" I sat down on the floor beside the basket. I picked up the dog. "Have you seen Maura? I'm getting worried about her."

"Woof." It was a very small woof. I pulled my terry-cloth bathrobe off the top of the basket. Maura reached for Poochie, rubbed the dog against her cheek. "Me hide," she said. "Annie go away."

I brushed a curl off her forehead. "Annie loves you," I said. "She wants you to go with her today. Do you want to do that, Maura? Go with Annie? For a little while?"

She shook her head solemnly. "Can we see Mama?"

Now what? Where was the owner's manual for this kid? I was flying without a net, blind, stupid.

"Annie will take you to see Mama, but Mama will really be asleep, because she went to be with the angels. Remember? Like I told you last night? Mama's gone to heaven. But Annie wants to take you to say bye-bye. In a church. Have you been to church, Maura?"

Her eyes got wider, but I could tell she didn't have any idea what I was talking about. Hell, I had no idea what I was talking about. How was I going to make it make sense to a three-year-old?

"No Annie," Maura said. "Me hide."

"I wish I'd thought of that," I said. Instead, I hefted her out of the basket, carried her in my arms into the kitchen.

"Maura, baby," Annette called, holding out her arms for Maura. Edna's face was pale, but her eyes were red-rimmed.

I tried to hand Maura over, but she clung tightly to me, burying her face in my neck, refusing to look at Annette. "No Annie," Maura cried.

"No."

Annette tried to disentangle Maura's arms. "Come, sweetheart," she said. "Annie's missed her little girl." She was really tugging hard at Maura.

I stepped away. Annette drew back her hand, as if to slap me. "Don't you dare," she hissed. "Don't you dare try to take her from me. She's all I've got now."

"You don't have her," Edna taunted.

"She's upset," I said. "The two of you were so busy screaming at each other, it scared her witless. You know where I found her? Hiding in the laundry basket. She was afraid to come out. I think she thinks you're mad at her."

"No!" Edna cried. She reached her arms out to Maura, but the child was having none of it, clinging to me like a barnacle.

I turned toward Annette. "Is this how you want her?" I asked. "She's frightened to death. Of both of you."

"That's nonsense," Annette said. "I've taken care of this child since the day she was born. If she's afraid, it's because you've made her that way. Put ideas in her head. You and Brian. All of you."

I decided to ignore her last shot. "My lawyer is contacting the judge, to protest the idea of letting Maura go to a funeral. We should have an answer by ten o'clock."

"The funeral's at eleven," Annette said angrily. "I'm not waiting any longer. Chuck said you have to hand her over. Or he'll ask the judge to hold you in contempt of court."

"The order doesn't say what time we have to give her to you, or for how long," I pointed out. "My lawyer says we need to have that clarified. And Maura's too upset to go anywhere right now. She's got to have breakfast and a bath, have a little time to calm down from all this fussin' you and Edna have subjected her to. But I'll tell you what. We'll have her at the church in plenty of time for the service. Just tell us where."

"She's going with me," Annette insisted, her voice rising an octave. "I won't leave her here another minute."

"Fine," I said, letting my arms fall to my side. Maura hung on, her arms wrapped tightly around my neck, her tiny fingers digging into the flesh of my back.

"You take her," I told Annette. "You be responsible."

"Noooooo," Maura cried pitifully. "Nooooo."

Annette tried again to pry the child away from me. Maura swatted at Annette with one hand. "Bad Annie," she cried.

Edna stayed right where she was. But her face had the look of an enraged bear whose only cub has just been threatened. "Don't you pull at her again," she said quietly. "We'll get her to that funeral. See that the decent thing is done. And that's the last time you make this child cry like this again. You hear me?"

Annette squared her shoulders, dug in her pocketbook, brought out a tissue, and dabbed at her soggy makeup with it. "Jonesboro First United Methodist," she said. "Eleven o'clock. I'll meet you out front, in the parking lot. You leave Maura with me, get the hell away. A Garrity's killed my daughter. I don't want any of 'em around at Shay's funeral. Not any."

19

Edna stirred the pot of grits. The hand that held the wooden spoon was trembling like a leaf. I put the cups and plates and silverware on the table one-handed, because I was toting Maura on my hip. Each time I tried to put her down she screamed and clutched at my robe.

Edna managed a half-smile. "She's really taken to you."

"I appreciate the sentiment," I said. "But I'm not cut out for this kind of thing."

"It's my fault," Edna said, staring down at the swirling cloud of grits. "I let my emotions get away from me. It's that woman, Jules. She does that to me. I just can't do it. I just can't let this child go to her."

Maura sniffled loudly. She knew we were talking about her again.

"We don't have a choice. Anyway, it's only for the day. Twenty-four hours."

After Annette left, we'd had two more phone conversations with Ferd, who'd finally reached Judge Bingham down in Jonesboro. The judge was willing to listen to the reasons we thought it would be harmful for Maura to attend Shay's funeral, but he wasn't willing to change his mind. In the end, we confirmed our agreement to have Maura at the church by eleven, and he stipulated that Annette would have Maura back at our house by nine o'clock Tuesday morning.

"Overnight?" When I told her, Edna couldn't believe it. "You can't let that woman have her overnight. She'll never bring her back. Besides, Ferd told us Brian has legal custody. Until after the hearing."

She grabbed the phone away from me.

"The hearing's been changed to Thursday," Ferd told her. "That's good. Gives us more time to prepare. And in the meantime, you have to give a little in order to get a little in this kind of situation. Have Maura at the church right on time. Try to keep her calm. That means you have to be calm, Edna."

"Easier said than done," my mother informed him.

I'd already packed Maura's things in her diaper bag. All except Poochie, whom Maura clutched tightly in the free hand that wasn't clutching me.

I heard a car door slam in the driveway, looked out the window.

"The girls are here," I reported.

Edna sighed. "I can't seem to get my mind on work today. All I can think about is this young'un."

"Where's the schedule book?" I asked. "I'll get 'em dispatched."

Neva Jean had picked up Baby and Sister at the senior citizen high-rise on the way in to work. Ruby pulled into the driveway right behind Neva Jean. I heard Cheezer's wheezy old mail truck pull up to the curb outside.

"Grits!" Neva Jean cried, taking a spoon and reaching for the pot.

"Just a little bit," Edna said, pushing her hand away. "These are for Maura. They're her favorite."

"Maura's going to spend the night with her other grandmother," I said, raising my eyebrows so the girls would get the message. "Granny Annie. She's going to say good-bye to her mama today."

"The funeral?" Ruby looked shocked. "They gonna take that little lamb to her mama's funeral?"

"That was my reaction, too," Edna said. "It can't be helped. The judge says we have to let her go."

"That's just some earthly judge," Ruby said. "Our heavenly judge, he wouldn't put no mess on a little baby like this. No ma'am."

Ruby reached out to Maura. "Come, lamb," she said softly. "Aunt Ruby wants to hear that song of yours. Can you sing me a song?"

Maura snuffed loudly, but allowed herself to be transferred to Ruby's loving embrace.

"See there?" Ruby asked, beaming, turning so the girls and Cheezer could see who Maura had chosen.

Ruby sat down at the kitchen table with Maura on her lap. "Twinkle, twinkle, . . . " she started.

"Little star," Maura added. She reached up and patted Ruby's soft brown cheek. "My mama's gone sleep," Maura whispered.

"I know, lamb," Ruby said sadly. "My mama's done gone, too."

The child ate a large bowl of grits swimming in butter, with just a sprinkle of sugar on top. She allowed Baby to feed her a piece of bacon, and gobbled up the toast Sister offered, in between singing "Twinkle, Twinkle" with Ruby.

We were coming down-to-the-wire on Christmas. All our clients wanted their homes to sparkle for the holidays, and at least for today, anyway, both Edna and I had other, non–House Mouse business to take care of. Once again, we were being squeezed in every direction.

Cheezer, God love him, offered to take four houses.

"You sure?" I asked. "I was going to hit the Dugans. We've cleaned for her before, and now she's thinking of having us come every week. It's a big house, three stories, five bedrooms, four baths. Her kids are all coming for the holidays, so she wants the deluxe treatment."

"I can handle it," Cheezer said.

"That Mr. Brian Dugan's house?" Sister asked, scraping the last of the grits from the bottom of the pan.

"Brian and Ann," I said, looking down at the appointment book. "Over in Druid Hills."

"I cleaned for them last Christmas," Sister said. "Me and Baby done that whole house. When we got done, he wouldn't let us take the bus. No sir. Drove us all the way home to the senior center in that big old Coupe de Ville. Fine car. Had us sittin' in the back like he's the driver and we're Mrs. Astor and Mrs. Vanderbilt. Ain't that right, Baby?"

"I remember that man," Baby said, slapping her knee. "Drove us right up to the front, got out, and opened the door. Give us each a ten-dollar tip. Cash money."

"You want us to go with Cheezer, show him how Miz Dugan likes things done?" Sister asked slyly. "That's the redheaded lady. She real particular 'bout her house. Can't do things just any ole way."

"Cool," Cheezer said. "Wait till you see my new silver polish. It's like a wadding compound, but I've been playing around with the formula. It's excellent. You should see what it did for the hubcaps on the mail truck. Like mirrors."

"You're sure it won't scratch the silver?" Edna asked sharply. "Mrs. Dugan thinks she's lace-curtain Irish. That silver of hers is the real thing. Sterling, eighteenth century, or so she claims. And she counts every piece of it before you get there and after you leave."

"You could wash your face with my silver polish," Cheezer promised. "That's how mild it is."

In the end, Cheezer promised to go easy on the silver polish, and to let Baby and Sister tag along on all his jobs. Neva Jean agreed to take on an extra condo, and Ruby decided she'd double up on that day's jobs, too.

"It's only for today," I assured them all. "Tomorrow things should be back to normal."

Nobody believed me, of course.

Edna got Maura into her black velvet dress, all the time making a face that showed just what she thought of Annette Gatlin's taste in children's clothing.

"Black velvet," she said, sniffing. "For a three-year-old. The woman's ghoulish." She flicked a dismissive finger at the sleeve. "Not even real velvet. Rayon. God. I'm gonna burn this thing as soon as we get her home."

I gave Edna a warning look. "You want to fight over dresses? Antagonize Annette some more? Or do you want to keep your mouth shut and let Ferd do his job?"

Edna fastened the strap on Maura's black patent leather shoe. She looked up at me, her face all set. "I'm staying right there at that funeral. The whole time. I'm not going to let this child out of my sight."

"You're doing more harm than good," I pointed out. "You can't go in the church. Ferd already told you that."

"I'll be right out there in the parking lot," Edna vowed. "Right behind Maura, wherever she goes." She reached into her pocketbook, pulled out a pair of binoculars. "I hope that Annette sees me, too," she said defiantly. "Let her know I've got my eye on her."

"You'll get yourself arrested for being a public nuisance," I said. "And don't call me to make your bail."

"I'll take care of myself," Edna said. She reached out her hand to Maura. "Grandma can take care of herself, can't she, Maura?"

"No," Maura said placidly.

I dropped the roll of film I'd shot at Shay's apartment off at a drugstore on Ponce de Leon. I asked for one-hour processing. Then I decided to drop by the Homicide Task Force office and see Bucky Deavers.

Shay had been killed in Clayton County, way out of the Atlanta P.D.'s jurisdiction, but it wouldn't hurt to see if my old buddy could shake some information loose. Besides, it had been a few months.

I picked up a dozen Krispy Kreme doughnuts and two Styrofoam cups of coffee on my way, to sweeten my welcome.

Deavers was at his desk, talking low into the phone. I dropped the box of doughnuts down in front of him. He looked up, surprised.

"OK, baby, I gotta go," he said. "Later."

I opened my container of coffee and took a long satisfying slurp.

Bucky sat back in his chair, helped himself to a doughnut. "What's shakin', Callahan?"

"Just a little visit to share some Christmas cheer," I said.

Bucky licked powdered sugar from his fingertips. He is a man who enjoys his groceries. That's what had cemented our friendship when we were both working out of the burglary office. Food. Deavers liked every kind. At first, he'd tried hitting on me, even though I'm five years older than he is. Bucky loves the ladies. After I shut him down, he decided I'd just make a good lunch partner. We'd stayed friends after I left the department, and he'd made detective in homicide. Mostly, we got together to feed our faces— usually while I was picking Bucky's brain for info about one of my cases.

He closed his eyes, looked up at the ceiling as though mining the heavens for inspiration. "Don't tell me. I'm a psychic. You're here because you need my help. You're here for information about a dead woman. Her name is . . ." He pressed his fingertips to his temples. "Shay. Shay Gatlin."

"You're wasting your time as a cop, Deavers," I said. "You ought to go on one of those psychic hotlines. Who called you about me? Was it that jerk Lawrence, down in Jonesboro?"

Deavers reached for another doughnut. "He's a big fan of yours. Actually, he called C. W. Hunsecker, and Hunsecker called me. C.W. wanted to know what you'd gotten yourself into. I called up Lawrence, he wanted to know all about you and your family. Says you found the murder victim."

"My family," I said, sighing. "What would I do without them?"

"Lawrence seems to think your brother stabbed his wife in the back," Deavers said casually. "I told him I didn't even know you had a brother."

"I've got two brothers. This one hasn't been around much," I admitted. "And from what Lawrence said, he hasn't been a model citizen, either."

Bucky sipped his coffee. "You know I can't mess around in that guy's case down there, Garrity. After Lawrence found out you were a P.I. and used to work here, he made a big point, warning me to mind my own business or he'd call the Major. He's a real territorial little shit, this Lawrence."

"You can't get me anything at all?" I asked, letting pretenses slide. "He really didn't kill this girl, Bucky."

"They're looking for a kitchen knife they think was the murder weapon," Deavers said. "One's missing from the kitchen. Your brother got any new knives?"

"He was married to the girl," I said. "His prints are probably on half the stuff in that apartment."

"Lawrence says the mother says the missing knife was new. Part of a set her daughter bought her for her birthday. In September. After your brother moved out.

I let that sink in. "What else? What else do they have?"

Bucky shook his head. His hair had grown out since the last time I'd seen him. He had it parted down the middle, with wire-rimmed glasses perched on his nose. He was wearing a perfectly conventional dark green shirt, striped tie, green tweed sportcoat. No earrings, no mohawk. Bucky Deavers had gone and gotten normal on me. It was a depressing turn of events in a so far surreally depressing day.

Bucky tapped a file folder on his desk. "You can't say nothing about this, OK? I'm only telling you because the guy pissed me off, talking to me like I should be careful the kind of people I hang with. Like I could lose my badge over my bad associations. Fuck him. I know who my associates are."

"What?" I asked, alarmed. "What are you talking about, Bucky?"

"Lawrence wanted some information from me," he said, reluctantly. "Wanted to know about an old unsolved case from 1989."

"What kind of case?" I asked, feeling the dread eating at my spine.

"Homicide," Bucky said. "Jane Doe. White, early twenties. Body was found down around Funtown. You know, the old amusement park?"

"Why you?" I asked. "You weren't working homicide then."

He shrugged. "You remember Acey Karpik?"

"Sure," I said. "Hotshot homicide detective for the city. Worked the missing and murdered kids investigation, a bunch of high-profile homicides. I thought he was retired."

"He is," Bucky said. "But he teaches advanced crime-scene analysis classes, through the academy. I took a class with him a year ago. He liked my work. I guess he's advising the city on this one."

"What happened to her?" I asked. "What's the connection? They can't be looking at Brian for another homicide. It's not possible, Bucky. This is my brother we're talking about here. I'm telling you, he's no angel, but he's no serial killer, either."

Bucky squirmed in his chair. "I know, Callahan. I'm sorry. I sent Lawrence a copy of our case file. I read it myself. There's nothing much in it. Couple of homeless guys, they were down there at Funtown, scavenging for recyclables, found the body. She'd been dead a week or so. She'd been beaten real bad. We put her photo out on the TV and newspaper, but nobody ever I.D.'d her."

"Why does Lawrence want to know about it?" I asked.

"Acey Karpik told him about it," Bucky said. "He moved down to Clayton County after he retired from the A.P.D. He drinks coffee every morning with these dinks down in Clayton County," Bucky said. "Apparently, he never forgot that Jane Doe. Jane of Funtown, they called her. After he retired, Karpik started collecting info about unsolved Jane Does. He thinks these two are related somehow. There's another one he's looking at, too, also young white female. Body found in a remote area, down in Henry County, starting to decompose. Two different jurisdictions, which is why they were never connected up."

"No," I said, leaning forward. "No way."

"Acey Karpik's been reading too many of them stories about the FBI profilers," Deavers said. "Got too much time on his hands. He's pissed off that the department made him take early retirement so they could give his job to a black guy with a college degree. He's got something to prove. He thinks he's got a serial killer on his hands."

"He's crazy," I said. I felt a little crazy myself "Shay's murder is nothing like those other two."

Deavers looked apologetic. "Karpik thinks they're related. That's why he called me about this Funtown case. He remembered me from that class I took with him. He and Lawrence are convinced they're connected. The South-side Serial Killer. That's what they're calling it."

20

Deavers's right hand kept rifling the pages of the file folder on his desk.

"That's the case file? On Funtown Jane?"

A flush of red crept up Bucky's neck. "Lawrence is pushing to have it reopened," he said. "Wants to form a South-side task force."

"And my brother is the target of all this," I said. "Incredible. Tell me how Acey Karpik takes a case like Shay Gatlin and makes it fit in a profile with those Jane Doe cases. What, my brother killed every young, white woman south of Buckhead? He's not that ambitious, Bucky."

"The bosses had a meeting this morning," Bucky said. "Us, Lawrence, and the chief of detectives from Henry County. Major Mackey told Lawrence he thinks it's all bullshit. He thinks Karpik's a senile old coot. Mackey was an uniformed officer when they found the body at Funtown. Talk at the time was that the girl was a hooker, got in the wrong car. A lot of the girls who worked the Stewart Avenue strip back then used to take their johns over there to Funtown." He grinned. "Sounds like a porno flick, huh? Johns at Funtown?"

"I'd laugh, but it's all too sick," I said. "While Lawrence was busy hooking Brian up for all these old homicides, did he bother to mention there's a little girl in the picture? Brian's three-year-old daughter Maura."

Deavers lost the grin. "Christ. I'm sorry. Who's got the kid?"

119

"We do, for now," I said. "Edna and I. Brian just changed jobs, got a new apartment. He's trying to get his act together. But Shay's mother Annette is going to fight us on custody. She's behind all this crap about Brian killing Shay."

"If your brother didn't kill Shay Gatlin, who did?" Bucky asked. "What's the motive? I mean, you gotta admit, Callahan, it looks like a classic domestic. Knife wounds, no sign of forced entry at the apartment. That's hardly stranger to stranger."

"I know what it looks like," I said. "But you don't know the life Shay and her mother were living. Men in and out of the apartment like it was a Motel Six. I saw the place, Bucky, it was filthy. Like a flophouse."

"Maybe your brother got pissed off about his kid living in those kind of conditions," Bucky reasoned. "Maybe that's why he killed her."

I reached over and plucked a tissue out of the box on Bucky's desk, used it to wipe the Krispy Kreme glaze off my hands. "He didn't do it. I'm gonna prove it."

He raised his hands in a gesture of helplessness. "Nothing I can do," he said. "You know that, right?"

"Of course," I said.

Even if Karpik couldn't get the South-side cases reopened, Brian was in serious trouble. Deavers's hands were tied. Anything he said or did on my behalf could jeopardize his job and arouse the attention of people like Lloyd Mackey and L. D. Lawrence and Acey Karpik down in Jonesboro.

God bless Bucky Deavers, who never let good sense get in the way of doing a favor for a friend. He did give me a copy of Brian's rap sheet, which Lawrence had faxed him. He wouldn't let me copy the Funtown file, but he did make himself conspicuously absent for a trip to the men's room, which was long enough for me to scan it.

As Bucky had promised, there wasn't much. An offense report, witness list, supplemental form, witness statements, crime scene drawing, property and evidence sheet, lab report, and autopsy report. A separate manila envelope held the crime scene photos. I got up, glanced around to make sure nobody would catch me peeking, and slid the photographs out of the envelope.

There were a dozen of them, eight-by-ten color glossies. The body had been crudely covered with an old, rotted mattress, which had been laid aside for the photo. The girl was blonde, and her face was bloodied, especially around the eyes and cheekbones. She was dressed in blue jeans and a T-shirt of some kind, which had been tied up to bare her abdomen.

At the back of the file I found several photocopies of the composite drawing the medical examiner's office had prepared and circulated in their search for their Jane Doe's identity.

It was an unremarkable face. Small, wide-set eyes, a longish nose with a pronounced bump at the base, a chipped front tooth, receding chin. The artist had drawn Jane with straight, light-colored hair parted on the right side. At the bottom of the page were Jane's statistics—Caucasian female, age 18–25, height 5' 4", weight approx. 110 pounds. I flipped back to the property and evidence list sheet. The investigating officers had inventoried a pair of blue jeans, the cotton T-shirt, a chain with medallion, and a key. No mention of shoes, purse, undergarments, I noticed.

I slipped one of the photocopies of the Jane Doe photograph into my purse.

Bucky coughed discreetly before he came back into the office, allowing me enough time to put the file back and act like I'd been busy studying my fingernails.

"Did Lawrence say how close they were to an arrest?" I asked.

He grimaced. "You know I can't say anything about that. Your brother takes off, the trail leads right back to me."

I got up to go. "You're right. Guess I'll have to work it myself. Thanks, Bucky. Really."

He got all flustered again. "I looked at that rap sheet. Your brother's no choir boy. You know?"

"He's no murderer," I said.

I called Brian's job site from my car phone. The guy who answered the phone sounded annoyed, put out. "He's busy," he said. "You'll have to try him at home."

"Tell him it's his sister," I said. "Tell him it's an emergency."

Pause. "Oh." And then. "Actually, he took the morning off. The funeral, you know."

I couldn't believe it. He'd gone to Shay's funeral. Annette would probably have him locked up on the spot.

"But he's coming back, right?"

"He better," the guy said. "I got a crew standing around here waiting on him."

"Tell him to call Callahan," I said. And then added. "Please."

Next I called Ferd at home. No answer. I hoped that meant something good. Like he was out finding ways to keep Maura out of Annette's clutches.

The intown traffic crept like sorghum syrup. I took the copy of Brian's rap sheet out of my purse, steadied it on the steering wheel, and read. There were some nasty surprises. For one thing, this was a different report than the one Lawrence had waved in our faces the day Ferd and I met with him. The first arrest came in 1980, while Brian was still in high school. He'd been arrested in the city of Atlanta. Possession of marijuana. Fine paid, sentence probated.

I swallowed hard, looked at the date again. Where was I in 1980 that I didn't know my baby brother had been busted for drugs?

Brian had been a typical teenage boy, seventeen or eighteen, probably, and I had been busy with my own life, getting out of college, deciding whether or not to go to law school. Had the bust occurred while I was in the police academy? Edna had obviously kept Brian's arrest a secret—at least from me. What else did she know about her baby boy that she wasn't sharing?

There was another arrest for marijuana in 1983, in Cobb County, but the arrest report didn't give a disposition. Maybe the charges had been dropped.

Two marijuana busts had obviously been enough for Brian. Either he'd quit messing with dope or he'd gotten smarter about hiding it, because he'd kept his nose clean for three more years, until 1986, when he'd been arrested in New Orleans for drunk and disorderly.

What a laugh—drunk and disorderly in New Orleans. I'd spent a New Year's Eve in New Orleans the year the University of Georgia played in the Sugar Bowl. As I recalled, drunk and disorderly was a way of life there. Brian had paid a fine and been released for time served. It looked like he'd spent maybe two weeks in jail.

A horn honked behind me. I looked up from my brother's past to see that my future had started to move. I gave an apologetic wave to the driver in my rearview mirror, put the rap sheet aside and got myself back into the flow of traffic.

21

Instinct, memory navigated. It had been a long time since I'd been on Stewart Avenue. Like most Atlantans, I still think of the street by that name, although the city, pressured by image and politics, calls it Metropolitan Avenue these days. Still, nobody can remember that name. Pestered by a lingering image as a cut-rate boulevard of cheesy strip joints, liquor stores, and violent crime, city fathers finally decided a couple of years ago that if they changed the street's name, nobody would remember how dangerous the street had become.

It wasn't that way when I was a kid. These were the pre-Disney, pre–Six Flags days. Stewart Avenue was solid, working class. And Funtown was why you saved your quarters and did the dishes when your mom told you to.

We didn't call it an amusement park. It was just Funtown.

The blue and yellow chevron-shaped sign pointed toward thrills and spills, Cokes over crushed ice drunk from paper cups, the big Ferris wheel, a roller coaster, and tinny music from loudspeakers.

It was the place you went when school was out for the summer, when you'd earned a big treat. I don't remember the first time my parents took us to Funtown, or the last. I can only remember in between, flashing lights, a big neon clown's head, feeling dizzy and exhilarated.

I remember in the mid-sixties, Funtown—already looking shabby and run-down at the edges—suffered a further blow when Rev. Martin Luther King showed up with his young children looking for a day on the roller coaster, but was turned away in those ugly times of segregation. Not long after King's assassination, Funtown was gone for good.

As a young patrol officer, I'd been on calls to Funtown. By then, the park was long abandoned, weeds grown up through the cracked asphalt, rides dismantled and sold, wading pool drained and cracked, concession buildings little more than concrete-block ruins. Thirty years after the clean-cut Garrity family arrived for a day of thrills, the new fun-seekers were mostly druggies, hookers, and bums.

The chevron sign was still there, sun-bleached, still silly. The old bowling alley had been reincarnated many times—country music palace, strip club, and urban nightclub. The sign out front called it Chocolate City. Spray paint, rotting bags of trash, and chains across the entrance said Chocolate City was long defunct.

I drove on, down the weedy old road. I felt a shudder down my spine, pushed the van's power-lock button. Pines and scrub oak crowded the edges of the road; roots pushed up through paving. Piles of trash dotted the landscape—dead-end roads make great dumps for tires, mattresses, and construction debris.

Finally, the road ran out. I shut the van's engine off and sat, looking out the window, trying to remember the way it had been. The old fairway was rubble now; chunks of concrete block scattered about were the only signs that this had once been someplace special. Only one building was left standing, the faded sign above the door said Tickets. The former cashier's window was caked with decades of grime; the wooden door was warped and rotted, but intact.

A smaller, wooden lean-to had been constructed ten yards away from the concession stand. Maybe six-by-eight, it had been thrown together from discarded sheets of plywood, insulated by sheets of rotted shag carpeting tacked onto the walls as siding. A junked car—a seventies model Mercury Marquis—was parked alongside it. The car's hood was up, and I could see cables snaking from the battery toward a huge sixty-gallon drum that stood beside the car.

I reached for my gun. Were squatters living back here? What was the car doing here? Had I stumbled onto some kind of bizarre moonshine operation?

From the corner of my eye, I caught a glimpse of movement, heard the faintest snap of brittle twigs, the brush of dried leaves. A possum, maybe, or a dog, foraging among the trash.

I tucked my gun into the waistband of my slacks, pulled my coat over it to conceal it. I watched for a few minutes before I got out of the car. If there were squatters living back here, if they were running some kind of criminal enterprise, I didn't want anybody mistaking me for a cop.

I tucked my hands in my pockets, got out, whistling merrily. I walked slowly around the area. Trees and underbrush hid two more sheds similar to the first one I'd spotted. There was a fire-ring where someone had obviously been doing some cooking.

"Hello?" I called. "Anybody home?"

Maybe Funtown's citizenry didn't like unexpected company.

I got back in the van, locked the doors, and took the photo of Jane Doe out of my purse, spreading it out on the seat next to me. Jane of Funtown. Close-set eyes, thin lips, told me nothing. The police reports speculated that she had been killed elsewhere, the body wrapped in the mattress, then dumped back here in this lonely grave-yard. I might have gotten out, walked around, looked for clues. Instead, I pulled the collar of my jacket closer around my neck, shuf-fled through the papers on the seat beside me, found Brian's arrest record.

Where had my brother been in 1988? It was the same year Daddy died. By his own account, Brian had spent most of the past decade drifting around, from New Orleans to Houston to California to Seattle.

There was a theft-by-taking charge in 1991, in Multonomah County, out in Washington. It looked like Brian had done three months in the county jail there. Another arrest, in the same county, came in 1993, possession of tools for commission of a crime and sim-ple battery. He'd done two months for that one.

The next time he was arrested was in 1994, in Atlanta, where he'd been charged with entering an auto and criminal damage to property, in DeKalb County. Had my brother hooked up with Shay by then? There was a simple battery charge in 1996, in Fulton County. Was Shay the victim? There was no way of telling from the arrest report.

I sighed, folded the report up, and stuck it under the seat of the van. This document, in black and white, was the blueprint for my brother's career as a drunken, inept criminal. Just knowing it existed would put my mother in an early grave. It wasn't doing much for my spirits, either.

At least, I told myself, most of Brian's career had been spent breaking into cars or houses, getting drunk, and acting stupid. There was nothing in his past that whispered murder. Nothing that I could see.

The parking lot at Twelve Oaks was nearly empty. No police cruisers, no new-looking unmarked Ford Tauruses. I walked up to Shay's door. No crime-scene tape. A small white business card was tucked in the doorjamb. I picked it out and read it. It was Lawrence's card, with the Clayton police department seal on it. Printed on the back were the words: PLEASE DO NOT ENTER PREMISES. That was all.

Of course I tried the knob. Of course it was locked. I rang the bell at the apartment next door, which had a brand new peephole drilled in it. Mrs. Jimmy James was a cautious lady.

"Who's that?" she called from the other side of the door.

"Callahan Garrity," I called, trying to keep my voice down. "I'm the one who—"

"Goodness gracious," she said, opening the door. "Come on in here."

I went back in the apartment, was almost knocked down with the intense heat.

"Took a chill over at that cemetery," Mrs. James said, gesturing for me to sit down. "Didn't see you at the funeral."

"I'm not exactly on good terms with Annette right now," I said, folding my hands in my lap. "She thinks my brother killed Shay."

Mrs. James nodded. "Lot of police at that funeral. And I saw my precious angel, Maura. Wearing a black dress! Who takes a baby to a funeral? That's what I want to know? I would have told Annette that, except for she was making such a show, carrying on."

"Has Annette been back to the apartment?" I asked.

"Chuck—that's the boyfriend—he come over here this morning," Mrs. James said. "That white police detective, he unlocked the door, went in with him. They come out with a whole bunch of clothes. Look like Annette's things, and some of Chuck's suits and stuff. I went over there and told him how sorry I was, asked when they might be coming back. Tell the truth, I was hoping they might be moving out. Get some quiet Christian folks living over there."

"What did he say?" I asked.

"He say they gonna move back in soon as the police let 'em have it cleaned up. Blood and all that. But then, Chuck said, they gonna start looking for a bigger place. A house maybe, with a yard so Maura can have a swing set and a dog or something."

She was watching my face for a reaction. "Guess Annette figures she gonna have Maura living with her."

I didn't see any reason to lie. Mrs. Jimmy James certainly didn't talk as though she were a big fan of Annette's.

"There's going to be a hearing before a judge. On Thursday. My brother's lawyer needs to prove that it's in Maura's best interest to live with us. To do that, we'll have to show that Annette would not be a fit guardian."

She smoothed her dress over her bony knees, looked up at the ceiling.

"Didn't you tell me they left Maura at that day-care center for long hours, while they were out partying?" I asked.

"Seem like she was there a lot," Mrs. James said, nodding.

"Would you be willing to tell that to the judge?" I asked, sitting forward on the edge of the chair. "Tell him that they didn't provide proper, nutritious meals for her, that she slept in the same room with Shay and her boyfriends?"

"Oh, my," Mrs. James said. "Where'd you hear something like that?"

"You told me all that," I reminded her. "The day we found Shay's body."

"I don't remember sayin' nuthin' like that," Mrs. James said smoothly. "I was kind of upset, probably, 'cause I didn't get much sleep the night before."

"Because they were over there partying and carrying on," I said. "That's what you told me. You told me you even called Annette and threatened to call the police if they didn't quiet down."

Mrs. James studied her fingernails. "Might have done that, but I can't really recall. I don't like to mess in other folks' bidness, you know."

• • •

I left my business card with Mrs. James, urged her to reconsider her sudden case of amnesia. "Maura's whole future depends on this," I said earnestly. "Shay grew up around the corner from me, when I was a kid. And Annette did her the same way, drinking and carousing, staying out late, always having boyfriends over. Annette was a lousy excuse for a mother. That's all Shay ever knew. So she was a lousy mother to Maura. You saw that firsthand, Mrs. James. And you and I saw how Shay ended up. We don't want that for Maura, Mrs. James. We want her to have a good life. A stable home, people who'll love her and look after her. Not stick her in some day care someplace. We don't want to give Annette another shot at ruining another little girl."

She blinked, gave me a hard stare. "I mind my own bidness."

22

Chuck Ingraham's law offices were on the wrong side of the railroad tracks. From my point of view, anyway. Jonesboro's downtown—what there was of it—was split in two by the Georgia Southern Railroad tracks. A series of modest brick and wood-frame houses lined one side of the road, lawyer's offices mostly.

I hadn't meant to try to speak to Ingraham. What I meant to do was to drop by the police department and see if I could get any information out of Lawrence—and ask him firsthand if he truly believed he could implicate my brother in two decades-old unsolved homicides.

But the small, yellow brick office caught my eye, as did the sign out front, reading Charles J. Ingraham, attorney at law. Only one car was in the parking lot, a shiny gun-metal gray Cadillac.

I parked, got out, paused in front of the door. Did I knock or just walk right in?

Chuck Ingraham saved me the trouble. He jerked the door open, obviously on his way out for the rest of the day. He carried a briefcase and under the other arm had a stack of file folders. He was dressed in a dark blue suit, white shirt, and dark red tie. Funeral clothes.

Ingraham frowned. Obviously, he would have preferred to see anybody except a Garrity.

"What do you want?" he said, scowling. "Your brother had the nerve to show up at the services for Shay today. Of all the sick, twisted bastards in the world, he's the sickest. Don't you people have any decency?"

"We people?" He was getting my Irish up. "We people are not the ones dragging a three-year-old to look at her dead mommy in a coffin.

"Fuck off," Ingraham said. He shifted the papers under his arm, made a dismissive gesture, like I should get the hell off his property.

"I'd like to talk to you," I said, with deliberate calm. "This bickering is terrible for Maura. She's already lost her mother, and I don't think it's good for her to see her family attacking each other. So I'd like to discuss this whole thing, see if we can't come to some agreement."

Edna would hate the idea, Brian would have a fit, but I was beginning to see this might be the only way. "I'd like to get Annette and Brian to talk about joint custody," I said. "Calmly, rationally. For Maura's sake. For Shay's sake, too."

His eyes narrowed, like he was trying to figure out if this was some trick. The shame of it was, it wasn't a trick.

"We intend to do our talking in court," Ingraham said. "Now, if you'll excuse me, I've got business to attend to."

"You people think you've got this thing all nicely packaged, don't you?" I asked, feeling myself start to steam again. "Big-deal lawyer in a small town like Jonesboro. Do you play golf with that judge, Judge Bingham? And how about the cops? You have coffee with them down at the courthouse café most mornings?"

Ingraham blinked. "I'm respected in this community, yes. I'm acquainted with Judge Bingham, yes. No, I don't have the police wrapped around my little finger. They don't make a homicide case because I ask them to."

"What about Annette?" I asked. "Is she a respected part of this community? A divorcée? Living in sin with her boyfriend? Partying till dawn over at the Marriott lounge? Seems like you were pretty tight with Shay, too, all of you living under one roof like that. This must be a pretty open-minded town down here. Because when Annette lived in my neighborhood, when I was growing up, she wasn't exactly June Cleaver, you know."

Ingraham laughed. "Annette Gatlin has had to work hard her whole life. Nobody ever gave her any breaks. She raised her daughter without any help from anybody, never asked anything from anybody. My relationship with Shay was purely as an adviser. I don't doubt a smug, self-righteous bunch of busybodies didn't approve of Shay or Annette. It does surprise me, however, that someone with your middle-class upbringing, your background in law enforcement, would approve of the kind of life Brian Garrity has lead."

"What would you know about that?" I asked.

"Your brother is a low-life scumbag maggot," Ingraham said. "A drunk, a malingerer, an abusive piece of shit. Annette tried to warn Shay, as soon as he started hanging around, but Shay wouldn't listen. When she got pregnant, Shay was afraid to tell him. He was out of work, as usual. Annette and I helped pay the hospital bills, gave her money for food and rent. We couldn't believe it when she married him after the baby was born. Annette made it clear to Shay, she absolutely did not need to marry Brian, that we would be there, to help her with Maura. The day after they were married, Shay knew it was a mistake. Everybody knew it was a mistake."

"Brian loved Shay," I said hotly. "No matter what happened later, he loved her."

"He loved her right into the emergency room at Southside General Hospital," Ingraham said rudely. "Don't think we don't intend to show the emergency room records to the judge. There are photographs, too. In living color. They had to get Shay to hold her hospital I.D. bracelet up to the camera, because her face was so badly battered, you couldn't tell who it was. You could barely tell it was a human being."

"I don't believe my brother did that," I retorted. "Anyway, it has nothing to do with Brian's suitability to raise his child. Our lawyer says the judge only considers what's in the child's best interest. And in this state, it's in the child's best interest to be raised by a parent. Brian's her father. He's made some mistakes, God knows, but he loves her. We love her."

"He's a killer," Ingraham said. "He abducted the child, then cut Shay up like a piece of Swiss steak. It's not his first kill, either. This is Clayton County, Miss Garrity, not Fulton or DeKalb. Look up the statistics. We don't let killers loose down here. We send them to the chair."

I shuddered involuntarily. "I'd heard Acey Karpik was behind this ridiculous serial murder thing," I said. "I should have known some-body else was egging him on. Somebody with something to gain."

"Everybody has something to gain out of seeing your brother taken out of decent society," Ingraham retorted. He turned, closed his office door, and locked it.

"See you in court," he said. He walked rapidly down the porch steps, put his files and briefcase in the backseat of the Cadillac, and spun out of the parking lot.

I called Ferd from my car phone, told him where I was and what I was doing, and about the conversation I'd had with Bucky Deavers.

"Two unsolved homicides," Ferd said. "Christ. They're making him the next Ted Bundy. And they're probably planning on laying it all out for the judge on Thursday."

"He hasn't been arrested," I pointed out. "Has he?"

"No," Ferd said. "He called me after he left Shay's funeral. He was pretty shook up. Annette tried to have him thrown out of the funeral home. Two of those Clayton detectives followed him back to his job site. They never spoke to him, never stopped him or questioned him, just parked at the entrance to the subdivision where Brian's working. He thinks one of them was videotaping him. It's harassment. I've called the police department to complain. They practically laughed me off the phone."

"They'd arrest him if they had something, wouldn't they?" I asked.

"In a second," Ferd said. "All they have is motive and opportunity. They don't have any proof. Not yet, anyway."

"Annette and Chuck keep bringing up this allegation that Brian beat Shay so badly she had to be hospitalized," I said. "Chuck just told me they plan to put it into evidence at the hearing. Can they do that?"

"They can try," Ferd said grimly.

"There're supposedly photographs of Shay," I said. "Taken at Southside General after she was admitted."

"He told you what hospital she was taken to?" Ferd asked.

"Yeah." Suddenly I got what he was driving at. "Might be worth taking a look at those medical records," I said. "If Annette has them, we ought to have them, too."

"You planning on going over there?" Ferd asked.

"I am now," I said. "Listen, we need to have a serious talk with my brother. A friend slipped me a copy of his arrest record. There's a whole lot on there that I never knew about. Nothing really violent, but there is one arrest for simple battery. I think we need to start talking to him about the possibility of joint custody."

"He'll never go for that. Not in his current state of mind," Ferd said. "I didn't want to bring it up, but when I talked to him, he sounded pretty shaky. Like maybe he'd been drinking."

"He went back to work that way?"

"I could be mistaken. He'd just been to his wife's funeral," Ferd said apologetically.

"Was he planning on coming over to our house tonight? To see Maura?"

Ferd hesitated. "I think he was planning on coming over and getting Maura and taking her back to his place," he said. "He mumbled something about getting tired of family interfering with his life."

"Interfering?" I felt like taking my fist and busting something. Like hunting my brother down and settling the old, unsolved beefs like rational adults—with my fists. I wanted to slap him into reality.

"He's not thinking rationally," Ferd said. "I told him I thought it wasn't a good idea for him to take Maura right now. She's had a rough time, been handed around a lot. I think I pissed him off, telling him that, but that's fine. I piss off my clients all the time."

"Better to be pissed off than pissed on," I remarked.

"Jack Garrity's favorite saying," Ferd said. "I miss your old man."

"Yeah," I said. "We all do. I'll call you and let you know what happens."

Southside General Hospital had a real bug up their rear about security.

As soon as I walked in the big double doors of the emergency room, a uniformed guard was in my face, asking me where I was going and what I was doing.

"I'm here about a bill," I said.

"Business office is in the main building," he said, pointing out the door and toward the right.

"It's an emergency room bill," I said.

"You'll still have to talk to the business office," he said, unmoved.

"But they say they don't have any record of my sister's visit," I said peevishly. "She's dead now, and I want to settle all her accounts. But the hospital never billed us for her visit. It's been three months, but still no bill."

He looked at me like I'd grown a second head. "That's a problem?"

"I've got to settle the estate," I insisted. "See all her accounts are settled. I can't go back to Boise until everything's taken care of."

He looked around to see if anybody was listening in, leaned foreword to impart some very important information.

"Listen to me, ma'am," he said. He was kind of nice-looking, young, with straight dark hair that fell over his eyebrows, and serious gray eyes. I wished he hadn't spoiled things by calling me ma'am. It made me feel like Mrs. Robinson. He looked good in his security guard uniform, too.

"This hospital, they charge you for every aspirin, every Band-Aid, every tongue depressor. Nobody gets out of here without a bill. This ain't no charity hospital. These people are experts at billing. So if your sister was treated here, she got a bill. Believe me."

"I'd like to," I said. Now I was leaning forward, to share my secret with him. "It's embarrassing," I said. "Her ex-husband beat her up. I've got to get this taken care of, before the hospital sends a bill and my mother finds out. She'd die if she knew what had happened to Shay."

"Spousal abuse?" He made a face. "These guys hit women, they oughta be locked up."

When I was a kid, Edna always preached the golden rule to me. "Always think of others," she'd say. "Put yourself in the other person's position, and you won't be willing to hurt them. Do onto others as you would have them do unto you."

Of course, she rarely practiced what she preached, being one of the more vindictive women God had ever put on earth. But I'd taken her lesson to heart. Putting yourself in the other person's shoes always worked well as an investigative technique. Especially when it comes to making up any story you can to get any information you need. Right now I was putting myself in Annette Gatlin's spike heels.

"I agree," I said, adding a flutter of the eyelashes. Thank God I'd put on mascara this morning. Fluttering only works if you're wearing at least three coats of jet black waterproof Maybelline.

"Shay's ex-husband was pond scum. But she's dead now. He can't hurt her anymore."

"Sorry for your loss," he said, lowering his thick, curly eyelashes. He really was quite a cute specimen. Too bad he was young enough to be my son.

"Can you do something for me?" I asked. "So I can get on a plane tonight, knowing I've done everything I can?"

"I don't see what I can do," he said. "It's up to the business department. If I were you, I'd just forget about it."

I pointed to the computer on the desk in front of him. "Can you check in there, see if there's any record she was admitted here?"

He looked dubious. "I'm just supposed to check and see what room people are in, hand out visitor's passes," he said.

"But the computer could tell you if she'd been in a room, couldn't it?"

"Yeah," he said. "Sometimes, people come over to see somebody, they've already been discharged. Or the bad thing, they come to see somebody, and they're dead. Oh, man, I hate having to tell somebody the patient is dead."

"How awful. You really have to do that?"

He shrugged, a valiant gesture. "Part of the job. We get training in grief counseling."

I ran my fingers through my curls and sighed. "If you were willing to check, my sister's name was Shay Garrity. I think she was admitted here back in September or October."

It was four o'clock. Slack time. The nurses at the desk behind him were sipping coffee, gossiping. There were only two people in the waiting room, both elderly black ladies who coughed continuously.

"I'll bet it's exciting working here," I said, laying it on even thicker. If he didn't hurry up and help me out, I was going to have to go to plan B. As soon as I figured out what Plan B was.

"Some days are better than others," he said. "Mondays are slow."

He tapped a key on the computer, and it started to hum.

"Spell that last name?"

I spelled it for him, helpfully added that my sister could have been admitted under her maiden name, which was Gatlin.

"Here it is," he said, reading the screen. "Shay Gatlin."

Shay had been admitted to the emergency room on September 15, at 3 A.M. He read over the computer screen and winced.

"Wow. She was hurt pretty bad. Spent the night, got an IV drip. They called in a plastic surgeon to stitch up her face. The attending docs took care of the other stuff."

He looked puzzled. "The notation on the bottom says your sister's bill was paid."

I blinked. "Are you sure there hasn't been some mistake? I didn't find any bill. And she never said a word about a plastic surgeon."

He tapped some buttons, kept reading. I could see a little tuft of fine black hair at the neckline of his gray uniform shirt. He had a mole right below the right corner of his lower lip. What was I doing? Lusting after some boytoy when I had the genuine article at my beck and call. Oh, well, if men can lust in their hearts, so can women.

"Just a minute," he said. He got up, walked away from the security desk. I prayed he wasn't going to get reinforcements, to have me thrown out.

Maybe it was time to get that Plan B in action.

Five minutes later, he was back, with a manila folder in hand.

He opened it, studied the first page. "This is your sister's chart," he said. "I'm not supposed to have this, you know."

"I know," I said warmly. "And I can't tell you how much I appreciate your assistance."

"The attending physician tried to have her swear out a complaint against the guy who did this to her," he said, looking down at the chart. "After they got her stitched up, she said it had all been a mistake. That she'd been injured when she tripped over one of her daughter's toys."

"She was embarrassed," I said, clucking my tongue. "Didn't want anybody to know how badly she was hurt."

"It was bad," he said. He held up a color Polaroid. "Real bad."

I put out my hand and he gave it to me.

Chuck Ingraham hadn't exaggerated. The woman in the photo had very blonde hair, and a very bloody, pulpy face. One eye was swollen shut; there were vivid red marks around her throat. One hand was held up beside her face. It was bandaged, but the hospital I.D. bracelet was readable. Clearly, it said Shay Garrity. She wore a blue and white hospital gown, the neckline pulled down to make the scratches and bruises on her chest visible to the camera. A small gold medallion hung between the bruised and bleeding breasts.

I wanted to throw up. How? How could my brother have inflicted these kinds of wounds on anybody? Any woman? Any mother of his own child? What was I doing, trying to help him win back another little girl? Another potential victim?

Gently, the guard took the photograph out of my hand, tucked it back in the folder. "Sorry you had to see that," he said. "I guess it's pretty upsetting for you."

I tried a smile. "Yes," I said. "It is." And this time, I wasn't lying.

"She gave as good as she got though," he added. "If it makes you feel any better."

I was still looking at the file, upside down on the desk in front of me. "What?" I said, confused.

"I found a Garrity file after all, right in front of your sister's file," he said. "I thought maybe it had something to do with your sister, so I brought it out."

He lifted the top folder, opened another. "Brian Garrity. Admitted the same night, same time as your sister. Is that the husband?"

I nodded, too startled to speak.

He laughed. "She scratched him up so bad they had to give him a tetanus shot. Bruised and cut, nose broken. The docs wanted to admit him, but he wouldn't do it. Let them bandage him up, then he left, just disappeared. Still hasn't paid his bill. His chart says it's been turned over to a collection agency."

23

I swiped the Polaroid of Brian while the security guard went to check on one of the elderly coughing women. When he got back, I was jotting notes on a yellow legal pad, a word-for-word list of all the injuries my brother had sustained: broken wrist, bruised ribs, fractured collarbone, stab wounds to the upper right arm and torso.

"Hey," the guard said. "I thought you were just interested in your sister's bill."

I put my pen away, flipped over the pages of the yellow legal pad.

"I am," I said. "But I need to know the kind of stunt that bastard ex-husband of hers might pull."

He closed the file and put them on the counter behind him. "You better go," he said, looking a trifle nervous. "The new charge nurse comes on at four, and she's a pistol. Doesn't like people just standing around in her emergency room, y'know what I mean?"

"I know," I said. I gave him a finger wave. "Thanks for your help. Now I can go back to Boise."

Out in the car, I looked down at the photo of my brother. He stared defiantly ahead at the camera, but his face had taken a pounding. His lips were so swollen they didn't cover his teeth, one of which appeared to be missing. Who'd given him this beating? Why had he never mentioned it when Shay began to level charges that he'd abused her?

There was still one person in this equation I knew little about. Shay's employer, Dyson Yount, who supposedly had the political pull to make things happen in Clayton County.

I dropped in at the only courthouse hangout I could find, a small storefront café half a block from the courthouse. That was its name, just Café.

It looked like they were getting ready to close for the day. I ordered a cup of coffee, selected a piece of pie from a twirling display case. "Chess pie," the waitress told me. "You're lucky. We only make it on Mondays, and usually all the lawyers hog it up."

"Those lawyers can be pie-eatin' pigs," I commented, sipping my coffee.

"Got a sweet tooth, every single one of 'em," she agreed. "We fix salads and soups and healthy stuff for the secretaries and clerks who are watching their weight, but the lawyers, they want their food salty, greasy, sweet, and fatty. Educated folks, you'd think they'd know better."

"I used to know a guy who went into business down here," I said. "We went to Georgia together. Dyson Yount. Is he still around?"

"Oh yeah," she said, bringing out a bottle of spray cleaner and spritzing the counter with it. "He's one of the Young Turks, people are calling him. Yount Realty, they own half this county. My sister rents her house from him."

"How about that?" I marveled. "When we were in college, he could barely make it to class more than once a week. Man was a serious partier."

"He likes the party, all right," the woman said. "Only now it's the Democratic Party. Old Maceo Holland, our state rep is retiring this year after forty years in the State House. Dyson Yount is right in line to take over for him. And if Holland says it's so, you better believe it's so."

I drank the rest of my coffee, set the cup down, put a dollar on the counter. "Well, good for Dyson," I said. "Couldn't happen to a greater guy."

"Hmm," the waitress said, scooping her tip up in a single fluid movement. "I like his wife a lot better. Real down-to-earth gal. She's president of the PTA over at the elementary school. My daughter baby-sits their little kids sometimes.

It wasn't hard to find Dyson Yount's office. It was a pale-yellow, two-story Victorian, on the good side of Main Street. A tasteful wooden plaque hung from a wrought-iron standard: Yount Realty. The boxwoods lining the walk to the house had been draped with tiny white lights and there was an evergreen wreath on the double front doors—only instead of the expected red ribbon, this was a wide black rosette. Somebody was in mourning.

I rang the doorbell and heard footsteps on the hardwood floors inside, and then the door opened.

Dyson Yount looked like he'd just been posing for the family Christmas card. Or maybe it was his campaign brochure. He wore a red and green Icelandic-looking sweater over a red plaid wool shirt, dark green corduroy slacks, polished penny loafers. His neatly combed dark hair was streaked gray at the temples, and a pair of tortoiseshell bifocals made him look wise and distinguished despite his youth. He was all of thirty-five, I guessed, brimming with promise.

He frowned when he saw me, but he motioned me inside the high-ceilinged foyer.

"You again," he said, looking me up and down. "Shay told me Brian had sisters. She said you were the nosy one."

I was tired of hearing about Shay's version of life with the Garritys, with her in the starring role of Snow White and the rest of us playing the various dwarves, Bitchy, Snotty, Goofy, Lazy, and Grumpy.

"Shay told a lot of people a lot of things about my family, apparently," I said. "She was a talented little liar, I'll give her credit for that. Busy, too. That's probably why she left Maura at that day-care center until ten o'clock at night three or four nights a week. Very busy. The real estate profession must be exhausting. Especially for a gal who dropped out of high school in her junior year."

Yount shook his head. "I don't appreciate character assassination of a young woman who's just been brutally murdered. A jury wouldn't, either. And I know Judge Bingham won't. He knew Shay. Lots of fine folks in this town knew and respected your sister-in-law."

"Most of them married men, it seems," I said, looking pointedly at the framed pictures of his wife and children on the desk in the reception area.

He flushed a little. "For the record, Shay was highly intelligent, highly motivated. Best assistant I ever had. She was working on getting her real estate license. And she'd already looked into getting into a paralegal program at Clayton State College. Your brother couldn't stand the idea of her getting ahead and leaving him behind, could he?"

I had my hands balled up by my side. I'd had all I could take of the "poor Shay, evil Brian" song they were singing in Shay's adopted hometown.

"My brother was confused," I said. "He thought he and Shay were supposed to be a married couple. He couldn't understand why she stayed out late, night after night. Or why she dumped their little girl with a baby-sitter all hours of the day. He couldn't understand why Shay's mother, Annette, and Chuck had such control over their lives."

"Shay was afraid of him," Yount said. "He beat her like a rug. Naturally, she turned to her family for help."

"You mean like that time in the fall, when Brian supposedly beat her so badly she was admitted to the hospital," I said.

"I told her to start divorce proceedings the next day. Tried to get her to sign a warrant for his arrest, but she wouldn't," Dyson said.

I fished the Polaroid of Brian out of my pocket, held it up for him to see. He moved to take it, but I moved it away.

"It's interesting to me how Shay is always the innocent victim in all that's happened here," I said. "I've seen those photos that were taken in September, when Shay was admitted to Southside General. But nobody seems to know too much about these photos of my brother, Brian."

"He got in another bar fight," Yount said. "Probably after he got done beating up Shay, he still needed to work out some aggression. Made the mistake of attacking somebody bigger than he was."

"I don't think so," I said. I pointed at the scratch marks on Brian's face and neck. "Shay had those long acrylic nails, didn't she? Those will leave hellish claw marks."

He sniffed. "You're saying Shay did all that to Brian? That's absurd."

"Not all of it," I said. "I think they got in a fight, exchanged blows. Shay fought the way her mama taught her—with her nails and teeth and feet. And then somebody else stepped in. I think somebody else was present at that fight. I think they beat the living shit out of my brother."

Yount sat down behind his desk, pulled a big black cigar out of a cedar box beside the phone. He held it up, turned it, and admired it. Cigars are all the rage now for yuppie twits like Dyson Yount who don't have the balls to smoke the kind of unfiltered Lucky Strikes my dad used to burn out his lungs.

"So now you've got a conspiracy theory going," he said.

"You think somebody beat up your brother. What? A boyfriend come to her rescue?"

"Something like that."

"Your brother's not a deaf-mute," Yount said. "Why don't you ask him what happened? He's probably got a long list of men he thought were sleeping with his wife."

"He does," I said. "Chuck Ingraham is on it. You're on it."

Yount yawned. "Keep one thing in mind when you talk to your brother, Miss Garrity. The man's a liar and a thief and a killer. Other than that, I'm sure he's a great guy."

24

Ferd's telephone greeting was a chest-racking cough. He gave me Brian's address with great reluctance. "He gave me this in confidence," he protested. "If he'd wanted you to have it, he would have given it to you."

"He needs to answer some questions," I said. "A lot of questions. I'm tired of his moodiness. I've been out busting my butt for three days, trying to save his ass, and he has done nothing to help me. In fact, he's done everything he could to keep me from finding out the truth about his life."

"Some things you don't want your family to know," Ferd said gently.

"It's a little late for that," I retorted. "Did you know that Brian was admitted to the same hospital, the same night he allegedly beat Shay? I saw the hospital chart, Ferd, I've got one of the Polaroids. Somebody beat him bad. And I don't think it was all Shay's doing. But why hasn't he mentioned that?"

"He's an odd guy," Ferd said. "Nothing like his mama or daddy or sisters or brother."

"He doesn't have to be like us," I said. "He doesn't even have to like us. But he does need to live up to his responsibilities. And one of those is Maura. Like it or not."

"One other thing," Ferd hesitated again. "Edna's been calling me. She's fit to be tied. Annette has disappeared with Maura."

143

"No. That's not possible," I said.

"Your mother hung around outside the church during the services, even followed the funeral procession to the cemetery. She said Annette was staring daggers at her the whole time. And Maura, apparently, just cried and cried."

"But the judge said they could only have her one day," I protested.

"And they're interpreting that as twenty-four hours," Ferd said. "Right after the graveside visitation was over, Annette jumped into a different car than the funeral home limo she'd come in, and they just took off. Your mama lost them at the first traffic light. She had me on the phone about fifteen seconds later. Like to have burnt my ear off."

"Oh God, Ferd, I'm sorry."

"Needless to say, Chuck Ingraham has not returned my calls."

"I saw him, just about an hour ago," I said. "He was leaving his law offices, with a lot of papers and files."

"Do you have any idea where he and Annette are staying?"

"None," I said helplessly. "I know they're not at the apartment. The police still haven't let them move back in."

"We'll just have to sit back and wait," Ferd said. "Your mama wants to put out an all points bulletin, of course. I tried to explain to her, but . . ."

"Edna only hears what she wants to hear," I told him. "How's Brian taking the news?"

"He was with Edna when Annette took off with Maura. I think that's why he went off on a toot before going back to work."

"This sucks," I said. "What do we do if they don't return Maura in twenty-four hours?"

"Go back to the judge," Ferd said.

Brian's "apartment" was actually a double-wide trailer in a fairly new-looking trailer park just off Old National Highway, less than a mile from the apartment Shay had shared with Annette. The trailers were parked close together, with beat-up pickup trucks and sedans nosed up close to the trailers, like one was nursing off the other.

His dusty black pickup truck, the bed full of toolboxes, a rain slicker, and a couple of bags of what looked like trash were parked alongside the tan and brown trailer.

The stoop was made of uneven concrete blocks. A pair of mud-covered work boots stood beside the partially open screen door. Music tumbled from within. Patsy Cline. I looked at the truck, looked at the metallic numbers on the side of the trailer, wondered if I'd made a mistake. The last music I'd heard my brother play was Pat Benatar, not Patsy Cline.

I knocked, pulled the door open. "Brian? It's me."

He was in the kitchen, frying something. Smoky grease wafted from that area. "Ferd gave you my address?"

"We need to talk," I explained.

The trailer had burnt-orange shag carpet, a bare box spring and mattress in the living room, and a card table with two folding chairs in the dinette area. Boxes were stacked everywhere. The music was coming from a boom box sitting on top of bookshelves made of concrete blocks and two-by-fours.

Brian stood in his stocking feet, at the stove, fork in one hand, beer bottle in the other. A cigarette hung from his lip.

He waved the fork at me. "Want some?"

"Are you still eating that shit?" I asked, shuddering. God. Spam. It had been a summertime staple when we were kids. We'd steal a can of Spam and a frying pan from the kitchen, sneak out in the woods, make a bonfire, and fry up a mess of the stuff, which we thought was the culinary equivalent of Porterhouse steak. Once, somebody'd gotten careless with the grease and we'd burned down some pine trees and a neighbor's doghouse. As punishment, Dad had spanked the four of us raw and restricted us to the yard for the rest of the summer. I'd lost my taste for Spam. And I'm still nervous about playing with matches.

"I'm not hungry," I said, which was a lie. No breakfast, no lunch, just a plateful of grief all day long. "I'd take a beer, though."

He nodded toward a forty-quart plastic cooler on the countertop. "Refrigerator doesn't work yet. Beer's in there." He stepped over to the boom box and turned it off.

I dug around in his makeshift larder, past a pound package of baloney, a jar of yellow French's mustard, a package of hotdogs, and a carton of chocolate milk, until I found a Pabst.

"Throw the cap anywhere," Brian said, flipping his Spam again. "Place is a mess. I'm not really settled yet."

I put the cap on the counter. He reached into a brown paper sack, brought out a loaf of Wonder bread, made himself a sandwich.

"You sure?" he gestured at the loaf, meaning there was plenty more.

"Just the beer," I said.

"Over here." He reached back into his grocery sack, came up with a bag of Fritos. He tore the end off with his teeth, sat down at the card table, sprinkled some pepper on his sandwich, and started to eat.

I helped myself to a handful of Fritos, which went down good with the beer. I crunched and sipped and tried to think about how to talk to my brother, who didn't like me and didn't like to talk.

He saved me the trouble. "What's up? You down here slumming?"

"I've talked to Ferd," I said. "He told me about this stunt Annette pulled, taking off with Maura."

"Fuckin' bitch," he said, between chews. "Now you know why I had to get out of there."

The direct approach sometimes works best. I got out the file folder of material I'd accumulated during the day, starting with his arrest record, the composite photo of Funtown Jane, and the Polaroid the hospital had taken when he was treated there.

He chewed, looked at the papers, chewed some more, drank. "What's this supposed to be? Some kind of mystery puzzle or something? I don't need this crap, Callahan. I just need you to help me get my baby. OK? Anything else you need to prove to yourself, you just keep it to yourself."

I shuffled the papers so that his arrest report was on top. "I don't need this crap, either, Brian. But now some cop down here in Clayton County wants to hook you up not just with Shay's murder, but with a bunch of old, unsolved homicides. They're looking at you as a serial murderer, brother dear. It's not just Annette and Chuck looking to take your baby away anymore. They're looking to send you to the electric chair."

He burped, wiped his mouth with the back of his hand. "Excuse me. You serious?"

I tapped his arrest report. "I got this from a friend who's a homicide detective with the Atlanta P.D. There's a retired homicide cop living down here, he thinks Shay's murder somehow resembles two other murders of young white females, some of them more than ten years old. He's trying to put together a task force, to reopen all the cases. They think it's you, Brian."

He looked up at me, his mouth ajar. "I keep telling you. I didn't kill Shay. I didn't kill anybody." He took another long swallow of beer. "Hell, I wasn't even around here ten years ago."

"All these arrests," I said, running my finger down the list. "Breaking and entering, public drunkenness, theft by taking. They start in Atlanta, they go out west, they take you back to Atlanta."

"I was an asshole," Brian said. "No college degree, no skills, you take the work where it comes. I was a kid, made some mistakes. I paid for 'em."

He still didn't understand the cumulative effect of an arrest record like his. So I tried to explain it to him.

"This is the classic profile of a serial murderer," I said. "Two murders on the south side of Atlanta. You were living here then, hanging out. We never saw you or knew what you were doing. Then you head out west. We still don't hear from you. Four years ago, you come back to Atlanta, and Shay ends up dead."

"And now I'm Son of Sam," he said. "'Cause my wife screws anything in pants and gets herself killed, I'm automatically guilty."

I moved the arrest report aside, showed him the drawing of the Jane Doe whose body had been found at Funtown.

"You ever see anybody who looks like her?"

"Is she somebody I'm supposed to have killed?"

"Just tell me."

"Yeah," he said, turning his head this way and that, looking at the drawing from different angles. "She kind of looks like somebody. I don't know, she looks like a lot of somebodys."

"Somebody specific," I said. "Somebody from Atlanta. Come on, Brian, think about it."

"Maybe," he said slowly. "Maybe somebody used to hang out someplace I used to hang out. I'm thinking a bar. Hell, I've been in every bar between here and LA. Thrown out of most of 'em."

"This girl's body was found here. Right here in Atlanta," I said. "Narrow it down to Atlanta."

He shrugged. "After high school, me and my buddies used to hang out at some places on Roswell Road. They're all gone now. And there was a country bar, down on the south side. Cowkickers. Lot of girls used to come in there. Maybe I saw her there."

"Where was Cowkickers?" I asked. I'd never heard of the place, but then it was obvious that my brother and I had been traveling in very different circles ever since the old neighborhood Spam-fries.

"Originally? Cowkickers was right where the skating rink used to be, there at I-20 and Moreland. That neighborhood went black. They moved it down onto Stewart Avenue. You'd never know it, but Stewart, that used to be all honky-tonks and nightclubs, some pretty high-class strip joints. Guys from all over Atlanta, even people from the north side, went down there. Now? Hell, I went down there once, right after I moved back here, I didn't know it had gotten so run-down. Two guys offered me crack and a hooker offered me a hand job, and that was all on the same red light. You'd have to take a battalion of marines make you feel safe over there now."

"What was Cowkickers near?" I asked. "The second time around?"

"Right there by Funtown" he said. "You remember the place?"

I took a deep breath. "I remember Funtown. This girl's body, her remains really, were found way back in there, back where the amusement park used to be. The body had been hidden under a mattress. The police never identified her. She'd been stabbed to death." Another deep breath. "The body was found in '88, Brian. You were still living here."

"Oh no," he said, getting up from the table. "Shit no." He reached into the cooler, got another beer, threw the empty bottle with such force it shattered against the far wall, making a dent in the sheetrock.

I cringed, fought the urge to leave, to run from this place and this alien being and life. "Do you really think you knew her?" I asked.

He snatched up the paper and waved it in my face. "Look at this," he cried. "This could be anybody. Shit! You didn't tell me it was somebody I was supposed to have killed."

"The cops have theorized she was maybe a hooker. Lots of them used to hang out down there. Still do. The really low-rent hookers wouldn't get a room. They'd just take their tricks back in there, back down that dead end into the woods."

He laughed. "Now you want to know if I've ever been with a hooker? Shit. You're my sister, Jules."

"I'm your sister, not your mother," I reminded him. "And I don't give a rat's ass if you've ever been with a hooker. The question is, do you think you've ever been with this girl, this hooker?"

"No," he said quickly. "I never had the money for a hooker. Anyway, I could usually use that famous Irish charm to get what I wanted with women. I never have had to pay for it."

Except with Shay, I thought to myself. Then you paid big.

I got one of Bucky Deavers's business cards, put it on the table. "This is my buddy the homicide cop. If they do reopen the Funtown case, it looks like the case will be his. Acey Karpik, the ex-cop putting all this together, wants Bucky to work on it. And if you can remember anything, anything at all about this girl, you should call Bucky. He knows you're my brother. He's a good guy."

Brian came back to the table, sat down again. He seemed a little calmer. Or maybe a little drunker. I couldn't tell which.

I put the Polaroid from the hospital in front of him. "I tracked this down at Southside General today. How come you didn't tell Ferd you'd been beaten the night you hit Shay?"

His face crumpled. He put the beer bottle down on the Polaroid. I took it off, put the Polaroid in front of me. "I saw the hospital charts, Brian," I said. "You were admitted the same time as Shay, with injuries as bad as, or worse, than she had. The doctors wanted to keep you. Instead, you just walked out. What happened?"

The old crooked smile. "I got whupped up on. Fight night at the Garritys."

"I don't believe it," I said. "I saw the photos they took of Shay, too. I don't care what anybody says. I know you're not capable of that kind of brutality."

His eyes dropped. "I did hit her, though."

"Not that hard."

He shrugged. "It's like being a little pregnant. If you hit a woman, you hit a woman. It's wrong. You're an animal. Your wife leaves, they take your kid away, pin a couple murders on you. Case closed."

I held out the Polaroid to him. "Shay weighed ninety pounds soaking wet. I can see she maybe did some of the scratches, maybe chewed you up a little bit, but not the rest of this. Come on, Brian, I was a cop. Give me some credit."

He crossed his arms and stared at the ceiling.

"Quit being such a macho asshole," I told him. "This photo and the hospital records, they may be what we need to start to prove you didn't kill Shay. That you're a fit father."

"Maybe I'm not a fit father," he muttered.

"What happened?" I repeated.

He let out a long, unhappy sigh. "It was Friday night. I'd just started a new job. Big subdivision they're building down at Lake Spivey. Six hundred houses. Good money, lots of possibilities. I got home at seven, there was a message on the answering machine, and she was going out drinking with the girls in the office. Fuck." He looked up, smiled. "The only other girl in her office was a nineteen-year-old Mexican chick named Sonya who did some typing for Tyson. I knew Shay was hanging out with Annette and her posse. The message on the machine said Maura was still at day care, and I needed to pick her up."

He swallowed, nodded. "I picked up a case of beer, a bucket of fried chicken for me, a Happy Meal for Maura. I got to day care, and the lady was busting my chops about how we owed extra money. She wanted ten bucks, cash, on the spot. Late fee. And she said Shay still owed her ten from the last Friday night when she picked Maura up late."

Brian beat a tattoo on the tabletop with his beer bottle. "We got a deal worked out. I pay the rent, utilities, and the note on Shay's car. She buys groceries, pays for day care. Only her idea of groceries is pizza and Burger King and wine coolers. And most Fridays, I get home, I gotta pick up Maura and they're looking to me to pay for all the times Shay picked her up late. And that's not all."

He blinked and I saw the tears he was trying to will away. "My little girl? She's had diarrhea all day. The day-care lady takes off the diaper and shows me. Her butt is just as red and raw as a piece of hamburger meat. She says she told Shay two days ago, told her to get some medicine to put on Maura's rash, but Shay never did. And the diapers. We have to buy the diapers and leave them at day care. The lady tells me they've been out since yesterday, and Shay promised to bring more, but she forgot. She gives me a bill, fifteen dollars for diapers. So I give her thirty-five bucks, and now I'm broke. It's Friday night, my wife is out partying with God knows who, and I'm broke."

I got up and helped myself to another beer. It was the last one, but I felt I was doing the sisterly thing by keeping it away from him.

"There weren't any diapers at home, either. I had to put a dish-towel around Maura, and put her to bed," Brian said. "I'd already spent all my money on day care, beer and chicken. No money left for diapers. I sat and watched TV and drank all the beer in the house. By midnight, I was hammered. Passed out on the sofa in the living room. But I woke up when I heard the key in the lock."

"Was she alone?" I asked.

"Guess not," he said. "The only light in the room was from the TV. Soon as she walked in, I sat up, started bitching her out. You know Shay, she's got a mouth on her. She just bitched me right back. Told me she had a right to do what she wanted. She earned her own money, and she was too young to sit around the apartment all day and wait on a loser like me."

"Is that when you hit her?"

"I guess. She was up in my face, calling me a loser, a nothing. Swear to God, I didn't mean to hit her. I was just, like, going to shove her, get her out of my face. Soon as I put my hand on her, she started screaming 'Wife-beater. Son-of-a-bitch wife-beater.'" Brian wrapped both hands around his beer bottle. "I hauled off and coldcocked her. God help me, Jules. I just wanted to shut her up and get her out of my face."

My eyes met his. It was the first time in a long time that my brother had been able to look me in the eyes. "Was it the first time you ever hit her?"

"Yeah," he said. "I wanted to before. But that night, I lost it. This sounds like I'm making it up, I know. But I think that's what she wanted me to do. She wanted to start something so I'd finish it."

"Did you?"

"She was still screaming, 'He beat me, he beat me,' and I was afraid she'd wake up Maura with all that screaming, so I grabbed her by the arm and hauled her up off the sofa, where she'd fell when I hit her. She just would not quit screaming, Jules. I put my hands on her neck, just to tell her to shut up."

"You choked her?"

"I didn't get a chance," Brian said. "Next thing I know, I've got what feels like a tire iron up against my head. Whack! Felt like my head was split in two. Then Shay's jumped on me, she's hitting and kicking and scratching. I coulda just shoved her away, but then somebody hits me again, right across the nose. When I came to, I was sitting in the emergency room, with a bloody towel wrapped around my head. The docs came in, looked at me, then I heard one of 'em saying they were gonna file a police report.

"I waited until they went out of the room, and I booked. Hitched a ride back to the apartment, threw my shit in the truck, and took off."

He ran a finger across the bridge of his nose. "The guy broke it good. I get really bad sinus headaches now."

"You have no idea who it was?"

"One of her boyfriends," he said. "Could be anybody."

"You told me before that you thought she was sleeping with her boss. Could it have been Dyson Yount?"

"That little dipshit wuss? No."

"Whoever beat you up, chances are good it was the same person who killed Shay."

"I thought about that," Brian said. "Chuck maybe? Hell, I'm telling you, it coulda been anybody hangs out over there at that Marriott lounge, or that health club Shay went to."

I let my mind drift back to the hospital charts I'd looked at earlier, at the Polaroids the hospital had taken of both the combatants. I wished I'd had the nerve to swipe one of the shots of Shay.

"You only hit her once? She had bruises all over her neck and chest, too," I pointed out.

"Just once."

I could still see the purplish clumps blooming on Shay's chest, her hospital gown pulled down to display them, the gold medallion hanging between her breasts.

"Who gave her the necklace?" I asked idly, wishing again for the photos.

"What necklace?"

"She had on some kind of medallion, on a gold chain around her neck," I said. "Like, maybe, I don't know, one of those astrology medals."

"Not me," Brian said. "I was spending all my money on diapers and day care. Ask one of her boyfriends."

"I will," I said.

25

By the time I got to the drugstore to pick up my film, I was wishing I'd taken Brian up on his offer of a Spam sandwich. Two beers, no food all day, my head was buzzing, my stomach growling. I resisted the call of the snack aisle, paying for an eighteen-ounce Diet Coke, a bottle of ibuprofen, and double prints before hurrying out of the drugstore.

Out in the van, I swallowed four ibuprofen, washed the caplets down with about eight ounces of Diet Coke. The old Callahan Garrity one-two punch for pain and suffering. I spread the photos out on the passenger seat, then got out my heavy-duty flashlight for a quick look.

The color was greenish, the focus imperfect. A photographer I'm not. But they were good enough for government work. Here was Shay's living room, festooned with overflowing ashtrays, unwashed laundry, shoes, toys, and junk mail. The kitchen shots were really fuzzy, but you could get the general idea from the sink full of dirty dishes and the overflowing trash can.

Just as I was getting ready to look at the photos of the bedroom a car door opened beside the van. Four teenagers piled out of a Toyota Celica and instead of going into the store, all four of them hopped on the hood of the car, firing up cigarettes.

Frustrated, I started the van's motor. I'd have to save the other photos for the privacy of my own home.

• • •

I saw Edna's silhouette at the front window as soon as I swung into the driveway. I knew what she was doing. Waiting for Maura.

She met me at the kitchen door. "You heard?" she asked, tight-lipped. "Annette kidnapped Maura."

I patted her arm. "Not kidnapped. Ferd says they just interpreted the judge's order a little too literally. If she's not back in the morning, he'll get the judge to issue an order."

Edna shook her head. "They could be anywhere. She could have left the country. We've got to get a new lawyer. Ferd is useless. He hasn't done a damn thing I asked him to."

I looked around the kitchen, sniffed hopefully. "Anything to eat? I'm starved."

"There's some Brunswick stew in the freezer that you could heat up. I've been too upset to cook. I've been by the phone ever since I got home today."

I pawed through the stuff in the freezer, found a Tupperware dish that looked suspiciously like Brunswick stew. Edna was sitting at the table, dealing herself a hand of solitaire.

"Do I heat it in the microwave or on the stove?"

"Doesn't matter," Edna said. Her fingers flew over the cards, flipping and sliding them into place. If they had been cigarettes, she would have been through half a pack already.

I dumped the stew into a saucepan, turned the burner on low, put the lid on, looked around for something to munch on.

My mother was really in a state. She'd been cleaning. We Garrity women do that when we're anxious. Binge-clean. From the looks of things, it would take an elephant tranquilizer to bring my mother down now. The kitchen reeked of ammonia and bleach. I opened a cupboard. All the cereal boxes and spices and mixes were lined up, big to small. The cans had been stacked in absolute pyramids. Everything was alphabetized and color-coded for God's sake.

I found a box of Ritz crackers and opened it up.

She gave me a sharp look. "Don't you dare drop a crumb on my clean floor."

"OK, Ma," I said, standing with my crackers over the sink. "What is it you want me to do?"

"Find Maura," she said. "Before something bad happens."

I shoved a cracker in my mouth, whole. "Find her, where?" I said, spitting crumbs as I spoke.

"You're a private investigator," she said. "So investigate."

The Brunswick stew was starting to sizzle a little bit. I got a wooden spoon out of the wooden spoon drawer. She'd sorted the drawers out, too. I'd never find anything again. I stirred the stew, watched the frozen lump start to dissipate.

"They could be anywhere," I said. "I've spent the whole day, nosing around down on the south side. I saw Chuck Ingraham around four o'clock. He had a bunch of files and papers. So I doubt they were skipping town."

"She'd leave without him," Edna said. "One man's as good as another to her. I should know."

I looked up sharply from the stew. "What's that supposed to mean?"

She cupped her right hand, slid all the cards off the tabletop with the left, and began shuffling rapid-fire. "Nothing."

"You really hate Annette," I said. "Not just idle hate. Bone-deep. And this is not all about Shay and Brian and Maura, either."

"Mind your own business," Edna said.

"I'd like to."

But I knew when I was licked. I called Brian. After eight or nine rings, a fuzzy-sounding voice answered. "Yeah?"

"Brian, it's me," I said. "Do you have Annette's work number?"

"Shit no," he said.

"Who does she work for?" I asked.

"I dunno."

"Come on," I said sharply. "You said she works security out at the airport. What's the name of the company? Think, OK? I'm trying to find out where she's keeping Maura."

"You think she's keeping Maura at the airport?"

Christ. I'd drunk his last beer, but he'd obviously gone out and bought some more. "No, I don't think that. I just want to call her work and find out if they know where she's been staying since Shay was killed. The cops still haven't let them move back into the apartment."

"Empire. Yeah, Empire Security. You think that'll help?"

"We'll see," I said, and I hung up.

"How's he holding up?" Edna asked.

"He's peachy," I said.

I got Empire Security's number from information, dialed, and got a long selection of voice-mail options. But I stayed on the line long enough and finally got an operator, who gave me Empire's office at Hartsfield International Airport.

My voice sounded crisper than I felt. "Hello," I said, as soon as a man picked up and answered "Empire Security."

"This is Martha Jo Winzeler with the Clayton County Department of Family and Children Services."

"Yes?" His voice was wary. Everybody is afraid of DFACS.

"I'm doing a verification of employment for an Annette Gatlin. Her child custody application states that she is employed by Empire Security. Is that correct?"

"I don't know," the man said. "You'll have to call the main office during the daytime."

"This is for an emergency application of custody," I said severely. "Tomorrow will be entirely too late. Now. Is Annette Gatlin employed by you people?"

"We got 432 people out here, lady," the guy groused.

"Annette Gatlin," I repeated. "I'll hold while you check."

Edna put her cards down and gave me the thumbs up. She's the only mother I know who encourages and supports serial lying.

I heard muttering and the sound of metal cabinets being opened and closed in the background.

"Hang on," the guy said. "I got the Gs here."

"Excellent," I told him.

"Yeah," he said. "We got an Annette Gatlin. Works out at the T Concourse. Been on the job here six years. OK?"

"Not quite," I said. "I'll need to verify her latest address and phone number."

"Shit." He breathed heavily into the phone. "Here." He gave me the address at Twelve Oaks.

"You're sure that's current?" I asked.

"I'm not sure of anything, except it's my break time," he said. "You want the phone number or not?"

He gave me the number. I said thanks and hung up. I handed the piece of paper with the number to my mother.

"Here," I said. "She hasn't given them a new address, but maybe she's had the phone forwarded. You do the rest. I'm hungry."

When the kitchen was filled with the smells of the warm chicken and tomato stew I dumped it into the biggest cereal bowl I could find. If my mother weren't in such a state, she would have fixed me a pan of corn bread to eat with my stew. And a glass of sweet tea. Instead, I got a handful of Ritz crackers and crumbled them into the stew, and finished off my Diet Coke.

Edna picked up the phone and started dialing. She hung it up in a hurry. "Busy," she said.

I got the photographs out of my purse and spread them out on the tabletop.

"What's that?" Edna asked, peering over her bifocals.

"The pictures I took at Shay's apartment. The day we found the body."

"Oh."

I made myself start at the beginning, looking closely at the first shots in the segment again. Living room, dining room, kitchen. I got up, put my dirty dishes in the sink and rinsed them out. Like I needed some kind of purifying ritual before I got down to the nitty-gritty.

Edna was looking at the photos when I got back to the table. Gently, I took the stack out of her hand.

"You don't want to see these," I told her. "They're not nice."

"I'm not a nice lady," she said evenly. "You of all people know that."

There were ten photos taken in the bedroom. The first showed the open door, nearly blocked by a plastic laundry basket heaped with unfolded clothes. I held it up, looked closely. Whoever had killed Shay had done a messy job. The stab wounds I'd seen had been deep, and many. It would have been a bloody awful mess. Had the killer dripped blood on leaving? The carpet was dark in color, blue or gray, and there was a heavy soil track leading from the doorway toward the center of the room. No blood visible in the photographs.

Here was the first photo of Shay. She was facedown, the way we'd found her, hair splayed over her face. Blood spatters on the comforter. I looked at the outflung hand. The fingers were clean. No blood. She'd been attacked in her sleep, on her back. No time for a struggle, probably.

"Mother of God." Edna was standing, looking over my shoulder, breathing heavily through her nose. "Sweet Mother of God," she repeated.

"I told you they weren't nice."

"I'm gonna be sick," she said, rushing from the room.

The next photo showed the rest of the bed and the headboard. Blood splatters on the right side of the white painted headboard and on the wall above it and beside it. Not that much on the comforter though. Whoever had cut her, I decided, had finished the job and then, out of some bizarre sense of fear or shame, covered the body up again with the comforter.

Another close-up of Shay. This one with the sheet pulled down enough to show Shay's back.

Suddenly, I wished I hadn't had that Brunswick stew.

The photos were, quite simply, ghastly. The slim narrow shoulders, pale, outstretched arm, the long tapered neck, all slashed, cuts so deep I could see bone in some places. I gagged, made myself keep looking.

She'd sustained the worst injuries right below the shoulder blade. Deep, slashing puncture wounds. Right through to the heart, I thought. That one, I hoped, had been first. The rest, I hoped, she hadn't been conscious to feel.

There was a deep wound at the base of the neck, another slash, and visible on her scalp, more slashes.

I got up from the table, got a drink of water. I opened the back door, took in a deep breath of the cold, night air. It was damp and slightly sweet. Edna had some kind of bush planted by the back door that bloomed in winter. Not showy, but with tiny white star-shaped flowers, and a fragrance that promised spring would come back. Wherever we'd lived, we'd always had a shrub like that planted by the back door, close to the house so the scent welcomed you when you were going out to hang some wash on the line, or take out the trash.

I allowed myself another lungful of the sweet white flowers, then I went back to look at the Kodachrome awfulness.

There were blood spatters on the left side of the bed too, but not as many. Clearly, Shay's killer had attacked from the right side of the bed. A blood trail lead away from the left side of the bed, though. I leafed through the photos till I found the next one in the segment.

The blood droplets formed a path, to a double dresser with a mirror above it. The droplets were smeared, as though someone had walked back over the trail. There was a closet on the wall next to the dresser, and the blood trail went there, too. Had the killer grabbed something to wipe off the blood? There was no trail leading away from the closet, unless the attacker had backtracked and gone out the way they had entered.

I looked again at the first photos leading into the room. There was no blood trail leading out. Whoever had killed Shay had stopped right there, in the bedroom, to clean her blood from their shoes.

"Are you done?" Edna's voice, weak, coming from the hallway. I looked up, saw her standing there, with a string of rosary beads in her hand. She'd had a sort of religious conversion in the past two years. Since my father died, we've been a family of lapsed Catholics, but two years ago, my mother had brokered some kind of private deal with God. She goes to mass now, but not at any one specific church. Doesn't want any uppity priests trying to tell her how to live her life. She goes just when she feels she needs it. And she does her laps on the beads. Religiously, you might say.

Edna saw me looking at the rosary and stuffed it in the pocket of her sweater. "That poor girl," she said. Her fingers went to her neck. She tugged at the little medal there, the gold St. Francis my father gave her when he knew he was dying. "Whoever did this, I hope they rot in hell."

"Even if it's Brian?"

"It's not Brian."

Edna came back into the kitchen. I took my photos and put them in the envelope from the drugstore. I made myself a bedtime toddy: Jack Daniel's and water and nine or ten ice cubes in a tall iced-tea glass.

My mother dialed the phone again. A malicious smile spread over her face.

"Annette? I know where you're staying," she started.

I waved goodnight. I'd had enough.

26

I called Mac from the line in my bedroom.

"You sleepin'?" I asked gently.

"You'll laugh," he said.

"Good," I said. "After the day I've had, I'm ready for a laugh."

"I'm building something. I've got the sawhorse and the Skilsaw set up in the living room, sawdust everywhere, the dogs are going nuts from the noise."

"What are you building?" I didn't even know he had a Skilsaw—not that I was surprised. Mac loves that kind of guy stuff. Tools and camping and fishing stuff.

"A dollhouse," he said. "For Maura."

"Maura?"

"For Christmas," he said. "I built one for Stephanie when she was six. Nothing fancy. Just a little fixer-upper cottage."

Stephanie was Mac's twenty-year-old daughter.

"A fixer-upper," I said dreamily. "I'd like a fixer-upper myself."

"Come on over to my house, baby," he said. "I'm your handyman." I appreciated the leer in his voice, even if it was showboating and we both knew it.

"Maybe tomorrow night," I said.

"How's it going?"

I told him about my visit with Bucky Deavers, and all the gumshoeing I'd accomplished today. I told him about Annette spiriting Maura away after the funeral and about my unsatisfactory session with my brother the low-rent criminal.

"What's the plan for tomorrow?" he asked. "Anything I can do?"

"The custody hearing is Thursday," I said. "I've got a lot of ground to cover before then."

"Give me something to do," he urged. "You know how government offices are the week before Christmas. Nobody's in their office, no work is getting done. It's all office parties and clandestine shopping trips. So put me to work, will you?"

"You know anybody down in Jonesboro?" I asked.

"I know everybody in Jonesboro," he said. "I work for the Atlanta Regional Commission, remember? Everybody in Clayton County owes me a favor."

"It's payback time," I told him. "You know how to use the records in the clerk's office? Criminal and civil indexes, plaintiff and defendant indexes, all that stuff?"

"I'm very good with clerks," he assured me.

"I'll bet you are. If you could run checks on Annette Gatlin, that would be a help. I want to know if she's ever been in court for anything, including liens, traffic tickets, anything at all. Go back ten years if you've got the time. And while you're at it, since she's living with Chuck Ingraham, do the same kind of check for him."

"Anything else?"

"I'm wondering about Dyson Yount. I heard he's thinking of running for the General Assembly. Brian thinks maybe Shay was sleeping with him. But he thinks Shay was sleeping with Chuck Ingraham, too. It'd take too long to do a complete check on him, and since he's not involved in the custody issue, I think we'll skip it."

"Don't worry about it," Mac urged me. "What counts is Maura."

27

I found Edna on the front porch, her bony butt parked on the morning paper to keep out the damp. She was sipping coffee, watching the lights come on all over the neighborhood.

Old Mr. Byerly's light had been on for hours. His front door popped open and Homer, his Boston terrier, came running out, speeding directly for the forsythia bush at the curb. I could almost hear the dog sigh with relief.

"He'll kill that bush, peeing on it every day," she said.

"I need to talk to you about Brian," I said. She gave me the sports section to sit on, which I took without comment.

"There are things you need to know." I handed her the copy of Brian's arrest report. It wasn't a very nice way to start the day, but there you go.

She saw what the report was, tossed it angrily back at me.

"Why do you keep harping on this stuff? Isn't it enough that he's not dead? He's not in prison someplace?"

"Annette's lawyers have this arrest report," I said. "They're going to use it in court. The cops have it, too."

"Ferd and I have already talked about that," Edna said. "The police haven't arrested Brian, they haven't even questioned him again."

"It's not just about Shay," I said.

"What else has he done?" she asked lightly. "Littering?"

"There are a couple of old, unsolved homicides down around the south side of town. In Atlanta and in Henry County," I started. "Both the victims were young white females. Bucky Deavers told me yesterday, those investigators down in Clayton County think they're connected, that they're the work of a serial killer."

She brightened. "If it was a serial murderer who killed Shay, that proves Brian is innocent. They can find the real murderer, leave Brian alone."

It was cold out on the porch, probably not even forty degrees. And the damp concrete was even colder beneath that sports section I was sitting on.

"It works the other way, too," I said finally. "Lawrence, that homicide investigator in Clayton? He and this retired Atlanta detective named Acey Karpik are trying to get a task force formed. Mom, Bucky says they think Brian is the south-side killer."

She put her coffee mug down so fast it spilled coffee all over the porch, seeping up into the newspaper we were both sitting on.

"For God's sakes!" she cried. "Bucky Deavers. You know him. He knows me. He knows I didn't raise a killer . . . "

"He thinks it's a bunch of bull and so does Lloyd Mackey, Atlanta's homicide commander," I said. "The problem is, Brian fits their idea of who a serial murderer is. All those years of wandering, the petty arrests—"

"He'd never hurt anybody!" Edna cried. "You know that."

"He hit Shay," I said. "I talked to him last night. Mama, Brian has a lot of problems. He drinks too much. He can't hold a job. Shay knew how to punch all his buttons, how to destroy him. He admits he hit her. Just once, but he admits it. And the hospital has Polaroids taken of her the night they had this big fight. Right before Brian left. Annette's got copies of the pictures. I've seen the Polaroids. They're bad."

Her shoulders slumped and she buried her face in her hands. "She'll make out that he's a monster. That he's dangerous or something." She turned to me, pleading. "What can we do?"

"Face facts, for one thing," I said. "Brian will listen to you. I think you should try to talk him into getting some counseling. There's no use in trying to pretend the abuse didn't happen. But if he goes before the judge on Thursday and says he's made some mistakes, and he's getting help—"

"I'll make him go to a therapist," Edna said fiercely. "He'll go if I have to drag him there by the nape of his neck. What else?"

"We've only got two days till the custody hearing," I said. "Two days to prove that it's in Maura's best welfare to be with us and Brian, and that Annette is not a fit guardian. Two days to prove Brian didn't kill Shay or those other women."

Maureen pulled up into the driveway in her new white Suburban at 8 A.M. sharp. She and her husband have no kids and live in a ranch house in Tucker, but they feel the need for a vehicle that could cross the Andes if necessary.

"What's she doing here?" I asked, looking out the kitchen window.

"Ferd says I should have somebody with me when I go to meet Annette to pick up Maura. Sort of a neutral party."

"She's not neutral," I pointed out. "She's your daughter."

Edna ignored that inconvenient fact. "Maureen's got her video camera. That way, she can be filming Annette in case she tries to pull anything funny. We're meeting at the Waffle House down by the airport. I told Annette on the phone last night: You try and pull anything funny, I'll fix it so you never see that child again."

I sighed. "Please don't threaten her. It doesn't help matters any. Why can't Ferd go with you?"

"He's busy," Edna said. "Getting all the stuff ready for court."

The back door opened and Maureen came sailing in. Her cheeks were pink with anticipation. "Ready?" she sang out to Edna.

"Hi," she said when she spotted me, sitting at the kitchen table.

I was still in my gray sweats, which, frankly, needed washing. My hair was standing up in tufts all over my head and I had a pimple forming on the tip of my chin. Maureen had herself all dolled up for the occasion. Red Christmas sweater, red slacks, even a red bow in her hair and little golden Christmas-tree drop earrings. She looked just as cute as pie.

"I can't wait to see Maura," Maureen told me. "Mama says she looks just like I did when I was that age."

"That's funny," I said. "Mom said she looked like me."

Edna got her purse and Maureen, always the suck-up, helped her into her jacket. "Did I?" Edna said innocently. "Oh. You both looked just alike at three."

"Only everybody always said Callahan looked like a little porkpie," Maureen said. "Daddy always called you that, remember? Porky Pig?"

My smile showed many more teeth than were strictly necessary.

"I remember Daddy's name for you," I said sweetly. "Elmer Fudd. 'Cause you were still bald when you were eight years old."

"Now girls," Edna warned.

"No scenes when you pick up Maura," I told Edna. "Be sweet now, you hear?"

After I got Cheezer and the girls dispatched to their jobs, I picked up another box of doughnuts and went back to the Homicide Task Force.

Bucky was not happy to see me.

"I told you I couldn't help you," he said. "Go away before Mackey sees you and starts giving me hell. It looks like we're reopening that Funtown case. Karpik wants me to reopen it."

I threw the envelope of photos from Shay's apartment on his desk. "Take a look at those," I said.

He fanned them out on his desk, went through them once, then again.

"How'd you get these?" he said. "You wanna get me fired?"

"I took them. Remember? I'm the one who found her."

"And you just happened to have a camera loaded with film."

"I went over there hoping to get some shots of the apartment, for the custody hearing. To show the judge what kind of conditions she and Maura were living in," I said. "I'd already shot half the roll before I opened the bedroom door and found the body. When the neighbor went next door to call the cops, I used up the rest of the roll."

"And contaminated a crime scene," Bucky said, disgusted. He pushed the photos onto the floor. "Get these outta here. I don't want to see or know what you did down there."

I gathered the photos off the floor, then sat, uninvited, in the chair by his desk.

"I need to see Clayton County's file on Shay's murder," I said. "I need to see the medical examiner's report and the supplemental and all the crime-scene drawings and photos. And I need copies of your Jane Doe file. Every scrap of it."

"They need ice water in hell, too," Bucky said, crossing his arms over his chest and leaning back in his chair.

"I've got something to trade," I said, smiling serenely.

"You've got nothing," Bucky challenged me. "Besides, you know I don't have access to another department's files. Cripes, especially not Clayton. You know how they are about anything the Atlanta P.D. wants."

"Everybody hates the big dog," I agreed. "But they want to make a big deal of this south-side killer—right? If they want your stuff, they gotta give you theirs."

"Me, not you."

"I can help you with Funtown," I said.

"Because your brother killed her? That's so sick I don't even want to think about it."

"He didn't kill her," I said. "But he recognized her—I think."

"Tell him to come talk to me," Bucky said, unmoved. "This is not a trading situation, Callahan."

"It's gotta be," I said. "Here's the deal. Brian and a bunch of his buddies hung out back then at a country bar called Cowkickers."

"Right there on the corner of Stewart Avenue and Bicksilver," Bucky said. "I used to go in there myself sometimes, when I got off shift. This was pre-Hooters, but the waitresses wore cowboy boots and these little cutoff blue jeans. Booty shorts they called them—"

"I'm sure they were attractive and elegant," I said, interrupting his fond memories. "I showed Brian the composite of your Jane Doe. He thinks he remembers seeing her somewhere down there."

This was an exaggeration, of course. What Brian remembered was vague, his memory fogged by all the beers and the years.

Bucky didn't know that. He was beginning to show signs of interest. "Did he say she was a hooker?"

"Did anybody from the medical examiner's ever try to come up with a drawing of how she'd have looked before the murder?"

I took out my copy of the drawing of Jane Doe.

"Where'd you get that?" he demanded.

"There were a lot of spares in the file," I said.

"I'm gonna have to frisk you every time you leave this damn office," Bucky said.

"This was done ten years ago," I reminded him. "Before a lot of the computer enhancements and digital imaging stuff was going on. You know, like computer special effects?"

"You been watching too much MTV," Bucky said. "This is Atlanta, not Hollywood. Who do you think the city has on payroll with those kinds of skills? We barely have radios that work. Hell, I pay for my own cell phone."

"I've got a client in the cell phone business," I said idly. "He gives me and the girls a corporate rate. Unbelievable, and it's all peak-hour stuff, too."

"How nice for you," Bucky said gloomily. "Bell South sticks it to me in the shorts every month."

"I could sign you on as one of my company units," I offered. "Mac's already on there. So is my sister Maureen."

"This is what you're trading me? Cell phone deals?"

I put the photos back on his desk. "I'm working a theory on Shay's murder. I've got to have access to that apartment, and to the file. Also to your Jane Doe file. If I figure anything out, I'll turn it all over to you, Bucky, swear to God. I just wanna help clear my brother, I'm not interested in being a hero."

"What's the theory?"

"Maybe Karpik's right. Maybe the south-side killer and Shay are connected. Not by my brother, though. Something down there at Funtown."

He nodded. "Was Shay Gatlin ever known to hang out down there?"

"I don't know," I said truthfully. "That's why I want to see the old witness lists and stuff, maybe see if anything matches up."

"You can't go around interviewing new witnesses," Bucky said. "See, that's why I can't give you these files. You'll go in there and kick up a lot of stuff and L. D. Lawrence will chew Mackey's ass and he'll chew mine."

"All right," I said. "I won't talk to anybody without talking to you first. You can go with me. You can ask the questions."

"That's pretty noble of you, considering that's my job in the first place," Bucky said.

I threw my hands up in the air. "For God's sake. Are you gonna do this or not? I got two days, and the meter's running."

He opened a drawer in his desk, slid out two files, handed them over to me. One was the Funtown paperwork, the other was copies of the paperwork on Shay Gatlin. He'd meant to give them to me all the time, was just yanking my chain for the hell of it. And there wasn't a damn thing I could do about it.

I opened Shay's file, started looking for the photos. They were in a separate folder. I slid them out, and turned them over, one by one. I was looking for a face-up photo. When I found it, I wished I hadn't.

Bucky looked over my shoulder. "Pretty girl. Somebody was mad at her."

Blood from the chest wound had pooled and smeared and dried across her chest. The blood had dripped around to the front of her neck and dried as thick brownish ribbons. I held the photo and looked closely. Got out my own photo and looked at it for comparison.

"That's funny," I told Bucky.

"What?"

I tapped the frontal view photo of Shay. "Look at all the blood on her neck and chest."

"Yeah. Some of those knife wounds went clean through. Definitely a passion killing." He picked up another document in the file. The medical examiner's report. He winced. "They found the tip of the knife embedded in her shoulder blade. The killer used such force, the knife tip broke off."

If I'd had Edna's rosary beads I would have said a decade myself, right there. Instead I tapped my index finger on the hollow of Shay's throat. It was covered with blood, except for one small, dime-shaped spot on her throat.

"Where's the blood?" I asked.

He looked at me. "It's everywhere. You want more blood?"

"No," I said, tapping the dime-shaped spot again. "Something's missing. She had a chain. With a medallion. See. She must have been wearing it when she was attacked. The blood pooled around it, but not under it."

"I don't see how you get that," Bucky said.

"She had a necklace," I insisted. "She was wearing it the night she and Brian had the fight, and she went to the emergency room. I saw it in the hospital files, Bucky. A gold medallion on a thin chain. Brian said he'd never seen it before."

Bucky took Shay's file from me, leafed through until he found a typed report. Now it was me looking over his shoulder.

It was the property and evidence list. Everything the police had found in the bedroom where Shay was killed was listed, down to the empty beer cans in the wastebasket, the coat hangers in her closet, the dirty clothes on her floor.

"No necklace," I said, skimming to the bottom.

"Maybe she wasn't wearing it," Bucky said.

"Maybe the killer took it."

28

Bucky called L. D. Lawrence on the speakerphone, so I could listen in on their conversation. I'd begged him to take me back to Shay's apartment, to walk through and get a closer look at the crime scene, but he was having none of it.

"L.D.?" Bucky said smoothly. "How y'all doin' down there? Uncovered any more serial murderer victims?"

"You're a riot, Deavers," Lawrence said sourly. "What do you want?"

"I've got Callahan Garrity here in my office," Bucky said. "She's brought some new information to my attention. Thought she could share it with the, uh, task force."

"What information?" Lawrence said. "You got civilians working your cases for you now?"

"I'm looking over the property list taken from the apartment at Twelve Oaks," Bucky said. "I'm on the page of stuff taken from the bedroom. Here it is: three boxes women's clothing, two boxes women's shoes, one box toys, ashtray, half pack of cigarettes, some gum wrappers, a woman's gold watch, a Diet Pepsi can, jewelry box, tube of black mascara—"

"Yeah, I remember the list," Lawrence said, yawning loudly. "What about it?"

"No necklace?" Deavers asked, "Kinda gold chain, with like, a little medal or something on it?"

"Christ," Lawrence muttered. "I don't remember nothing like that. Let me get the list. I know we returned a jewelry box of some kind to Shay Gatlin's mother. How's this got anything to do with Garrity?"

"Tell you in a minute," Deavers said. "You see any mention of it? Maybe I overlooked it?"

Deavers was Mr. Tact. Mr. Charm. "Thought maybe it was in the jewelry box. You said you returned the jewelry box to the mother. But nobody inventoried what was in there?"

"Tuohy did the evidence processing," Lawrence said. "You'd have to ask him about a necklace. I don't remember seeing one. Certainly not on the victim. She was nude. No wedding ring, no necklace, nothing.

I remembered Tuohy. The gym rat.

"Here's the thing," Bucky said. "Brian Garrity's lawyers have dug up a Polaroid photo taken of Shay Garrity in September, when she was admitted to the Emergency Room at Southside General. In that photo, she's wearing a little gold necklace. The husband claims to know nothing about it. Of course, he moved out right after the assault. But now, the other thing Garrity noticed on the crime-scene photos—"

"Who showed her those?" Lawrence demanded. "Are you fuckin' nuts? I'm calling your commander. Those are confidential police files, Deavers."

"Hi, Detective Lawrence," I said brightly. "It's not Deavers's fault. See, I noticed, on the photo showing the close-up of Shay, and there's this little dime-shaped place in the hollow of her throat. I—uh, we— were thinking, maybe she was wearing that necklace when she was killed. There's this one little place on her skin that looks like it was sort of masked from the blood? But the property list doesn't say anything about a necklace. And I don't remember seeing one on Shay when I found her body. Deavers was saying, maybe it was removed postmortem. By the killer."

"Like a souvenir?" Lawrence liked the idea. I didn't have to tell him it fit in neatly with his serial killer theory. "I've seen cases like that," he admitted. "Let me talk to Tuohy, see if he remembers a necklace. Of course, if our suspect took it, he's long since gotten rid of it, especially since his sister the detective was so obliging as to tell him about it."

"I did ask him about it," I volunteered. "Didn't think there was any harm, since none of your detectives noticed the necklace. My brother believes one of Shay's boyfriends gave her the necklace. He'd never seen it before. I believe him."

Deavers nodded, kept on leafing through the file, like he was just now getting around to that. He sorted through the bedroom photographs, looked closely at the photos of Shay. We could hear Lawrence waiting, impatiently, on the other end of the line.

"No signs the victim had recent sexual activity?" Deavers asked. "No sign of a struggle? Reason I ask is, my Jane Doe at Funtown, the coroner thought she'd had sex recently. I'm hearing the same thing about the victim in Henry County, too. A pattern, you know?"

"Could be," Lawrence said.

Bucky looked back in the file. "Nothing in the files I was given about any signs of sexual trauma," he said, pulling out the medical examiner's report. "But you looked at all that in the autopsy, right?"

"Right," Lawrence said.

"Hey." Bucky put his finger on a line on the medical examiner's report. "Says here they found signs of recent sexual activity. What's that supposed to mean? Was there semen or not?"

I hugged myself tightly. Brian would not have raped his own wife. If Shay had sex shortly before she was killed, it had to have been with someone else.

"There were swabs done," Lawrence said finally.

"And?"

"Let's wrap this up. I gotta be in court in thirty minutes, and I ain't had lunch."

"Come on, Lawrence," Bucky said. "This is a task force, right? Those other two unsolved, including my Jane Doe, we're thinking they're sex crimes. I need to know what you've got on your end."

"There was semen," Lawrence admitted. "It's at the crime lab. You know how long it takes to get results." He laughed. "We've called the ex-husband. Brian Garrity. Asked him to make a little deposit at the sperm bank. See if it matches up."

"What about other suspects?" I demanded. "Shay Garrity was no saint. Even the next-door neighbor could tell you that. She had an active, quote, 'dating life.' They were having a party over there the night Shay was killed. Mrs. James told me she had to threaten to call the cops to get them to quiet down that night. Why don't you ask Chuck Ingraham for a sample? He was living right here in the same apartment. Or her boss, Dyson Yount. Why not get a sperm sample from him?"

Lawrence laughed. "Yeah, I'll just do that next time I see him. Hey, Mr. Yount, Mr. Pillar of the Community. You got a minute? Get a life Garrity, and get outta my case."

"This case concerns me," Bucky said, shooting daggers at me. "I'd like to see copies of all the crime lab reports as soon as they come in," he said.

"Yeah, all right," Lawrence said. "Whatever. Only keep Nancy Drew out of it, OK? Her brother's a suspect."

Bucky hung up and shook his head. "You couldn't keep quiet, could you? Now you've made everything worse. Lawrence already didn't trust you. Now he thinks I'm running to you with confidential case information."

"I'm sorry," I said. "But I can't believe they were trying to withhold the stuff about the sexual activity. Lawrence knows that changes everything. Of course, I figured Shay had been screwing somebody. But it didn't dawn on me, the DNA testing and all that. God. This could be the one thing that clears Brian. And ties all these cases together."

"Unless he'd been screwing her, too," Bucky said.

"They were separated. Barely speaking," I said.

"You think ex-wives don't sleep with their ex-husbands?" Bucky asked, snorting at my naïveté.

I blushed. I was thinking back to a couple of years ago, when I found out, first person, that Mac had slept with his ex-wife. It was only one time, but it nearly killed our relationship—put a strain on it that we almost didn't overcome. Since then I've learned that certain marriages have a boomerang effect. The partners occasionally reunite sexually when it's the last thing they really want or need.

"Brian wasn't there that night," I told him. "I showed his picture to the next door neighbor. She said she hadn't seen him there."

"Have you checked his alibi? Personally?"

"Not yet," I admitted. "Brian told me that he worked late the night Shay was killed. Picked up his paycheck, went to move into his new trailer, and the power wasn't on. The phone wasn't working. He got a pizza and went to bed."

"You talked to his boss?" Bucky asked.

"Not yet." It was embarrassing to admit.

"He works construction, right? Somewhere around here?"

"I've got the phone number," I said.

"Might want to do that," he said.

"I will."

He stood up and got his coat from a hook on the wall. "Wanta take a ride with me?" he asked.

"Something to do with Shay's murder?" I asked. "Or is this just a food run?"

He tried to look casual. "I called the crime lab yesterday. To see what happened to the evidence from the Funtown homicide. They kept the stuff a couple years, then shipped it back to A.P.D. It should be in the property room. Thought I'd take a look. Just, you know, see if there's something Karpik missed the first time around."

29

Thank God for computers. Bucky gave the clerk the case file number, then stood at the counter to fill out the paperwork while the property clerk went to look for an eleven-year-old bag of evidence.

Ten minutes later she came wheeling around the corner with a gray plastic cart like the kind they use to bus dishes in restaurants. Two large brown paper sacks rested on the cart. Somehow, this wasn't the kind of take-out I was expecting.

We took the bags back to the homicide office. Bucky got a pair of disposable rubber gloves from a drawer in his desk and handed a pair to me. He unsealed the bag and spilled the contents out onto his desktop.

The necklace fell out first. Wrapped in a small plastic bag, with its own evidence number. Bucky picked it up, unwrapped it, and handed it to me.

The chain was gold, cobweb fine, maybe sixteen inches long. The medallion was one of those hollow, lopsided hearts that you see advertised around Valentine's Day. It was cheap, the gold rubbed off on the edges. I dangled it from the fingers of my left hand, let it catch the weak late afternoon sunlight.

"I had a necklace like this in the seventh grade," I told Bucky. "My best friend and I bought them, just alike, at a jewelry store at the mall. I bet we paid ten bucks apiece for them. Mine gave me a rash my mother swore was ringworm. I wonder what ever happened to it?"

"Dunno," Bucky said. "I've still got my I.D. bracelet from eighth grade. Genuine stainless steel." He picked his way through the rest of Jane Doe's belongings. A plastic Ziploc bag contained a dirty white rag that would have been Jane's T-shirt. Bucky spread the fragile white fragment out flat on the desktop. The knit neckband was intact with the print on the label—Beefy-T, Size M—faded but readable, but the rest was a shred. The blue jeans, in a separate bag, were in just as fragile. The jeans label said Sergio Valenti. They were a size five.

He opened the other evidence bag. There was a faded foil wrapper—for a condom. Trojan, ribbed. "That's one of the things made them think maybe she was a hooker," Bucky said, nodding at the condom. "It was in the jeans pocket."

A white canvas tennis shoe, the bottom tread nearly worn out, the canvas stained and muddy. In yet another plastic bag was a faded paper card with MARTA written across the front.

"Were they able to do anything with the MARTA card?" I asked.

"You kidding?" Bucky said. "MARTA sells thousands of those cards every week. No telling where it was bought, or by who, or where it was used, or anything else. All it says is that maybe our Jane Doe took a train or a bus, somewhere in Atlanta, some time."

"Might explain how she got to Funtown," I pointed out.

"They thought of that," Bucky said, reading through the detective's supplementary reports. "They checked at every bus stop within a two-mile radius of the area where the body was found. Showed the drawing to bus drivers, other commuters, anybody who worked or even drove by a bus stop. Nothing."

I fingered the waistband of the jeans. "Did they test the clothes, you know, for blood or semen or anything?"

"We didn't have DNA testing back then, remember?" He turned the page of the report he was reading. "Blood on the shirt was 0-positive," he said. "Nothing found on the jeans, but you can see how they are. That body was exposed to the elements for at least a week."

"Where is her underwear?" I asked.

He looked up at me. "They never found any. Not on the body, not in the area. That was another thing that made them categorize it as a sex crime."

"Doesn't look like a lot to go on here," I said, gesturing toward the evidence spread across his desktop.

"There's a couple things we can do," Bucky said. "The technology's better now. We can take the photograph of Jane Doe, put it on the Internet and stuff like that. I've got a call in to Kelly Pike, over at the GBI crime lab, to see if there's any new tests they can run on the remains, anything we missed the first time around. Henry County is supposed to be doing the same thing with their victim."

I cupped the gold chain in my hand. "This girl, the victim in Henry County, and Shay Gatlin. Murdered more than ten years apart. Totally different circumstances. You really think it could be the same perp?"

"Your brother is the main link," he said. "We both know that. And it's a tentative link. Personally, I think Acey Karpik is seeing things that aren't there. But I haven't seen the case files from Henry yet. Karpik's coordinating all that. He told me he just wants me concentrating on the Funtown victim. Major Mackey says we're all supposed to have a sit-down, next Monday. Hash all this stuff out.

"Lawrence is convinced your brother is our perp," Bucky said calmly. "If I were you, I'd check your brother's alibi. Make sure it's solid. If Lawrence and Karpik can match him up with the semen from his ex-wife, he's up shit creek."

The sign promoting Scarborough Faire promised it would be an Impressive and Elegant Community of Estate Homes from $275,000. Right now Scarborough Faire looked like a big ugly gash in the road, with a rash of newly poured concrete foundations. I followed the gravel construction road around to a group of trailers that housed the developer's offices and found Randy Prior, the project supervisor, in the trailer marked Scarborough Properties, Inc.

I opened the door, stuck my head in. He was on the phone. "I'm Callahan Garrity," I whispered. "Brian's sister."

He motioned for me to come in and take a seat. The only other one in the trailer was a metal folding chair.

Prier was chewing somebody out on the other end of the line for trying to sell him a load of bad lumber. "Hell, that stuff was nothing but knots and warps. You call that finish grade white pine? I didn't even let the driver unload it. Send me another load of crap like that and we're done. I'll take my business to Ply Mart."

He hung up the phone, folded his hands in front of him, like a pupil about to be called on in school.

"What can I do you for?" he asked. "Brian's not here. He had an errand to run. Said he'd be back around four. Your brother's a hell of a guy. I think he's been getting a bad deal out of this whole thing with his ex. Hear you're trying to help him out."

"I'm trying," I said. "But Brian's pretty private. Doesn't like to answer a lot of questions. He's always been like that."

"Can I give him a reference, something like that?" Prier asked. "I told him, whatever you need, buddy, you got it. Just say the word."

"Have the police been around to talk to you?" I asked. "About Saturday?"

"Oh yeah," Prier said. He opened a drawer of his desk, took out a business card and showed it to me. "Detective Lawrence. I told him how the girl in bookkeeping had screwed up Brian's paycheck. He came in on Saturday, did some stuff on the site here, and then, when we found his check, it didn't have the overtime he'd worked. He was pretty insistent about getting the overtime money, 'cause he was moving into a new place. He'd been counting on it."

"Was he upset about the check?" I asked.

Prier laughed. "He wasn't happy. There was no place around where he could get his check cashed. I ended up taking him to the instant teller at my own bank and getting him five hundred in cash out of my personal account. If we'd waited on bookkeeping, it would have been another two weeks before he got his money."

"Do you remember what time he left here that day?" I asked.

"Late," Prier said. "I remember it was already dark. Must have been after six. I helped Brian put some scrap lumber in the back of his truck. He wanted to make some bookshelves at the new place. He said he'd see me Monday, and he left."

"You know where he was going?"

"Probably to finish moving into the new place," Prier said. "He had some of his stuff in the back of the truck when he came in that day. A mattress, some furniture, that kind of stuff."

"Where had he been living before?" I asked.

"What do you mean?"

"Between the time he and Shay broke up and the time he moved into the trailer," I said. "Before last Friday."

Prier blinked. "I don't know. He, uh, I guess he was staying with friends."

"He didn't give you the address?"

Prier swiveled his chair around so that it faced a metal file cabinet behind his desk. He pulled out a drawer, found a file folder, pulled it halfway out, and took out a single sheet of paper. He read it, put it back.

"Last address was the one over there on Tara Boulevard," he said. "Probably slipped his mind, about giving me his new address. Sometimes the guys do that, when they're in between places. You know, record-keeping, that's not what you're worrying about when you're pouring concrete."

"The friend he was staying with, was that somebody who worked here with him?"

"Sorry," Prier said, "I don't know. It's a big site."

And Brian was famous for keeping himself to himself.

"Saturday night, after he left here, Brian said he went to a pizza place. You know which one that might have been?"

Prier shrugged. "Afraid I'm not a lot of help. I don't eat pizza. Allergic to the cheese. But the guys have a place somewhere near here they go. Place delivers to the site. Not many restaurants will do that."

"There's a shopping center about a mile from here," I said, retracing the route I'd taken. "There's an Italian restaurant in there. Could that be the place?"

"Sounds right," Prier said. "They only get forty-five minutes for lunch, so they can't go too far when they do leave the site."

The phone rang. He put his hand on the receiver, looked up at me. "Anything else?"

"Shay," I said. "Brian says she came down here, more than once, looking for her child support money. Is that true?"

Prier made a face. "The lady was a piece of work. Embarrassing as hell for Brian. She showed up Friday afternoon, an hour before quitting time. Brian was helping frame up the roof for the Scarborough Faire model. She stood over there and screamed at him. Called him a deadbeat, accused him of running out on his kid. If it had been me, I'd have dropped a hammer on the lady's head."

He picked up the phone, said, "Hold on a minute." He covered the receiver with his right hand.

"How did Brian act?"

"Furious," Prier said. "He tried to tell her he couldn't get to the bank to cash his check. The bank up on the corner is the one the company does business with, so they cash his check as a courtesy to us. Brian told her she'd just have to wait. That made her even madder. She come stomping in here, demanding that I cash her husband's check right then and there, because if I didn't, she was gonna have his wages garnisheed. He come in right behind her, told her to get the hell out before she got him fired. Finally, I told him go cash it right now."

I winced. It sounded like an ugly, ugly scene.

Prier paused. "She took the money, counted it, like he might short her or something. Then she told him he couldn't see the baby that Saturday, 'cause she was taking her out of town. What a bitch! Good-looking woman, I'll admit. But the mouth on her? I've got guys on my crews don't talk as bad as that. And I'm talking journeymen plumbers and electricians. You talk worse than a plumber, you got a mouth on you."

The pizza place around the corner was called Mario's. A Vietnamese guy sat at the cashier's desk by the front door, watching the television mounted above the bar. The Home Shopping Network was running a Christmas special on women's silk pantsuits. The Vietnamese guy looked fascinated.

I pulled out the picture of my brother, asked him if he'd seen him in there before.

"This guy." The Vietnamese shrugged. "Cops come in here asking about this guy. I say, we get a lotta guys work around here." There was a pencil stuck behind his ear. He looked at the TV screen, jotted something down, and looked back at the pantsuit parade.

"Did he come in here?" I repeated. "Last Saturday night? Sometime after six?"

"Yeah," the cashier said. "Probably. I tell the cops yes. He here alla time. I think he like pizza pretty good. Beer, too."

The Vietnamese guy couldn't tell me definitely what time my brother had come in that night, or what time he'd left, only that he thought he'd seen him. It was better than nothing.

I still needed to talk to the manager of the trailer park to check out Brian's story about how the trailer wasn't ready when he went to move in the previous week, and how the power hadn't been hooked up.

The park manager lived in a white double-wide that had a set of peeling wooden columns tacked on either side of the aluminum front door. Taped to the door was one of those signs with the clock hands. Back at six, it said. The office sign had a phone number on it. I wrote it down, got back in my car, and headed north toward home.

Neva Jean's car was already in the driveway, Cheezer's mail truck parked beside it. Both of them were in the garage, refilling their caddies with supplies.

"Long day, huh?" Neva Jean asked, eyeing my bedraggled state. I'd put on wool slacks and a good tweed blazer that morning, but that seemed like a lifetime ago now. My silk blouse had a spot of doughnut grease on the front, I'd chewed off any lipstick, pushed my hands through my hair a hundred times out of the sheer frustration of running into so many dead ends.

"You gotta let me help," Neva Jean said. "Come on, Callahan. Let me do a little snooping. I'm subtle. You know that."

She was as subtle as the gallon of ammonia she was loading onto her cart, but maybe this one time, subtle didn't count.

"OK," I said. I got my billfold out of my purse, handed her two twenties. "I need some info on Shay and Annette. Brian insists they liked to party a lot. There's a Marriott over by the airport. He says they hung out in the lounge over there. And a health club somewhere. It's down near their apartment, on Tara Boulevard. It'll be one of those ones that cater to singles—you know, with a bar and the whole works. Get me the real deal. Who they come in with, who they leave with. Names, dates, everything. See if you can find out if they were out partying last Saturday night. Shay's neighbor said they were making a lot of racket at the apartment, but maybe they started out at the bars and took somebody home with them."

I gave her a snapshot of Shay and Annette that Brian had given me. It had been taken at Maura's first birthday party. Maura was in a high chair, wearing a silly pink party hat with elastic under her chin, birthday cake smeared all over her face. One day she'd hate them for making her wear that hat. "Don't lose that picture," I warned. "It's the only one I've got."

Neva Jean ruffled the bills under Cheezer's nose. "Expense money," she trilled. "Nothing spends like expense money."

"Don't spend it all in one place," I warned.

Cheezer finished reloading his cleaning caddy. Squared his shoulders.

"I want to help, too," he said. "Remember, you said I'm a pretty good guy in a pinch."

I shoved my hands in the pocket of my blazer, considering.

"Ever been to Funtown?" I asked.

30

Sometimes I forget about my gun. Mostly, I don't need it to run the House Mouse. Bleach, yes; firearm, no. But occasionally the need arises. Then I have to remember the last place I hid the darned thing, which is a Smith & Wesson 9 mm.

I went into my bedroom and opened the jewelry box on my dresser. Since I never throw anything away, the box is loaded with all my old junk jewelry, mixed up with the very few pieces of good stuff, most of which Mac has given me as gifts over the years. I wondered again about the heart-shaped chain from seventh grade. What had happened to it? On the bottom of the jewelry box I found what I was looking for. A bunch of keys, mostly to locks I no longer own.

The strongbox was on the top shelf of my closet, inside a suitcase. I unlocked the suitcase, then the strongbox. The clip for my S&W was inside, along with my lucky two-dollar bill and the title to my new van.

The 9 mm. itself was in a tiny floor safe I'd had installed in the back of my closet, after I became neurotic about hiding the gun in the oatmeal box in the kitchen. I put the two-dollar bill in my billfold, so my luck would be closer. Also I put the clip in the pistol, just in case the luck was slow.

Cheezer was behind the wheel of the van, the motor running. He was wearing his black leather Harley-Davidson jacket and a black knit cap, your traditional burglar topper. It was only the second time I've seen him wearing a jacket. Cheezer has the basal body temperature of a polar bear. He's never cold.

"I'll drive, OK?" he asked eagerly.

"Please," I said, groaning as I got back in the front seat.

He got as far as the corner of Oakdale, my street, and McClendon. "Now where?"

"You've never been to Funtown?"

"Never even heard of it before. How do I get there?"

"Take Moreland to I-20 west, get off on Stewart Avenue. Look close. You'll see the old Funtown sign on the right." I glanced over at him. "Are you really that young?"

He grinned.

"Or am I really that old?"

"No comment," Cheezer said.

It had gotten dark. All the headlights on all the cars on the interstate twinkled festively as drivers fumed and cussed at the unseen annoyance slowing their trip home.

I closed my eyes to take a short rest. Cheezer switched on the radio. A rock band was playing. The group included a bass viola and a piano and the singer's voice was pleasant and the lyrics told a story I could understand. "What is that?" I asked Cheezer.

"Ben Folds Five," he said, humming along. "You like?"

"Yeah, I do. Sounds almost like music."

"See, you're not that old."

"Callahan. Uh, is this it?"

I yawned, stretched, and blinked my eyes open. He'd pulled into the parking lot at the old bowling alley at Funtown.

"This is it," I said. I reached over and pushed the power-lock button, put my fully loaded pocketbook in my lap.

Cheezer nodded knowingly at the pocketbook. "Are we really going to need that?"

"Sure," I told him. "My lucky two-dollar bill is in there."

"Where's the amusement park?" he asked. "Didn't you say it used to be kind of like Six Flags?"

"Actually, it was more like one of those roadside carnivals they used to have down at Panama City when I was a kid," I said. "But that was before Six Flags. Before DisneyWorld. We didn't know it was cheesy and third-rate. It's been closed a long time. Probably close to thirty years."

I directed him out of the parking lot, told him to take a right, turn on the brights, and take it slow.

As soon as we started rolling down the access road we saw figures in the headlights. A hooker and her trick, strolling arm in arm down the middle of the cracked, trash-strewn road. She was tall, black, with marcelled Jean Harlow hair and toothpick legs dangling out of a red leather skirt so short it was really more like a belt. He was shorter, whiter, fatter, with a baseball cap pushed to the back of his head. He had one arm wrapped around her, the other held onto a quart bottle of malt liquor. They stopped when they saw the van's headlights. Stood there, watching, to make sure we weren't cops, then lurched away.

Cheezer rolled the window down an inch. "Get a room!" he hollered.

We saw two more couples emerge from the woods as we made our way toward the entrance to the old park, another black hooker and white john, and then a short, fat redheaded transvestite with a black teenager so stoned she had to pull him along to get him to walk.

We parked the van where the road ran out.

"Now what?" Cheezer wanted to know. He had both arms stretched across the steering wheel, leaning forward, looking around at all the wildlife.

I told him about Jane Doe, a pretty, slender blonde hooker who'd been knifed to death, her body left hidden under a mattress here at Funtown. I told her my brother Brian thought maybe he'd seen the girl at a nearby nightclub, and that some retired cop had a notion that three blonde girls, one here, one in Henry County, and the other, my sister-in-law, had all been victims of the same killer.

"Except for Shay, this was all a long time ago," I told Cheezer. "You were probably still in Little League."

I tucked the pistol into my jacket pocket and got out of the van. He got out, too, and stood close beside me, his hands tucked into his jacket pockets, his long brown ponytail whipping about in the breeze blowing through the tall pines.

"I never played Little League," he said.

"Soccer, then," I said.

"No sports, nothing normal like that."

He'd never heard of Funtown. Didn't play sports. What did I know about this kid who knew so much about so many different things? Almost nothing. That was the way he seemed to want it.

"What did you do when you were a kid?" I asked. "You weren't one of those library dweebs, were you?"

"Never had a library card in my whole life until I went to Georgia Tech," he said. "Where were all the rides? Was this a cool place?"

I pointed out the wading pool to him. "That was for the babies." Even in the dark you could see the peeling, turquoise paint. "There was a miniature golf course back there," I said, pointing toward the entrance. "There were these concrete dinosaurs you had to hit the ball through. Sort of a Flintstones rip-off, I guess. Over there," I pointed toward the back of the park, "they had the Tilt-A-Whirl. And that," I pointed toward the left, "was the roller coaster. The Wild Mouse. Used to be, you could see the old wooden tracks from the interstate. It was here for a long time after they closed the park down."

"A mouse? Sounds kinda tame," Cheezer said.

"Oh, honey," I told him. "You've obviously never seen a cornered mouse. This ride was great. High and tight, and you'd come whipping out of the curves in a loop-the-loop and for five seconds you thought you were safe, then you'd swoop right up again and plunge down so fast you thought you might scream till your tonsils fell out."

I got my flashlight out of the van, and we walked slowly around the perimeter of the ruined park. Small animals, possums, probably, scurried in the dried leaves, and the wind rattled in the treetops, blowing pine needles down on our heads.

He was fascinated with the huts. As I swung my flashlight over them, we could see three of them clustered close together. The abandoned car I'd seen on my last trip had its motor running, but this time there was no moonshine drum. I pointed at it. "What do you think they're doing?"

Cheezer laughed, pointed at one of the sheds, where a small glow of light was discernible from behind the window layer of discarded wall-to-wall carpet. He pointed at the cables snaking out from the car's battery toward the shacks. "They're generating electricity," he said, laughing. "Pretty damn clever."

"What would the big drums be for?" I asked. He glanced around the clearing until he spotted one. "Either they were steeping tea or they were heating hot water," Cheezer said. "See the fire hydrant over there? They've left it open so they can have running water." He nodded his head in appreciation. "Decent little set-up they got here."

I shivered and pulled my coat tighter around my neck. "All the comforts of home," I said. "Come on, I'll show you something not as cozy."

Jane Doe's remains had been found at the back of the park, behind the building that had once housed the bathrooms. Ten years later, all that was left was a three-foot-high concrete block wall. I played the flashlight over the mound rising in back of the wall. Somebody had decided the spot made a good trash dump. Old tires, paint cans, a chunk of concrete that looked like it might once have been the head of a Tyrannosaurus rex, several car batteries.

"How was she killed?" Cheezer said, his voice very still.

"Multiple stab wounds to the face and neck," I said. "The body was here at least a week. They got lucky finding it. The girl killed down in Henry County? Her body had been out in a field for at least a year when they found her remains."

He shrugged. "Probably some whore."

"Could be," I said. "There've been hot sheet joints up and down this street for years. You ever hear of the Alamo Pass?"

"Isn't there a place here on Stewart Avenue? I've seen it before and wondered about it. The front is fake stucco, looks kind of like the real Alamo?"

"That was the place," I said. "When I was a patrol officer, I can't tell you how many times I responded to calls at the Alamo. Some Friday nights, you could ride down Stewart Avenue, see the guys lined up outside the rooms. The place got so notorious the city finally closed it down a couple years ago. It's supposedly been cleaned up now. They don't even call it Alamo Pass any more."

We turned around and were walking back toward the van. The wind ruffled my hair and I turned up the collar of my jacket. What were we doing out here?

"At the time, the cops figured Jane couldn't afford a room the night she died. Not even twenty-five dollars for the Alamo. Girl couldn't afford a room, she'd bring a trick back in here. Funtown, right?"

"If she didn't do the guy in the car," Cheezer said. He kicked at a pinecone, sent it scudding into the underbrush.

I played the flashlight around again. "Somebody around here knew her," I said. "She had a name. Somebody must have known it. Hookers are territorial. They like the same bars, the same street corners—"

"The same backseats," Cheezer said. His face was expressionless. "The same fuckin' losers they shack up with, the same rat-hole apartments, all the same excuses. If she had a name, I bet nobody cared."

I thought about that gold chain with the lopsided heart back in the evidence locker. "Somebody cared. Once."

There was a flicker of movement from one of the shacks. A curtain lifted, then dropped.

"We're being watched," Cheezer said. "You think these guys are dangerous?"

I let my hand rest on my gun. "Probably not."

I made a lot of noise approaching the main shack. Its occupant had been admirably inventive when it came to setting up housekeeping. Three of the concrete blocks from the concession stand had been pried out of their mortar, and now stood as a front porch for the largest of the plywood shacks.

I played my flashlight over the front of the shack. In black spray paint, someone had written The Chamber. I took a step backward. Had I stumbled into some coven of homeless role-players?

A door opened, a man emerged. His hair was shoulder-length, matted with dirt, nearly hiding a gaunt, filthy face. He wore orange zip-front coveralls, the prison issue kind.

He stood in his doorway, arms crossed. "You the police?"

"Me? No. Uh, how you doing?"

"What you want out here? We ain't breaking no law."

Cheezer walked up beside me. "I like your house," he said, gesturing at the shack. The young can be so guileless. "How come it says The Chamber?"

The orange-suited man shrugged. "Happens I'm a John Grisham fan. Read the book over at the Labor Pool. *The Chamber*—you get it?"

I got it, even if Cheezer did not. "Have you lived here a long time?" I asked.

He shrugged. "Since the Olympics. City made us move out from the I-75 underpass. Bunch of us, we found this place. Some fellas from Tech, they helped us fix it up."

"The Madhousers?" Cheezer asked.

"You know those boys?" The Chamber's owner asked.

"I knew one of them at Tech," Cheezer said.

"They're the ones give us the cable and stuff to wire up. And they bring us the gas for the car every week, so we can run the generator," he said.

I'd brought out the picture of Jane Doe, but it was useless to show it to him. He saw it in my hand. "What you got there?"

I showed it to him. "It's a picture. Of a young girl. Her body was found here ten years ago. She'd been killed, the body dumped. We're trying to find out who she was, who killed her."

He frowned. "Thought you said you weren't cops."

"We're not," I assured him. "It's personal."

"We don't need cops back in here," he said. "They call me Sarge. That's 'cause I don't put up with no shit. We don't put up with stealing or drugs or any of that shit. We just want to be left alone. Cops come back in here, pretty soon we got city inspectors and welfare and all kinds of crap."

"How many people live back in here?" Cheezer asked.

The Sarge looked around. "Maybe sixteen right now. Guy just left. Somebody else moved into his place."

He handed me back the photo of Jane Doe. "We got lots of hookers coming back here. Crack dealers, too. We usually chase 'em off. Never saw a girl looked like her."

"Thanks," I told him.

We drove around the back of the old bowling alley, our headlights sending night people hurrying out of the shadows.

"My brother hung out down here when it was a bar called Cow-kickers," I told Cheezer. "He thinks maybe he saw the dead girl, here or one of the other bars on Stewart. The cops canvassed with the composite drawing, came up with nothing. And it's changed. It's all changed so much, just in ten years."

"You need somebody who didn't change. Somebody who stayed."

There was a MARTA bus stop down to the right. Two elderly black women huddled together under the Plexiglas shelter, trying to stay out of the wind. When the bus came lumbering up to the stop they hurried to the curb. The smaller one of the two helped her friend step up. After a minute, the bus shifted gears and rolled forward.

I reached over and flipped the turn signal the other way. "Follow that bus."

Everywhere the bus stopped, we stopped. We took turns with the composite drawing, one of us staying in the van, doors locked, the other going inside to show around the picture of Jane Doe.

We hit three convenience stores, six liquor stores, and three of the hot sheets, including the Sleepy Inn Motor Court, and the former Alamo Pass, where the desk clerk was all of eighteen years old and wore a shoulder holster with a .38 right on top of his sweatshirt. Nobody knew Jane Doe. By the time we got to the red-brick Faithful Harvest Baptist Church, Tuesday night prayer services were nearly underway.

An elderly gentleman with a baby blue polyester suit and a dark blue silk shirt stood at the front door, directing people to their pews. There were maybe two dozen people scattered around the pews, most of them middle-aged or older, although I did see a couple of little girls in frilly dresses, skipping up and down the side aisle. They had a small electric organ up on the altar and a husky woman in a choir robe and red turban was playing the snappiest version of "We Three Kings" I'd ever heard. Of course, I'm Catholic, so snappy isn't exactly part of my church music experience.

The blue-suited gentleman gave me a big smile. "Welcome to Faithful Harvest!" He pumped my hand in his. "I'm Brother Wayne. Now, you just go right down front, little lady."

"I wish I could stay," I told him. "But I'm actually trying to find somebody who might recognize this woman." I pulled out the picture of Jane Doe and showed it to him. "From a long time ago. Ten years. Would anybody tonight have been here ten years ago?"

He chuckled. "Young lady, we don't get a lot of newcomers here. Just about everybody here tonight been here a long, long time." He looked at the drawing. "Not too many white folks worship with us. Not that we exclude."

"I understand," I said. "Still. She might have lived or worked around here. Maybe shopped in the same stores?"

He pursed his lips. "Maybe. Most of our congregation, you understand, doesn't live in this community anymore. No. Things have gotten rough in this neighborhood. Real rough. Some of the ladies, they
don't even come to Tuesday night services anymore. Don't come over
here at night, period. What about you? Does your husband approve
of your coming over to this kind of neighborhood after dark like
this?"

I felt bad about lying in church, but some things are unavoidable.
"He's out in the car," I said. "Can you think of anybody here tonight
who might have seen this girl, known her ten years ago?"

He was old, but he wasn't dense. "What happened to her?"

"She got killed," I said. "They found her body. Back in the woods
behind Funtown. Nobody knew who she was. I'm trying to find out."

"Just a minute," he said. He walked slowly to the front of the
room, up to the altar to the woman in the red turban. He whispered
something to her, she nodded her head, finished the last chord with a
prolonged keyboard flourish, then got up and followed Brother
Wayne to the back of the church where I was standing. She had a din-
ner-plate-sized orchid pinned to her choir robe and it bobbed with
each step.

"This is First Lady Billingsley," the usher said. "She is our music
director, and the director of youth activities and the wife of our pastor, the Reverend Billingsley."

Some people had come in behind me. He hurried over to help
them to their seats.

First Lady Billingsley gave me a gracious smile. She towered over
me by six inches. "May I see the picture?" she said.

I handed it to her. She nodded and the turban slipped a little.
"This young lady, Brother Wayne said she passed away some time
ago?"

"She was killed," I said. "Down the street. At Funtown."

The church was starting to fill up. Quiet conversation hummed
around us. She pulled me over to the side, away from the door.

"Was this young woman, um, involved in things?" She was watching me for a reaction. Her skin was quite smooth, with only the
faintest lines radiating out from the corners of her eyes toward a hair-
line that showed white beneath the edges of the turban.

"She may have been a prostitute," I said. "Do you know her?"

"I knew girls like her," Mrs. Billingsley said. "From our outreach program." She looked apologetic. "We had more members back then. More ambition. We thought we could change the neighborhood. Instead, it changed us. Made us afraid. We prayed over that mission. But Jesus wanted us to change lives in a different way."

"AIDS?"

She nodded. "And the crack. The young ladies didn't want our sandwiches or our counsel. They just wanted something they could sell so they could buy more of that crack. One of them brought a gun to the outreach center, put it right up against my head, threatening to kill me if I didn't give her the money from the Sunday collection. Pastor Billingsley made me give up the center after that."

"You didn't know her, but what about some of the other prostitutes? Are any of them still around?"

Mrs. Billingsley looked sad. "Ten years is a long time for a girl on the streets down here. Most of them, I only knew a street name. You know, Candi or Brandi, those made-up names. Up until a few years ago, I'd see them sometimes, at the bus stop maybe."

I was getting desperate. "Anybody? Can you think of anybody who might have known her?"

She thought about it. Brother Wayne came up, nodded at me, nodded at the clock on the wall. It was time for services to start.

"We used to give them meal vouchers sometimes," Mrs. Billingsley said. "Instead of money, so they couldn't spend it on liquor or that crack. Of course, later, we realized they'd just trade the vouchers, to other girls, or customers or dealers, for what they wanted. There were two places that would accept the vouchers. The Nightowl, it closed, years ago. But the other place, Aundray's, on Cambellton Road, it's still open. If Aundray were still there, maybe he'd know her. Aundray, he was nice to those girls."

31

Cheezer looked relieved when I emerged from the church. "I thought maybe something happened in there," he said. "I was getting ready to come in and look for you."

"It's cold," I said. "Let's go get some coffee."

"Here?" He clicked the door lock.

"Not here," I said. "Aundray's. On Campbellton Road."

No music this time. Something was on his mind. "You think we'll find out who that girl was?"

"Maybe. It's a long shot. That church back there, they used to have a sort of day shelter. Some of the prostitutes would come in sometimes, use the phone, cadge meals or cigarette money. This restaurant we're going to, they used to accept the girls' meal vouchers. Maybe the owner knows our Jane."

"We lived in a shelter once," Cheezer said. "In Pensacola. When I was in fourth grade. I went to the same school from Halloween right through to May. We had our own room. Right in the Sunday School building. But the church closed the shelter down in May. To get ready for Vacation Bible School. You ever go to Vacation Bible School?"

"Yeah," I said. "The Methodists had a good one. They liked to try to convert Catholic kids. We illustrated gospel stories with construction paper and cotton balls and toothpicks and glitter. Methodists were big on glitter. I never lived in a shelter, though."

"The shelter was nice," Cheezer said.

"Compared to what?"

"The rest of it." He threw me a quick look. "I guess you're wondering."

"Who wouldn't?" I said. "You feel like explaining?"

"Let's get some coffee first." We were in front of a neon yellow A-frame restaurant. It looked vaguely like some fast-food franchise from the past. Maybe a chicken place. The sign out front still said Hot To Go, but underneath it, in faded red letters, it said Aundray's.

People were still eating their dinner. It was one smallish dining room, with a lunch counter and a wall of booths and some tables in between. We ordered coffee. Cheezer asked for pie, too. The waitress assured us it was fresh and homemade, and that Aundray was in the office, working on the books. She would tell him somebody wanted to talk to him.

We got our coffee and Cheezer got a slab of pecan pie with a scoop of vanilla ice cream on top.

"Officially, my mom was a secretary," he said, taking a sip of the coffee. "That's what I always put on the school forms. Secretary. I didn't figure out until I was fifteen that most secretaries didn't live in single-room occupancy hotels, or go to work at midnight, or move every three months." He smiled weakly over his coffee cup. Cheezer had a not-quite dimple in his left cheek, and the softest brown eyes. If you looked very close, you could see some acne scars on his cheeks.

I nodded understanding. "What happened when you were fifteen?"

"She got arrested in Macon. Couldn't make bail. When I got home from school, my granddad's car was in front of the motel where we were staying. He told me I was coming to stay with him. In Kissimmee. The middle of nowhere."

"What happened to your mom?"

He sliced off the end of the pie with the edge of his fork, separated it carefully away from the rest of the wedge, and then ate it, chewing slowly. Here was a man who liked pie.

"I think my granddad paid the bail," he said. "All he'd tell me was that my mom was working, trying to get her life straightened out. She sent me ten dollars for my sisteenth birthday, from Memphis.

Right before I graduated from high school, she called me up one night, late, after my granddad had already gone to bed. He was a mailman, so he went to bed early. I picked up the phone one night and it was her."

"And you all lived happily ever after?"

"Like you? With a mom and a dad and a house of your own and a bike and summer camp? No. She was high. Kept giggling, saying she couldn't believe my voice had changed already. I was sixteen, for Christ's sake! After high school, my granddad got me a job at the post office. I sorted mail for a year, took my SATs, went to Leon Community College for a year, did good enough to get accepted to Tech."

An uncomfortable silence drifted over us.

"You never heard from her again?"

He'd finished the pie, pushed the plate away. "No. She could be somebody's Jane Doe. "

"You were looking for me?" The black man had a shiny bald dome and a shiny gold tooth in the front. His accent sounded West Indian. He wore a spotless white uniform, with the name Aundray embroidered over the shirt pocket.

I introduced Cheezer and myself. Told him we were looking for a girl who'd been dead for ten years. "Mrs. Billingsley at Faithful Harvest Church said maybe you could help," I said. "She said some of the girls from her outreach center used to eat over here."

"Yes? They don't send them no more. Things got too rough over there. I close up at ten now. Decent folks, they eat dinner by then."

I handed him the photograph of Jane Doe.

"Funny kind of picture," he said, puzzled.

"She'd been dead a long time when they found the body, so it might not be an exact likeness."

He pulled a chair up from another table, sat down, gestured for the waitress to bring more coffee. She brought another cup, filled his, refilled ours.

"Maybe," he said dubiously. "She wore a lot of makeup, the girl I'm thinking of. So long ago. I can't say."

But he'd seen something in the picture. "She wore a gold chain with a heart medallion," I said. "They found it on the body."

He frowned. "A boy's name, I think. The other girls didn't like her. One time, they beat her up outside, in the parking lot. She came inside, crying and bleeding from a cut lip, and I let her clean up in the bathroom and called a cab for her. Tell the driver it's so-and-so, she say. A boy's name, I think."

"Joey?" Cheezer asked. "Frankie? Eddie?"

"No-o-o," Aundray said.

"Billie? Bobbi?" I suggested. They were two of the three girls from the old *Petticoat Junction* show on TV. Call it cultural bias.

"Marty," he said suddenly. "I think she was called Marty."

The three of us stared at the photo of Jane. I'd come to think of her as Jane. Marty didn't seem to suit her. Marty. Short for Martha? Marianne?

"What was she like?" Cheezer asked. "Was she really a hooker?"

Aundray looked unsettled. "I'm a married man," he protested. "A Christian." He pointed at the waitress, who was behind the counter now, stacking dirty dishes on a plastic tray. "That's my wife."

"No, no," I said. "We just wanted to know something, anything else about her."

"She's dead?"

"Murdered. You never saw her picture in the paper? The police never came around and asked about her?"

"Police? No. I don't know her. Just Marty. That's all I know."

It was more than I'd expected, really.

His wife came over to the table with the coffeepot, even though our cups were still nearly full. She was middle-aged, trim-figured. Dying to know what Aundray was talking to us about. Her presence was making him nervous.

"OK?" he said heartily, getting up to leave. "Good."

Cheezer's face fell. It was his first real stab at detecting. We'd gotten a hot lead, and now all of a sudden things had cooled very fast.

I took some money out of my billfold, twice what the bill should come to. I laid the money on the table. "Mr. Aundray? The night you called the cab for Marty, were you here when it came for her?"

He shrugged. "I can't remember. So long ago."

"I remember." His wife put the coffeepot down on the table.

Aundray frowned at his wife. "You don't know her."

"This girl," Mrs. Aundray said, looking down at the photograph still on the table, beside the money. "Marty. She needed a bath. All dirty and beat up. The cab driver, when he come and seen it was a hooker, he didn't want to take her, said she'd bleed all over his car. She got the money out and gave it to him, right here. Five dollars. 'It's only over at the Panda,' she say." Mrs. Aundray gave her husband a smug look. "The Panda Inn. That's where she stayed. Lot of those girls stayed there."

Cheezer waited until we were in the van, then he offered me a high five. "You're good," he marveled. "I mean it. Better than Jim Rockford."

He started the car and I patted my purse with the lucky two-dollar bill inside.

32

The luck ran out at the Panda Inn.

The desk clerk was dark-skinned, Pakistani, maybe. Definitely uninterested in a hooker named Marty who'd been dead for ten years.

He pointed to a flyspecked sign over the check-in counter. Under New Management. "You see? The old owners, they move to California. Three years now, I am here. No girls living here now. Only business people and nice families."

Two hookers walked through the lobby, their high heels clacking against the tile floors. Each gave the manager a friendly family-type wave.

"Anybody else here who used to work for the old owner?" I asked.

"No. Everybody who works here now is my family. My wife, my children, my aunts . . . "

"Never mind," I said.

As we were pulling out of the parking lot, a MARTA bus paused at the stop out front, let some teenagers off.

"Where now?" Cheezer asked. He was ready to spend the rest of the evening hunting our quarry. I was ready to call it a night.

"Home," I said. "I'll call Deavers in the morning. We've got a first name for Jane Doe, where she lived, some of the places she hung out. That's a lot."

• • •

I heard laughter coming from the bathroom. I followed the giggles and splashing noises. Edna had the lid down on the commode, sitting there, snapping photos of Maura in her bubblebath.

The little girl was covered in suds. She had a suds hat and a suds beard and the little pink toes were suds-covered, too.

"Say hi to Callahan," Edna told her.

"Ca'han," Maura said, stumbling a little over the name. "Hi, Ca'han."

"Aren't we having fun?" I asked, looking at my watch. It was past ten.

Edna snapped another picture. "Wave, honey!" she instructed Maura.

Maura flipped a handful of bubbles at her and Edna chuckled and snapped some more.

"I've spent all damn day messing with you-know-who," Edna said.

"Shouldn't she be in bed?" I asked.

"Bath first," Edna said. "She's been at 'Granny Annie's' for two days. I need to give her a good bath before I put her to bed."

I nodded, understanding slowly dawning. "So this is some sort of ritual cleansing?"

"Not just ritual," Edna said, annoyed.

"Close your eyes, honey, so you don't get water in them," she instructed. Edna took a little plastic sand bucket, which she filled with warm water and poured over Maura's head to rinse the suds out of her hair. Maura squealed happily. "Rain!"

Edna handed me the camera. She lifted Maura out of the tub and stood her up on the bath mat. She took a fluffy white bath towel and began drying Maura off. She worked slowly, patting and rubbing and, I noticed, making the child turn, examining every inch of her little pink body.

I shook my head. "Looking for bruises?"

My mother pursed her lips. "You forget who we're dealing with. She's been with those people. You-know-who and her boyfriend."

"So that's why the camera? Documentation?"

"I just wanted some snapshots of my granddaughter," Edna said. "No crime in that, is there?"

A little white iron daybed had been installed in the corner of Edna's bedroom. It had a pink and white quilt and a new nightie all laid out. And a stack of picture books. "Aunt Maureen bought all this," Edna said, slipping the nightgown over Maura's head.

She looked over at me. "Maura adores Maureen. You'd think she'd known her all her life."

We took turns reading the stories. Maura liked *Goodnight Moon* so much we had to read it twice, in between *The Runaway Bunny*. Then Edna had her say her "Now I lay me's." She'd fallen asleep before we got to the God-bless list.

I fixed us both a Jack Daniel's and water and we took them into the living room to sit by the fire.

"What happened?" I asked.

Edna crunched an ice cube and made a face. "That woman. If Maureen hadn't been there with me, Jules, I would have gone after her tooth and toenail."

"She pulled something?"

"Did she ever," Edna said.

"We got to the Waffle House right when we were supposed to. Waited an hour, no sign of Annette or my grandbaby. I got on the phone to Ferd. Annette and Chuck didn't answer their phone. Ferd had to call that Dyson Yount—the man Shay worked for? Of course, this Yount character claimed he didn't know anything about it and didn't know how to reach Annette."

"While you were doing a slow burn," I said, trying to suppress the image of my mother and sister, hanging around a Waffle House all morning waiting for Annette Gatlin to make a grand entrance.

"Do you know where she was?" Edna asked, her rage building. She didn't wait for me to answer. "She took Maura to a doctor. A pediatrician. To make sure that . . . Brian . . . we . . . "

"Hadn't physically abused her?" Edna couldn't bring herself to say the words, but I could.

Edna got up and took the poker and stabbed viciously at the logs in the fireplace, sending sparks flying against the screen. "How dare she? Subject a three-year-old to that kind of thing. And do you know what she said to me when she finally showed up? With that boyfriend in tow? She announced, right there in that restaurant, for everybody to hear, that the police had asked Brian to give a . . . a . . . sample of his body fluids to compare with the fluids they found on Shay."

She whacked the burning logs again, and then again. She took her glass and drained it. "You know what she's trying to say, don't you?

That Brian raped Shay and raped his own baby daughter. Jules, I've never been so angry, so humiliated in my whole life. Your sister had to give me one of her tranquilizers to calm me down, I was shaking so hard."

We would be in court, before a judge of Annette's choosing in less than two days for the custody hearing. I didn't want to tell Edna it would probably get worse. Much, much worse.

So I told her what I'd found out about Bucky's Jane Doe. And about talking to the cashier at the pizza place and to Brian's boss. "He's very supportive of Brian," I said, wanting to have some good news to share. "And he and the pizza guy both confirmed what Brian told me about working late the night Shay was killed."

"Of course he did," Edna snapped. "It was the truth. Why would he lie?"

Why wouldn't he lie, I wondered. The phone rang. "I'll get it in my room," I told her.

"I'm going to bed," Edna announced.

It was Mac. I propped myself up on a stack of pillows, kicked off my shoes, and lay back on the bed.

"Didn't we have a date tonight?" he asked.

"I'm not allowed to date on school nights," I said primly. "And my mother certainly wouldn't allow me to see a man as old as you are."

"OK, forget it," he said. "I'll just throw away all this info I spent the day digging up."

"I'm sorry. I just got in a little while ago," I said. "Really long day."

"Why don't you come out here and let me rub your back? And I'll bring you up to speed on what I found out at the courthouse."

I was tempted. My neck and shoulders were in knots. "Why don't you come into town?" I countered. "And I'll bring you up to speed."

"Can't. I've got an early meeting in Canton in the morning. And the dogs have got to be fed. Somebody's got to give Maybelline her medicine. Have you eaten?"

"Not in a long time," I admitted. "Edna's not in a cooking mood these days. We've had to medicate her to keep her from throttling Annette Gatlin."

"I've got steak and eggs and hash browns and cold beer," Mac offered.

"Can I eat it in bed? And you swear you'll rub my back? For thirty minutes?"

"At least twenty." Mac likes to bargain.

I got up and started throwing clothes in my overnight bag. "See you in half an hour."

Rufus, Mac's freeloading black lab, begged and whined until I gave him the scraps of my steak. I tried to slip it to him surreptitiously, but Mac caught me.

"That's positive reinforcement," he said, squeezing some lotion out of the bottle into the palm of his hands. "You want him to end up in juvenile hall?"

"I want him to end up outside after he's eaten all that steak," I said, pushing my hair off the nape of my neck so he could rub there. "That dog's got some powerful gas."

"He'll be nice," Mac promised, giving Rufus a stern look. "Won't you?"

The dog thumped his tail on the rug by the foot of the bed. Maybelline was already asleep.

"You're all knotted up here," Mac said, kneading my shoulder muscles, his fingertips pushing deep into my flesh.

"You can unknot me," I said, putting my plate on the bedside table. "While you tell me what you found at the courthouse."

"You'll be proud of me," Mac promised. "First. Granny Annie. I know a gal at Georgia Power. She checked the records. Annette's lived at that apartment at Twelve Oaks Plaza for six years. Prior to that, she lived in Hapeville, closer to the airport. Her name is the only one on the lease for the Twelve Oaks apartment. I know Edna will be disappointed, but she doesn't have a criminal record. Only thing I could find in the dockets at Clayton was a judgment issued against her for an unpaid Rich's credit card bill in 1989. She'd run up a bill of $1,500, the judge ordered her to pay the bill plus collection fees; it was paid in full by 1990. There was also an apparent rent dispute with her old landlord in 1993. He got a judgment against her for $1,800 in damages to her apartment, after she moved out. As far as I could tell, the judgment was never settled."

"Exciting stuff," I said. "No outstanding murder warrants though, huh?"

"Nope," Mac said. "Not in Clayton County." He was working with both hands on my right biceps. "She's worked for that security company at the airport for six years. Ingraham represented her on both the civil cases."

"Wish my boyfriend were an attorney," I said. "So I could check his briefs."

Mac gave my shoulder a playful punch, then rubbed some more lotion on me. It was cold, but it smelled good, like grass or something fresh and green, and the hands-on technique was even better.

"Charles Ingraham has an interesting secret in his past," Mac said.

I turned around to look at him. "Really?"

"He's married," Mac said.

"Oh." I was hoping for more.

"Ingraham got out of law school at UGA in 1971," Mac said. "I had to make a long-distance call to Athens to get that, you know."

"Put it on my bill," I said.

"He was married in 1969. To a woman named Deborah Shrakes. No record of them ever divorcing."

"Maybe he forgot."

"He opened his law practice in Jonesboro in 1984," Mac said. "One beef against him. On the civil side. In 1990, a client sued, claimed Ingraham had neglected to turn over the money from the sale of some property from an escrow account. The docket says the case was dismissed, six months later."

"Ingraham does a lot of real estate law," Mac said. "Guess who his biggest client is?"

"Dyson Yount."

"You peeked," Mac said.

"Tell me about Mr. Yount," I said.

"You're not gonna like this," he told me. "Dyson Yount is a solid citizen. No civil or criminal complaints. All the girls in the clerk's office just love him. Every desk down there has a big poinsettia on it—each one with a card wishing them Merry Christmas from Dyson Yount Realty."

Mac switched arms. As he rubbed and pounded and stroked, I felt myself slowly begin to relax.

"Yount and Ingraham have been doing business together for years," Mac continued. "And they belong to Rotary together. Let's see, hmm . . . what else? My notes are in the other room."

"Just keep rubbing and talking," I murmured. "It'll all come to you."

"The girls in the clerk's office seemed to know Shay," he said. "They said she'd been working for Yount for a couple years. He had her doing title searches, I think. One of them rolled their eyes when I described her as Yount's secretary. Don't think she made a big impression with them."

"They're women, right? She usually saved the impressing for men."

"Right. Yount was elected to the County Commission four years ago. Funny thing about Dyson Yount. He's supposed to be a political comer, didn't you say?"

"A young turk," I agreed.

"Everybody thought he was going to run for the General Assembly two years ago. Supposedly it was all set. Then, nothing. My source says he didn't get the nod from Maceo Holland, the guy who was supposed to retire and bequeath his seat to Dyson Yount."

I thought about that for a minute while Mac had me lie down on my stomach so he could work my lower back.

"Well, what are the rumors?" In a town like Jonesboro, there are always rumors.

"The usual," Mac said. "Dyson is gay, according to one camp. According to another camp, he's screwing around on his wife. There are rumors that he's a closet Republican. And then there are rumors that he sleeps around with gay closet Republicans."

I turned my head to look at him. "Which is it?"

Mac grinned. He was very pleased with himself.

"Did you know Shay was planning on moving out of that apartment she was living in with her mother?"

Pay dirt. "Really?"

"She'd put a down payment on a condo. In Fayetteville."

"A single mother? With an ex-husband behind on the child support? On a secretary's salary? Where'd she get the money for a condo?"

"She paid five thousand down, got the mortgage through Tara Savings and Loan. It would have closed February 1."

"So?"

"Dyson Yount is on the board of directors of Tara Savings and Loan."

"Maybe a condo was part of Shay's benefits package?" I suggested, propping myself up on one elbow.

Mac was rubbing my lower spine with both thumbs, pushing away the tension bubbles.

"Mrs. Yount spent Thanksgiving with her parents in Alabama."

"Yeah?"

"Took the little Younts with her. Mr. Yount stayed at home in Jonesboro. Pressing work schedule. Mrs. Yount is still in Alabama."

I rolled over, put my arms around Mac's neck and pulled him down toward me. "You are one talented dick," I whispered in his ear.

He put the lotion down. "I'd like that in writing, if you don't mind."

33

Maura waved at me when she saw me coming in the back door of the kitchen, overnight bag in hand. "Ca'han! Want some 'nanner?"

Her high chair tray was a smorgasbord of finger foods. Froot Loops, Cheerios, Ritz crackers, grapes, a biscuit half dripping with honey. The banana she was offering me had been peeled and gnawed at and was turning dark. I parked a kiss on the top of her head. She smelled like soap and Froot Loops. "No thanks, Maura. Did you leave me any biscuits?"

Edna looked up from the newspaper. "I finally found something she'll eat. Biscuits. I should have known. Brian always loved biscuits."

"He'd hog the whole pan if you didn't watch him," I said, putting down my bag and pouring myself a cup of coffee.

"Neva Jean called," Edna said, pushing the biscuit basket across the table at me. "She says she's got dirt. I told her it's her job to get rid of dirt. She just laughed. What's that supposed to mean?"

I split a biscuit open, laid on a slice of butter and squeezed some of the honey all over the surface, then mashed the biscuit halves together and waited. When the butter started dripping, I took a bite. Heavenly.

"She did a little detecting for me last night," I said, dabbing at the honey dripping down my chin. "Asking around at the lounges where Brian says Annette and Shay liked to spend time."

Edna's face fell. "I coulda done that."

"You were busy with Maura, remember? Besides, it was right up Neva Jean's alley."

"That's true," Edna said. She propped her chin on her fist and looked over at Maura, who was applying the banana to her face like an oversized lipstick. "Where do you think she saw that?"

Neva Jean, not to put too fine a point on it, looked like hell. Her bright yellow hair was teased and snarled and perfectly flat on one side, she had mascara globules clumped under both eyes and she wore two different kinds of tennis shoes. But she was ready to bust with her news.

She swept into the kitchen, got herself a Mountain Dew out of the refrigerator, and flung herself down at the table.

"Your sister-in-law liked wine coolers, baked potato skins, and older men," she announced. "Her mother didn't like junk food, but she sure as hell liked to drink and screw."

"Shh!" Edna said, gesturing toward Maura, who was stuffing Froot Loops down the front of her shirt. "Little pitchers!" Edna leaned forward, gracing Neva Jean with an enchanting smile. "Have a biscuit, Neva Jean," she said. "Spill your guts. Just lower your voice, please."

Neva Jean heaped three biscuits onto her plate and took a preparatory swallow of Mountain Dew.

"You were right about the Marriott lounge," she told me. "I talked to the cocktail waitress—her name is Diane. Diane Holt. She told me Shay came in there a lot on Wednesday nights 'cause that was Ladies Night—dollar drinks. There's another place, in a shopping center on Tara Boulevard, Bleachers, it's a sports bar? She liked to go in there on Mondays, hit up on all the guys who came in to watch Monday night football."

"What about Saturday night? Where was she last Saturday night?" Edna wanted to know.

Neva Jean grinned. "Right there in the lounge at the Marriott hotel. She'd been there Friday night, too. Her mama came in there and met her after she got off work. Diane said Annette did that a lot. They had people thinking they were sisters."

"That's a laugh," Edna said dryly.

"They liked to match each other drink for drink," Neva Jean said. "It sounds like they made a little game of it. Usually, they tried to get some out-of-town business type to pick up their tabs."

"I'll bet that's not the only thing they got those men to pick up," Edna hissed.

I got up and poured myself another cup of coffee. "Did they ever leave with these guys? Any sort of regulars?"

"Shay did," Neva Jean said. "Not with locals though. I guess she had more fun with guys she knew she wasn't going to see again. Diane said just Friday night, a guy put Shay's tab on his room bill and they left together. She was pretty sure they were going upstairs to his room."

She handed me back the photo I'd given her of Annette and Shay. "I described that Dyson Yount and Chuck Ingraham. Nobody I talked to had ever seen Dyson Yount. But they had seen Annette in there with Chuck sometimes."

"What happened Saturday night? Give it to me step by step."

Neva Jean reached into the biscuit basket, looked disappointed to see it was empty. "Shay came in alone. She got real drunk, real fast. There was a guy in there, Diane thinks he's somebody local, she'd seen him around, and he knew Shay's name. Shay flirted with him, let him buy her a drink, even used his cell phone."

"Did the waitress know who she was calling?"

"The guy made some big joke about it better not be long distance. Shay laughed and said 'Don't I wish it was long distance.'"

"What happened then?" Edna asked.

"She left right after she got off the phone. Alone. Sometime around eight P.M. The waitress couldn't be real sure, because a bunch of people from a hardware convention came in and they got real busy."

"Did the waitress have any idea who the guy was with the cell phone?" I asked.

She shook her head. "No. Just a guy. Sport shirt, slacks, probably in his late forties."

"Ca'han?"

I looked up. Maura was standing up in her high chair, pushing at the tray, trying to climb down. "Potty, Ca'han," she said urgently.

"That's my girl!" Edna cried. "Take Maura to the potty, Callahan. And don't forget the paperwork."

Neva Jean sniggered. I took my niece by the hand and headed for the bathroom.

"By the way," Neva Jean called after me. "Those police detectives have been in both those bars already, making pests of themselves asking the employees about Shay. They were asking about your brother, too."

"Brian? Did anybody see him?" I asked.

"Ca'han." Maura tugged at my hand. Her face was scrunched up, all concentration.

Neva Jean looked at Edna, bit her lip. "A couple times."

I waited until Maura had completed her toilette, then delivered her back to Edna and Neva Jean. I slipped into my bedroom and called Brian at work. A long time passed before he came to the phone.

"This is Garrity," he said briskly.

"It's Callahan," I said.

"Can't talk," he said. "Call me tonight, at home."

"I'm working, too," I told him. "Listen, did you ever meet Shay at the bar at the Marriott by the airport?"

"Maybe. She hung out there all the time. I coulda met her there. To talk about Maura or the divorce or something."

"What about the night Shay was killed? Were you there that night?"

"I told you where I was that night," Brian's voice crackled with impatience. "I gotta go now. And hey, don't come out here talking to people about me again—you hear?"

"Brian!" I said sharply. "I might have a line on that girl they found at Funtown. I showed her picture around yesterday. Marty. Does that name ring a bell?"

"No," he said. "Bye."

"Ferd?"

He yawned the yawn of a fat man. "God. What time is it?"

"It's nine o'clock," I said. "Can I come out there? To talk to you? It's really important."

"What for?"

"About Shay Gatlin, for one thing. I pulled some strings, got a look at the homicide case file, talked over some things with Bucky Deavers and L. D. Lawrence. I saw the crime-scene photos, the close-ups of Shay."

He yawned again.

"The killer took a souvenir, Ferd. From Shay. A gold necklace."

That woke him up. "How do you know that? Did the cops tell you that?"

"She was wearing it in the Polaroids they took at the emergency room—back in the fall. It's a gold chain with a medallion. I can't tell what the medallion is, just that it's oval. And in the crime-scene photos, the close-ups, you can tell it's oval-shaped. There are blood splatters all over her neck except for one spot, right at her throat, where the medal must have been. Only she wasn't wearing it when the police got there. The killer must have taken it."

Ferd was silent, waiting for me to continue.

"I've seen the evidence inventory," I said. "The cops didn't find it. After the cops processed the apartment, they let Annette take Shay's valuables, her watch and her jewelry box. I'm wondering—were they supposed to do that? I mean, shouldn't that stuff go to Maura?"

"What's your point here?" he asked. "If the killer took the necklace, it's not in her jewelry box, right? Shay died intestate. Annette was her next of kin."

"All right," I agreed. "But I've done some checking around. For one thing, both Annette and Shay were spending a lot of time at that Marriott bar. Two, three nights a week. Shay left with men several times. Maybe one of them killed her."

He sighed. "We've got a custody hearing tomorrow morning. You're wasting a lot of time and energy with all these theories about who killed Shay. All we have to do is make the judge believe one thing—that Brian didn't. And that Annette is not a fitting or proper custodian for Maura. The stuff about her being in bars might be useful. Have you got a name?"

I gave him Diane Holt's name.

"Anything else?"

"Annette got kicked out of an apartment down in Jonesboro. Years ago. And she had a delinquent credit card at Rich's. Took a long time to pay off the balance."

I could hear scratching sounds coming from the other end of the line.

"Shay had put a down payment on a condo," I added. "At a bank in Jonesboro. Dyson Yount is on the bank's board of directors. And it looks like maybe he and his wife are separated. I think Brian is right. I think something was going on between Shay and Yount."

"Busy gal," Ferd said. "You suspect she was sleeping with Chuck Ingraham, too. You found anybody she wasn't sleeping with yet?"

It was a sobering thought. "The cops found semen during Shay's autopsy. They're running tests on it. Lawrence said they're going to ask Brian to submit a sample. It could be a way to clear him, Ferd."

He coughed. "I'm aware of what the cops are requesting," he said.

"He'll do it, won't he? To prove he hadn't had sex with her the night she was killed?"

Ferd had a sudden spell of coughing. Then there was a silence. No more scratching. "I can't discuss that with you," Ferd said.

"Why not?" I demanded.

"You're not my client. Brian is my client, and this is a confidential matter."

I drummed my fingers on my bedside table. "I hired you, Ferd. Edna and I are paying you. Maura is staying with us. We have a right to some answers."

"You have a right to ask your brother questions, and if he wants to answer, he may," Ferd said. "I can't discuss this any more, Callahan."

I was gripping the phone tightly. "Ferd, this is not just about Shay. They're going to come at Brian for those south-side murders. I think I've got a strong lead on the I.D. of that girl at Funtown. She was a hooker. Her name was Marty. Did Brian know her?"

"Ask him," Ferd said. "I'll see you in court tomorrow."

34

Bucky Deavers's face darkened when he saw me enter the room. He stood up, strode across the room in half a dozen steps. "Outside," he said.

"It's cold out there," I protested.

He took me by the elbow and steered me toward the front door. "I said, outside."

Another one of the homicide detectives was standing in the doorway, finishing off a cigarette. Bucky nodded at him, we stood there silently until the guy stubbed out the cigarette on the concrete walkway. "See ya," he said.

I hugged my coat around me. Bucky's eyes narrowed and looked somewhere off behind me, his lips set in a pale, rigid slash.

"You pissed Lawrence off, telling him you'd seen the crime-scene photos of Shay Garrity. Lawrence called Mackey, Mackey called me in for an hour this morning, chewing my ass for letting a civilian get involved in an active homicide investigation."

"Don't forget, I'm the one who gave you information."

"You gave me a pain in the ass," Bucky said. "I trusted you. Karpik wants Mackey to pull me off the Funtown investigation. He says you've compromised the case's integrity."

"I've practically solved the case," I said heatedly. "Your Jane Doe's name was Marty. It was that MARTA card. Cheezer and I followed a

MARTA bus last night. We asked at all the bus stops. We found a church shelter where she used to use the phone. They sent me to a restaurant. Aundray's. The owner recognized her from the drawing. Her name was Marty and she lived at the Panda Inn."

He wouldn't look at me. "Marty. That's a big lead."

"It's more than you had," I pointed out. "Somebody out there at the Panda Inn knew her. Hell, call somebody who worked Vice back then. Tell them her name was Marty and she worked Stewart Avenue in the late eighties. The other girls didn't like her."

Bucky thought about it. He didn't like it, and at that moment, he didn't like me, but he's a good cop. He hates an unsolved case. "You know," he said, "your brother still might be good for these murders. We're gonna submit the girl's clothes for DNA testing. Lawrence says they're trying to get a sample from Brian. If they match up, he's toast."

I nodded.

"Get the hell out of here," Bucky said, turning away from me. I was turning to go, but he reached out and grabbed my sleeve. "And stay away from Funtown. I mean it, Garrity."

I sat in my car in the parking lot at the Homicide Task Force feeling sorry for myself for about thirty seconds.

Then I got mad. I could have kicked myself for not managing to shoplift Bucky's Jane Doe file. Ten years ago, the detectives working the case had canvassed the neighborhood around Funtown with little more than a sketch. Now I had a first name and an address—but in the interim years, everything on Stewart Avenue had changed. Or had it?

According to the route schedule I'd picked up at the MARTA offices on Piedmont Avenue, Bus #82 should have been pulling into the Arts Center train station at 10:15 A.M. I parked across the street from the station in a pay lot, crossed against traffic, and managed to get to the stop just as the bus was pulling in.

The driver lolled back in her seat, sipping from a plastic bottle of mineral water.

"Sylvia Wesson?"

"Yes?" She was in her early fifties, with blonde hair, and she'd logged a lot of miles on a tanning bed somewhere.

"I understand you used to drive a route down on Stewart Avenue, in the late eighties. I'm looking for somebody who might have been a regular rider back then."

She sighed. "Have you cleared this through the main office? I'm not allowed to talk to anybody without going through the main office."

I took the Jane Doe photo out of my purse and handed it to the driver. "Don't worry. She can't sue you. She's dead. I'm just trying to find out her name."

She looked at the photo. "Why?"

"I'm a private investigator," I said. "The case has been unsolved for ten years. Do you recognize her?"

"Her hair looks pretty awful. Course, she never knew how to fix it right," Sylvia said. "I cut hair part-time." She handed me a business card. It said Hair-Tamers Salon, and it had her name and phone number. "You've got good hair," she said, "but if I was cutting it, I'd feather it more, so you didn't look so moon-faced."

I pocketed the card. "I'll keep it in mind," I said. "But you do recognize the girl?"

"She looked better as a blonde," Sylvia said.

My hand shook a little. "Did you know her name?"

She frowned. "Let me think. She used to go downtown, to the Hyatt, when the big trade shows were in town. It was a much nicer class of client there. Otherwise, I always saw her on my route, around the clubs and bars, places like that."

"Marty? Was that her name?" I asked.

She snapped her fingers. "Marty! That's it. Marty what? She was from up north. She said Atlanta weather was nothing compared to up home. Now what the heck was her name?"

Sylvia drank deeply from the water bottle, the effort making hollows of her oven-baked cheeks. "Italian name. We got to talking one night. It was raining real hard, business was bad, so she took the bus back to the hotel she stayed at."

"Her last name was Italian?" I said, trying to get the driver back on track.

She slapped her knee with the flat of her hand. "Good Times. That was it!"

"Her name was Good Times?" It was obviously her street name. I tried to keep the disappointment from my voice.

"She said her name meant that. In Italian. It was Bona-something. Bona means good in Italian, right?"

"That sounds right," I said, smiling broadly. Half a last name. Maybe I'd have to get her I.D. one syllable at a time. "Somebody else told me she might have lived at the Panda Inn?"

"That's right," Sylvia said.

"The police found a necklace. A gold chain, with a lopsided heart pendant. Do you remember seeing her wear something like that?"

"She wore lots of gold jewelry, I don't remember anything specific."

"What about a pimp? Did she ever mention her pimp?"

"Told me she worked for herself," Sylvia said. "She wasn't what you'd call a high-class girl." She took one last look at the photo. "And you say she's dead? Funny. I just figured she'd gotten herself a car."

I tried to call Bucky from my car phone, but I got hooked up with his voice-mail. "Marty Bona-something," I said, not bothering to explain. "From up north somewhere. The last name means 'good times' in Italian."

Ferd sighed when I told him what I wanted. "The issue here is custody of Maura," he said. "I thought you understood that Brian is my client."

"I do understand, dammit," I said. "But Shay is dead. The chances are good that whoever killed her was somebody close. I want to take a look at that jewelry box of Shay's. Can't we make Annette hand it over? Since it actually belongs to Maura now?"

"We can ask," Ferd said. "But the lady isn't going to do anything without a court order. And that takes time. Time away from the brief I'm supposed to be writing to see that Annette doesn't get custody of your niece."

"Just do it, please?"

"Only if that's OK with Brian," Ferd said.

The van snaked through the treacherous downtown traffic. The local newspaper is always saying how downtown is deserted, but if that's true, why is traffic always such a bitch? The worst parking, of course, is in and around the state-county-city government complex. Every time I have to go there, it chafes me, seeing all the free parking spots reserved for bureaucrats and none for the taxpayers. After three loops around the complex I finally snagged a metered space at the curb, then still had to hike three blocks back to the Fulton County courthouse, through a stiff, biting wind blowing through the concrete caverns on Courtland Street.

Annette was the reason we had to win this custody hearing on Thursday. We had to find something that would persuade even a biased judge that Annette wasn't fit to raise Maura. After all, look what had happened to Shay, her only child. We'd checked Annette's past in Clayton County, but it wasn't until just now that I remembered all those years Annette lived in Sandy Springs—in Fulton County. She was definitely a lady with a past. It was just a matter of helping her past catch up with her.

They were having a little Christmas feast in the court clerk's office. A buffet was spread out on a desk behind the counter, and people were wandering around, gossiping, noshing, sipping from paper cups, and generally having a nice time. The smell of pigs-in-a-blanket wafted over the usual courthouse signature smells of copier fluid and institutional disinfectant.

The computer lead me through a series of prompts, then asked me to type in a name for it to search. Without thinking, I typed in Shay Gatlin.

Shay had been left to fend for herself since the time she was Maura's age. Anytime a bike disappeared in our neighborhood, the theft would be blamed on Shay. Shay always had candy, plenty of school supplies, jewelry, makeup, anything small enough to fit into her quick little, hot little, hands.

Line by line, the computer screen began to fill. Arrested for shoplifting at the age of seventeen, she'd been given three months to serve, concurrent with another sentence. Another sentence? Juvenile records are shielded in Georgia. Shay must have had an arrest record dating back before her seventeenth birthday. There were more shoplifting arrests. She liked Kmarts and Rich's, but kept getting caught there. I counted two bad check charges, and two charges of criminal trespass and one charge of theft by taking. The arrests seemed to have tapered off three years ago, about the time she'd become pregnant with Maura. Mostly, Shay had been a petty thief. Someday, maybe that would be a small comfort to Maura when she found out about her mother. We would say, "Yes, she was a thief, but she never stole anything that would require heavy lifting."

I put some quarters in the slot and the computer printed out Shay Gatlin's arrest record.

Search more? The computer prompt asked.

I typed in Annette Gatlin.

Two arrests. Maybe Annette had been too busy keeping Shay out of trouble to get into any real trouble herself. Then I began to read, and what I read made me dig in the bottom of my purse for more quarters for the printer.

Way back in 1984, Annette Gatlin had made a mistake. She'd solicited an undercover Atlanta vice officer and instead of making a quick fifty bucks for a low-rent rendezvous, she'd gotten slapped with an arrest for solicitation for prostitution. The charges had been dropped, but she'd slipped up again in 1986 with a second arrest for prostitution.

No more arrests after that, but those two, I felt sure, should be enough for any judge.

I printed out the pages, circled the docket number on each arrest. I took the numbers and stood at the front counter. The clerks were buzzing around a walnut-studded cheese ball. I coughed loudly. A young girl wearing a red fur Santa cap rolled her eyes, but came to the counter.

"Staff party," she said, pouting.

I handed her the docket numbers. "I'd like to see the disposition on these cases, please."

She gestured toward the bank of computers on the opposite wall. "You know how to use a computer?"

"I do," I said pleasantly. "That's how I got these docket numbers in the first place. But the sign says the computerized records only go back to July of '86. These arrests were before that."

She sighed heavily. "It'll take a moment."

"I'll wait."

Santa's helper stopped by the cheese ball for another tidbit, then strolled back into the file room. Five minutes later she was back with the photocopied pages. "It's a dollar a page," she said pointedly.

I paid, got a receipt, then went and sat at the tables with the computers to read the dispositions of Annette's two brushes with the law.

In the 1984 incident, she'd been arrested after propositioning an undercover officer in the lounge at the Peachtree Plaza Hotel. She'd paid a $250 fine and spent a week in jail. The second time, the arrest came after she'd approached a car in the parking lot of Cowkickers on Stewart Avenue and offered a group rate for its occupants—three out-of-uniform cops working security for a neighboring bar.

Annette's lawyer had claimed she'd been enticed into making the offer, enticed and then entrapped by three bored cops. He'd gotten the charge dropped. Pretty sharp lawyer. His name was Chuck Ingraham.

35

They had a fax machine in the lobby of the courthouse. Two dollars a page local transmission charges. What with the dollar-a-page photocopying it was charging, the county should have dropped our property tax rates and given everybody a free ham.

I called Ferd to let him know what I had found. "Ferd?" I was looking down at Annette and Shay's past. "I'm sending you a fax. Early Christmas present."

"Wonderful," he said. "That could make the difference, Callahan. Sure, Brian has a record, but none of them were sex crimes. None of them involved the possibility of him bringing another criminal into the home where Maura would be living."

"The arrests were a long time ago, though," I pointed out. "Looks like she cleaned up her act after that second arrest. Did I tell you who her lawyer was?"

"No."

"Chuck Ingraham. I'd been wondering where a lowlife like Annette would meet a lawyer like him. Now we know. They met while Annette was trying to get out of jail. You think she paid him in kind?"

"You've got a very smutty mind, Julia Callahan Garrity," Ferd said. "I like that in a woman. You still want me to try and get Shay's jewelry box?

"It's a long shot, but I do," I said.

"Soon as you fax those records over to me, I'm gonna fax them over to Chuck Ingraham's office," Ferd said, chuckling. "Maybe Annette will decide to drop the custody request once she gets a load of what we've found in her background."

"There's still the matter of finding Shay's killer," I reminded him. "Of clearing Brian's name. What about the sperm test?"

"You've done the best you could and that's great," Ferd said evenly. "Now, leave the rest up to me. I'm looking out for my client's best interests."

It was the equivalent of a pat on the head and a sweet dismissal, and it was infuriating.

Did Brian have something to hide? We'd blindly accepted his pledge of innocence. But why was he so hostile about having his alibi for last Saturday night checked out? Why wouldn't he even discuss a simple test that might rule him out as a suspect in Shay's murder? And what did he really know about a girl named Marty who did business in the tangled ruins of Funtown?

Annette, I reminded myself, might know something. She'd been arrested herself a year before Marty's body was discovered, trying to sell herself in the parking lot at Cowkickers. It had to be more than a coincidence.

The sky overhead was a brilliant blue. The sun had come out of hiding and the air felt crystalline and pure. With Maura in the house, I'd taken a chance and left my semi-automatic under the seat of the van the night before.

It was warm enough to go without the overcoat, but I liked having the heft of the 9 mm. in my coat pocket, close at hand. The van splashed through the puddles left from all the rain and I thought some of the trash piles by the road into Funtown were new ones.

I found the old ticket booth Cheezer and I had noticed the night before. In the daytime, though, I noticed something else. The only window in the hut was the front one. Its glass had long ago been broken, but a rough slab of plywood had been shoved in front of the opening.

I had a pair of wool gloves in the pocket of my coat. I pulled them on, tried the door of the ticket booth. The knob turned, but the door was rotted and warped. I leaned on the door and pushed. It opened slowly, the warped sill rubbing on the concrete-block floor.

It wasn't the Ritz, but the booth had been home to somebody, and recently. A white plastic five-gallon paint bucket was upended in one corner; a water-stained mattress took up most of the rest of the room. A bed and a chair—and a roof to keep out the rain—what more could a person want?

Back outside, I kicked one of the plastic bags of trash that had been piled near the door. Nothing moved or kicked back, which is always a good sign. I bent down, opened a bag with one gloved hand. Empty fried chicken boxes, beer bottles, old newspapers, a plastic liter soda bottle, and orange rinds. An empty Spam can.

I wiped my gloves on one of the newspapers, then smoothed them out. The oldest one was from September 20, the newest from December 15th. Funtown's most recent tenant had checked out.

"Hey!" I jumped. Sarge was standing over me, glaring at me. "Thought you were done here."

I found a folded five-dollar bill in my coat pocket, offered it to him. "I just need to know one more thing. You said somebody moved out recently. Was it, uh, a guy named Brian? Drove a black pickup truck?"

"Yeah, Brian. He's got a good job. Got an apartment. You know the guy?" Sarge asked, taking the money and shoving it in his pocket.

"I used to."

I'd run raids on my brother's lair as a kid. He was totally predictable; the nudie mags hidden under the mattress, dope tucked into the toe of the shoes he never wore, the clothes he'd stolen from Kevin, my other brother, hidden at the back of the closet.

A dog was chained to a tree on the lot next to Brian's at the trailer park. He barked and snarled, but he couldn't go far. The chain looked good and tight, but I hurried anyway.

The lock on Brian's trailer was toylike in its simplicity. I popped it with a pick I'd bought from a mail-order catalog, stepped quickly inside, hoping the next door neighbor's dog would forget he'd seen me.

The trailer was tiny, little more than a tin can on concrete blocks, but Brian had turned into a neat housekeeper. Maybe it was a reaction to the years he'd spent living with Shay. The living room had a worn-looking sofa and desk chair, the kitchen furniture consisted of a dinette and two chairs so old they looked like something you might find discarded in back of the Goodwill. I opened the two kitchen cabinets, found my brother's meager groceries and housekeeping supplies; two plates, some plastic take-out cups from fast food restaurants, and a plastic dish containing paper packets of salt, pepper, ketchup, and mustard. In the drawer with the silverware, I found a butcher knife. I picked it up for a closer look. The handle was cheap plastic, the blade dull. And the tip was intact. "Good boy," I said aloud. Brian had gotten a refrigerator since my last visit, but he was still using it mostly as a beer cooler. Nothing on top of the refrigerator, nothing under the sofa cushions, nothing taped to the underside of his kitchen table. No dirty dishes or glasses with telltale lipstick stains. No mail of any kind. I did find one magazine, a two-year-old issue of *Penthouse*, in the bathroom.

The bedroom was barely big enough for the bed, which consisted of a mattress and a box spring. The bed was neatly made, with a spare blanket folded at the foot. There was a dresser of cheap pine, and a nightstand that held an alarm clock, with an ashtray full of pennies. Half a dozen flannel shirts hung from the metal rod in the closet. In the back of the closet there was a large cardboard carton. I pulled it out to get a better look. It was a portable crib, still in its original packing. A bed for Maura.

I put the crib back. The dresser drawers held neatly folded clean clothes, jeans, shirts, socks, underwear. In the bottom drawer, under a sweatshirt, I found a cigar box.

I sat down on the foot of the bed, opened the box. It was if my brother had reduced all the personal effects in his life to a pile that would fit in one, small, flat box. Snapshots, scraps of paper, receipts. His high school ring was here, the green gemstone shining dully. The plastic photo holder from an old billfold was my brother's photo gallery. A greenish color snapshot of the Garritys, taken one Easter in the sixties. Edna and Maureen and I wore floppy flowered Easter hats, Daddy and the boys wore black pants with white dress shirts and bow ties. Brian grinned, showing a gap in his front teeth, Kevin looked annoyed. There was a color photo of Shay, holding a red, wrinkled newborn up to the camera. Another shot of Brian and Shay, smiling up from a beach blanket, the sun in their eyes. A baby picture of Maura, one of those studio shots you get done at discount stores. She must have been around one, clutching her still-furry Poochie in the photo.

Under the photo gallery I found receipts for money orders—Shay's child support, probably. And a laminated plastic card. The image was of a pair of praying hands, the gold lettering said Mass of Christian Burial, Raymond John Garrity, Aug. 16, 1988. Our Lady, Pray for Us.

Pray for us now, especially, I thought. I picked through the scraps of paper. Old movie ticket stubs, more money order carbons. A foil-wrapped condom. Trojan. A Southern Bell cash receipt, for service initiation. It was dated 12–17–98. Thursday. Brian's phone had been hooked up on Thursday, but he'd told me it was still not in service on Saturday night. More scraps of paper. A pink message slip with my phone number on it, one of Ferd's business cards. Another pink message slip. Please call SG. And the phone number.

I took the number into the living room, where Brian's phone sat on the kitchen counter. I dialed. A woman's voice answered "Marriott airport lounge."

"Wrong number," I told her. Wrong damn number.

36

I was thinking about that phone call the bartender at the Marriott had seen Shay make on some guy's cell phone. Is that when she'd called Brian? At work maybe? To ask him to call her back, maybe arrange for a quickie? It explained a lot. The condom, the lying about the phone. Even Brian's refusal to submit a sperm sample to rule him out as someone who'd had contact with Shay immediately before her death. Why? Why was he seeing this woman he professed to hate? Why hadn't he let us know he'd been living the life of a vagrant, down in Funtown? I couldn't understand Brian. Or the lies.

Brian had been seeing Shay right up until she was killed. As Bucky had pointed out, it's not usually smart for a man to sleep with his ex-wife, but it's not unheard, of either. So, why lie?

Given that I'd expended this much energy on my brother's behalf based on a pile of lies, I decided to use his phone to call him on it. But he wasn't there. Randy Pryor said he'd gone off on an errand. "Tell him to call his sister," I said angrily. "Tell him I said he's a lying sack of shit."

"Whatever," Pryor said.

Next I called Ferd, who wasn't in, or wasn't answering his phone. I called our house. Cheezer answered.

"Hey," he said, sounding surprised. "We thought maybe you were Edna."

"Where's Edna?" I asked. It was 4 P.M. Time for her TV talk shows.

"She had a meeting with the lawyer," Cheezer said. "But she was supposed to be back by now. I was just, uh, getting a little worried. I mean, we can handle Maura. She's real good. But she uh, she's kind of, uh, wet."

"Well, duh! Change her. You can do that, can't you?"

"There's a problem," he said, whispering. "Miss Sister pulled all the tape off all the diapers. The whole box."

"Is that Edna?" a voice called from the background. It was Sister. "Tell Edna bring home some diapers for that child. This mess she left ain't no good."

"Do the best you can," I said, sighing. "I'll pick some up on my way home. I didn't know Baby and Sister were going to work today."

"They need some extra Christmas money. I just got here a little while ago. Thought maybe I could pick up one more job before I call it quits for the day. Before she left, Edna told them they could clean some lady's house in Decatur. Mrs. Whitcomb. But they need a ride over there. I told 'em I'd take 'em, but what do we do about Maura?"

I thought about it. I could call my sister and have her take over with Maura, but then we'd have Maureen to deal with all night. She'd probably want us all to come over and have dinner and play some stupid board game. I'd have to talk to her moronic husband Steve, who owns his own ambulance and thinks that makes him Young Doctor Kildare. Young Doctor Kevorkian was more like it.

"Do you have any seat belts in that mail truck of yours?" I asked.

"There's one up front," Cheezer said proudly.

"Would you mind dropping the girls off, then coming back and keeping an eye on Maura? Just until Edna gets back? I'll pay you, of course."

"No problem," Cheezer said. "Miss Baby's been wanting me to take her for a ride in my truck anyway. I think she's got a thing for mailmen."

"She probably does," I said. "You don't have a uniform, do you?"

"No."

"Good. You've got to watch out for Miss Baby around uniforms. The UPS man won't even deliver in their building anymore, she's gotten so bad."

"I'll keep that in mind," Cheezer said gravely.

• • •

I called Bucky on my cell phone, from the parking lot at the Homicide Task Force office.

"Come outside," I said, as soon as he picked up his phone.

"No fuckin' way," he said. "I can't be seen with you."

"Then I'll come in there," I said. "I'm right outside. I'll just come strolling in the front door, right past Major Mackey's door."

"I'm on my way," he said. "Fuck."

He shook his head. "You're nuts. Certifiable."

"Did you try running Marty Bono-something? Come on, Bucky. I know you're mad at me. You can stay mad. You have my permission. But this is a chance to solve a ten-year-old case. A chance to rub it in Acey Karpik's face. Not to mention those guys in Clayton and Henry counties. So what about it?"

He put his hand into the inner pocket of his leather jacket, brought out a computer printout. "Nobody in vice remembered your girl. I got a hunch. If she had a MARTA card, chances are she also had a Grady card somewhere. So I went over to Grady. Talked to this nurse in the infectious diseases unit. They got a special clinic for STDs, you know, sexually transmitted diseases. They supply hookers with condoms, do regular VD and AIDS tests. This nurse, Judy, she's been at the hospital since the mayor of Atlanta was a white guy. She remembered a Marty. From up north. Came down here that summer, she told Judy, with a girlfriend. To work the Democratic Convention."

"I knew it," I said. "Tell me."

"Judy checked the Grady computer for me. Her name was Marianne Bonaventura. DOB 3–25–69. The Grady records list her address as the Alamo Pass. Guess she must have moved, later."

"What about a record?" I asked. "Did you find an arrest record?"

"If this is our girl, she had four arrests, all for solicitation," Bucky said, looking down at the printout.

"It's gotta be her," I said.

"I showed Judy the photograph, she wasn't positive," Bucky said. "But Grady had an address for her next of kin. Guy named Nick Bonaventura in Trenton, New Jersey. It's Marianne's brother. He promised to find a photo of his sister, see if he could get it faxed down to me."

"Did he know she was dead?"

Bucky shrugged. "He said they weren't a close family. She moved out of town, their Mom died, he hadn't heard from her."

I thought about the jeans and T-shirt sitting in an evidence locker at the Atlanta Police Department for the past ten years. Those could have been my brother's. We wouldn't have known, either.

"Can I see the rap sheet?" I asked, putting out my hand.

"That's a felony in this state," Bucky said, snatching it away from me.

"You hold it, let me read over your shoulder," I said, glaring at him.

As he'd said, Marianne Bonaventura had been arrested four times, all for solicitation of prostitution, all by members of the Atlanta Police Department. The arrests had started in January of 1987, the last one had come in July of 1988.

Bucky pointed at the last arrest. "I looked up the docket number. She was arrested at Cowkickers in 1986."

I pulled out my file of notes from under the front seat, flipped through until I found the record of Annette Gatlin's arrest. It was the same date.

"Shay's mother, Annette, was arrested for prostitution at Cowkickers, that same date," I said. "Christ."

"Lots of people were arrested all that summer," Bucky said. "The city fathers didn't want hookers messing up the street corners. Vice ran sweeps almost every night. Forty or fifty arrests every Friday and Saturday night."

"Did you bring me a copy of the case file?" I asked, trying not to sound as eager as I was.

"You're lucky I even came out of the damn office," Bucky said. "I gotta get back. I'm waiting on that fax from New Jersey."

"What then?" I asked.

"We find out who killed Jane Doe. And whether the killer had anything to do with those other homicides. Including Shay Gatlin." He gave me an odd look. "You've been real busy. You find out anything else you wanna share with me?"

I thought of my brother's stay at Funtown, where Marty Bonaventura's body had been discovered. My stomach lurched. "No."

"I called up a buddy at the crime lab," Bucky said, casually, like it was an afterthought. "They're not done running everything from that crime scene where your sister-in-law was killed. He says they found something interesting on the bed sheet."

"Yeah?"

"Two different blood types. B and O. Shay Gatlin's blood type was O-positive. The killer must have cut his hand, while he was stabbing her. Type B. Something to think about."

I thought about it the whole way home. My blood type was B, but I had no idea what Edna's blood type was, and whatever I'd learned about blood typing and genetics in high school had disappeared along with all that other important stuff they'd tried to cram into our heads.

But I knew somebody who should know a lot about blood and how it works. Somebody who'd worked for fifteen years in the busiest hospital emergency room in the Southeast.

"Maureen?" My brother-in-law Steve acted like he'd never heard the name before. "She's on another line right now."

"Steve, it's me. Callahan. Tell her it's important. I need to talk to her right now."

"OK," he said reluctantly. "But it's your mom she's talking to. And she sounds kind of upset."

"Callahan?" Maureen screeched. "How did this happen?"

"What? What are you talking about? Quit screaming. I just need to ask you some questions. You know, medical questions. Listen, what's your blood type?"

"You're crazy," Maureen said. "You let that Annette woman just abduct my niece, and then you call up and want to talk about blood?"

"What are you saying?" I repeated.

"While you were running around town playing detective this afternoon, Annette Gatlin got some kind of court order from some kind of Mickey Mouse judge, giving her custody of Maura. Mama just got home and found out one of your stupid lackeys just handed Maura over to Annette. Mama's beside herself. I'm going over there right now to try to calm her down. I suggest you get your behind home to help me," Maureen said. "Honestly!"

Cheezer sat on the front porch, his face buried in his hands. He looked up when he heard my footsteps.

"God, Callahan," he said mournfully. "I didn't know. She showed up here, and I was the only one. Just me and Maura. We were watching *Barney* together. Annette came to the front door. I wouldn't let her come in. But she had this court order. It was signed, looked real official. I told her she'd have to wait for you or Edna to get home, and she was hollering at me, saying she was the child's grandmother. I guess Maura heard her voice. She came running out the door, 'Granny Annie!' she was saying."

He chewed his knuckle. "She wouldn't leave. Wouldn't put Maura down, and you know how cold it was getting around five. Cold and dark. So I told her she could come in, while I tried to call you, or Edna. She said Maura was wet. She was going to take her in the bathroom to change her."

Cheezer ducked his head. "I can't lie to you. Maura had, sort of, uh, the runs. She was pretty smelly. And I couldn't get the diapers to stay on. Finally, I just wrapped some duct tape around her waist. But then the diapers were a bitch to get off. When Annette offered to change Maura, man, I guess I jumped at it."

I patted his hand. "It's OK. Nobody likes the stinky ones. Not even Edna. What happened next?"

"I went into the kitchen to try to call you, and as soon as I did, I heard footsteps. I ran to the front door, and she was already in her car. She just threw Maura in the front seat, didn't even buckle her seat belt," he said indignantly. "I went running out, to try to stop her. I ran out in front of her car, even, but she just swerved around me. Went right up over Mr. Byerly's yard, and then she tore off. Trenched Mr. Byerly's yard bad. I got in the mail truck, and tried to catch up with her. But hell, that thing's top speed is only about thirty-five. She had that car floored."

More headlights in the driveway. It was Maureen, in her Suburban. Cheezer looked like he wished he could disappear. I wished we could both disappear.

37

Edna was on the phone. "Ferd? Annette's taken Maura. What the hell is going on?"

She listened for about thirty seconds. "Annette showed up here about five thirty, after I'd already left your office and was on the way home. She showed one of my employees some court order saying she'd been awarded temporary custody. What?"

Edna turned as she saw us enter the kitchen, Cheezer skulking in like a purse-snatcher who'd been nabbed with the goods in his back pocket. "Did you keep the court order? Where is it?"

"It was right there on the hall table," he said. "I put it there when I went to call you. It's gone. She must have taken it with her."

"Is this legal?" Edna asked. "Why are we going through the motions of having a hearing tomorrow if she can just snatch Maura tonight? Ferd, why didn't you see this coming?"

She put the phone down with a bang. "He says Annette must have gotten desperate after she saw we had a copy of her old arrest report. Ferd thinks it's some kind of delaying tactic. He's calling Chuck Ingraham right now. Then he says he'll try to get hold of Judge Bingham at home. He says if I call Annette, it'll just make matters worse."

Maureen fluttered around the kitchen, trying to help. "Let me fix you a cup of tea," she begged.

For myself, I preferred a taste of Tennessee tea. I got the Jack Daniel's bottle and poured a thick slug onto a tumbler full of ice cubes. I held the bottle up, but Cheezer shook his head.

"It's my fault," he kept saying. "All my fault."

Maureen cut her eyes at him, letting him know she thought it really was all his fault.

"Can you remember whose signature was on the court order?" I asked, sitting down at the table. "Was it Judge Bingham? Payne Bingham?"

"That doesn't sound right," he said. "God, I'm sorry."

Where else would Annette have gotten some kind of court document that would give her custody of Maura? Would she have had the nerve to cook up something by herself?

"What about Chuck Ingraham?" I said. "He's a lawyer. He'd know how to make something look official. Does that ring a bell, Cheezer?"

Cheezer looked hopeful. "Yeah. Ingraham. That sounds like the name. I only saw it for a few seconds, before Maura came running in, but that sounds kinda like the name I read."

Edna walked over to the table and helped herself to my Jack and water. "Never mind the tea," she told Maureen. "Fix me a drink. If Ferd can't do it, I will. I'm calling Annette Gatlin right now."

She slammed the phone down again, and the three of us winced. Mayflies have a longer life span than the phones in our house.

"She's got Maura," Edna fumed. "Lord knows where they could be. Sitting in a bar somewhere, picking up men." Her eyes widened. "What if she's skipping town? She knows we've got the goods on her. What if she decided not to wait for a hearing? What if she just trumped up a piece of paper that looked official?"

Maureen patted Edna's shoulder. "Don't get yourself all worked up. Ferd is working on it. He'll find out what this is all about. Just give him a little time."

"Time, hell," Edna said.

I got my coat. "I'll go look for them," I said.

"Me, too," Cheezer said, jumping up to join me.

I wanted a face-to-face with Chuck Ingraham. The light was on at his office, but nobody was home. I banged on the door and rang the doorbell. I had Cheezer stand lookout while I checked the back of the office. My picklock was still in my coat pocket, but the office was on Jonesboro's main thoroughfare, a block from the sheriff's office, with all those official-looking cruisers.

I still had no idea where Chuck and Annette had been staying since they'd left Twelve Oaks Plaza. I thought about Dyson Yount. He and Ingraham were tight. And something had been going on between Shay and Yount. Why else would he have arranged to give her a condo?

Dyson Yount's address was in the phone directory. Sycamore Street was easy to find. The homes were the kind of mansions you see on those home tours we love in the South, enormous magnolias flanking the driveway, even a discreetly lit sign—Oakleigh 1922. It wasn't even close to antebellum, but there wasn't much left in General Sherman's wake that did date back to the Confederacy.

A Volvo station wagon was parked halfway up the driveway at Oakleigh, its tailgate raised, all four doors open. A petite dark-haired woman in blue jeans and a red polar fleece jacket was unloading the car. She looked up, shaded her eyes to try to see who was pulling into her driveway.

"Mrs. Yount?"

She smiled warmly. "Yes?"

"I'm looking for your husband. It's sort of urgent."

She pulled a suitcase out of the cargo area and set it down. "He's not home," she said. "Can I help?" She was anxious, trying to figure out if it was safe to talk to a woman who drove around in a van with a pony-tailed hippie like Cheezer.

"I'm Shay's sister-in-law," I said. "I'm looking for my niece."

"Oh." She went back to the car, pulled out another suitcase and, with a bag in each hand, headed toward the back of the house. I followed right behind her. She glanced over her shoulder, but kept going, until she reached the back door, which seemed to open onto a glassed-in sun porch. She set the bags down on the brick floor.

"You can probably reach Dyson at his office, in the morning," she said, thinking to dismiss me.

"The morning will be too late," I said. "Shay's mother, Annette, and her lawyer Chuck Ingraham have cooked up some kind of order, giving custody of Maura to Shay's mother, Annette. The problem is,

Ingraham isn't a judge. Why would he do something like this, Mrs. Yount?"

"I don't know anything about any of this," Mrs. Yount whispered. "How would Dyson know anything about these people? He's a real estate broker. He doesn't kidnap children."

"Mom?" A young girl, not quite a teen, came out of the house onto the sun porch. She had her mother's dark hair and trim build, and her father's prominent jawline. Even the same kind of tortoiseshell glasses. Maybe they got a family discount at the optometrist.

"Not now, Sarah," Mrs. Yount said hastily. "Take these suitcases in, please. Tell your brother to take his upstairs."

The girl stared, but obeyed.

"What's your name?" Mrs. Yount asked, flipping a strand of hair behind one ear.

"Callahan Garrity. Shay was married to my brother, Brian."

"I know about your brother. My husband said he's a criminal."

"What do you know about your husband?" I asked, since we were discussing family issues. "Did he tell you his bank approved a mortgage loan for Shay? Has he admitted to you that he was sleeping with Shay? Or maybe you already knew that. Maybe that's why you left him. She's dead now. Is that why you came back to live with your husband?"

The sunporch was unheated, chilly, half-lit. Dyson Yount's wife turned away. She was in the doorway.

"Did he kill Shay? Was he with her last Saturday night?"

When she turned around, her face was very pale.

"Tomorrow is Christmas Eve," she whispered. "My children missed their father. I missed my husband. I'm sorry Shay is dead. I don't know where Maura is. There's nothing more I can tell you."

"Would you bring your children home to a man who stabbed a woman in her sleep?" I asked. "Would you sleep in the same bed with him?"

"Dyson had nothing to do with that," she said, her voice trembling.

"You were out of town," I pointed out.

"He called me at my parents' house," she said. "He called me every night while I was away. Dyson teaches a class in domestic law. At the police academy. Saturday was the last class. Afterward, he and his students had a get-together. At Harold's Barbecue. He called me afterwards. He was pleased with how well the class went. You should go now."

But I wasn't ready to go. Not yet. "Does Annette know something about Shay's affair with your husband?" I asked. "Is she blackmailing him? Is that why he's helping her try to get custody of Maura?"

"Leave us alone," Mrs. Yount said. She stepped inside the house, closed the door. I heard the lock click. And then the lights went out across the back of the house.

There were lots of lights at Twelve Oaks Plaza. Balconies were strung with colored lights that twinkled and raced, brightly lit trees glowed through every window, and management had even sprung for red and green spotlights and an eight-foot-tall plastic Nativity scene in front of the Twelve Oaks sign. A loudspeaker played "Jinglebell Rock." There is nothing like a white-trash Christmas.

Mrs. Jimmy James was not in residence. I knocked at the door to Annette's apartment, but there was no answer there, either.

We found a cardboard carton in the back of the van and dumped out the twelve bottles of window cleaner it had contained. We stuffed it full of newspaper, and then I wrote Annette Gatlin's name and address across the top of the box.

"Lemme do something, please," Cheezer begged. "It's my fault. You gotta let me make it right."

We cruised through the complex until we found a door marked Resident Manager. A faint blue glow emanated from the front window.

Cheezer's bony wrists dangled from the sleeves of his T-shirt, which was faded and dirt-streaked. I took my jacket off, made him put it on and tuck his ponytail underneath the collar. It made him look a little less like the Boston Strangler.

"Tell the manager you've got to deliver this package to Mrs. Gatlin," I coached. "It's urgent. You've got to have the new address where she's staying. Right?"

He nodded enthusiastically. "He shouldn't call to ask her if it's all right, because we don't want to spoil the big surprise. Right?"

I watched as he knocked on the door, stepped back, squared his shoulders, put on his expectant, hopeful face. The door opened, a woman popped her head out. She did not pop back in and she did not reappear with a shotgun. So far, so good. They talked, then she went inside. When she came back, she handed him a slip of paper. On his way back to the van, he shot me a thumbs-up. All systems go.

38

The address was in Hapeville, for a place called Silver Dollar Court. Cheezer found it on my metro Atlanta map book. He navigated, I drove. "It looks like it's really close to the airport," he reported.

In fact, most of the rest of Silver Dollar Court seemed about to become airport. The street was a narrow cul-de-sac, lined with dumpy red-brick houses, all of them numbingly alike. Barbed wire fencing stretched across both sides of the road. Every hundred yards signs were posted: Warning: This Property Condemned By Atlanta Airport Authority. Only two houses, at the end of the cul-de-sac, were not fenced off. Both had For Sale By Owner signs in the front yard. One was the house we were looking for, number 325.

Jets thundered overhead, swooping so low to the horizon that I swore I could see the pilot's dental work. The sky seemed strung with an endless chain of the blinking white and red lights from jets, circling, stacked four and five high, waiting to land at Hartsfield. The cul-de-sac backed up to the interstate, so close we could see more lights—white headlights, red brake lights. Traffic was at a standstill. With Christmas little more than a day away, it seemed as if half the world was trying to get a plane out of Atlanta. The other half was circling overhead, waiting to get in.

Like the others, the house at 325 Silver Dollar Court looked empty and abandoned.

I called the number for Annette that Edna had given me as I was running out the door. Nobody answered. "Her car's not here," Cheezer pointed out. "She was driving a white Pontiac Firebird."

It was 9 P.M. Annette Gatlin could have been anywhere. If she were alone. But to the best of our knowledge, she wasn't alone. She was toting a three-year-old little girl, who at this hour would be tired and, according to Cheezer, as ripe as a week-old banana.

I was about to make a command decision. Call off the search—let Ferd do the job we were paying him to do. Besides, I needed to know more about what Ferd really knew about Brian's involvement with Shay.

"We could break in," Cheezer said, in a small voice.

"You know how to burglarize a residence?" I asked, trying to sound shocked.

"My mom," he said. "Sometimes, if we were behind on the rent and the landlord locked us out, we'd go back in to get our stuff. Sometimes we'd stay an extra night, too. She did it all the time. I guess she thought I wasn't paying attention."

"Something tells me you paid attention all the time," I said.

We pulled the van up into the driveway at the house next door. It wasn't hidden from the street, but it wasn't parked out front with that sign that screamed House Mouse, either.

The front door of 325 had a padlock, which seemed to surprise Cheezer. "Oh," he said, faintly.

I handed him my picklock. "Be my guest."

He didn't ask, I didn't tell.

The house was cold and only half-furnished. A combination living room–dining room held a sofa decorated with a pillow and the yellow knit afghan I'd seen hanging on Maura's crib in Shay's bedroom. There was a television and stacked on top were three videos. *Die Hard. Cinderella. Barney.* My scalp prickled.

"Stand by the window," I told Cheezer. "Let me know if you see any cars coming down the street. Maybe we can jump out and throw a surprise party for Annette."

There were two bedrooms. One held nothing but cardboard boxes, which proved to be full of women's clothes.

The other was a functioning bedroom, with a king-sized waterbed, dresser, and open suitcases lying around on the floor. The closet door was open—inside hung a rack of navy blue uniforms. The patch on the shoulders all said the same thing. Empire Airport Security.

"See anybody?" I called to Cheezer.

"All's quiet," he called back.

I rifled quickly through the suitcases. They'd been neatly packed, two with women's clothes, one with small pink and white and pale blue outfits. A threadbare stuffed dog had been tossed on top. Poochie. All the signs pointed to Annette and Maura. But what about Chuck? Where did he fit into Annette's scheme?

I found reassurance in the bathroom. Annette's cosmetic bag, bulging with foundation, mascara, moisturizer, powder, lipstick, the works. If Annette Gatlin's makeup was here, she was coming back. Another flowered, zippered bag sat atop the hamper. It clinked. I sat down on the floor, unzipped the bag and poured out its contents. Jewelry. A watch that didn't keep time, lots of earrings, bracelets, a couple of pins, a thin gold wedding band. Was it Shay's? There were necklaces, strings of cheap pearls, plenty of tacky costume stuff. Nothing that looked remotely like the necklace Shay had been wearing in the hospital photo.

The tile floor was cold and I was tired. Annette would probably be back, but when? And what would I do when she got back?

I put everything back where I'd found it. Straightened the suitcases I'd rifled, gave Poochie a final pat. "See ya later, pal."

Maura's day-care center was off Riverdale Road. KidzKare. Drop-Ins Welcome.

"Like, people just dump kids here and take off?" Cheezer asked. "Is that legal?"

"It's called day care. A very popular concept. You can even buy a franchise."

KidzKare was spanking clean. Like a hospital. The young woman at the reception desk wore one of those telephone headsets. The door buzzed when we walked in, and she looked up and gave us a smile featuring glittering orthodontia. "Welcome to KidzKare! I'm Sherry."

"Hi, Sherry. I'm looking for Maura Garrity," I said, smiling back. "Her grandmother asked me to pick her up." I don't actually have an aversion to lying, but this was the truth. "Her grandmother has got to work an extra shift tonight."

"Maura?" Recognition flickered in her eyes, which were framed, Cleopatra-style, with blue eyeliner. She picked up a clipboard with a sign-in sheet and frowned.

"I can't talk to you about Maura," she said.

"That's all right," I said. "I'll just sign her out and take her off your hands. She's got a little tummy bug, you know."

Her eyebrow twitched. "You're the people who kidnapped Maura before. My cousin lost her job because of you people." She picked up the telephone. "I'm calling the police."

"Go ahead," Cheezer taunted. "Make my day."

I put my hand on hers. "Don't do that."

She pulled away violently. "There's a video camera recording everything you do," she said, her voice high and tight.

"Is she here?" I asked wearily. "Just tell me if she's here."

"I'm calling the cops now," she repeated.

"Never mind, we're leaving," I said.

Cheezer was still sputtering as we got in the van. "You could've taken her, easy. I'll bet you anything Maura was in there."

"So what?" I asked. "We knock over a day-care center, steal the kid—with video cameras staring us in the face? You want me to pull a gun on a baby-sitter? Cheezer, this is not TV. I am not Batgirl and you are not Robin."

"What do we tell Edna?"

"I'll deal with her," I said, starting the van.

It was after eleven, but the house was ablaze with color and light. It was all so damned cheerful I nearly turned around and left.

She'd made a fire in the living room and she was curled up on the sofa with a quilt over her legs, sipping a cup of tea, watching the flames lick at the white oak logs from the tree that had fallen in the big Halloween storm last year.

To make things worse, she didn't say a word when I walked in and sat on the armchair facing the sofa. She didn't yell or cry or curse. Just kept sipping her tea, keeping her eyes on the flames.

"I'm sorry," I told her. "But it's not over. Tomorrow, we'll raise hell with that judge. Get the sheriff's deputies with a warrant or something. The important thing is, Annette can't win. She's staying in some hovel on a street that's been condemned for the airport's new runway. We'll go back there, get some photos to show the judge she's unstable, unfit to raise a child. We'll get a new lawyer, maybe an expert in child custody issues."

"Tomorrow is Christmas Eve," Edna said tonelessly.

"I know."

She swung her legs off the sofa, stood uneasily. "I want to show you something," she said, facing me for the first time.

I followed her down the hall, marveling again at how steadily she'd physically diminished over the past three years, since her heart attack. Always, my mother had seemed larger than life, even if she was really only five-foot-four. Big hair, big talk, big ideas, had been her credo. Now I felt like a giant, lumbering in the wake of a dwarf.

The carved walnut bed stood squarely in the middle of her bedroom, one of my grandmother's feed-sack quilts smoothed over the starched white sheets. She'd laid everything out on the foot of the bed, just the way she'd always laid out her outfit when she and Daddy were getting ready to go to a fancy party. Cocktail dress, stockings, slip, shoes, bag, jewelry.

But this dress was child-sized, and instead of nylons, she'd laid out a tiny pair of white tights and a pair of shiny black patent leather Mary Janes with grosgrain bows on the insteps.

"Remember this?" she asked, presenting the dress on a fancy satin padded coathanger.

The dress was red plaid taffeta, with a white bib collar trimmed in crocheted lace. I fingered the shiny skirt fabric. It smelled of Woolite and a steam iron.

"It was scratchy," I told her. "I hated this dress. But I loved the new Mary Janes every year. Nothing slides over a wooden floor like a new pair of Mary Janes."

"If you put a very fine coating of floor wax on the patent leather, it doesn't scuff," Edna said. "Did I ever tell you that?"

"I'll keep it in mind," I said, although my current lifestyle didn't frequently necessitate black patent leather.

She fluffed the skirt. "It was the crinoline that made it so scratchy," Edna said. "I dressed you and Maureen exactly alike. Every Christmas and Easter. Sister dresses. Your Aunt Julia sent the money for them, and afterwards, I sent the family pictures, so she could see how nice everybody looked. The year you two wore these dresses you took your crinoline off and kicked it under Daddy's car in the parking lot at church. I could have whipped your behind, if it wasn't Christmas and the whole church wasn't watching."

"Maureen loved those crinolines," I said. "She always did love to priss around and have her picture taken. She was stealing your lipstick and perfume when she was only eight years old."

"This one was Maureen's," Edna said, putting the dress back on the bed. "Like new, isn't it? All I had to do was freshen it up with a new red velvet sash. I found yours in the cedar chest, but it wasn't fit for a dishrag by the time you got done with it. You never did keep things nice like Maureen."

Edna opened the top drawer of her dresser. She still keeps things like handkerchiefs and dress shields and lavender sachets in there. But now she brought out a small disposable camera.

"It's the kind with a flash," she explained. "So I could take a picture of Maura in her dress. You know, before midnight mass. With the whole family. Maureen promised she'd make Steve go. I haven't brought it up with Brian yet, but I know I can talk him into it. Kevin called. I have a feeling they might show up, to surprise me. Then, in the morning, I can finish the roll of film when she's opening up all her presents. I think she's old enough to take to midnight Mass, don't you?"

All those years of midnight Mass. We'd stay up late on Christmas Eve, listening to music, maybe watching Daddy's favorite movie, *White Christmas* on TV. Daddy thought Bing Crosby was a living saint. Around 10 P.M., Edna would hustle the four of us into our Christmas outfits. We'd pose for pictures for Aunt Julia, drink some eggnog and nibble at cookies, then load into the car, which Daddy had gotten warmed up while we dressed.

The church was always a crush. "Christmas Catholics," my father would mutter. Organ music trilled, the choir warbled "Adeste Fideles," even after Vatican II decreed that Latin was finished. The priests dressed in their fanciest cassocks and the flicker of candles threw shadows on the stone walls. We kids picked out our favorite figures in the Italian manger scene on the altar.

After we got home, we'd be hustled off to bed so that the two of them could finish assembling the toys and filling the stockings.

I can't remember when all of that changed—when we gave up midnight Mass and started sleeping late Christmas morning. Probably the year Kevin announced he was no longer Catholic, but a druid. Or maybe it was the next year, when it seemed more important to me, at sixteen, to party with friends on Christmas Eve than to get dressed up and take family pictures. Nobody thought to take any family pictures the last time we were all together, at Daddy's funeral.

Edna gave the dress a final pat, then took it and hung it carefully in her closet. She put the camera back in the top dresser drawer. "We'll save her presents until we get Maura back. Save Christmas until then."

39

Ferd knocked once, lightly on the kitchen door, then stepped inside. Brian, right behind him, hesitated a moment, as if to seek permission before entering his mother's home.

"It's gonna snow," Ferd said heartily. He gave Edna a peck on the cheek. "We're gonna have a white Christmas, Edna Mae."

"It never snows in Atlanta at Christmas," Edna said, turning to Brian, who hung back, near the door. "You ever remember a white Christmas in Georgia?"

"No ma'am," Brian said.

Edna ruffled his hair, letting her hand linger a moment on his scratchy beard, straightening the frayed collar of his flannel shirt.

"No coat and tie for court?" She clucked her tongue. "That won't make a very good impression on the judge."

"No ma'am," Brian said, staring down at his muddy work boots.

Her hand fell away. She took a step back. "What's going on?" she demanded. "Why aren't you dressed for this custody hearing?"

Brian was staring at me, a red flush creeping up his neck. I knew that flush too well, suffering all my life from emotional transparency in times of stress.

Ferd coughed. His color was bad. He coughed again, a dry, hacking sound. "Brian?"

"I'm not going to court, Mama. It's, uh, complicated. The time's not right for me to get Maura."

Edna clutched his arm, steely-faced. "What do you mean? Maura can't stay with that woman. With those people."

She looked at Ferd in desperation. "Did you tell him about Annette? That she was a prostitute?"

Ferd nodded.

"Do you know the kind of environment your daughter would be raised in? Left in a day-care center all day and all night? Living with a woman with the morals of an alley cat? A woman who picks up men in bars and brings them home? Is that the life you want for your little girl?"

The only sound in the kitchen was the steady drip of the coffeemaker.

"I gotta go to work," Brian blurted. He bolted for the door.

Edna's face crumpled. She sank down in a kitchen chair, buried her face in her hands. One weak sob. It tore my gut like a knife.

I flew out the door, caught up with Brian as he was getting into his dusty black pickup. I jerked his arm and whipped him around to face me.

"Goddamn it, you're not running away again," I said angrily.

He brushed my hand away. "Get offa me."

"You killed her, didn't you? You killed Shay and now you're just going to walk away. You're going to let Maura pay because you're such a selfish shit."

"You don't know anything," Brian snarled.

"I know some things," I shot back. "I know you're incapable of telling the truth, even to yourself. After you left Shay, you weren't staying with friends, you were living down in that hut at Funtown. You could have asked us for help, but you wouldn't. I know you were still sleeping with Shay, even after one of her boyfriends beat you up. You screwed her that night, too. That's why you won't give a sperm sample to clear this up. You screwed her and then you killed her."

"I don't need your fuckin' help," Brian said. "All of this was a mistake. I came home because I thought I could get my kid back, start over—"

"You want your kid back? You never had Maura. Shay had her. The day care had her. Edna and I had her. Where were you?"

He shoved me hard, sent me sprawling onto the driveway. He was breathing hard, his fists clenched. Maybe he would hit me, like he'd hit Shay.

But he couldn't shut me up.

"Maura's not a thing, Brian. She's not some toy you latch onto just to keep another kid from having her. Why don't you do the right thing for once? Why don't you tell the truth? Ask for help? Fix it so Maura won't grow up to be another Annette? Another Shay?"

"Fuck you."

I had to scramble to clear the driveway before he shoved the truck into reverse and went blasting away.

Ferd sat at the table, sipping coffee. He'd kept his overcoat on. Edna sat opposite him, staring daggers.

"You knew he was going to do something like this, didn't you?" she said.

He sighed. "Did I know the boy had mixed feelings about what he'd have to go through to get custody of Maura? Yes. Did I know he'd back out? No. You're his mama. You know him better than me."

"We don't know him," I said dully. "He won't let us."

Ferd put his coffee mug down. He was puffy-eyed, ill. Why had we not seen it before? He was old and sick. He'd tried to tell us, but we hadn't wanted to listen.

"I'm sorry," he said. "About all of it. Don't worry about a bill. I feel bad about Maura. I really do."

"It's not over," Edna said. "I'll take her. She's my grandchild. It's my responsibility to see that she's raised right."

He shook his head. "Brian is her surviving parent. I believe the judge was ready to award him permanent physical custody. But without his name on the petition . . . I don't know."

"Can't you leave his name on the petition?" I asked. "Does Brian have to be in court today? Can't we just say he had to work, or something like that?"

"Just fix it so the judge lets us keep her till after Christmas," Edna pleaded. "Till we get Brian back on his feet again."

Ferd shook his head. My mother was the only one in the room who didn't know that Brian would never get back on his feet. "I'm sorry."

He kept saying that. "It's too late. We'd have to file new briefs, get supporting documentation . . . It all takes time."

He coughed and, this time, he couldn't catch his breath. I got up, brought him a glass of water. He sipped, coughed again. "I don't have a lot of time right now," he said, his voice coming out as a wheeze. "After today, I was going to suggest you get another lawyer. I've got some names I could suggest."

Listening to his labored breathing was agonizing. "Never mind," Edna said gently. "You tried. You're a good friend, Ferd Bryce. If Jack Garrity were alive, he'd buy you a beer."

Ferd smiled ruefully. "A generic beer, probably. He damn sure wouldn't have paid me, the old cheapskate."

It was still early for such a crushing disappointment. I was all dressed up in my good black pantsuit. All ready for court, to make a good impression for Maura's sake. Edna was carefully dressed, too, in dark green wool, with a little Santa Claus–face pin Ruby had crocheted for her a couple of Christmases ago.

"Stay here," I told her. "Listen out for the phones. I've got Ferd's files. I'm going down there to Clayton County. I'll bring Maura back in time. I promise." And then I remembered the old family joke. "What time is midnight Mass?"

The hearing was set for 9 A.M. I checked the directory in the courthouse lobby, found Judge Bingham's office. I went through the metal detectors in front of the elevators, went up two flights, then followed arrows until I was sure I'd walked completely around the building.

Judge Bingham's secretary was on the phone. She motioned me to sit down, kept talking. "The judge is leaving at noon sharp," I heard her say. "The whole family's going down to Sea Island for the holidays, and his wife will skin me alive if I don't get him out of here in time."

She hung up, looked at me quizzically. "If it's not on our calendar today, I really can't deal with you, ma'am."

"It's on the judge's calendar," I said. "I'm Callahan Garrity. My brother is Brian Garrity, and I'm here for the custody hearing for my niece, Maura Garrity."

She looked down at her wristwatch. "Are you one of the attorneys?"

"No," I said. "Our attorney is ill. That's what I wanted to talk to the judge about. Somebody showed up at our house yesterday, with a custody order. But I can't understand why he would have signed an order when we had this hearing scheduled today."

"The judge hasn't signed any new orders in the Garrity custody action," she said crisply. "He'll hear the case at nine A.M.," she said firmly. "The bailiff will have unlocked the courtroom by now. You can wait in there."

Chuck Ingraham had concocted the fake custody order, making it look just authentic enough to get Maura away from us. But he and Annette had to know their ruse wouldn't last for long. What were they up to? The courtroom was bone cold, and windowless. I sat in the front row, mentally rehearsing what I would tell the judge. Edna, I decided, would not mind my describing her as an ailing, elderly, heartbroken widow, if it meant getting Maura.

At a quarter till the bailiff came in, fiddled with the thermostat on the wall. Soon after, a court reporter set up in front of the judge's bench. Another bailiff came in, put some papers on the judge's desk, and left through a door behind the bench. The secretary came out, looked around.

"Is your attorney present?" she asked.

"No ma'am," I said. "He's ill. I'll be representing my brother."

She looked down at her watch again. "The judge isn't going to like this."

Nine o'clock came and went. The bailiff wandered around the courtroom. The court reporter leafed through a magazine. Another bailiff came out. "You're Miss Garrity?"

"Yes," I said, standing up.

"Judge Bingham wants all parties in this courtroom within the next five minutes," the bailiff said. He turned around and disappeared again.

A bead of sweat trickled down my back. Where was Annette? Where was Chuck Ingraham? More important, where was Maura?

Five minutes later, I was in the judge's office, pleading with the secretary. "I've got to talk to the judge," I told her. "There's no sign of the other parties in this case. I think they've abducted my niece."

"Who's the attorney?" she asked.

"Chuck Ingraham," I said. "He and the grandmother, Annette Gatlin, were the ones who falsified that custody order."

"I'll let the judge know," she said. "You can wait outside in the hallway. The bailiff has already called his next case. You may have to wait a while."

I found the pay phone and called Edna. "They're not here," I said. "The judge has already called the next case."

"She's gone," Edna said bleakly. "She's taken Maura. We'll never see her again."

"Don't start panicking," I said, although I'd been feeling panicky ever since I hit the courthouse. "It's only been fifteen minutes. I'm going to wait til this next case is done, then see if the judge will just go ahead and sign the permanent custody order. Once we've got that, we've got the weight of the law behind us. If Annette doesn't hand Maura over, we can get her arrested for violating the order."

"If we can find her," Edna said.

I wandered around the hallway for a while, reading bulletin boards, wringing my hands, checking the clock. At 10 A.M. I wandered back into the courtroom. Judge Bingham turned out to have intensely blue eyes and a shiny bald head. Lawyers clustered around both sides of the bench, and a man and a woman sat, separately, at the lawyer's tables.

"Judge, my client was given this animal for a twenty-fifth anniversary gift," a pudgy female attorney said. "She was expecting a Lexus, but be that as it may, she has bonded with the dog, and we would expect that Scooter would be awarded her in any property settlement, just as she should be awarded her diamond engagement ring, the lake home, and alimony in the amount of five thousand dollars a month."

"Your honor!" The lawyer on the husband's side jumped up, all excited. "My client was the one who chose Scooter, who cared for her, took her to the vet, had her spayed. Scooter's emotional attachment is to Mr. Douglas, not Mrs. Douglas."

Judge Bingham yawned. "Who took the dog for walks every night? Who's had the dog since this couple has been legally separated?"

I got up and walked out of the courtroom. Mac was standing on the other side of the door. He'd been watching through the glass insert in the door.

"What are you doing here?" I asked, glad, for once, to have reinforcements. Canine custody hearings can get pretty hairy.

He had a foil-wrapped poinsettia under one arm and a honey-baked ham under the other.

"Edna told me what's been going on," he said, handing me the poinsettia. "C'mon. Let's go see the judge's secretary."

"She won't listen to me," I said, trying not to sound too whiny. "She says I have to wait until the judge has finished hearing this next case."

"I'm a bureaucrat, remember?" Mac said. "I made some phone calls on the way over here. Judge Bingham's secretary is Mackenzie Waller. She used to work in the Clayton Planning and Zoning office. She used to think I was a pretty hot ticket."

"If this woman thinks you're such a hot ticket, why do we need a poinsettia and a ham?"

"Lagniappe," Mac said. "It's an old courthouse tradition."

Mackenzie Waller's disposition changed when Mac walked in the office. "Well, hey there, stranger," she said, twinkling. "Is this official business?"

"Business and pleasure," Mac said, setting the ham on her desk. "Could we have a moment of your time?"

Sexism cuts both ways. Sometimes, you just have to go with it. Mac explained our dilemma and she listened attentively, even going so far as to open the file of papers Ferd had prepared for the hearing. She nodded as she leafed through, frowned when she saw Annette Gatlin's arrest report.

But she was no dummy. "The child's mother was murdered? Has there been an arrest yet?"

"No," Mac said without batting an eye. "The police are still investigating. But in the meantime, we think Maura's endangered."

"Three years old?" Mackenzie asked. She stood up, took the file. "Be back in a few minutes."

She bustled back in five minutes later. "Judge Bingham's going to recess at eleven A.M. His bladder won't hold any longer than that. I've explained the situation, and he's asked me to draw up the order."

"Giving us permanent custody?" I asked.

"Temporary," she said. "He wants to know more about what happened to the child's mother."

The judge strode through his outer office, robes flapping, face set firmly. The secretary gave him ten minutes. She went in with the file, came out with a three-page document awarding temporary custody to my brother Brian.

"The child's grandmother isn't going to want to turn her over to us," I said, clutching the order. "She's already pulled a bunch of funny business."

Mackenzie Waller's interest in us was waning. "You've got your order. If the woman doesn't comply, call the police. But don't call me. As soon as Judge Bingham leaves at noon, I'm gone. A whole week in Key West. No lawyers, no clerks, no coats."

Mac blew her a kiss. "Don't forget the sun block."

We left my van in the courthouse parking lot, after I'd taken my gun from its hiding place under the seat.

"You're not planning to use that?" Mac asked, seeing me tuck it in my overcoat.

"I'm planning to use that court order," I said. "But sometimes things don't go the way I plan."

The padlock was gone from the house on Silver Dollar Court. I pushed the door open. "Annette?" I called. No answer.

The living room was bare. "Gone," I said, cursing. I ran into the master bedroom. The suitcases were missing. In the bathroom, no makeup case.

"This room's empty," Mac called from the other bedroom.

"Damn," I said, shaking my head. "We spooked her, sending Ingraham copies of those arrest reports yesterday. Her stuff was here last night. And I bet Maura was at that day care. I should have snatched her then. The hell with technicalities. This woman's deranged. I think she killed that woman at Funtown. She knew her, Mac. They were arrested the same place, the same night."

"Who killed Shay?" Mac asked.

He knew what was coming, but I had to make myself say it anyway. "I think Brian killed her."

"Where would Annette go?" Mac asked.

"If I know Annette, she's with a man," I said. "Chuck Ingraham."

40

I called L. D. Lawrence from my cell phone. The secretary told me he wasn't in. "He's off until Monday."

"Can he be reached by phone? It's really important."

"Give me your name and number, and I'll try to have him call you back," she said, sounding dubious.

We'd had to get back on the interstate to get to Jonesboro. Should have been too early for rush hour, but it wasn't.

I gave Mac directions and fumed.

The phone buzzed and I clicked the "on" button. "Captain Lawrence?"

"Garrity? You messing around in my homicide again? I thought we were pretty clear on your staying out of my way."

"I came across a piece of information I thought you should have."

"What would that be?" His voice dripped sarcasm.

"Annette Gatlin," I said. "Shay's mother."

"I know the lady."

"She's involved in the Jane Doe homicide at Funtown."

"You mean Marianne Bonaventura."

He'd talked to Bucky. It meant I had a little less to trade. Actually, I probably had nothing to trade anyway, so now it was bluff time.

"Annette Gatlin was picked up for soliciting. The same night Marianne Bonaventura was picked up, at the very same place. Cow-kickers Saloon. Right there at Funtown. Same arresting officers, too."

"That was a long time ago," Lawrence said. "Old news. The lady's been clean since then. Works security at the airport, I recall."

"Check and see who Marianne's attorney was on that arrest," I said, grasping at straws.

"Why would I do that?"

"Chuck Ingraham. Annette's lawyer. Marianne's lawyer. He's Annette's boyfriend. He was living with her and Shay."

"Doesn't fit, Garrity," he said flatly. "Nice try. Now, why would Annette Gatlin kill a hooker?"

"I don't know," I admitted. "I do know the other hookers working that area had it in for Marianne Bonaventura. They beat her up once."

"Stick to the cleaning business, Garrity. As a detective, you suck."

"Look," I said, letting the remark pass, "I really do have a problem. And I need some police assistance."

"I don't fix tickets."

"Annette's got my niece. Maura. Judge Bingham has given us legal custody, but Annette snatched her yesterday."

"What makes you think that?"

"She got Chuck Ingraham to draw up some bogus paper yesterday, then she picked Maura up and they disappeared. She and Ingraham missed the court date this morning. I checked the house where she's been staying. Her stuff is gone."

"You're supposed to be a detective," Lawrence said lazily. "Find her."

A few minutes ago, he'd been telling me to stay out of his hair. Now he was telling me to do his work.

"Annette Gatlin killed a woman," I said. "She's abducted a three-year-old. Isn't this the kind of thing the police usually do? What about putting out a warrant for her arrest?"

"Warrant?" he hooted derisively. "We don't have jack shit that she killed anybody. Speaking of which, your brother is looking better and better on this. You want to talk about catching a killer, you tell us what you know about Brian Garrity. In the meantime, if you catch up with Annette Gatlin, give us a holler. If you really do have an order from Judge Bingham, we'll talk."

"Thanks for nothing," I said.

"Hey, Garrity? Don't call me on Christmas. I'm a family man."

• • •

Dyson Yount's involvement with Shay was still troubling me. He was a happily married man with a wide-open political career in front of him. The only reason he would have given her a condo was if she were blackmailing him. Would he have risked it all on a silly piece of fluff like Shay?

"Let's go see a man about a condo," I suggested.

"Sounds good," Mac agreed. "Will he be glad to see us?"

"Probably not."

This time, when we got to his office, I didn't bother knocking. Mac and I strolled right in. The little desk in the vestibule where Shay had once sat feeling important was empty. She'd obviously been an irreplaceable cog in the Dyson Yount machine. Either that or his wife was shopping for ugly and smart this time around.

The house was one of those double-parlor jobs. On the left, the parlor was intact, with walnut pocket doors slid in the open position. A merry gas-log fire burned in the Victorian cast-iron fireplace. On the right, the pocket doors were closed.

I slid them open. The twin fireplace in Dyson's office was also burning merrily away. Yount was supplementing the fire with wads of paper, which he was balling up and tossing onto the flames.

"Feliz Navidad!" I said.

"That means Merry Christmas in Spanish," Mac said helpfully.

Yount's face darkened. "You saw my wife," he said. "You went to my home. You had no right."

"You had no right to sleep with my brother's wife and then beat him senseless when he caught you doing it."

Dyson slid a stack of paper into the fireplace, then folded his hands on his desk. "I don't know what you're talking about."

"You can burn everything in this office if you want," I said. "I've got the piece of paper I need. It's public record. You gave Shay a piece of real estate. And your wife knows about it, too. Did you pay Shay money, too? Or was it Annette who demanded cash? What will Maceo Holland and the other boys down at the Gold Dome think when they hear the nasty little mess you've gotten yourself involved in?"

He got a little green around the gills when I mentioned the man whose legislative seat he hoped to inherit, but he had remarkable recovery time. I thought I was a smooth liar, but I'd forgotten what line of work Dyson Yount was in.

"Annette Gatlin is unbalanced," he said. "And Chuck Ingraham, unfortunately, has gotten wrapped up in her personal problems. I warned him Judge Bingham would have him arrested for fraud, but Annette's got him as crazy as she is."

I leaned over, placing both hands on his desk, until I was right in his face. "Annette Gatlin is a murderer. Chuck Ingraham is, at the very least, accessory to her crimes. If Annette leaves town with my niece, I'm not going to be very understanding. And if she crosses the state line, that's felony child abduction."

He leaned away from my hot breath. He was starting to look a little wilted. "There's no proof of any of this," he said, gesturing toward the fireplace.

"You paid Annette off," Mac said. "Blackmail."

"Shay's death benefits," he said, shrugging. "She was an employee. Annette is entitled."

"Maura is entitled," I said. "Annette is a murdering psychopath. Where is Annette?" I asked, pounding the desk to get his attention.

"I don't know," he said coolly.

Time to play Batgirl. I took out my 9 mm. and laid the muzzle tenderly behind Dyson Yount's right ear.

"No, Callahan," Mac screamed. "For Christ's sake. The killing has to stop. Not again!"

Yount's breathing was shallow. He was very still. "You people are insane. I'm glad I beat your brother. He would have killed Shay. I should have finished him off."

"Don't do it, Callahan," Mac begged.

"All the Garritys have hair-trigger tempers. Literally." I gave Yount a firm but meaningful knock on the cheekbone with the butt of the gun. He screamed with pain and disbelief. Facial cuts bleed really convincingly. And the sight of his own blood was enough to convince Dyson Yount.

"You hit me," he whispered. "I'm bleeding."

"You're still not telling me what I need to hear," I said, laying the gun beside his other cheek.

He recoiled. "I gave her all the money I could get my hands on. Fifty thousand dollars. They're leaving. Florida, or maybe California. Someplace warm, that's all I know."

• • •

254

"The airport," I said. "If it's California, they'd have to fly."

"Sounds right," Mac agreed. "But what if it's Florida?"

"They may have already left. Let's split up. I'll drop you at the airport. Then I'll double back and check Chuck's law office. We'll meet again in, what, an hour?"

"Five o'clock," Mac agreed. "In front of the Delta International ticket area."

"What are you gonna do if you see them?" I asked, unsure of what I would do, especially in a crowded airport.

"I'll do the manly thing," Mac said.

"Which is?"

"Grab the kid and run like hell."

I gave him the copy of the court order Judge Bingham had signed. "It might be just as well to stop a cop and explain the situation to them. So it doesn't look like the dirty old man is trying to steal the cute little girl," I suggested.

"Makes more sense," he agreed. "But it's not as manly."

It was four o'clock, and the interstate was jammed even worse. Traffic was backed up at the airport exit. "Keep on going," Mac urged. "Up to the next exit, drop me at the MARTA station and I'll take the train."

It took us twenty minutes to get to the Hapeville station. I leaned over and gave him a quick kiss, then headed back south to Jonesboro.

Banks of pink-and-gold streaked clouds that seemed to tumble over one another were edging the bright blue sky. Snow clouds, Ferd had called them. The temperature had been dropping all day. Earlier, it had looked like rain, which would have spoiled any chance of snow. Now, the clouds seemed to pile higher. The drone of jets was constant. Please, I thought, please don't let Annette and Maura be on one of those jets. I kept thinking of Edna, waiting, at home. How would I tell her we had won the battle but lost the war?

The only lights at Chuck Ingraham's law offices came from the plastic snowman propped on the front porch. The paint had rubbed off the plastic in places, and now there was something menacing about his cute little button eyes and carrot nose.

Cars whizzed by on the road in front of the house, but nobody slowed to say howdy or Merry Christmas. I scooted around to the back of the house and found the kitchen door, which popped rather easily, after I cut the screen door loose from its wooden frame.

At first I tiptoed. "Hello?" My voice echoed in the small but high-ceilinged rooms. I got bolder. "Anybody home, you assholes?"

Not a creature was stirring, not even a mouse.

Ingraham's office was lined with file cabinets. There was a closet full of file storage boxes. It would take weeks to look through them all. And I didn't really know what I was looking for. I sat down at the chair behind his desk and tackled the drawers. I tried the middle drawer first. Nothing much there. Pencils, pens, books of stamps, a tiny key on a knotted red ribbon.

I turned the key over in my hand, looked around the room. The other drawers in the desk opened easily, revealing office supplies and phone books. I pulled all the framed photographs of Ingraham with celebrities off the wall. No hidden compartments.

The former dining room of the home had been converted to a conference room. Nothing there but a bunch of dark mahogany tables and chairs and a credenza that turned out to be full of liquor bottles. I went back into the kitchen, where I'd entered the house. The cabinets were mostly empty, except for coffee-making supplies and some elderly-looking loaves of Claxton Fruit Cake, which had probably been there since the house was built in the forties.

There were two bedrooms, both of which were being used for file storage. The rooms were lined with cardboard archive boxes, each marked with the dates and numbers of the files they held.

That left the bathroom. It had pistachio green tile and postwar green fixtures. There was a cabinet under the sink. Cleaning supplies, a scrub brush, and a lockbox. Bingo.

I took the box back to Ingraham's office, sat in his chair, fitted the key to the lock. He had a much more impressive stash of hideables than my brother. There were some property deeds, including two to houses on Silver Dollar Court, a wad of cash, all of it twenties, some stock certificates, a heavy steel notary public stamp, some Plexiglas-encased coins, silver and gold half-dollars, business-sized envelopes, and a videotape.

There was a television set with a VCR in the conference room. I picked up the lockbox and carried it into the conference room. I popped the tape in and hit the play button on the remote control.

The lighting was lousy, the plot unimaginative. The players were the only things of real interest. Shay, in a black lace teddy, was doing a drunken bump and grind to some raunchy Janet Jackson song, oozing around a man dressed only in baggy plaid boxer shorts and some kind of science-fiction looking headgear. I got up close to the television and hit the freeze-frame. My God, it was a Power Ranger helmet. I'd had to run all over town to buy one for one of Kevin's sons for his birthday last year. The kid had specified red Power Ranger. The man in the boxers wore a blue one. Very hard to find.

I hit the play button and the dance continued. Whoever was holding the videotape called encouragement. "Good. All right! Sexy! Now, Shay, hold it. That's right. You're turning him on. Dyson, for God's sake, lose the shorts!" The action continued, with both of them disrobing, and the cameraman shouting directions, until Shay and the helmeted man were on the floor writhing around, naked. The camera bumped a little, there was a break in the action, and now, the man in the Power Ranger helmet had been replaced with a new costar. Chuck Ingraham, stark naked, obviously aroused. The new cameraman was Dyson Yount.

I turned the videotape off and slid it back into its plastic case. Then I went in the kitchen and washed my hands and took a long drink of water. If there had been any bleach in the room, I would have used it to disinfect myself.

I went back into the conference room to finish examining the box's contents. The last thing I took out was a white legal-sized envelope, with Ingraham's letterhead in the corner. I opened it and poured the contents onto the desktop.

It was a thin gold chain with an oval-shaped gold medallion. The symbol was astrological. Libra. I slipped the necklace back into the envelope and reached for the phone. It rang before I could dial.

The answering machine picked up on the third ring.

"Chuck? Where the hell are you? I'm at the airport, and I'm leaving as soon as I get my paycheck. Meet me here, or we'll leave without you."

I threw the videotape and the necklace into my purse and raced out the back door.

• • •

I called Delta on my car phone, asking to have Andrew MacAuliffe paged. They paged three times, but nobody ever picked up the phone. I hadn't really expected Mac to hear, because I can never make out what they're saying in those airport pages.

The Christmas Eve traffic was the worst I'd ever seen. Worse than the Olympics, worse than the traffic around the stadium the year the Braves won the World Series. After forty-five minutes, I managed to get onto the airport exit ramp, but the immediate signs were not good. Cars had been left abandoned on the shoulder of the airport access road; taxis and buses blocked all the lanes. I pounded the steering wheel in frustration.

I called L. D. Lawrence's office number, got a recording, saying he'd be back in the office on Monday. I called Deavers, too. Another message. Voice-mail is one of the great abominations of the late twentieth century.

Inching along, I finally got within sight of the Delta terminal. Cops were everywhere, blowing their whistles, screaming at drivers to get out of the lanes and keep going. I parked at the passenger drop-off and a woman cop was in my face immediately.

"Ma'am! You can't leave this vehicle here."

"It's an emergency," I pleaded.

"The tow-truck's right behind you," she said, and she waved it forward.

"Bitch," I said, between clenched teeth. I kept inching forward until I came to a slot at the curb, parallel to the taxi and limousine staging area. The sign said No Parking By Order Of Atlanta Police. Towaway Zone. Strictly Enforced. It was the kind of parking spot you dream about at the airport. The kind you can get shot for using.

I reached over my sun visor, got out the square of white cardboard I keep there for just such emergencies. Robert G. Deavers, Detective, Criminal Investigations Division, Atlanta Police Department, it said. It even had an embossed gold seal of the city. I kissed it for good luck, and stuck it on the dashboard facing the front window. My get-out-of-jail-free card.

• • •

I ran for the Delta ticket counter, but Mac was nowhere to be seen. The main terminal was clogged with people and luggage. I found a Delta reservations agent, shouldered aside a young mother with three kids clinging to her who'd been pleading for him to put her on the next flight to Indianapolis.

"Excuse me," I said. "I'm a detective. I'm looking for a woman, a fugitive. She's abducted a small child and I have reason to believe she's catching a flight out of here tonight. Her name is Annette Gatlin." I looked at the computer screen on his desk. "Can you check the computer? Find out what flight she's booked on?"

He looked interested. "Really? A detective? What kind of detective? Do you have your badge?"

"No," I said. "I'm private. But the police are looking for her, too. And her companion. A man named Chuck Ingraham. They're wanted in connection with a murder. A brutal stabbing."

He pointed across the terminal, to a counter below a sign that said Information. "You'll have to go over there. Maybe they could help," he said. "Or you could go down to the second level, to the A.P.D. Airport Precinct. Ask for Officer Carr."

I'd already lost forty-five minutes. Where the hell was Annette? I stopped to think. The message she'd left said something about picking up her paycheck. I went to the main security point, where three dozen private security guards were busy herding people through the metal detectors.

"Your office," I said, tapping one on the shoulder. "Where's the main security office?"

"Like, Empire Airport Security?"

"Like, the company you work for," I said. "Where is it?"

She pointed behind me. "Up there, third level of the atrium. But they ain't hiring right now."

"Do you know a woman named Annette Gatlin, works for Empire Security?"

She thought about it, called to somebody who was busy running a handheld scanner over a harried-looking businessman who kept setting off the detector. "Lenisha. You know somebody named Annette Gatlin? That the lady works out there on the D Concourse?"

Lenisha shrugged. "I don't know. If she don't be working up here, I don't be knowing her.'

"Never mind." I found the elevator column in the atrium, took it up to the third floor. Glass-fronted offices ringed the outer wall. Empire Security was in the middle of the ring.

The office was full of blue-uniformed Empire Security guards. A man sat at a desk with a huge stack of envelopes, handing them out. Payday.

I elbowed my way to the front of the throng. "Annette Gatlin," I said. "Have you seen her today? Has she been in here?"

A tall black woman with braids wound around her head in a perfect cone nodded. "You just missed her. Annette just left out of here. On vacation for two weeks."

"Where was she going?" I asked. "What gate was she leaving from?"

"Gate?" the woman sniggered. "Annette don't be flying. She afraid of planes. You ever heard of somebody afraid of planes working at an airport?"

"Where was she going?" I repeated.

"I don't know," the woman shrugged. "She got that cute little grandgirl of hers. They talking 'bout Disneyland."

"Disneyland? In California? Or DisneyWorld in Florida?"

"Same thing to me," the cone-headed woman said.

The elevator down to the ground floor of the terminal was crowded with blue-uniformed Empire Security Guards going off shift. They were excited, talking about holiday plans, last-minute shopping for their kids.

Throngs milled through the security checkpoints, toward the baggage check, out the doors to the MARTA station, cabs, and shuttle buses. I felt my shoulders slumped, felt the energy sapped. I had been so close. Now she was gone. I walked out the south entrance of the terminal and saw half a dozen Empire Security Guards standing at the curb. They were all women, their hips bristling with thick leather belts holding their radios, black riot batons, and handcuffs. One had a blonde-haired child by the hand. My pulse quickened. I ran to the curb. The child turned around. Not Maura. Not even a little girl. A shuttle bus pulled up. Blue and white, like the Empire Security uniforms. The marquee across the front of the bus said Empire Employee Parking Shuttle. The women stepped up to the bus. I went with them.

The driver gave me an odd look. For the first time, I noticed the other women wore white plastic security badges around their necks. As the bus jolted from the curb, they took turns swiping their tag through a code box.

"Miss?" the driver said. "This isn't a public bus. You've got to be an Empire Employee. We go to a restricted access parking lot. If you don't have your I.D. with you, I'm gonna have to let you off up ahead here, before we get on the South Loop Road."

I pulled a sad face. It wasn't hard. This was my last shot at finding Annette. If this didn't work, I'd have to go home to my mother and explain how I'd let her granddaughter slip through my fingers.

"They fired me," I said, breaking into tears. "The son of a bitch fired me. On Christmas Eve. I went in for my grievance hearing, and the bastard told me I was fired. They made me turn in my badge and my radio. Everything."

It was all too much. I broke down in the aisle of that bus, sinking to the floor and clutching the base of the chrome grab-rail for balance. I lost it. It felt good, too. "My car's in the employee lot," I wailed. "I don't even know if it'll start. What am I gonna do?"

A woman with long, diamond-tipped fingernails sat on the bench beside me and rubbed my back. "Go ahead, sister-friend," she urged. "We all done been there. The man done messed with all of us. Go ahead, girlfriend." She glared at the driver. "This lady ain't hurting you or nobody else. Just drive the bus and do what they pay you to do."

I kept my face covered with my hands, sniffing and bawling like a baby.

"Sit up here, honey," my sister-friend insisted. "Ain't nobody gonna mess with you no more."

The bus passed the sign for the I-85 entrance ramp. Next came signs for the rental car return lots, Big Peach Park and Ride, and finally, slowing, the bus took a right onto a road marked Airport Employee Parking.

We passed three employee lots crammed with cars, and then the shuttle slowed. The driver pulled the bus up to an electronic gate, swiped his own I.D. through it, and waited until the mechanical arm swung up.

I wanted to cry some more. The Empire Security lot must have taken up five acres. Row after row of parked cars. The sun was setting. I had no idea where to look for Annette Gatlin.

The driver pulled through the first row of cars. "Here," somebody from the back shouted. He slowed, and a gray-haired man hopped off the bus. The driver started up again and cruised down two more rows.

"Here," my sister-friend shouted. She stood up, reached inside her hooded blue Empire Security windbreaker. "Good luck," she whispered, pressing something into my hand. Then she jumped off and the bus was moving again.

I opened my hand to examine what she'd given me. It was a ten-dollar bill. Now I'd have to rethink my position that all security guards were neo-Nazis.

The driver slowly cruised rows. I stood up and held onto the grabrail, searching for a white car like Annette's. But they were all either minivans or other white cars.

I was the last one on the bus. The driver kept throwing glances my way. "Forget where you parked?"

"I was upset this morning," I said. "I'm sure it's here somewhere."

Women drivers, I could hear him thinking.

"Three more rows, then I gotta head back to the terminal for my next run," the driver said. "You'll have to get off there. I don't care what your friend says. It's rules."

"Let me off here," I said, spying a white car that looked the right size, at the far end of the last row. "You passed it back there. I'll just walk."

"Suit yourself," he said. He hit the switch and the doors opened. I jumped out into the freezing cold. The bus was moving away before I'd even hit the ground.

I pulled my jacket tight around my neck, thought about my gloves, but reached instead for my gun. I quickened my step as I drew nearer to the white car. It had tinted windows like Annette's. The security company hadn't bothered to extend the lights to this row. It was dark and I was terrible with car models, but it looked the right size to be Annette's. I slowed down when I saw what was parked right next to it. A dusty black pickup truck. Brian's truck.

I glanced over at the white car again. Was it Annette's? I walked around to the back, to try to look through the tinted window. The car sat funny. I looked down. Both rear tires were flat as pancakes. I squatted down to get a better look at the right rear tire. The valve stem had been neatly sliced off.

And then, something hard and cold was around my neck, squeezing, squeezing so tight I could hear myself gasping for air. And a small voice. "Ca'han." Then I blacked out.

41

I felt the truck take a hard fast left that sent my body slamming against the far side of the truck bed. My cheek scraped against something gritty, and when I reached up to feel it my hand came away wet and warm.

The rest of me was bloody cold. Wind-driven snow flurries whirled around in the cold dry air. I tried to crawl to a kneeling position to see what was happening. Through the back window of the cab I saw only the back of the driver's head, cloaked in a navy blue hood. The truck made another hard left and I was once again flung against the side of the truck, bouncing my hip hard against the wheel well.

Overhead I saw the sign that said we were on the entrance ramp to Interstate 85, headed north. An hour earlier, traffic on the interstate had been at a standstill. Now, it seemed, everything had suddenly come unclogged. The truck was speeding, passing the other cars on the highway, darting and crazily weaving from lane to lane.

I pulled myself to my knees to get another look. This time, what I saw sent a chill down my spine that had nothing to do with the air temperature. The snow whirled thickly, stinging my eyes from the impact, but I could see a tiny blonde head, bobbing up and down on the front seat of the truck's cab. For her it was a thrill ride. Fast but safe, because she was with her daddy. Maura. In the cab of a truck with a killer. I ducked down quickly, to keep out of sight.

Both out lives might depend on that driver thinking I was still unconscious.

My exposed hands and ears burned from the cold. I hunched back down again, searching in the pockets of my coat for my gun. Gone, of course. My gloves were still there, though. I pulled them on and reminded myself to feel grateful for small blessings.

I pushed myself up against the back of the truck cab, tucking my head down to keep the frigid wind from cutting through me. I couldn't see where we were going, only where we'd already been.

Now I was watching the overhead signs. We whizzed past Virginia Avenue in the far left lane, then whipped hard to the right, cutting across two lanes of traffic, slowing not at all. And then we were on an exit ramp, but I couldn't tell where, couldn't remember what northbound ramp came after Virginia. We never stopped at the top of the ramp, veering sharp right again. We were somewhere on the city's rundown south side. Cleveland Avenue maybe? After another block, at the first intersection, we turned left, running the red light, narrowly avoiding collision with a two-tone red and white Cadillac Eldorado. I didn't need signs now to know where we were. It was Stewart Avenue. And now I knew not only where we'd been, but also where we were going.

Only another mile, and I could see the red and blue directional signs for I-20. The truck slowed. Traffic was heavier here, Stewart lined with shopping centers and liquor stores and check-cashing outlets. Cars pulled in and out of the highway. I risked raising my head. Maura was standing up in the front seat, her face pressed to her window.

The driver pointed to the sign, or maybe it was just the unexpected sight of a wasteland covered in a thin frosting of new-fallen snow. The faded blue sign had once raced with red-and-yellow circus lights, the arrow pointing to the left, toward Funtown; now kudzu vines crawled up the rusty iron stanchions and the only lights were from the streetlights on the I-20 overpass.

We swerved left, jumping the curb, then swinging onto the old entry road to Funtown. No more traffic. I could jump free without the risk of being run over by another car. And Maura would still be in the truck.

Suddenly, the race of an engine, bouncing over the same curb, and now a streak of pink, flashing on the left side of the truck, horn blaring. The headlights were off, but a person knows her own van, even when it's being driven by somebody who's apparently trying to run her off the road. The truck jerked right, and I clung with cold hands to the wheel well, trying to gain my balance. We jounced along the broken asphalt, fishtailing from pothole to pothole. I heard a scream coming from the cab, pulled myself to my knees, and peered through the curtain of snow. Maura's head was no longer visible.

Now the van was beside us again, forcing us farther to the right, until we were off the roadbed, clipping pine saplings, ripping kudzu vines from overhanging trees, but still we lurched forward. The truck slowed, zigzagging around garbage dumps and bigger trees. Branches and leaves rained down into the truck bed and I heard another scream and a long, impassioned wail. Without thinking, I turned around and began banging on the window of the cab. "Stop it, damn it, stop it!"

And then the driver slammed on the brakes, fishtailing us sideways into a pine tree. I heard the sickening crunch of metal folding onto itself, then felt myself hurtle up and over the side of the truck bed, landing in a heap on a kudzu-covered clump of privet. Everything was upside down. My chest felt as though the truck had fallen on it. I gasped for breath, flailing my arms, the small sharp privet leaves tearing at the flesh of my face and hands and legs.

I had to get up, get Maura out of the truck. I dragged myself to my knees, felt the sharp pain in my right ankle.

"Callahan?" Mac's voice. I heard his footfalls in the underbrush. "Are you OK?"

"Maura's in the truck," I screamed. "Brian's got Maura. He'll hurt her."

He was beside me now, bending over. I grabbed onto his shoulder, pulled myself up.

"He's got Maura," I repeated.

"It's not Brian," Mac said. "It's Annette."

He got to the truck only a few seconds before me. The driver's side door was open, but the cab was empty.

We heard her, tearing through the underbrush, running parallel to the access road, down toward the abandoned amusement park. "Nooo," Maura wailed. "No, Annie."

Mac had a good ten-yard lead on me. "Go back to the van," he yelled over his shoulder.

I kept going. "She's got Maura. She's got my gun."

He disappeared into the treeline. My ankle was throbbing but I pushed through. We were on a rise, the ground sloping down sharply below up. I caught glimpses of Mac's yellow windbreaker, shining through the snow, and up ahead, Annette, a sixty-year-old woman, running with a three-year-old who must have weighed twenty-five pounds.

The ground was wet with mushy snow. My foot slipped once, but I regained my balance and kept going. I heard Mac grunt, then saw the yellow jacket tumbling headlong down the steep embankment. At the same time I saw him go, I caught sight of Annette. She was still on her feet but sliding sideways, down the embankment, Maura clutched tightly in her arms.

Ten yards in front of me. Ten yards away. "Let her go!" I screamed. Annette looked back, just for an instant, and she went down, suddenly and hard, and Maura went down, too, tumbling fast and free down the snow-covered hillside.

It was my last chance. I took a flying leap, landing nearly on top of Annette. She was struggling to stand. I wrapped my arms around her knees and pulled her down.

I'd never wrestled with a grandmother before. She was skinny and she was vicious, but I was bigger and younger. She fought trailer-trash style, kicking me in the gut, clawing at my eyes. But I'd seen professional wrestling on television and survived two brothers. She reached for my eyes again; I grabbed her wrist and twisted it backwards. Annette cried out in pain.

"Shay," I said, the words coming out as a gasp. "You killed Shay. Your own flesh and blood."

Annette's boots kicked up clods of mud as she tried to scuttle backwards out of my hold. I put my knee on her chest and pressed down hard. She choked and I let up a little. Tears ran sideways down her face.

"Shay didn't have any blood. Never did. Cold. That was her. She knew Chuck was the only man I ever loved." She gulped and when she exhaled, it came out as a strangled sob. "Shay took him. Didn't even want him. It was Dyson Yount she really wanted. Chuck was somebody else to party with. Then, Yount finally admitted he was gonna run for office, and he wouldn't leave his wife because of the scandal. I think he got cold feet after Brian caught them that night.

267

He bought her that townhouse, but it wasn't enough. That's when she made up her mind to take Chuck.

"Chuck," she spat his name. "I shoulda known. He's a man. He's got a prick, he's gonna put it where it hadn't oughtta be."

She saw the disgust on my face.

"I'll bet you think that boyfriend of yours is different. You think the Garritys are different. Let me tell you, Miss Julia Callahan Garrity, even that goody-goody daddy of yours, he wasn't all that good when nobody was looking."

"Liar!" I screamed.

"Ask your mama what Jack Garrity told her when he was in the hospital dying of cancer," Annette said smugly. "You just ask her."

I jammed the heel of my hand under the tip of her nose and pushed until I felt something snap behind the soft cartilage.

She fell back onto the ground. The blood streaming from her face made a bright-red pool on the snow beneath her. Still she tried to scramble away. I pinned her by the shoulders, my breath shallow and labored.

"And all that time she was messin' with my man, Shay was stringing Brian along, too. Even after he nearly beat her to death, she was sneakin' off, sleepin' with him. She thought it was all a big joke. She came home that night, drunk, told me what all they'd been doing. And she showed me the necklace, made sure I knew Chuck gave it to her. He bought her a goddamn necklace," Annette cried. "Shay was dead drunk, laughing and giggling. Next minute, she was asleep, snoring like a sailor. I put on the stereo, made like we were all par-tyin'. That old bag next door called to complain, and I slammed the door, so she'd think everybody was leaving."

"And you stabbed her," I said, wonderingly. "Your own daughter."

"Whoever said blood was thicker than water, they didn't know Shay Gatlin," Annette said wheezily. "The only good thing she ever did was get herself knocked up with Maura." She set her lips in a cruel smile. "Maura's mine. She's loved me from the start. You might have her now, but she'll come back to me. I guarantee it. She loves her Granny Annie. I'm the only family she ever had."

"You're gonna rot in prison," I said with satisfaction. "I found that necklace. At Chuck's house. It's probably got your fingerprints on it. And some of Shay's blood."

"I took it off her afterwards," Annette said. "Gave it back to him. So he'd know I knew."

"You'd killed for him before," I said. "Marianne Bonaventure."

"You mean Marty? That whore. I'm the one gave her Chuck's phone number, when she needed a lawyer. A month later, Chuck met me at Cowkickers for a drink. He left before me. I came out and saw him in his car with the little whore. Afterwards, I caught up with her. He'd given her a necklace. A heart. Just like he'd given me. I told her to come on down here, back by the concession stand. I'd bring a trick back here for her. I had the knife. Chuck gave me that knife— did you know that?"

"Is that why you came back here to Funtown tonight? To dump another body?"

Her eyes blazed. "If you people had minded your own business, we'd be on our way to Florida now. I came off the bus in the parking lot, and caught that asshole brother of yours, cutting my tires valves. Thought he'd take Maura from me. And then, if you hadn't come along, I woulda got rid of Brian for good. He'd been staying down here. He told Shay about it, she told me. It would have been natural as anything, him getting depressed about not getting his baby back, feeling guilty about killing Shay. I was gonna show Maura the rides," Annette said. "Like we were gonna ride at DisneyWorld. Dump you off, go back and pick up my car, and take my little girl to Disney-World."

"I've got her," Mac said, trudging back up the hill. He held Maura tightly, her arms wound in a choke hold around his neck.

"Come to Annie," Annette called weakly. I pressed my knee down on her chest until she couldn't speak anymore, then I flipped her over, and got my gun and the riot holster she'd throttled me with. I reached up under her jacket and got the handcuffs off her belt and slapped them around her wrists.

"Where's Brian?" I asked Mac. "What happened? How did you get my van?"

"Annie," Maura cried. "Annie's hurt."

"Get her out of here, please," I told Mac. "She's been through enough."

Mac looked down at Annette, who stared back, stone-faced, blood-smeared. "What happened to her?"

"She must have broken her nose when she fell," I said. "Don't worry about her. She's too mean to die. Take Maura up to the van. I'll be along with Granny Annie in a minute."

Mac carried Maura back to the van. I waited a while, then force-marched Annette back up the hill.

He had Maura inside the van with the heater going. We put Annette in the cab of the wrecked truck. The fender was crumpled where it had hit the tree, but the motor cranked and we were able to get the heat going.

"I called 911 on your cell phone," Mac reported. "Brian's in the back of the van. I think he's got a concussion."

"What happened?" I asked. "It's not that I'm not grateful, but how the hell did you get my van? How did you figure out what was going on?"

"I looked all over the airport for you, and for Annette," Mac said. "I'd tried to have you paged, but it was such bedlam in the terminal, nobody could hear anything. I was going to just take a cab back to your house. Then, as I walked outside, I saw the House Mouse van parked at the curb. A tow truck was backing up to it. So I gave the driver twenty bucks, showed him I had the keys, and got in. I circled around three times looking for you to come out. The third time, I saw you come out the south terminal door, but then I saw you get on that security company shuttle bus. I figured you were tailing Annette, so I tailed you."

"Pretty clever," I said. "I may have to sign you on to the force. Teach you the secret P.I. handshake. How did you get in the parking lot without an I.D.?"

"Told the security guard my girlfriend had a dead battery and she'd called me to come give her a jumpstart," Mac said. "He stood there and argued with me for a while, that's why I wasn't right behind you. But as cold as it was outside, he wasn't going to volunteer to leave that nice heated guard shack. Finally, he waved me in, said if I wasn't back out in five minutes he'd come looking for me. I saw Brian's truck come whizzing out the exit, and I went looking for you. Instead I found Brian, with a welt on the side of his head. I saw the flat tires, figured he must have tried to stop Annette himself. I threw him in the back of the van and just prayed I could catch up with the truck."

"She could have killed Maura," I said soberly.

We heard the sirens then. Two of them.

• • •

I called Bucky Deavers from the Emergency Room at Grady Hospital.

Maura was hysterical. One of the nurses finally came out and fed her a little white paper cup of Tylenol with codeine. She allowed Mac to hold her on his lap and read her an old copy of *Sports Illustrated.* She was fast asleep before they got to the table of contents.

Bucky showed up fifteen minutes later, while we were sitting in the waiting area.

"They're treating my brother for a concussion," I said. "Annette Gatlin tried to kill him, and me. She confessed, Bucky. She killed Shay. And she killed your Funtown Jane Doe, too. Funny, huh? Acey Karpik's instincts were right. The murders were related. Annette killed both women—for sleeping with her man."

"Why call me?" Bucky asked. "Not that I mind getting credit for cleaning up the Funtown homicide."

"It all went down tonight, at Funtown. That's Atlanta, right?"

He got out his notebook, started taking my statement.

"I need another favor," I said, rubbing my ankle.

He shook his head. "I'm out of favors."

"It's nine o'clock, right? I'll give you a statement, Mac will give you a statement, and Brian, as soon as he's feeling alert, will give you a statement. I'll tell L. D. Lawrence everything I know. Tomorrow."

"Where do you think you're going?" Bucky snorted. "You're the corroborating witness in two homicides."

I thought about the Robert Frost poem I'd memorized for an eighth grade English class. Something about "promises to keep, and miles to go before I sleep."

"I'm going to mass," I said. "Midnight mass."

It was nearly eleven before they let us leave the emergency room. They wouldn't release Brian at all, said they had to keep him under observation for twelve hours. Maura was motionless in my arms.

I found her dress and tights and shoes laid out on the bed in Edna's room. It was like dressing a doll. She lay limp on the bed while I threaded her legs into the tights, then slipped the taffeta dress over

271

her head. Edna had thought of everything, including a brand new crinoline. But I wouldn't do that to a kid. After I got her face washed and her hair combed, I left her on her daybed.

The shower stung all the tiny cuts on my arms and legs, but soap and hot water made me feel better. I toweled off and went into my bedroom.

Edna had been a busy little beaver. Laid across the foot of my bed was a new, Callahan-sized outfit: form-fitting dark green velvet dress, new black suede heels, and a new pair of sheer black stockings. The card said: I knew you'd do it. See you at mass. Love, Mom.

Mac whistled with appreciation when I finally emerged with my sleeping niece in my arms. "Wanna get right with Jesus?" I asked, keeping my voice light.

He shook his head no. "It's a family thing," he said. "Besides, I've got to finish gluing the shingles on Maura's dollhouse. I'll see you first thing in the morning."

It was standing room only at Blessed Sacrament Church. I squeezed past a throng of pissed-off late-arriving Christmas Catholics, craning my neck for Edna. Finally, my brother-in-law Steve stood up and waved for me. The organ was playing the opening strains of "Oh, Holy Night" as I edged down the pew, the drowsing Maura draped over my shoulder.

My brother Kevin and his boys were sitting on the aisle, the boys red-faced from the scrubbing my mother had probably given them. I hadn't seen Kevin in months. He kissed my cheek, stroked Maura's hair. Edna was sitting next to him. Her hair glowed faintly blue— she'd been to the beauty parlor. She was wearing her good red wool dress, and draped around her neck was something I hadn't seen in fifteen years. Her fox fur stole.

Daddy had given it to her for her fiftieth birthday. It was too good, she protested. So she wore it to midnight mass, and to occasional cocktail parties, and the rest of its life it spent zippered up in the special vinyl Rich's bag in the back of her closet.

She beamed at the sight of Maura, then craned her head to look for the child's father. "Where's Brian?" she asked worriedly. "He called the house looking for you, I told him you'd gone to the airport to look for Maura and Annette."

That answered one question. "You know Brian and church," I said, shrugging. "He promised he'd meet us back at the house, in the morning." My Christmas gift tonight, I'd already decided, would be peace of mind. There would be time to hear the rest of it tomorrow. And as for Annette Gatlin's accusation about my father, I would put that out of my mind, too.

Maureen was sitting beside my mother. She stood up and put out her arms to take Maura. That's when I realized it. She was wearing the same exact green velvet dress as me. Only three sizes smaller.

"Merry Christmas," Edna whispered.

EPILOGUE

Christmas Day

Edna's camera worked well. We have the photos to prove the moment happened, and she keeps them in a small leatherbound album in her purse, convenient for ambushing unsuspecting friends and strangers.

That one morning, we were family once again. Maureen and Steve spent Christmas Eve, so they could be there when Maura woke up and discovered the wonders of Santa Claus. Mac arrived at six with bleary eyes and paint-stained hands and a wooden dollhouse with wallpaper and working lights and a doorbell that rang when you pressed the button. Kevin and the boys arrived just as the first pot of coffee finished perking.

We feasted on Maura's excitement. There were toys and dolls and the EZ Bake Oven, coffee cake and battery-operated machines of war for the boys, and silk neckties and flannel nightgowns and silly joke gifts, and by nine o'clock the living room was ankle-deep in wrapping paper and empty boxes and grown-ups already woozy from brandy-laced coffee. The boys took Maura outside and they built a Maura-sized snowgirl, then rode around on the new pink tricycle, which was much too big for her, of course.

I'd given Edna a blow-by-blow account of what had happened at the airport and Funtown, and reassured her a dozen times that Brian's

274

injuries were not severe. She knew all of this, but her eyes never wandered far from the front door all morning long.

"Don't put that coffee cake away," she told us half a dozen times, "It's Brian's favorite. Cinnamon-pecan."

Maureen and I rolled our eyes, and did the dishes together. "Have you ever seen Mama happier?" she asked, stacking the cups in the dishwasher.

I thought about it. "Not since the day you got married. Not since we all turned around and saw you coming down the aisle on Daddy's arm."

At noon, I went into my bedroom and called the hospital to ask when my brother would be released.

"Brian Garrity?" the clerk asked. I heard the clicking of computer keys. She had me repeat the spelling, and then asked if I could hold for a moment. Less than a minute passed. Mac had given me a new watch for Christmas, with a yellow-gold face and an alligator strap. I watched the second hand sweep around and vowed that starting now, I would be a punctual person.

This time a man came on the line. "This is Dr. K. B. Ligon," he said. "You were inquiring about Brian Garrity?"

"Yes."

"He's gone."

"You've released him?"

"No," Dr. Ligon said. "His bed was empty when the nurse went to check his vital signs this morning. There's a police officer here who's been asking for him. Detective Lawrence. Are you family?"

I watched the seconds tick off smartly on my new watch. "I guess not," I said. "Would you put Detective Lawrence on the phone, please?"

At one o'clock our Christmas Day celebration sputtered and died. When I told my mother Brian would not be coming home she turned off the oven that was roasting our turkey, and took to her bed.

At exactly two o'clock I arrived at the Clayton County police department.

L. D. Lawrence and Acey Karpik were waiting for me in the criminal investigation office. Lawrence wore permanent press blue jeans and a striped shirt that still had the folds in it. Acey Karpik had on a set of dark brown handyman's overalls and a blue A.P.D. baseball cap.

Karpik stood up when I entered the room, even reached out to shake my hand. He was tall and rangy, with wild tufts of gray hair sticking out from the sides of his cap. "Quite a night you had last night," he said. "Pretty good work. Two homicides cleared."

Lawrence cleared his throat.

"Probably," Karpik said. "Maybe. Still leaves that Jane Doe in Henry County unsolved. It's unrelated, I'm guessing now."

I took a chair and looked at Lawrence. "Is my brother gone?"

Lawrence nodded. "His place is cleaned out. He didn't tell you he was leaving town?"

"No," I said. "Have you talked to Annette Gatlin? Did she make a statement?"

"Won't say a damn word," Lawrence said. "On her lawyer's advice."

"Chuck Ingraham?"

"No," Lawrence said. "Some woman lawyer. A real ball-buster."

"What about Ingraham?" I asked. "Did you find him, or did he skip town, too?"

Lawrence laughed. "He called in a burglary report last night. Says somebody broke into his office and ransacked the place. He says there's a wad of cash and some valuable jewelry missing. He also denies having any knowledge of Annette Gatlin's intentions. Doesn't remember anybody named Marianne Bonaventura."

"Did you get the answering machine tape from his office? With the message from Annette, telling him to meet her at the airport?"

"It had been erased," Lawrence said. "Chuck Ingraham is slimy, but he's not stupid."

I'd put the zodiac necklace in my jacket pocket. I took it out now and handed it to Karpik. "I couldn't leave it there," I said apologetically. "He would have destroyed it. Like the answering machine tape."

Karpik shrugged. "Your friend Deavers says evidence has a tendency to disappear around you. He says you have sticky fingers."

I blushed. The videotape I'd found in Ingraham's office was stuffed under the front seat of my van. For now, it could just stay there.

"Dyson Yount?" I asked. "He admitted to me that he gave Annette fifty thousand dollars. Shay was blackmailing him. Her mama finished the job she'd started. I saw him burning documents. In his office."

"Mr. Yount and his family left town last night. Skiing trip to Colorado. We've left messages at his hotel," Lawrence said.

"What about the cash he gave Annette? Was it in her car?" I asked.

"Money? No. Suitcases, and the kid's stuff. No money."

Lawrence gave me the fish-eye. "That's a lot of money. Maybe your brother took it. Maybe we'll look him up and ask him about it." There were a lot of things I wanted to ask Brian. I doubted I'd get that chance.

Monday, Feast of the Holy Innocents

At 9 A.M. I told Edna I had some errands to run. She gave me one of her sharp looks, but didn't ask any questions.

I took myself over to St. Joseph's Hospital and had my mammogram. Two days later, my new surgeon, Barrie Aycock, took a look at the scar from my lumpectomy. "Everything's normal," she said. "Totally boring. Totally healthy."

"No cancer?" I needed to hear her say it.

"Not cancer. Just a bunch of fibro-fatty breast tissue."

New Year's Eve

It took one week before Edna admitted defeat. She'd come down with a cold on Christmas Day, and by Christmas night, both she and Maura had bad coughs and low grade fever. Maura bounced back in two days.

"School, Ca'han," she'd say, every morning, pulling me toward the front door. "I go school now." She was bored. It was all both of us could do to keep up with her. In the meantime, Maureen had a plan. My sister always had a plan.

"Let me take Maura," she begged Edna. "There's a preschool right around the corner from the house. She needs to be with other children, Mama. And I can work a Baylor plan at the hospital, be home with her four weekdays, then work a three-day weekend, when Steve could be home. Or she could come over here on weekends, to be with you and Callahan."

Edna blew her nose loudly into a handkerchief. "I don't want her left all day and all night at day care. Raised by strangers."

"She could go to Mother's Morning Out. It's only three mornings a week, just till noon," Maureen said. "I'd be home with her the rest of the day. It's a wonderful program. Episcopalian."

"What about Annette?" Edna asked.

Despite being held in the Clayton County jail, charged with two counts of murder, Annette was still refusing to admit defeat. Her lawyer, a woman named Elizabeth Brown, had already filed an appeal to Judge Bingham's custody order, based on the fact that Brian had disappeared. Annette herself had called the house twice, begging to speak to Maura. I hung up both times.

"Steve and I want to adopt her. Legally," Maureen said.

"And what happens when Brian comes back?" Edna asked, glancing around the living room. She'd left all the Christmas decorations up, even the stockings on the mantel. And the patched and leaky snow globe with its skewed vision of home held pride of place once again.

Maureen cut her eyes over at me. My turn.

"Is that what you want for Maura?" I asked quietly.

Edna thought about it. She folded her hands in her lap. "She keeps the name Garrity," she said finally.

Epiphany

Maureen came over at two o'clock. Maura had on a purple snowsuit and purple sneakers and purple barrettes in her blonde hair. As soon as she came in the kitchen, she started pulling out the pots and pans. "Cook, Gramma," she told Edna. "Let's cook."

Edna took the EZ Bake Oven off the counter and put it in the corner of the kitchen that had been declared Maura's territory.

"Callahan?" Maureen touched my sleeve. "Come out to the car. I want to show you the wagon I bought for Maura today."

I followed my sister out to the car. She was pale and shaky. "What's wrong?" I asked. "Something with the lawyers? Did Brian call?"

She shook her head. "I took Maura to the pediatrician. She has to have a physical exam, get caught up with all her shots, before I can enroll her in preschool."

I felt physically sick. "What's wrong with her?" I asked. "Is she sick?"

Maureen bit the skin around her thumbnail. "You can't tell Mama. Swear to God."

"I swear."

"Nobody," Maureen insisted. "You can't tell anybody. Not Mac, not Steve, not anybody."

"OK," I said. "Swear to God."

"On Daddy's grave."

"On his grave."

"The pediatrician gave me copies of all the tests, everything. Her blood type. It's impossible. She's not Brian's, Callahan. She's not ours."

I looked in through the kitchen window. I could see Edna, bent over the EZ Bake Oven, helping Maura bake a tiny cake.

"She is now," I said.